TURNING
SECRETS

Stonechild and Rouleau Mysteries
Cold Mourning
Butterfly Kills
Tumbled Graves
Shallow End
Bleeding Darkness
Turning Secrets

BRENDA CHAPMAN

TURNING SECRETS

A STONECHILD AND ROULEAU MYSTERY

DUNDURN

TORONTO

Cover image: shutterstock.com/JustBreak
Printer: Webcom

Library and Archives Canada Cataloguing in Publication

Chapman, Brenda, 1955-, author
    Turning secrets / Brenda Chapman.

(A Stonechild and Rouleau mystery)
Issued in print and electronic formats.
ISBN 978-1-4597-4181-2 (softcover).--ISBN 978-1-4597-4182-9 (PDF).--
ISBN 978-1-4597-4183-6 (EPUB)

    I. Title. II. Series: Chapman, Brenda, 1955- . Stonechild and
Rouleau mystery.

PS8605.H36T87 2019   C813'.6   C2018-904996-0
                                             C2018-904997-9

1 2 3 4 5   23 22 21 20 19

 Conseil des Arts du Canada   Canada Council for the Arts   Canadä    ONTARIO ARTS COUNCIL CONSEIL DES ARTS DE L'ONTARIO an Ontario government agency un organisme du gouvernement de l'Ontario

We acknowledge the support of the **Canada Council for the Arts**, which last year invested $153 million to bring the arts to Canadians throughout the country, and the **Ontario Arts Council** for our publishing program. We also acknowledge the financial support of the **Government of Ontario**, through the **Ontario Book Publishing Tax Credit** and **Ontario Creates**, and the **Government of Canada**.

Nous remercions le **Conseil des arts du Canada** de son soutien. L'an dernier, le Conseil a investi 153 millions de dollars pour mettre de l'art dans la vie des Canadiennes et des Canadiens de tout le pays.

Care has been taken to trace the ownership of copyright material used in this book. The author and the publisher welcome any information enabling them to rectify any references or credits in subsequent editions.

The publisher is not responsible for websites or their content unless they are owned by the publisher.

Printed and bound in Canada.

VISIT US AT

dundurn.com | @dundurnpress | dundurnpress | dundurnpress

Dundurn
3 Church Street, Suite 500
Toronto, Ontario, Canada
M5E 1M2

For Ted

By that sin fell the angels.
— William Shakespeare, *Henry VIII*

Cruelty, like every other vice, requires no motive outside of itself; it only requires opportunity.
— George Eliot

CHAPTER ONE

Fisher Dumont stopped in front of the window on his way to the kitchen with one last tray full of dirty dishes. He gazed out at the grey April day now sinking into a cool Toronto evening, where on the street, the shift change was well underway. Office workers in power suits were hurrying past on their way to the subway, oblivious to their nighttime replacements. Misha the Amazon transwoman swayed by on stiletto heels heading to her usual corner while Flip, a panhandler who could have been forty or seventy, squatted on the sidewalk next to a hot air grate. Two college girls crossed to the opposite side of the street, their faces flushed and animated. Fisher imagined they were meeting up with friends at the Firkin, set for a night of beer and fried finger food. The sight of the girls was like a stoner's fix; they made him want … want something clean and soft to make him forget the empty hours that made up his life — but he wouldn't let his dreams go there. Not now. He turned away from the street dance and shifted the heavy tray.

Fisher hated this time of the afternoon. The shadows and thinning sunlight brought on the loneliness.

The dying hour.

"Your buddies are waiting for you out front," said Nico, interrupting his thoughts with the noise of clinking glass as he pushed aside the strings of red beads in the doorway. Nico's greased-back hair momentarily caught a shaft of sunlight on his way past the window. "Raff just arrived if you wanna split a few minutes early. He can do that load."

Fisher looked down at the tray of dishes and hurried ahead of Nico into the steamy kitchen. He set the tray on the counter next to the dishwasher and slipped off his apron, hanging it on the hook near the fridge. Gina waved a spoon coated in tomato sauce at him from where she stood at the stove. Rhonda was chopping carrots near the sink and ignored him, as per usual. Bitch thought she was above the job because she'd had a year of university. He'd like to tell her to wipe that stuck-up look off her pointy face, but she was the vindictive kind who'd make sure they put him back inside if she could make up a reason. He wouldn't put it past her.

He glanced back down the long hallway toward the ruby beads and the two men he knew were waiting for him. Luckily, his coat was hanging in the corridor; he grabbed it on his way to the rear exit. The alarm was busted and he made it outside without alerting anybody. He ran past the garbage bins in the alleyway, calling hello to the stray cat chewing on something it had dragged out of a bag dumped at the end of the lane. The cat's green eyes locked onto him as it picked up the treasure with sharp teeth and scuttled deeper into the shadow of the building.

He didn't know how long he'd be able to keep avoiding Loot and Ronnie, and he shivered at the thought of what they'd do when they finally caught up to him. Maybe he'd have some of their money by then and could talk his way into a reprieve for the rest. Maybe they'd give him more time to make good on what he owed and wouldn't beat him to a pulp. And maybe a flying pot-bellied pig would land on the blue moon.

At the corner, he stopped and looked back. He was glad now for the shadows and coming darkness. It was getting tougher to stay away from all his old haunts but he had a few safe places they hadn't figured out yet. Marie had said he could crash at her dump another night. He turned left onto Dalhousie to take the back streets north to Gerrard. He'd buy a twenty-sixer of rye on his way as payment for another night on her mattress. With any luck, she'd pass out before she pressed her bony hips onto his and he was forced again to return her hospitality in another way.

CHAPTER TWO

Paul Gundersund pulled his vintage Mustang alongside Kala Stonechild's black truck and put the gearshift into park. The clock read 8:20 a.m. but it felt much earlier. He was still running on West Coast time. The construction site had been overtaken by police cars and first responders. A fire truck blocked his view of the body that he knew was lying on the concrete slab in front of the hulking skeleton of the half-finished hotel. A red light pulsed from the hood of the fire truck. A white van with *Mortimer Construction* spray-painted across the side panels was in his sightline with its four-ways on. He looked up. Seven stories tall, the concrete walls and floors of the new construction were in place but the finishing had yet to be started. A boom truck sat dark and silent at the western corner, its crane hovering above the tallest point of the structure.

Gundersund caught sight of his bloodshot eyes in the rear-view mirror and tried to flatten his damp, tangled hair with the heels of his palms. He'd meant to get a haircut but had never gotten around to it. A month's leave and one day had run into the next. He'd spent three weeks travelling the West Coast, renting a motorcycle in Monterey and camping in the Big Sur. Record-high temperatures and days of blazing sun. Upon arriving home three days ago, he'd been surprised to find Fiona in his living room. She was on study week; she'd sublet her Kingston apartment when she'd gone to Calgary to teach forensics on a sabbatical. He should have told her to book a hotel room but they were still married and this had seemed ungenerous. She'd lost weight and her face was drawn and pale. She'd seemed anxious about something but changed the subject when he asked if anything was wrong. He knew her well enough to believe that her anxiety wasn't feigned.

Stonechild must have found out that Fiona was at his place. She'd cancelled dinner the night of his return and hadn't replied to his voice mails. Hadn't contacted him at all until the call twenty minutes earlier, asking him to meet her at this location. He'd been in the shower when the house phone rang. Fiona had answered and passed the message along.

Bedouin greeted him as he eased himself out of the car. "You're a sight for sore eyes, buddy. Good holiday, I'm guessing, from your tan and beach-boy flowing hair."

"Me and the open road."

"Sorry it had to end this way." Bedouin started walking toward the paramedics standing at the tail end of the fire truck. "The construction workers found her lying there at six-thirty this morning and phoned it in. Must have jumped during the night."

"Any ID on the body?" Gundersund asked, catching up to him. "There were no details in the message I got to show up here."

"Nothing. Stonechild had the coroner look a second time because she couldn't believe the girl had nothing on her. No purse or backpack found yet, either."

"A jumper?"

"Looks that way but Rouleau asked us to secure the scene while we confirm the leap was voluntary. He's on his way."

Gundersund scanned the construction site. "This is an odd place for a girl to kill herself. It would have taken some effort to get through the fence and climb up there in the dark," he said, voicing his initial misgivings. Bedouin nodded his head to let him know he'd thought the same.

Bedouin shrugged. "But not impossible. We found a gap in the fence at the east side of the site."

They skirted around the first responders, getting close enough to see the body. The girl lay on her stomach, arms and legs spread wide with her face turned away from them. Blood pooled around her, garish red against the dull grey concrete. Gundersund took in her physical details, not letting her death affect him so that he couldn't do his job: tall with the lean build of a runner, soiled tight jeans, red running shoes, black jacket. Hair dyed midnight black. Multiple piercings lining the one ear that he could see.

He took a deep breath before shifting his eyes to Stonechild and the new coroner, squatting next to each other and talking. He must have been hired while Gundersund was away. The coroner drew a cover over the girl's body before standing. He saw Gundersund and said something to Stonechild, who was still on her haunches writing in her notepad. She lifted her head and looked directly into Gundersund's eyes. He wasn't sure what he saw in the black depths of hers but he knew it wasn't warmth.

Bedouin pointed toward the building. "Landed face first. Nose and cheeks flattened, skin rubbed right off. Going to be tough to get a photo for an ID if nobody claims her."

Gundersund flinched and forced himself to focus. No need to have a closer look now, he decided. The photographer would have explicit pictures if this death needed follow-up. "Odd to land head first," he said.

"Most jumpers aim to land on their head since it's the best way to ensure a fatal end. This girl took a flat dive." Bedouin spread his arms out. "Like a swan." He frowned. "But she didn't break impact with her arms."

"Hopefully she blacked out on the way down."

"It'd have been quick, anyhow."

Gundersund watched Stonechild tuck her notebook into her jacket pocket and start making her way toward them. Her long, black hair was loose and her turquoise-beaded earrings shimmered when the wind blew back her hair. In her jeans, black leather jacket, and deep-blue turtleneck, she appeared simultaneously down to earth and unattainable.

He'd taken a three-week journey along the West Coast to clear his head and get some perspective on his failed marriage. He'd known halfway up the Big

Sur highway that the woman now walking toward him was the one. He'd come home ready to take the next step with Stonechild. Fiona's visit had only delayed his trip to Stonechild's house ... or so he'd thought. He had a sudden urge to grab Stonechild by the arm and force her to talk to him but held back. He knew Fiona's week-long visit was at the root but nothing had gone on between them. The opposite, in fact. He'd finally gotten Fiona to agree to a divorce, which would be negotiated when she returned for good in a few months after the school term ended. He would have told Stonechild if she'd returned any of his calls.

"Welcome back," she said without smiling when she reached him. She turned and spoke to Bedouin. "Coroner says she probably jumped but he's going to run a tox screen and do the full autopsy." She kicked at a clump of dirt. "The girl was young."

"How young?" asked Bedouin.

"Late teens, early twenties." She looked past them. "I'm wondering if she was a Queen's student. She had no ID. Nothing to identify her at all. Not even a cellphone."

Gundersund knew Stonechild's detachment was forced. She was a master at keeping her thoughts and feelings tucked away where nobody had access. Two more cars pulled up and they all turned in unison. Rouleau was walking toward them. *Whig-Standard* reporter Marci Stokes and a photographer got out of the second car.

Bedouin muttered, "Not really fooling anybody, are they?"

"And not our business," said Stonechild, giving him a cold look before starting across the yard to meet Rouleau. They chatted and Gundersund listened while keeping an eye on Marci and the photographer to make sure they stayed out of earshot. One of the construction workers tossed his cigarette onto the ground and broke away from the group. He was shorter than the other men, but burly with grey hair poking out from under a white hard hat. Above his beard, his skin was tanned and leathery from long days working outside.

"Can the lads get back to work once she … the body's gone?" he asked Rouleau. "We're on a tight deadline."

Somehow, he'd known Rouleau was in charge. Gundersund would have picked Rouleau too, if he'd had to guess, but the man might also have seen Rouleau on the local news. As head of Major Crimes, Rouleau was often departmental spokesperson for high-profile cases or missing person alerts. He'd also recently finished a stint as acting chief that had given him even more airtime.

Rouleau turned away from Stonechild and spoke directly to the man. "You'll have to shut down today. Sorry, but we need to make a complete search. Your name is?"

"Bill Lapointe. I'm the site foreman. Why would you shut us down if she jumped? All you got to do is clear her away." Lapointe's face reddened, perhaps aware of how callous he sounded, although he didn't make any attempt to backtrack.

"I wish it were that simple. We need to follow standard procedure. You can tell the men to go home after we get their names and statements. Officer Bedouin will take your phone number and we'll call you with an update later today."

"Mortimer's going to be pissed." Lapointe pulled a phone out of his pocket and checked the texts. "He's on his way. Workplace safety and union reps will be here soon too."

The words felt like a threat to Gundersund but Rouleau remained unruffled. "I can have a word with them when they arrive. We'll treat this as a crime scene until we know for certain otherwise. Officers Bedouin and Stonechild will go with you to get those statements so your men can leave for the day."

"Your call." Lapointe's voice let them know he wouldn't be in Rouleau's shoes for love or money once the cavalry showed up. He strode back to his workers with Stonechild and Bedouin following close behind.

Gundersund walked with Rouleau toward the body. He glanced back and Marci and the photographer were setting up for a shot with the building in the background. They'd called Lapointe over as well as the construction worker who'd found the girl. His bad fortune would get him on the eleven o'clock news.

"Why this place to kill yourself?" Rouleau asked, craning his neck to look up at the unfinished frame of the hotel. "It's not an obvious choice, so far from anywhere. Was a vehicle found?"

"Not that anyone said."

"Organize a search for her car, and if none is located, have the buses checked to see if a driver remembers dropping her off. She could have walked, but not likely."

"She might have come by taxi or Uber."

"Let's go with the obvious first. Have any of her belongings been gathered up?"

"Bedouin said they haven't found anything. It's as if someone stripped her clean of identification."

"People setting out to kill themselves are known to leave their wallets and jewellery at home, but you're right. You'd think she'd have something." Rouleau squinted when the sun came out from behind a cloud. "Have Forensics go through the building. Are we positive the fall killed her?"

"We're not one hundred percent certain yet, but the coroner said by the angle and impact, it's likely she dropped from the sixth or seventh floor."

The fire truck was pulling away and they waited for it to move on to the roadway. Once gone, the girl's body was revealed like a curtain had been pulled open. Rouleau stood still for a moment and Gundersund waited with him before they walked toward her. Rouleau spoke quietly to the coroner, who rolled back the sheet to give them a look. The paramedics were waiting with a gurney, and after Rouleau had bent down to inspect the girl, he rose slowly from his crouched position and signalled them to take her away.

He looked at Gundersund. "The priority is to locate her family and make sure she doesn't end up a Jane Doe. We need to find out exactly how she died and why."

Gundersund nodded and Rouleau walked back to his car. Gundersund waited for the ambulance to pull away before he went in search of Bedouin. They had a long day ahead of them.

CHAPTER THREE

Dawn met Emily and Chelsea after class on the front steps of the high school. The wind was steady and the sky was increasingly overcast, but the sun was warm on her face when it came out from behind the clouds. She felt a lightness inside at the approaching longer days that would glide into summer months. She usually didn't mind winter but Kingston winters were damp and unpredictable. She'd gotten tired of walking in slush and shivering in the cold wind off the lake.

"Want to go for a coffee?" asked Emily. "I can drive."

Chelsea nodded and Dawn said okay. She looked back at the front door of the school. "Aren't we waiting for Vanessa?"

Chelsea frowned. "Van's been seeing some guy but doesn't want anybody to know — well, anybody besides us. She says her parents would freak if they found out."

Dawn fell into step with them as they walked toward the parking lot at the back of the building. "Does he go to our school?"

Chelsea shook her head. "He's older."

"University?"

"Van hasn't said much but I get the idea he's out of school and working. She said he drives a new car."

Emily gave Dawn a look that she couldn't interpret before climbing into the driver's seat. She was still surprised to find herself hanging out with these popular girls; the reason they included her was that she'd been helping Emily pass math. They'd been having private tutorials after class in the library since the year before. Emily seemed to like her but she knew that Chelsea and Vanessa only tolerated her presence because Emily wanted her there.

Thick black rain clouds rolled in while they sat drinking cappuccinos at their favourite table by the window in the Tim Hortons on Princess. Kala had warned Dawn before school about a thunderstorm later in the afternoon and told her to pack a raincoat, but she'd forgotten. She was going to get soaked walking from the bus to their house on Old Front Road. She looked over at Emily, who listened to the end of Chelsea's monologue about some show she'd watched the night before on Netflix before shifting her eyes to return Dawn's stare.

"Plans for the weekend, Dawn?" Emily asked.

"Not sure. It depends on my aunt Kala. We were planning to go to Montreal on Saturday." *To visit my mother in prison.* So far, she'd avoided telling Emily about her convict parents and her mom's convict boyfriend and wasn't planning to anytime soon. She knew the knowledge *would* change how they treated her. Vanessa and Chelsea would have more ammunition to convince Emily that she wasn't worthy. "But I got a text that she's going to be late, which means she probably has a new case, and that'll nix our trip."

"Want to see a movie Saturday night if you're around?"

Chelsea twisted a strand of hair round and round in her fingers and said, "I thought you and Van and I were going to hang out, Em. Sleep over at my place."

"Well, Dawn could come too."

Chelsea took her time answering. "I guess."

Dawn pretended not to notice Chelsea's reluctance. "No, that's okay, but thanks anyway, Chelsea." She picked up her empty cup and stood. "I need to get moving. A storm is coming in and I have to take the dog out."

Emily started to put on her jacket. "I'll drive you to the bus stop."

"You don't need to."

Chelsea checked her phone and looked up at Emily. "Vanessa texted that she's being dropped off here in half an hour."

Emily stood as she struggled to get her arm into the second sleeve. "I'll be back way before then, Chels. You can wait here in case she's early. Maybe you'll even get to meet the mystery boyfriend."

When they reached the front door, Emily said over her shoulder, "I think it's already raining."

"Lovely."

They were merging into traffic on Princess when Emily said, "Chelsea and Vanessa can be idiots. They think I'm going to dump them to hang out with you so they get all weird."

"I'm not offended."

"Well, I am. I probably would dump their sorry asses if we hadn't been friends since kindergarten. I feel this loyalty to them even if they sometimes act like jealous bitches." Emily flashed her a wide grin before looking back at the road. "Vanessa's parents are getting a divorce and it's ugly. She lives with her mom and her two brothers are with her dad. He's some big-deal architect so there's lots of money and property to fight over."

"I didn't know."

"She thinks if she doesn't talk about the divorce, it's not really happening. Like her parents will make up and move back in together. She forgets about all the screaming and fighting when they were living under the same roof."

Dawn had only ever thought of Chelsea and Vanessa as shallow, faded versions of Emily — when she thought about them at all. Emily was the one she liked, the reason she spent time with the three of them. Realizing Vanessa was going through a difficult time at home put her in a new, uncertain light.

After Emily drove away, Dawn stood in the misty rain at the bus stop scanning both sides of the street. She knew he wouldn't be there but part of her was still disappointed. She pulled her phone out of her pocket and scrolled down to his last message.

Will try to get to Kingston on the weekend.

She raised her head when she heard the rumble of the bus getting closer. She knew she should tell

Kala that her father had made contact, but for now, she wanted to keep him a secret. When she'd seen him waiting on the sidewalk across from her school, his aloneness had made her forget Kala's and her mother's warnings. She'd known who he was before she went over to him, before he even opened his mouth.

She'd seen him twice before, standing by himself in the same spot as if he was waiting for somebody. Nobody had joined him either time and she hadn't been able to shake the feeling that he was there for her. Snow had started falling when she finally crossed the street to talk to him for the first time, and he'd been shivering in his wet coat and running shoes. He'd flicked away the stub of a glowing cigarette and met her stare. His dark eyes were searching, needing something from her that she couldn't name. She'd been the one to break the silence.

"I'm Dawn," she'd said. "Are you waiting for me?"

He'd nodded and reached out his hand. "I'm Fisher. Your dad." He gave a phlegmy, self-conscious laugh. "Been a long time."

Fisher Dumont. Absent father. Convict.

The warnings to stay away from him had echoed in her head. She'd understood the danger, and yet, she couldn't stop herself from walking with him to a coffee shop so she could get him somewhere warm. She'd bought him a coffee, and they'd sat together for twenty minutes before she'd rushed outside to catch her bus home. It was enough time for him to tell her that he regretted not being in her life. Enough time for her to give him her cell-phone number.

She hoped she hadn't made a big mistake.

Kala rested her chin on her hand and looked through Rouleau's open office door. They were the last two working at their desks and she was about to call it a day. Rouleau had been on the phone for a while but was now reading something on his computer. She put on her leather jacket and walked over to say goodnight on her way out.

"Sit down for a minute if you've got time," Rouleau said, swivelling his chair away from the computer screen to face her. "I'd like a moment to catch up."

She took the seat across from his desk. "You're working late."

"You as well. Any progress identifying the girl?"

"I've put word out to the university and college but nothing so far. No new missing person reports either."

"We could issue a bulletin to the public."

"If nobody reports her missing tomorrow, we might not have any other option but to go to the media." Kala considered warning him about the chatter surrounding his relationship with Marci Stokes but decided against it. He had to know that sleeping with the *Whig*'s crime reporter would put them both under scrutiny.

"The girl could have been passing through Kingston," he said.

"And decided to jump off an unfinished, out-of-the-way hotel after ditching all her personal belongings?"

Rouleau smiled. "Far-fetched, I grant you."

"Unusual behaviour at the very least." She could see that Rouleau wanted to raise something with her but looked uncomfortable. After a brief silence, she asked, "Glad to be back as head of Major Crimes?"

"I am. Less paperwork and not as many meetings as when I was acting chief. Plus, I can be involved in the cases hands-on."

"Well, the team is glad you've returned. What do you think of the new acting chief?"

"Willy Ellington? A good old boy. I suppose he'll do as a placeholder until Heath gets back at the end of the year.

If he gets back.

They exchanged looks, but neither mentioned the elephant. Instead, she said, "I get the feeling Vera isn't thrilled being Ellington's assistant."

"No."

She's unhappy about having to exchange you for a chauvinist. Not to mention losing you to Marci Stokes. Kala watched him for a moment more before slapping her hands on her thighs and standing up. "Time I got home to Dawn. You should be on your way too."

"One last file to review and I'll be right behind you. I promised Dad we'd watch a movie on Netflix and order in pizza."

Kala smiled. "Dawn loves helping your dad with his research. He's given her some work to do at home."

"Dad's grown very fond of her too."

The rain had soaked her hair by the time Kala reached her truck in the station parking lot. She drove west out of town; the roads were oily black, slick with rain. Between buildings on her left, she glimpsed the grey-blue lake through the blowing sheet of rain. Whitecaps were crashing like giant fists on the shoreline. She could hear the harbour bell clanging out its warning. *I love this*, she thought. *The wildness. The force that won't be tamed.*

She turned off Front Road onto Old Front Road. Gundersund's Mustang was halfway down his driveway. Fiona drove his second car, a Camaro, when she was in town. It wasn't in the laneway; likely it was tucked away in the garage. Kala turned her face in time to see a woman staring out the window facing the road. She recognized Fiona's long blond hair as she disappeared into the room. Kala quickly looked back at the road.

Fiona had dropped by unexpectedly with a bouquet of flowers the day before Gundersund returned from holidays. It would have been ungracious not to invite her inside for tea. *Paul has been telling me how much he misses me so I decided to surprise him. A week isn't nearly long enough, but my sabbatical will be over in a few months and I'll be home permanently.* Fiona had slipped the words into the conversation as smooth as silk, not waiting for Kala to respond before starting on another line of thought. But it was enough to shake any hope Kala had allowed herself that Gundersund would soon be free to start a relationship with her. He'd talked convincingly to her about getting a divorce before his holiday but he must be waffling or Fiona would have backed off by now. It was time for Kala to protect herself.

Taiku greeted Kala at the back door. He took one look outside into the rainy darkness, whined, and turned tail into the kitchen.

"I can't say I blame you, boy," said Kala, taking off her boots and jacket.

Dawn was sitting at the kitchen table reading. She got up to hug Kala and to pour her a cup of tea from the pot on the stove. "Sit down, Aunt Kala, and I'll get your supper out of the oven. I kept a plate warm."

"How did I ever survive without you?" Kala squeezed past Taiku — now stretched out on the floor — and happily settled into a chair. "Good day?" she asked, sipping the tea.

Dawn stopped halfway to the table with a plate covered in foil. She tilted her head and smiled in Kala's direction. "Yeah, it was an okay day. I went for coffee with Emily and Chelsea." She set the plate in front of Kala and removed the foil. "Voilà. Chicken strips and fries. Sorry it's kind of a crappy meal."

"This is exactly what I've been craving."

"I doubt it, but nice of you to say." Dawn sat back down, rested her elbows on the table, and watched her eat. "Will we be able to visit my mother this Saturday?" she asked after a while.

Kala swallowed part of a fry. "We'll have to play it by ear but likely yes. It's a good sign that your mom agreed to a second visit."

"She must have understood that I'm not traumatized by seeing her in prison."

"And are you upset at all?"

"I wish she wasn't in there. I guess I've realized that she didn't have much say about helping Gil hold up the liquor store. He was controlling her."

"Your mom regrets ever getting tangled up with him." Kala tried to sound offhand. "She worries that you're going to be approached by your dad now that he's on parole, even though it's unlikely after all this time."

Dawn slid her elbows off the table and leaned back. She stared at Kala and frowned. "I don't get why that worries her. Fisher was good enough to get pregnant with."

"She said that he often finds himself in the middle of trouble. She's concerned that he could bring some your way."

"Well, that's not going to happen. I'm not stupid. Why would she even care if I saw my dad? It's not like I can't be trusted."

"I know that. She knows that." Kala wondered at how quickly Dawn's back had gone up and the flash of anger in her eyes. Both seemed extreme reactions to a casual comment about the father she wouldn't even remember since he'd left when she was a toddler. "Your mom wants to keep you safe. Maybe she's fretting too much because she's stuck where she is."

"A little late for her to worry about me. She might have considered raising her standards *before* hooking up with Fisher or Gil. She wasn't exactly being mother of the year when she robbed that liquor store with me in the back seat." Dawn stood up, her mouth set. "I'm going to do my homework."

Kala studied Dawn's face and decided now was not the time to get into Rose's sins or the reasons for them. If Rose hadn't shared the details of her miserable childhood with her daughter, then Kala wasn't about to break her confidence while she was in prison — or make excuses for her reckless behaviour.

She reached up and touched Dawn's arm. "We can talk more later when we're not both so tired. I'll clean the kitchen while you get your homework done. Thanks for supper."

Dawn's shoulders relaxed. "Okay, Aunt Kala."

Kala listened to Dawn clump up the stairs before picking up a cold chicken finger. She chewed it slowly while she thought about Dawn and all she'd been through. She had a right to get angry — hell, the kid had a right to scream and throw things and rage for days on end. Up until now she'd been amazingly placid for someone her age with this amount of baggage. Maybe this show of spirit was a good thing. She'd become secure in her place in the world and felt strong enough to vent her emotions.

Kala reached down to pet Taiku's head. The feel of his fur under her fingers always made her calmer. He was the constant in her life and the thought that she'd outlive him weighed heavy when she considered how long they'd been together. He was eight years old. Fifty-six in dog years. She got down on the floor beside him and ran her hands across his silky back.

"This has been one long, distressing day, old pup," she whispered into his ear. "Let's hope it isn't a prelude to what's yet to come."

She lay her head on Taiku's side and listened to the steady beat of his heart. She was feeling restless as the winter turned into spring. She'd have liked to head north with Taiku and her canoe and disappear into the woods for a month, but now she had a house and Dawn to keep her here.

"This is enough," she said into the softness of Taiku's neck. "This has to be enough."

CHAPTER FOUR

Teagan McPherson woke to the sound of crying. It took a moment to orient herself and to remember that baby Hugo was sleeping in a travelling cot at the foot of her bed. She heard her daughter, Shelley, scream for her from the other room as she rolled over and swung her feet onto the floor.

"I'll be right there!" She called back, lifting the squirming baby off the thin mattress. "My goodness, could your bottom be any wetter?" She rubbed his back and shushed him with soothing noises. "Let's get you changed and then some milk."

After putting a clean diaper and sleeper on him, she carried Hugo into the kitchen on her hip. Shelley and Aiden were sitting at the small table under the window eating cocoa puffs. Milk dripped from the side of the table onto the floor where Mittens the cat was busy lapping it up. Raindrops splattered against the windowpane and the air in the kitchen felt close and damp.

"How long are we keeping Hugo?" asked Shelley before she slurped milk from her spoon.

"Nadia will be here by eight to pick him up," said Teagan. "Lucky I kept your old high chair." She buckled Hugo in and he settled down after she poured a handful of Cheerios onto the tray. She plugged in the kettle for a cup of instant coffee and poured a bottle of formula for Hugo. She'd forgotten how much work babies were and she thanked her lucky stars that Aiden and Shelley were past the toddler stage. At least Clyde had been around for the first few years of their lives. She didn't envy Nadia having to raise a child alone. Her life was only going to get tougher.

Aiden and Shelley took an extra long time getting dressed for school. One of Aiden's rainboots was missing and he remembered only at the last minute that he'd been playing with it in his bedroom. Teagan hurried him into his raincoat after he'd pulled on his boots, and they raced down the hallway to the stairs. She carried Hugo on her hip down to the lobby to watch them get onto the school bus. The driver was idling in front of the building; Shelley breathed a sigh of relief. Another minute and they'd have missed the bus altogether. Then she'd have had to find a jacket for Hugo so they could walk the kids to school in the pouring rain. Not how she wanted to spend her morning off.

She climbed the stairs to the third floor, Hugo a dead weight in her arms, and knocked on Nadia's door. When there was no answer, she leaned her ear against the wood and listened for sounds from within. A radio was blasting. She wondered if Nadia was in the shower.

"We'll give your mama half an hour, shall we?" she said to Hugo, opening the door to the stairwell to descend to her second-floor apartment.

The building was cleaner than it had been thanks to Jeff taking over from the previous management company. The greasy cooking smells still lingered in the air and the hallways needed a fresh coat of paint, but this place would never qualify as luxury digs, no matter how much they tarted it up. She saw Jeff around a couple of times a week and he'd once even asked her if she needed anything fixed. Nobody knew much about him except that he'd been living in the States and had returned to Canada just before Christmas. His brother Murray owned the apartment building and had given him the job. Jeff was a big, quiet guy with a nice smile. He moved around the building without being noticed for the most part. Short blond hair. Glasses. Hunched shoulders. She placed him in his late twenties at the most. Early on she'd thought he might be a good match for Nadia, but as she'd gotten to know both of them, she realized that was a crazy idea. Nadia would never go for a guy with so few prospects even though she wasn't high up the social ladder herself. Teagan could tell Nadia had ambition. She'd said she wasn't planning on staying in Bellevue Towers much longer — but everyone in the building had sworn that at one time or another.

Back in her apartment, she set up Hugo on a blanket with some blocks and a plastic bath book left over from her kids' baby years and phoned the number Nadia had given her. It was the first time she'd ever called Nadia's cell, never having had a reason to before. She wasn't surprised when it went straight to voice mail. She left a message asking Nadia to check in and let her know when she planned to get Hugo, then tossed her phone on the counter and began cleaning up the morning mess.

Teagan waited until after lunch, when Hugo was fast asleep in the cot, before climbing the stairs to knock again on Nadia's door. The kids would be home in a few hours and she was eager to have some time to herself before she had to go downstairs and wait to meet their bus. Hugo was sleeping but she was still on duty and couldn't leave for a walk to buy sausages and apples for supper. She'd promised Aiden his favourite meal as a reward for making his bed all week.

She knocked lightly at first. Waited. Knocked again. Called out Nadia's name. She leaned an ear against the door and heard music. *This is really beyond the pale*, she thought. *It's not as if I even know you well.* Was Nadia holed up in there with some guy she'd met in a bar the night before? Teagan was willing to cut her some slack but that would be too much. She'd refuse to take Hugo next time.

She turned as the door to the stairwell opened. The front of a stepladder appeared first, followed by Jeff in his grey work shirt and matching pants. A honking big circle of keys hung from his belt and jangled as he moved.

"You're on the wrong floor," he said. "Is there a problem?"

"No, I don't think so." She pointed at the ladder. "Fixing something?"

"Light's burned out at the end of the hall." He started to walk past her.

Teagan thought about her few remaining hours of freedom before the kids came home and a swell of desperation rose in her chest. She held out a hand to stop him. "The thing is, I've been looking after Nadia's baby and she's supposed to have picked him up this morning. I'm not sure if she's in her apartment but I hear music."

"Have you tried knocking?"

What, do I look stupid? "Yeah, a few times. I also left a voice mail on her phone but she hasn't answered."

"What do you want me to do?"

"You have a key to all the apartments … maybe you could open her door so I can do a quick check that she's okay?"

Jeff frowned and his mouth set in a stubborn line. "I'm not allowed to go into anyone's apartment without prior notice. Those are the rules."

"I wouldn't ordinarily ask but she missed picking up her son. It's not like her." Actually, Teagan had no idea what Nadia was or was not like. They'd been alone together in the elevator once and Teagan had invited Nadia for coffee but the offer hadn't been taken up. The request to look after Hugo for the night had come out of the blue. The creeping suspicion that Nadia was taking advantage of her made Teagan add, "And I'd be able to grab some diapers for Hugo and some baby food because he's running out. I hadn't expected to have him this long." And it wasn't up to her to go buy the stuff.

Jeff set the ladder on the floor against the wall. "Let me knock. Maybe you weren't loud enough."

He pounded on the door. Waited. Pounded again. "She's not answering," he said, turning. He started back toward his ladder.

Not the brightest bulb, are you? Teagan thought, realization dawning. She had to take control. "Nadia could be hurt or unable to come to the door. We need to get inside and make sure she's not in distress. If we go in together, we're insurance for each other that neither one of us has done anything wrong. I'll also tell people that concern for her well-being was the only reason I convinced you to open her door."

Her words had come out in a flood and Jeff appeared to be working through what she'd said. "My brother Murray will be angry if I go into anyone's apartment without prior notice. He made me promise."

"I'll take any blame squarely on my shoulders. Besides, your brother won't even know."

"I could call him."

"Or you could make this decision now, yourself. You *are* the building super, aren't you? From what I hear, everyone thinks you're doing a terrific job."

She almost felt guilty at the flash of delight that filled his eyes at her praise. He tilted his head as if giving the matter deep thought, his mouth open. "Well … okay. But just this once. And we leave right away if she's there."

"Deal."

"And we don't touch anything except diapers and baby food."

"Agreed."

He took what felt like forever to find the right key and rattle it in the lock. When the door finally sprang open Teagan almost pushed him down to get inside. She looked around the barely furnished living room. Baby toys scattered across the floor. Small TV on a stand. Blue couch that had seen better days. The galley kitchen sink was filled with dirty dishes and the garbage can in the corner was overflowing, its smell making Teagan wrinkle her nose in distaste. She moved quickly into the bedroom, the location of the blaring radio that now played Rihanna's latest hit. The double bed was unmade and a crib was wedged between it and the wall. A bag spilled out diapers onto the floor next to an antique dresser whose top was covered in a plastic change mat.

Teagan crossed to the bed and lifted the blankets, checking to make certain Nadia wasn't buried under the messy heap. She turned off the radio and spun around to see Jeff standing in the doorway looking over the room.

"She's not here," he said. "She should take her garbage out. She could get bugs."

"I agree. I'll take this bag of diapers and see if she has some jars of baby food. Then we can leave."

Jeff carefully locked the door once they were back in the hall. "She won't be mad that I let you in?" he asked, his earlier confidence gone.

"No, of course not," said Teagan. "We did the right thing."

Jeff picked up the ladder and continued down the hall without saying anything more. Teagan jostled the diaper bag and jars of food in her hands on her way to the stairwell. It looked like she was stuck with Hugo for the afternoon.

What are you playing at, Nadia? she thought. *Just where the hell are you?*

CHAPTER FIVE

Tanya Morrison handed Kala the press bulletin requesting the public's help in identifying the dead girl. "Could you have a look before I send this to Rouleau?" she asked.

Kala looked up and smiled. "Sure. Pull up a chair." She read through the paragraph and crossed out a couple of words but otherwise didn't make any suggestions. "You've got the tone right and all the important details. Good to go."

"Thanks." Morrison remained seated.

"Is there something else?" Kala asked.

Morrison bit her bottom lip and took a few seconds to think before saying, "Do you want to take a break and get a coffee?"

"I've got to place a few calls …" Kala looked at Morrison's worried face. "Ten minutes?"

"Perfect. I'll meet you at the café."

"Sounds good."

After Kala checked to see if anyone fitting the dead girl's description had been reported missing that morning, she sent a note to the team letting them know the girl's ID was still a mystery. She made one of her return phone calls and was a bit late meeting Morrison. Kala bought a coffee and joined Morrison at the end of a long table on the far side of the room.

"Are you avoiding the riff-raff?" she asked, sliding in across from her. "This is about as far away from the regulars as you can get."

Morrison laughed. "I didn't want us to be overheard."

"I'd say you've succeeded in that." Kala took a sip of coffee, set the mug on the table, folded her arms across her chest, and waited.

"The thing is, I saw something I wasn't meant to see and now I don't know quite what I should do about it." Morrison twisted a ring on her finger back and forth.

Kala inwardly groaned. She hated being anyone's confidante if it meant helping them decide between two paths forward. Her experience was that no matter what opinion she gave, the person inevitably blamed her for whatever mess they got themselves into. "Are you sure this is something that you need to share with me?" she asked.

"No, but I need advice and you're the most discreet and sensible person I know."

"Not always." Kala sighed and picked up the coffee cup. "So what is it?"

"Rouleau is dating that journalist."

"Marci Stokes. What of it?"

"No, I don't care about him dating her, except I'm not sure about her motives."

Kala tried to read between the lines but couldn't. "I have no idea what you're talking about."

Morrison did a visual survey of the room before looking back at Kala. "I saw her meeting with our very own officer Woodhouse. I was at the Delta because a girlfriend was in town on business, staying there overnight. When I was walking through the lobby on my way to the elevator, I spotted them together."

"It might have been innocent. They could have met up accidentally."

"Maybe."

"But you don't believe that."

"No. They had their heads together and he passed her a piece of paper. I'd stopped behind a pillar to watch them. She put the paper into her purse and he then picked up his beer and sauntered over to the bar as casual as can be, without looking back. I got on the elevator and went up to get my friend. When we came down five minutes later, they were both gone."

Woodhouse and Marci Stokes? Could Woodhouse be feeding her information about cases? There'd been rumours of a leak but she hadn't seriously considered the informant might be on their small team. She didn't want to entertain the idea that Marci was using Rouleau to further her career — yet knew she couldn't rule it out. Marci was likeable enough but Kala didn't know much about her, except that she was a career journalist known for doing whatever it took to get a story. *Shit*. For the first time since she'd known him, Rouleau was happy, and now she had to question whether his relationship with Marci was built on lies.

"Leave this with me," Kala said, attempting to sound unconcerned. "I'll try to uncover whether

Woodhouse is up to something before we raise this with Rouleau."

Morrison's face relaxed. "Thanks, Kala. I've been struggling with whether to bury this or warn Rouleau."

"Let's hope it never comes to that."

Kala's cellphone vibrated in her pocket. She pulled it out and looked at the screen. "Gundersund is looking for me. I've got to meet him in ten minutes for the autopsy."

Morrison pushed back her chair. "And I've got to get upstairs and issue that media release when Rouleau gives the go-ahead."

Kala took the stairs to the basement and entered the lab. Gundersund was already inside and he tilted his head by way of greeting as she took a spot next to him. She nodded hello to the new young coroner, Trevor Cavanaugh, who was making an examination of the girl's corpse. Kala glanced over at his assistant dressed in green scrubs and was surprised to see Fiona Gundersund organizing the tools.

"Fiona's here another day and offered to help with the autopsy. Trevor said he was happy for another set of eyes." Gundersund spoke quietly to Kala as he ran a hand across his forehead. "I only just met him. He seems a competent enough bloke."

Kala studied Gundersund for a moment. "Have you got a headache?"

"Woke up with it. The painkiller should kick in soon."

Fiona walked over to join them. "Nice to see you, Kala. As we told Paul already, based on the height of the girl's fall, she was going approximately seventy kilometres an hour on impact. People have been known to walk away from seven-storey falls but usually they've landed on soft earth or something with some give. Not many survive hitting a concrete slab at that velocity."

"I'd imagine not."

"All set," said Cavanaugh.

Fiona smiled at Gundersund. "Then let's get started."

Kala tried to detach herself from the cutting and the organ removal going on in front of her while listening to the running dialogue and the observations being recorded as Cavanaugh and Fiona worked. She was hyper aware of Gundersund standing next to her but she couldn't read his mood. A couple of times, he reached up and massaged his temple.

"I can take this alone if you want to go for a break," she said about an hour in as they watched the saw grinding into the girl's chest.

"I'm okay."

"If you say so."

Two more uncomfortable hours passed before Cavanaugh removed the mask covering his mouth and nose. "I'll tidy up here and we can meet in my office, say in ten minutes, if you want to grab some coffee from the pot. It was fresh a few hours ago."

Kala and Gundersund declined the coffee but took the opportunity to step into the hall to breathe some fresh air.

"God, those never get easier," said Gundersund. He leaned against the wall and closed his eyes.

"Maybe you should go home and lie down. I can sit in on the debrief." Sweat beaded on his forehead and there was bluish bruising underneath his eyes. Kala pulled up her sleeve to look at her watch. "It's going on four o'clock and we missed lunch. Maybe you need to eat something."

"I'll push through."

They stood waiting without talking until Fiona poked her head out the door and called them in. Gundersund trailed Kala into the office at the back of the lab. The space was cramped with a large desk, bookshelves, and filing cabinets and it smelled of formaldehyde and stale coffee. Kala motioned Gundersund to take the visitor chair while she wedged herself into a corner. Fiona positioned herself on the corner of the desk facing Gundersund and Trevor Cavanaugh took the chair. Fiona had taken off her lab coat and let her long blond hair loose from its bun. Her silk shirtdress rode up on her thighs when she crossed her legs.

Kala kept her eyes averted from Fiona's swinging legs and focused on Trevor's face. He had friendly eyes in a narrow face capped with straight ginger-coloured hair. He cleared his throat. "Right. We put Jane Doe at twenty-two years of age, five foot seven — or one hundred and seventy point one eight centimetres tall — weighing fifty-two kilograms or one hundred and fifteen pounds. In good health, albeit slightly anemic. She landed face first, angled to the right, and broke her nose and jaw and the right cheekbone. Most of the facial skin was scraped off when she slid forward on impact across the rough concrete. Her internal organs were damaged, particularly the heart, spleen, and liver. Her ribs were shattered. Without the complete lab test results, cause of death can be attributed to severance of brachial arteries and internal hemorrhaging, including in the brain. In other words, a fall from a great height." He paused. "We noticed bruising on her left biceps and wrist, and old scars on her back that were not caused by the fall. She'd also given birth less than a year ago. Caesarian, by the scar."

"Was there a wedding ring?" Kala asked.

"No, and she wasn't wearing any rings on her digits, although she had multiple earrings in both ears and a crystal stud above her lip on the right side."

"If she kept the child, one has to wonder where it is." Kala hoped the bulletin had gone out. She was suddenly anxious for this meeting to finish up so she could check.

"Wonder whether she killed the baby as well as herself, you mean," said Fiona. "The girl had to be desperate to jump off that building. Based on her old wounds, her partner was beating her. I'd guess she'd had enough."

Kala wanted to keep options open. "That would be a worst-case scenario but we aren't there yet."

"Let's not jump to any conclusions without evidence, Fiona," Gundersund cut in. "Probably the child was adopted or is safely at home with this girl's mother or another family member."

"Then who was beating her? Because that's what we can conclude from the marks on her skin."

Cavanaugh coughed and took a moment to clear phlegm from his throat. "Sorry," he said. "Getting over a cold. I'm having a tox scan done on her blood and running more tests. We're checking with dentists' offices to see if we can get a match for her teeth, at least the ones still intact. I've put a rush on the requests."

"Anything else to report now?" asked Gundersund.

"Nothing that will help identify her. I'll have the written report to you by end of day."

"In that case" — Gundersund slapped his thighs and pushed himself to his feet — "I have to let Rouleau know the results so far. Coming, Stonechild?"

"Sure."

She thanked Trevor and Fiona and followed Gundersund into the hall. As they walked toward the stairwell, he said, "By the look on your face, I'd say you've got doubts about the suicide."

"I didn't know I was so readable."

"I've gotten to know you."

She ignored the intimacy in his lowered voice. "Well, I have questions."

"Such as?"

"How did she get to the construction site and why even pick it to start with? Most women carry a purse or wear a watch or have a cellphone. Why did she have absolutely nothing? If she got there by bus, where was her bus pass if she wasn't carrying money?"

"She might have planned to kill herself so she left everything behind. People often leave their wallet, watch, jewellery, phone, whatever at home before setting out to commit suicide."

"I don't know. This entire scenario doesn't sit right." She led the way into the stairwell. "Especially her being a mother and having those old scars on her body."

"That could be her motivation for ending it all. Maybe her partner was beating her. Maybe she had postpartum depression."

"Or maybe it was somebody else's motivation to throw her over." She stopped mid step and looked back at him. "You think I'm dreaming up something that isn't there."

"No, I'm playing devil's advocate. I agree that there are oddities, especially because I know how intuitive you are."

Until that moment, she hadn't realized how much tension she was carrying in her shoulders. She relaxed her mouth and smiled. "Thanks for the vote of confidence. I could very well be wrong but my gut tells me I'm not."

He smiled back. "Your gut should be surgically removed and used as a teaching tool for new recruits."

"God, Gundersund. What an image after the autopsy."

"Sorry. I never sleep well after watching the fileting and removal of organs. I'm going to need a few beers to change channels and get those images out of my memory bank and the smell of that place out of my nose."

"Attending an autopsy is nothing compared to what the victim went through. I remind myself of that and think of witnessing the autopsy as a sacred duty." She turned back to continue up the stairs. A moment later, she felt the pressure of Gundersund's hand on the small of her back.

"You're right," he said. "I've never looked at an autopsy that way before but think I will in future."

"A spiritual outlook helps to cope with the worst trauma," said Kala, "and it keeps me able to do this job."

CHAPTER SIX

The clock clicked over to 7:00 p.m. Kala had waited until the office was empty before shutting down her computer and putting on her coat. She checked the hallway, then crossed the room to Woodhouse's desk. He had a prime spot next to the wall and was lucky enough to have a bulletin board, which he'd covered with photos of comic book superheroes, wrestling champions, and sports cars. His desk was clear except for the obligatory computer; a plastic Mighty Mouse figurine wearing a Superman cape, one arm thrust skyward as if in flight; an Ultimate Warrior coffee mug filled with pens and pencils; and a phone accompanied by a notepad for taking messages. Kala picked up the mug and shook her head. The wild-haired man depicted on it was bare-chested, his bulging arms flexed, his eyes glaring out from a blue-and-red mask and his oversized muscles close to exploding. She set the mug back in place.

You are one predictable dude, Woodhouse.

She took a last look toward the door before methodically going through his desk drawers. He wasn't a pack rat so the search was easy — minimal paperwork to sort through and what there was of it routine. She wasn't certain what she'd expected to find. Maybe a smoking gun linking Woodhouse to Marci Stokes? But in hindsight, she knew he was too smart for that. She didn't bother to turn on his computer. It would be password protected and if she guessed wrong a message would notify him that someone had tried to log in. She'd have to wait until he happened to leave the computer open and stepped out of the office. Risky at best.

She stood up as the door to the office started to open. By the time Desk Sergeant Fred Taylor stepped into the room, she was almost back at her own desk, her heart pounding like a metronome on speed.

"You're still here," Taylor said. "I didn't bother to ring through because I thought everyone had gone."

"I'm on my way." She was glad she'd thought to put on her jacket before carrying out the search. She hoped he wouldn't notice that she was breathing hard from the exertion of distancing herself from Woodhouse's desk. "I had a few reports to finish. Have you got something?"

"Not sure. There's a worried young lady at the front desk who says she's here about a possible missing friend. She seems uncertain about anything but with the Jane Doe suicide case … I thought maybe the two could be connected. Rouleau said to keep the case top of mind when processing public enquiries."

"The bulletin went out this afternoon and calls have been flooding in with no real information. This sounds like another dead end but I can talk to her. Give me a sec to make a call first."

"I'll tell her you're on your way."

He left and Kala fished her phone out of her jacket pocket. She texted Dawn with a message to go ahead with supper because something had come up and she'd be home even later than she'd indicated in her last text. She waited a minute to see if Dawn would message her back and briefly considered calling before throwing the phone into her bag. She had to stop worrying about the kid; she'd never been anything but responsible. Kala would have a quick chat with this woman and get home to Dawn and Taiku before 8:00 p.m.

Based on Taylor's description, Kala had expected someone younger than the woman who rose from her seat in the waiting area to greet her. Teagan McPherson had frizzy red hair, drawn features, and slightly bulging eyes. Her coat was stained and her jeans were too snug over her wide hips.

"Sorry to have kept you waiting," Kala said after shaking her hand. "I'm Officer Stonechild. Let's find a quiet place where we can talk."

In an empty meeting room they took seats kitty corner to each other at the end of the long table.

"I haven't got much time," Teagan said in an Irish accent after refusing tea or coffee. "I've left the children with a lass from across the hall. She has school tomorrow."

"Then let's get right into it." Kala took out a notepad and pen. "Who do you believe is missing and for how long?"

"Her name is Nadia Armstrong and she lives in apartment 302, a floor above me in Bellevue Towers. The building is located at 60 Alfred Street at the corner of York. Nadia asked me to mind her baby overnight. She went out last evening and hasn't been home all day. I even got the super to let me into her apartment to check."

Kala raised her head. "Can you tell me what Nadia looks like?"

"Early twenties. Black hair. Slender and tall ... well, not short. She had a diamond stud above her lip. Pretty."

"Where was she going last evening?"

"I have no idea. Like, we weren't friends or anything. She moved into the building late last year and she wasn't overly friendly. I was surprised when she asked me to look after her wee babe Hugo yesterday, quite frankly."

Kala tucked her notebook into her pocket and stood. "Wait here for a moment while I make a call."

"Do you know where Nadia is?"

I believe I do. Kala hesitated. "I have to check with my team and we'll go from there."

Teagan sighed and slumped back into the chair. "As long as this doesn't take too long. My son, Aiden, can be a pure handful at bedtime and I promised the wee sitter I'd be home to tuck him in."

Rouleau answered on the second ring. "I'm on my way. Call Gundersund and get him back to HQ. I'll line up Trevor Cavanaugh for a viewing. If the dead girl is Nadia Armstrong, we'll want to lock down her apartment until Forensics has a look in the morning."

"You think the girl was murdered?"

"Not sure yet, but it never hurts to dot the i's until we have conclusive proof one way or the other."

"For what it's worth, sir, I agree with you."

They signed off and she sent another quick text to Dawn to let her know she'd now be home very late. She ignored the flutter of worry that Dawn hadn't answered her previous text and returned to break the bad news to Teagan. She'd have to stay another hour at least to identify the dead girl.

Dawn had meant to catch the bus home right after class ended. In fact, she was at her locker putting on her jacket when Emily came to talk to her.

"I have a math test tomorrow that I forgot about and I need help. Do you have an hour to spare?"

Dawn considered the timing for a second before agreeing. After all, Kala wouldn't be home for at least another hour and Taiku was fine indoors for a few more. They found seats in the library and Emily struggled through some problems before finally announcing that she got the concept. They worked through a few more problems to be certain, then Dawn checked the clock above the librarian's desk.

"I have to get home," she said, gathering up her books. "Are you meeting up with Chelsea and Vanessa?"

"Chelsea's sick today." Emily checked her phone. "Vanessa's with her mystery boyfriend. Do you have time to go for coffee? I could drive you home afterward. The rain has started up again so it'll save you getting wet."

"If we go somewhere close by."

They chose the Tim Hortons on the way to Dawn's house and settled in with cups of hot chocolate. Dawn checked her phone while Emily went to the washroom. Another message from her father. Should she delete it and cut the tie now or see what he wanted? She waffled, knowing that Kala and her mother would be upset if they knew Fisher had been contacting her. Feeling guilty, she opened her aunt's message first. Another arrived while she was reading the first.

"Anyone exciting?" asked Emily, sliding into the seat across from her.

Dawn set her phone on the table. "Just my aunt letting me know she's got to work on a case and won't be home for a while."

"So you can stay longer?"

"Not too long. I have to get home to take the dog out."

Emily seemed to be mulling something over. She asked, "Why do you live with your aunt instead of your parents?"

Dawn had known she'd be questioned at some point and she had her answer ready. "My parents are divorced and out of the city a lot. It's easier to live with my aunt while I'm going to school."

"Still, must be hard not seeing them much."

"Sometimes."

"Vanessa's not taking her parents' divorce well.

She's gotten all secretive and this new boyfriend seems … I don't know … sketchy."

"Have you met him?"

"I saw him when he picked her up once, but only from a distance. He looks older. Like maybe too old to be dating a fifteen-year-old."

"How old is he?"

"She won't tell me." Emily picked up her hot chocolate. "I've tried talking to her. Chelsea tried. Vanessa is being evasive, you know? It's so not like her."

"She probably wants to be sure of their relationship before she brings him into the circle. She'll come around."

"I hope so."

"Does he have a name?"

"Leo somebody. She never told me his last name."

Dawn didn't know Vanessa well enough to offer to talk to her, let alone to offer advice on dating or even on parents divorcing, for that matter. Dawn could commiserate about the loneliness that came from feeling you didn't belong anywhere but it wasn't like Vanessa was becoming an orphan. She'd end up with two homes and at least one parent who cared about her. She'd still be blond, white, and privileged. Dawn finished her hot chocolate. "I should be getting home."

Emily was looking at her phone. "Speak of the devil. Vanessa wants me to pick her up downtown."

"Then you should go. I'll be fine on the bus. The stop is on the next block."

"No, I can take you home."

"Listen, this might give you a chance to find out

about the guy Vanessa's dating. Really, I'm fine getting home on the bus."

"I guess. I'll drive you home next time for sure."

They parted at the door and Dawn pulled up her hood as she started down the street. The day was darker than usual because of the heavy cloud cover. Sunset was more than an hour away, yet it felt as if it had already begun. The wind blew a spring chill through her jacket and she shivered when she reached the bus stop and stopped moving. She'd planned to message Kala but didn't want to pull out her phone with the rain pouring down. By the time the bus pulled up ten minutes later, she was soaked and cold and not thinking about texting. She sat at the front of the nearly empty bus and the driver chatted to her about the rain keeping people home and off his route. He let her off at the intersection of Front Road and Old Front Road and she walked home through the gathering dusk.

Taiku was happy to see her. She let him out while she changed into dry clothes. It was only after she'd fed him supper and made a pot of tea that she remembered Fisher's unopened message. She sat staring at the rain snaking its way down the kitchen window while she considered what she should do. Listen to her mother and Kala or give him a chance to be part of her life? Taiku seemed to sense her worry. He padded across the floor and rested his head on her thigh. "What should I do, boy?" she asked, rubbing his head. "Cut my dad loose or try to help him?" She picked up her phone. After a moment's hesitation, she opened his text. She read it through twice before typing her reply.

CHAPTER SEVEN

Rouleau's father, Henri, was waiting up with a bottle of Scotch on the table when he finally arrived home just before midnight. "Sit down *mon fils*. Take your shoes off and let me pour you a few fingers," Henri said, getting up to take a tumbler from the sideboard. "How did the evening go?"

Rouleau sighed as he stretched out his legs and settled into the easy chair. "I believe we're dealing with the murder of a young mother." He took the proffered glass from his father. "*Merci, mon père.*"

"*De rien.*" Henri topped up his own glass and sat in the chair angled to face his son's. He sipped and studied Rouleau over the top of the glass. "Why only believe? Aren't the facts conclusive?"

"A few mitigating factors point to murder, including testimony from the woman minding the dead girl's child." He took a sip of Scotch and let the burn slide down his throat. "The woman said that she barely knew the victim, Nadia Armstrong, but that she hadn't been acting suicidal. Nadia told her that she needed a night out and would be by first thing in the morning for her baby, an eight-month-old named Hugo. Apparently, she'd been smiling and bright-faced, like any young twentysomething let loose on the town for an evening of fun. She was dedicated to the baby."

"Was she meeting someone?"

"If she was, she never said, but I believe she must have done. The alternative is that she met a stranger, which would mean an altogether different level of concern for the public."

"*Mon Dieu.* The poor child."

"This woman that Nadia left her baby with said there was never any man about that she saw. Nadia wasn't married. Her parents live in Manotick, on the western edge of Ottawa. I've sent two officers to break the news. They should be arriving any time now."

"Kala Stonechild?"

"Paul Gunderson and Tanya Morrison. They volunteered. Hopefully, the parents won't be in too bad a condition after learning their daughter has died to give us information."

"It is a parent's worst nightmare to have a child die before them, especially a violent death."

"I know."

"What will become of this dead girl's baby?"

"I expect her parents will take him. Child Services is involved."

Henri drained the last of his drink and set the glass on the side table. "I must go to bed and I suggest you do the same." He rested his hands on his knees. His eyes were apologetic and his voice hesitant. "You know, son, if you prefer to spend nights with Marci, I'm fine on my own."

Rouleau knew that Henri must have debated saying this for some time. He wanted to put his father's mind at ease without making him feel a burden so he chose his words carefully. "I may spend the occasional night with her, Dad, but for now, we're happy leading our own lives for the most part. We enjoy each other's company but we also have other interests and work to keep us busy. It's also a good idea to stay apart as a new case unfolds, optics being what they are when a Homicide staff sergeant is dating a crime reporter."

Henri's eyes searched Rouleau's face. "So long as I'm not the one standing in the way, I'm fine with whatever you decide."

"You aren't." Rouleau smiled at his father. "Go get some sleep, Dad, and I'll be right behind you. I'll be leaving early in the morning — I'll try not to wake you."

"Then have a good day tomorrow. I hope you find out what happened to the girl and who's responsible without any further difficulty."

"From your mouth." Rouleau tilted back his head and raised his glass toward the ceiling.

After Rouleau heard the bedsprings creak, signalling that his father was safely in bed, he topped up his glass, put on his coat, and stepped onto the balcony. He sat down, moving the deck chair away from the railing so he was out of the rain but could still see the water and hear the waves sloshing onto the breakwall. A fine mist settled around him, dampening his face and clothes. He knew the stars and moon were above him but they were impossible to see through the dark, low-hanging clouds. Frances would have loved sitting out here with him, if only she were alive and they'd still been married. She'd liked nothing better than putting on her coat and walking along the pathways during a spring rainstorm. When he closed his eyes, he could hear her voice.

Just smell that, Jacques. The fresh spring rain and black earth and new life. The purple crocuses. The daffodils. The grass magically changing from brown to green overnight. This is what it is to be reborn and I don't want to miss a moment.

In the end, she'd had far too few springs. This was his second with her gone from the world. Frances had had a way of seeing into the hearts of people. She'd have liked Marci Stokes, he knew. Sometimes he even thought that Frances had sent Marci to get him back into the swing of life. Marci tackled the world head on, as Frances had, with intelligence, wit, and empathy. He considered himself a blessed man to have had two such women in his life.

A gust of wind rattled the glass behind him and he felt a damp chill through his jacket. He drank the last mouthful of Scotch and stood looking down at the parking lot. He thought of the dead girl. *Nadia Armstrong.* Morrison and Gundersund were at this moment getting information from her parents to fill in some of the gaps in her background. The team would be working through the weekend to retrace her movements that night. They'd need to act quickly while memories were fresh.

Before the killer — or killers — had time to cover their tracks, if indeed she had been murdered, as Stonechild believed.

The cold rain in Toronto ended before Fisher finished his evening shift. With an hour left, he took a smoke break in the back alley. Water dripped from the crooked gutter and made a steady patter on the pavement. He jumped when the exit door opened, but it was only Nico sneaking outside for a few puffs. Nico sidled up next to him and pulled a pack from the pocket inside his suit jacket. He lit up and exhaled, squinting as the smoke drifted into his eyes.

"Slow night," Fisher commented. He didn't feel like speaking but stating the obvious wasn't exactly a conversation.

"Blue Jays are in town. Wait until the game ends."

And then what? We'll be flooded with baseball fans looking for a plate of spaghetti? Fisher thought this a tad optimistic given that the Venice Café wasn't exactly a destination restaurant for anyone outside the hood. He decided not to get into it though. At one time, he might have challenged Nico's absurd statement, but all the prison therapy had taught him to pull back in no-win situations.

The stray cat was creeping closer to them, probably hoping they'd drop some food. Nico stomped his foot and yelled at it to get lost. He picked up a stone and lobbed it skyward. The cat skittered backwards and found a spot in the shadows to lie in wait. "I hate that fuckin' cat," said Nico. "Fuckin' scavenger." He took a quick puff and flicked the cigarette onto the pavement. "Got to get back inside. You're in my debt, by the way."

"Oh yeah? How so?"

"Your two buddies came back last night after you left. I told them you didn't work here anymore."

The brief flash of relief was followed by the usual sick feeling. Fisher knew Loot and Ronnie might be put off for a day or two but they'd be back. He owed them too much money for them to give up. Money he'd foolishly bet and lost.

Nico's eyes narrowed when he appeared to realize that no expression of thanks was forthcoming. "What have they got on you anyway?"

"Nothing. I borrowed a few bucks and they want it back … with interest."

"Man, why don't you pay them off?"

"Yeah, I'll just do that." *Asshole.*

"'Cause they look like they could beat you senseless, no problem." Nico grinned, a feat that stretched muscles clearly not used to getting a workout. "How do you even know them?"

Fisher answered while picturing himself lying on the sidewalk, two sets of boots taking turns kicking him in the ribs. "I shared a cell with the black guy, Loot."

"What, do they house you by colour now? He's a darker shade of brown but you're from the same paint chip." Nico laughed. "What was he in for?"

Keep control. "Pimping, selling drugs. The usual."

"Maybe in your world." Nico's eyes dismissed Fisher as if he were in the same category of low-lifes as the two men tracking him down. "See you inside."

Fisher finished his cigarette and returned to the kitchen a few minutes after Nico. An hour more of hauling trays of dirty dishes and filling and emptying the dishwasher, and he was free for another long, empty evening. He draped his apron on the hook, said goodbye to Gina, who was using the quiet time to make a big pan of manicotti, and saluted Rhonda on his way out. She lifted her head but lowered it as quickly.

Yeah, you want me bad, Fisher mouthed to the top of her head.

Outside, he inhaled the night air deep into his lungs. He scanned the alleyway to make sure nobody was waiting to jump out at him before he started walking toward the street. The cat slunk out from the dark side of the building but kept its distance. Fisher squatted down and held out a piece of cooked meatball he'd taken from the fridge. The cat sat and stared, its slitted eyes glinting yellow-green. "Wasn't me threw the rock," Fisher said, "so don't give me that look. Come get your supper." The cat moved closer but wouldn't take the food until Fisher stepped away. "I'm planning a vacation," he said. "So you'll have to fend for yourself for a bit until I get back. See that you behave yourself."

He continued to the street and looked both ways before stepping out from the shadows and turning toward Dalhousie on his way to Marie's. One more night crashing with her, a trip to his parole officer, and he'd be on his way to Kingston on the afternoon bus. He'd have to remember to call in sick to the restaurant to make sure he still had a job in a week's time — although losing it wouldn't be the end of the world. He could always find another minimum-wage, dead-end job. Might even be a good thing to start working somewhere else to throw Loot off his trail.

CHAPTER EIGHT

As soon as he got in to work the following morning, Rouleau answered a call to update the acting chief. He walked past Vera as she put down the phone and looked up from her desk. She smiled, but the lustre wasn't as bright as usual. He knew from stories around the water cooler that Willy Ellington usually had that impact on people.

"Everything okay, Vera?"

"Yes." She rolled her eyes. "He's expecting you."

"Wish me luck."

"You're going to need it." She swung her chair sideways to face her computer. She mumbled something to herself that sounded like a string of curse words.

Ellington put down the pages he was reading and removed his half-moon glasses as Rouleau knocked and walked into his office. "Take a seat," Ellington said. "I've told Vera to bring coffee. I hear we have a suicide on our hands."

"Thanks." Rouleau settled himself in the leather chair. "We haven't ruled out foul play yet. A twenty-two-year-old girl named Nadia Armstrong. She lived with her eight-month-old baby in Bellevue

Towers, a low-rise apartment building at the corner of Alfred and York, north of the university campus. Apparently she moved in six months ago. Woodhouse and Morrison went to see her parents in Manotick last night to notify them and find out her history. They arrived home early morning, so I told them to sleep in. They should be here in an hour or so to update us."

"Suicide looks like the obvious cause of death, from what I've been told."

"I can't shut the file until we have conclusive proof one way or the other."

Ellington raised both palms as if conceding. "Do what you have to do, but we shouldn't waste much time on this. If it walks like a duck it probably is one. Suicide is nasty, but young people do it all the time."

The door opened and Vera entered carrying two mugs of coffee. Rouleau followed Ellington's eyes as he tracked her across the room. He reminded Rouleau of a Buddha statue: heavy-lidded eyes, wide lips, and a balding dome. He was close to six feet tall, but his substantial, once muscular body had softened from sitting behind a desk. Vera set the mugs down in front of them and rolled her eyes again at Rouleau before straightening and turning to leave. Rouleau observed Ellington watch her go, his eyes zeroed in on her long legs and tight skirt. Rouleau didn't anticipate Vera tolerating Ellington for long before she put him in his place. He hoped he'd be present to witness it.

"I'll need you to approve more resources if the time comes," Rouleau said, drawing Ellington's grey-blue eyes back to face him. "Past experience has shown that we need to be prepared."

"Do you know who fathered her baby? A love affair gone sour could make someone depressed."

"I'm hopeful that Gundersund will have that information when he debriefs later."

They both sipped from their mugs. Ellington wiped his mouth with the back of his hand. "Shit, she makes one lousy cup of coffee."

Rouleau let the comment slide past him. "We might have to set up a tip line if we need to go to the public to trace her movements that night. We'll see what the canvassing unearths first. There will be overtime hours to budget for." He could see that Ellington wasn't convinced about the need to dig deeper, so he added, "Hopefully, we'll be able to wrap up our inquiries quickly."

"There must be forms for you to submit to Vera for my sign-off."

"Yes, and I'll get started on them this afternoon."

"Very good. Anything else?"

"No." He could feel an awkwardness in the silence. Some kind of nicety appeared to be in order. "Are you settling in okay, sir?"

"No problems so far. As you know, I worked Drugs on the Kingston force for fifteen years before going to Hamilton for five years, and then spent the last few years in Ottawa as assistant chief, so I know this town and this police force, for that matter." He paused. "I heard through the grapevine that you didn't want the acting."

Rouleau felt Ellington assessing his response.

Rouleau kept his own gaze steady. "I have no aspirations to be in charge," he said. "I prefer working in Major Crimes."

Ellington threw back his head and laughed heartily. "Just making sure I'm not cutting your grass. Always good to know if someone's looking for an opportunity to bring out a knife and plunge it between your shoulder blades."

"Rest assured."

"Well, then, we should get along just fine. I value loyalty in uniform above all else."

"An important quality."

They stood at the same time and Ellington walked him to the door. "Keep me updated and let me know when it's time to give a press briefing. I'll want you there at my side." He grabbed Rouleau's shoulder with a hand that tightened like a clamp. Rouleau knew the pressure was meant to be a message.

"Of course."

The door shut behind him with a thump. Vera was standing at the window with her arms crossed when he reached her desk. Her white-blond hair was glowing in the shaft of sunlight pouring through the glass.

"Have you been dabbling in the medical field?" he asked.

She spun around. She'd wound her hair into a bun since her coffee run. "Whatever do you mean?"

"Because I suspect you've been doctoring someone's coffee."

"Oh, that." She waved a hand as if swatting a mosquito. "A little salt with the sugar makes for an interesting flavour."

"So Ellington said." He lowered his voice. "Be careful, Vera. He's got a temper, by all accounts."

She smiled. "Well, that makes two of us."

She kept her thoughtful eyes steady on his for a fraction of a second longer before she lifted her chin and turned to stare back out the window.

"See you later, sir," she said over her shoulder. "Have yourself a nice day."

Gundersund and Morrison arrived back in the office before lunch. Rouleau gathered the team together in their makeshift meeting area, the photos from the construction site already posted on the bulletin board. He asked Gundersund to lead the briefing.

"Nadia's parents live on the western edge of Ottawa in the village of Manotick in a large two-storey home. Clarence is a government policy analyst at National Defence and Greta works as an administrative assistant at Health Canada. They have another daughter, Lorraine, who lives in Brockville with her husband, Peter Billings. Peter manages a Jiffy Lube franchise and Lorraine stays home with their two young children. We didn't have a chance to interview Lorraine, but it would be a good idea."

While he listed the family members, Morrison had written their names and relationships on the whiteboard. She swivelled to face the others and added, "We caught the parents at home before they left for work."

"A couple of government wonks living in the burbs," said Woodhouse. "Viva the vanilla life."

"Not that you'd have any experience in that department," said Bedouin.

"My life is all about the excitement." Woodhouse yawned. "But let's not make this about me. What did you learn about Nadia?"

Gundersund shook his head at Woodhouse before continuing. "She was the younger daughter and was adopted at the age of five after being in a couple of foster homes. She had learning problems and self-confidence issues. When she turned thirteen, she got in with a bad crowd at school and her parents had trouble controlling her. She ran away when she was fifteen, and from then on, she'd return home off and on for short periods of time, usually after breaking up with a boyfriend. She showed up pregnant almost two years ago at the age of twenty and had a terrible argument with her father. He said that the tough love seemed to work because she got herself off drugs and alcohol and moved in with her sister in Brockville for six months before giving birth to a boy eight months ago. He said that he regrets their last altercation and he seemed genuinely broken up when he heard she'd died."

"Was she still involved with the father of her baby?" Rouleau asked.

"The parents don't know. Nadia all but cut them out of her life after the argument, but they considered her relationship with Lorraine a start and hoped she'd let them in eventually. They never met the grandchild."

"What about the people she was hanging around with?"

"Again, the parents don't know." Gundersund looked at his notes and then up at Morrison.

She straightened and said to the team, "We looked in the basement bedroom that she stayed in whenever she came home. We couldn't find anything personal aside from a few clothes and a teddy bear."

Stonechild had been sitting quietly, taking everything in. She leaned forward. "How did she end up in Kingston?"

"That we don't know yet," said Gundersund. "My suggestion is that we go interview the sister in Brockville right away."

Rouleau nodded his agreement. "Stonechild and Morrison can go to Brockville after lunch. Gundersund, you organize the door-to-door with Bennett, Bedouin, and Woodhouse. Retrace Nadia's steps that night. I'll be getting the paperwork going for more resources. We need to find out more about her life, the people she associated with, and her final days."

Kala walked with Morrison to her desk after the briefing had ended.

"I'd like to get on the road right away," she said. "We can grab something to eat at the highway rest stop in Mallorytown."

"Just let me make a trip to the washroom and I'll be set."

Kala drove her truck. They made good time on the 401, even with a detour for sandwiches and coffee. The skies had cleared during the course of the morning, and a warm breeze was blowing in from the southwest.

They both opened their windows and fresh air filled the cab. The annoying sound of wind rushing past the open windows was worth it for this taste of spring.

"I wish we could play hooky and find a restaurant with a patio overlooking the water. It'd be a treat to enjoy this first real day of spring and soak up some vitamin D," said Morrison, popping the last bite of chicken sandwich into her mouth.

Kala looked across at her and smiled before turning her eyes back to the road. "Nice to dream. I was going to take Dawn to Montreal on Saturday but I had to tell her last night that I'd be working all weekend … again."

"I know. Policing is tough on marriages and families." Morrison's wide smile disappeared and she was quiet for a few kilometres, her face averted to stare out the side window. The smile returned when she looked back at Kala. "I was glad to hear that Child Services returned Dawn to you. How's she doing?"

"Good. She helps Rouleau's father with research at the university and takes art classes downtown. She's even made friends with a couple of girls." Kala had to trust that she wasn't tempting fate with her hopefulness. She forced herself to be realistic. "Dawn hides her feelings from me, though. Doesn't show anger or give me the normal teenage drama because she's always working to please. I know this sounds strange, but I worry she's being too good."

"Parents of teenagers the world over would happily trade a day of your relationship for a month of theirs. My kids are only in their tweens and all of our lives are becoming unbearable already."

"Sons or daughters?"

"Twins. Sara and Jack. They're too young and goofy to befriend your Dawn, but maybe in a few years. They could teach her a thing or two about misbehaving. They live with their father when I'm working. He's better with them now that he's been forced to parent. He pretty much ignored them when I was there to change diapers and wipe noses." Morrison struggled to open the lid of her coffee and slopped some onto her lap. "*Merde.* Good thing I'm wearing black pants." She slurped the coffee and dabbed at her pants with the end of her jacket. She added, "Nadia began acting out when she became a teenager. Not all that unusual, I guess."

Kala thought about the timing. "The new peer group must have made her feel like she belonged. Kids are impressionable at that age, especially if they're having trouble in school or at home."

She pulled into the outside lane and sped up to pass a trio of transport trucks hauling their loads cross country, the need to concentrate allowing her to distance herself from her thoughts. Driving normally soothed her, but today she couldn't push down the anxiety that had flared up when she'd heard that Nadia had spent her first five years in foster care. Kala had her own memories of waking up calling for her mother, not understanding why she'd been taken away to live with strangers. The pain was in her even now, and she felt connected to Nadia in a way she couldn't begin to explain. She could have ended up like Nadia if Roger hadn't found her on the street in Sudbury and gotten her back on track.

She hadn't known that he was keeping track of her whereabouts after she left the rez to live in another foster home — one of many in a long string. He told her later that when her last foster parents told him she'd run away, he'd never felt such despair.

"The turnoff is up ahead," said Morrison. She had her phone out and was checking the map. "Beley Street is in a subdivision north of the 401."

Kala exited the highway and drove until she reached Centennial Road, which she followed east. Thick forest lined the left side of the road, with new builds carved out of the woods on the right. Morrison directed her into the subdivision, and a few minutes later, Kala pulled up in front of a two-storey red faux-brick house with a garage protruding like a snout onto a short driveway. Every house on the street was a similar style with little space between them and postage-stamp-sized front yards. Most of the trees were newly planted and it would be many years before they provided much shade. An older red Chevy Cavalier was parked in the driveway. It looked to have been recently repainted.

Kala sidled up to the curb and shut off the engine. "You ready for this?" she asked, resting her arms on the steering wheel and turning to look at Morrison.

"I'm your backup, so yeah, I'm ready if you are."

"The sister, Lorraine, appears to have been the one closest to Nadia, and I expect she'll be in shock. Let's hope she's up to talking."

"She couldn't possibly know less about Nadia than her parents did."

CHAPTER NINE

Lorraine had the coffee on and she served them cups in the sunroom at the back of the house, a windowed add-on to the original structure; the floor was a step down from the kitchen. Kala didn't need any more caffeine but accepted a mug to put Lorraine at ease. She watched Lorraine settle into the flowered cushions of the wicker couch and shifted on her own tufted cushion, trying to find a comfortable position. Morrison had taken a chair off to the side facing the bank of windows. A large spider plant hung dangerously close to her head but she appeared unfazed. Kala faced Lorraine and the inside wall but knew she wasn't missing much of a view. On her way to sit down, she'd glanced out at the back of another row of houses with identical decks and bits of lawn.

Lorraine looked, understandably, nothing like her adopted sister. Where Nadia was tall and slender, Lorraine was petite and — if Kala was any judge of height — topped out at five three. She had straight, shoulder-length hair the same shade as her hazel eyes, which now stared back at Kala. Pain and fatigue made her appear older than thirty-two.

"We're very sorry for the loss of your sister," said Kala. "I understand she lived with you during her pregnancy. Can you tell us more about her?"

"Nadia was finally getting her act together. She loved her baby and had cut free of all the garbage holding her down. I really thought she was going to make it." Lorraine's voice cracked and she stopped talking, fanning a hand in front of her face to give herself a moment. She croaked, "I'm sorry."

"Take your time," said Kala. "I know how difficult this is."

Lorraine swiped away a tear and took a deep breath, exhaling before she spoke. "She lived with us for the last half of her pregnancy and until Hugo was two months old. I didn't want them to leave but Nad thought it was time to stand on her own two feet and make a home for Hugo. She picked Kingston because it wasn't too big and she could go to college once she got her high school certificate. She was taking online courses as a mature student, or at least that was her plan. What's going to happen to Hugo now? I left a message with Children's Services but nobody's called me back."

"Do you know if Nadia had a will?"

"Are you kidding me? Nadia wasn't exactly in that headspace." She smiled, either at the memory of her sister or at the thought of what she said next. "We'd like to adopt Hugo. Peter and I talked it over last night and we think it's the right thing to do. He wanted to be here today, but he had to see about an emergency at his shop. He manages a Jiffy Lube."

Kala had been hoping that the family would take in Hugo. The alternative didn't have a high success rate. "I'm sure you'll provide a good home," she said. "Hugo will need lots of love and support."

"We hadn't planned to have another but I don't like to think of Hugo with strangers."

"No." What kid in the system was ever happy to be there? Living in a series of foster families. Belonging nowhere. Constantly grieving for the parents who gave you away. Kala took a second to rid her mind of memories of her own past. "Is Hugo's father a possibility?"

"Nadia didn't name anybody on the birth certificate, so I'm guessing the father doesn't even know he has a kid. I won't spend any time looking for him, that's for sure."

"She never said who he was?"

"Nope."

"Can you name any of the people who Nadia hung around with?"

"You mean before she came to live with us?"

"Yes."

Lorraine shifted in her seat and looked past Kala out the window, seeming to stall for time. She took a few moments before focusing back on Kala. "A guy named Danny and his friends. There was a group of them. They were into getting stoned and drunk and not much else. I never met them, thank God. We were all relieved when she decided to come here and get away from them."

"Do you have Danny's last name?"

"She told me once, but I can't remember now."

"And the others in the group?"

"Sorry, nothing comes to mind."

Kala studied Lorraine to see if she was lying and thought that perhaps she was. Kala leaned in so that Lorraine couldn't avoid looking directly into her eyes. "Look, I know that you don't want us to think the worst of Nadia, but her past life in Ottawa and the people she associated with could have something to do with her death."

"But she'd broken away from them. She was living in Kingston and starting over."

"You can't ever escape your past entirely. People can find you, and Ottawa is only a few hours from Kingston."

Lorraine looked past her out the window. She pushed out her jaw. "Peter and I are going to go see her body when he gets home. Mom and Dad aren't up to it yet."

"There was damage in the fall from the building. You need to know that so you can prepare yourself."

"I still want to see her. I know you're checking dental records and DNA. Dad told me."

"How was Nadia supporting herself?"

"Waitressing." Lorraine's eyes travelled back to Kala's. "She only had her grade nine but she had dreams, Officer. She wasn't a bad person, even if she'd screwed up for a while. A lot of kids do before they find their way." She chewed on a fingernail before dropping both hands into her lap. "I can't believe she'd kill herself. Not with Hugo and all her plans."

"We're not judging Nadia or the life she led. Our only reason for asking these questions is to find out what caused her death." Kala hesitated. "We're considering the possibility that someone killed her."

Morrison looked up and Kala tried to reassure her with her eyes. She needed to get more out of Lorraine, who wasn't going to talk if she believed her sister was under attack. Morrison dropped her head and continued writing in her notepad.

"Do you honestly have reason to believe she was murdered?" Lorraine asked.

"Yes. The day she died, she left Hugo with a downstairs neighbour and promised to pick him up in the morning. She was happy and she was a good mother. Hugo was healthy and well looked after." Kala could see Lorraine's shoulders relax and the tight line of her mouth loosen. Kala kept her voice neutral. "Was your sister involved in anything illegal? Say, prostitution or dealing drugs? We need to know, Lorraine, so that we can piece together her life at the end."

"No." Lorraine shook her head back and forth. "No, she took drugs before she got pregnant, but she didn't deal. She didn't turn tricks either." She pounded her fist into the seat cushion. "I would have known. I would have helped her."

"Is there anything else you can tell us about Nadia that might aid us with our enquiries? Did she leave any belongings when she moved away?"

"No. She took everything with her, which wasn't much. I'm sorry. Maybe after I've had a few days to digest that she's dead ... suicide was horrible enough, and now the idea that she might have been murdered ... I'm having trouble thinking about anything right now. My head's pounding from all the crying and I haven't been able to keep any food down since I heard."

"Losing a sister is difficult, especially under these circumstances." Kala chose her next words carefully. "We need to know where you and Peter were on Wednesday evening to get a full picture of everyone's movements that day."

Lorraine's body tensed again but she didn't protest the obvious intent of the question. "Peter took our eldest daughter to her soccer game for seven o'clock. I was home working on a quilt and put Susie to bed at eight-thirty. Peter brought Katie home at nine and went to meet his friends at the pub, as he does every Wednesday. I fell asleep on the couch watching *The National* at ten. It was over when I woke up at eleven so I went to bed."

"Was Peter home when you woke up?"

"He might have been in his workshop in the basement. I didn't hear him come in but I was half out of it when I woke up."

"Thank you, Lorraine. You've been very helpful. We may have more questions later but we'll leave it here for now. If you have any questions for us at any time, don't hesitate to call me. I'll do my best to keep you informed when we have anything new to share."

"Did you catch the underlying anger when she spoke about her husband being at the pub? I swear there's some tension going on in that marriage," said Morrison, sliding into the passenger seat. "I know the signs."

"Oh yeah?" Kala glanced over at her. Against her better judgment, she asked, "Anything you want to talk about?"

"Let's just say Allen and I had our ups and downs over the twelve years of wedded bliss. We're separated at the moment, while he's off finding himself. The search involves younger women, from what Sara tells me."

"I'm sorry to hear that."

"Sometimes I am too. Other times, I'm happy not to have to see Allen's gloomy face at my breakfast table."

Kala started driving back the way they'd come. "Run a search on the Jiffy Lube location."

"You plan to pay Peter a visit?"

"I'd like to have a look at him. At the very least, we can get the names of his pub mates to confirm his whereabouts the night Nadia died."

"You have a mighty suspicious nature, you know that, Officer Stonechild? He is the victim's brother-in-law, after all."

"The nearest and dearest are always the first place we look."

"I hate to say it, but after our last few cases, I've come around to the same suspicious way of thinking. I just wish it wasn't so."

"Familiarity breeds murder."

Morrison looked up from her cellphone. "The Jiffy Lube is on Stewart Boulevard near the Home Depot. Let's go see if this Peter fellow looks like a killer."

They met Peter Billings on his way out of the Jiffy Lube's front door. "You'll have to book an appointment for later in the week," he said. "We're full up today and tomorrow." He pointed to the kid standing behind the counter. "Charlie can help you out."

Kala was closest to him. "Peter Billings?" He nodded, and she said, "We're not here about a vehicle. I'm Officer Stonechild and this is Officer Morrison from the Kingston Police. We'd like to speak with you for a moment about Nadia."

Peter ran a hand through his greased hair. It was shaved close at the sides of his head but long and slicked back on top. "I was on my way to pick up my wife. We're going to Kingston to see Nadia's body."

Kala watched his eyes as he spoke. They remained steady on hers, dark brown and arresting. A girl would let him buy her a drink based on his eyes alone. "This won't take a minute," she said. "Is there somewhere private we can go?"

"My office is in the back."

They followed him down a short hallway to a room that doubled as a storage space, glimpsing the activity in the double bays on their way past a large plate-glass window. Kala's eyes fixed on the green bird tattooed on the back of his neck.

He invited them to sit in the two chairs, pulling one out from behind his desk.

"We'll stand," said Kala. She added, "This won't take long."

Peter crossed his arms over his chest and leaned against the desk. "So ask away."

"What can you tell us about Nadia?"

"She was a troubled girl. Lorraine wanted to believe the best of her, but I wasn't convinced she'd given up the rough life forever. She was good with the baby, though. I'll give her that."

"Why did you think Nadia would return to that life?"

"She was an addict. Sure, she'd stopped using, but she had that look, like she was restless and hungry. I don't know how to explain it."

"Did she deal drugs?"

"Not that I knew."

"How about turn tricks?"

"No idea."

"Do you know anybody who might have wanted to hurt her?"

Peter laughed. "She had some low-life friends in Ottawa. I'm not sure what any of them would be capable of, let's put it that way."

"Do you have any names?"

"Danny ... somebody. She cut them off when she moved in with us. Lorraine insisted."

"Why did Nadia move to Kingston?"

He took a moment to answer. "She said that she wanted to make a clean start in a new town, but I've got to say that I believe she sensed that we wanted her to leave."

"That's not what your wife said."

"Oh?"

"She told us that she wanted Nadia to stay longer."

"She's having trouble with guilt now that Nadia's dead. If we'd kept her living with us another year or so, she'd be alive — that's how Lorraine's mind is working. She chooses to forget how cramped we were and the sleepless nights with the baby crying and the lack of privacy. Nadia lived with us for eight months and didn't pay us anything — not that we begrudged her that if it meant she got on her feet."

"Did you help Nadia move to Kingston?"

"No, Lorraine drove her. It's not all that far."

"Had Nadia already found a place to live before she moved out?"

"Yeah, she found a cheap apartment online and met the landlord when she went to Kingston. I guess she struck a deal because her welfare cheque covered first and last month's rent. He must have taken pity on her. She knew how to work people to get what she wanted."

Kala made a mental note to speak with the landlord. She could see Peter looking at his watch and over at the door. "One more question," she said. "Where were you on Wednesday night?"

"You can't honestly suspect me?"

"We need to know people's movements. I'm asking everyone where they were so we can cross-reference later."

"I went to the pub with the boys like I do every Wednesday night. I got home late and Lorraine was sleeping in the living room. Our daughters were in bed asleep."

"Officer Morrison will take the names of your friends and the pub, and that will be all for now." Kala motioned to Morrison and took out her cellphone. "I'll be in the truck making a call."

Kala left the Jiffy Lube and got into her truck. She opened a text message from Dawn. She was going to tutor Emily after school and would be late getting home. *And so will I*, thought Kala while she texted a reply. The next message she opened came from Trevor Cavanaugh.

Opioids and alcohol in Nadia's system. Re-examined heart and found signs of heart attack. Moved from another location after death. Dead before the fall.

Kala's pulse quickened. She took a second to absorb his words, knowing now that her intuition hadn't failed her. Nadia Armstrong had been dead before she was brought to the unfinished hotel and thrown from the seventh floor like a sack of garbage. Somebody else was involved in her death. The relief Kala felt at having correctly suspected foul play from the start fed into a gnawing sense of unease. Why would somebody go to all that trouble to make her death look like suicide? And the more pressing question: what had Nadia been doing that evening that had led to her death?

CHAPTER TEN

Woodhouse knocked on the door across the hall from Nadia Armstrong's apartment. He was positive that he'd heard noises coming from inside, but nobody was answering. He knocked again, harder this time, with the side of his fist. "C'mon. Open up."

The dead girl's apartment was getting the full forensics treatment, every fingerprint, electronic device, and scrap of paper being bagged and accounted for. Woodhouse hadn't gone inside yet, but he would once Forensics left. He jumped when he felt a hand on his shoulder and whirled around to face some overgrown boy-man staring at him with his mouth half-open. "How the hell did you get on this floor?" Woodhouse asked.

"I work here. I'm the super."

"Name?"

"Jeff Simmons. My brother Murray owns the building."

"Has anyone interviewed you, Jeff?"

"No. I got here late today. I had a dentist appointment."

"So, you don't live on the premises?"

"You mean here?"

"That's what 'the premises' means, doesn't it?"

"I have a room I sleep in sometimes, in the basement. Usually I stay with my mother. I slept at her place last night."

Woodhouse saw Gundersund talking to another cop inside the Armstrong apartment. He wasn't going to be scooped this time. He grabbed Jeff Simmons by the arm. "Let's go check out your basement pad, shall we? Then you can tell me everything you know about Nadia Armstrong, the woman who lived in that apartment." If he saw anything suspicious in the basement, he'd get a warrant for a thorough search.

"My brother Murray is coming. I phoned him."

"Perfect. We'll wait for him near the entrance after I see the basement."

Woodhouse let Jeff lead the way through the exit door and down the concrete stairs. The garage was through another exit door. Jeff used a key from his ring to open a metal door to the left of it. They entered a furnace room lit by an overhead bulb. Tucked behind the large furnace against the back wall was a cot with a ratty-looking wool blanket draped over the end. An iPad, a flashlight, a package of Smarties, a selection of chocolate bars, and a bottle of water all sat on an upended crate next to the cot. Woodhouse did a quick search, making sure nothing was hidden in any cobwebby nooks or crannies. Jeff stood stock-still behind him the entire time. The place smelled like a boys' locker room marinating in machine oil: hot, greasy, and suffocating. Woodhouse would have liked to have found something he could tie to the girl's murder, but unless Jeff had put her into a diabetic coma with all the candy he had lying around, Woodhouse had nothing.

"We'll wait for your brother in the lobby," he said, motioning toward the door while loosening his collar. Jeff speared him with an accusing stare but said nothing. In the stairwell, Woodhouse sucked in dry, stale air that was a hell of a ways better than what he'd had to breathe in the furnace room.

They took the two visitor chairs in the small space, positioned across from the elevator so that everybody entering the building would have to walk past them. Woodhouse tried to figure out what the story was with Jeff Simmons.

"How long you worked in this building?"

Jeff didn't react to the question until Woodhouse repeated it more loudly. He kept his face turned toward the elevator as he answered. "Three months and twenty-four days."

"What did you do before that?"

"I lived in Nebraska with my other brother, Lenny."

"What did you do in Nebraska?"

"Nothing."

"I can't believe you did nothing. How long were you living there?"

"One year, eight months, and four days."

Woodhouse stared at Jeff's profile. The guy was a mouth-breather and apparently not very bright.

He pulled out his notebook. "Where does your mother live?"

"1365 McDonald Avenue."

"Her name?"

"Edna Simmons."

"What can you tell me about Nadia Armstrong?"

"She lived in 302. She moved in six months and three days ago. She has a baby. Eight months, six days old."

"You got a thing for numbers, bud?"

Jeff turned his odd grey eyes Woodhouse's way. "Numbers don't lie."

"Did you ever talk to her? Nadia?"

"She wanted me to fix her tap in the kitchen. I did, last week at 3:23 p.m. It took forty-two minutes. I have it in my log."

"And aside from that?"

"I said hello when I saw her in the lobby." He seemed to think of something that scared him. "I never went into her apartment when she wasn't home, except with Teagan McPherson in 201 to get diapers."

"When was that?"

"Thursday afternoon at 2:15 p.m. We made sure she wasn't there and Teagan got what she needed for the baby. That's all we took."

The front door opened and Jeff jumped up, looking as if he'd just been let out of school. "There's my brother Murray. You can talk to him."

The man walking toward them crackled with energy. He was wiry and bald, with the same grey eyes as his brother, except his had the sharpness that Jeff's lacked. He sized up Woodhouse and Jeff quickly, then he moved between the two of them.

"What's going on, Jeff?" he asked, keeping his stare fixed on Woodhouse.

"I'm Officer Woodhouse. We're here investigating the death of Nadia Armstrong, who lived on the third floor. You own this building?"

Murray's stare shifted sideways to his brother. "Why didn't you tell me about the police when you called?"

"They weren't here yet."

"Was she killed in her apartment?" Murray asked Woodhouse.

"No."

"Thank Christ for that."

"Did you know her, Murray?"

"Yeah, I knew her. I rented the apartment to Nadia and collected the rent."

"She paid on time?"

"Sure."

"Did you know anything about her friends?"

"No. She was only a tenant, Officer. It was a business arrangement."

"So you have no idea who could have killed her?"

"Nope."

"You said that very quickly. Do you need a minute to think about your answer?"

"I don't need to think about it."

"They're searching her apartment," said Jeff.

"Do you have a warrant?" asked Murray, looking hard at Woodhouse.

"We do."

"Well then, I'm going to take Jeff for lunch around the corner. Here's my cell number if you need any follow-up." Murray handed him a business card.

Woodhouse couldn't think of a good reason not to let them go. "Stay in the vicinity," he said.

Murray waved a dismissive hand over his head as he strode away.

Woodhouse watched them walk toward the main door. Murray put a hand on his brother's shoulder before he shoved the door open. Murray came off as heartless when it came to Nadia, but protective of the dummy brother — well, dummy except for the savant bit with the numbers. Woodhouse could understand Murray's reaction when it came to the death of a tenant; he might have had the same reaction himself if he were her landlord. But shouldn't Murray have been more surprised by the news than he was, since apparently Jeff hadn't told him anything? The elevator opened as the brothers were stepping outside. Bennett exited the elevator and pointed at their retreating backs. "Who's that?"

"The owner of the building and his brother, the super. I just interviewed the two of them. They don't know anything."

"You should have called me to help with the interviews."

"Nothing I couldn't handle. Where you been, anyway?"

"Door to door. Nobody knew much about her, but then, she only lived in the building six months. Rouleau said to start combing the neighbourhood after we finish here. Bedouin and a couple of uniforms are meeting us outside to divvy up the streets. You're to do the divvying."

"Just another day in paradise. Get ready to take some notes." Woodhouse pulled out his cellphone and clicked on a map of the neighbourhood. He'd start with the closest streets and spread out the search after the first results came in. At least Rouleau had had the sense to put him in charge. He much preferred coordinating over knocking on doors and talking to idiots.

CHAPTER ELEVEN

Fisher looked at his parole officer, Dennis Wilburn, and smiled. Wilburn was grizzled around the edges and close to retirement. He'd been in the business too long to be fooled by the average con, and he said things straight up with a cynical understanding that his job wasn't going to save the world. Fisher respected that about him.

Wilburn had Fisher's file spread out in front of him and was reading when Fisher entered and plunked down in the chair across the desk from him. Wilburn looked up and said, "You got a good report from your employer. Staying off the drugs and alcohol?"

"I am." *Well, drugs, anyhow.*

"Very good." Wilburn tossed the page that he was holding onto the pile and put his hands behind his head, leaning back in his chair. He kept his gaze focused on Fisher while his tongue worked a toothpick back and forth between his teeth. "Have you given any thought to getting your high school levels, as we discussed?"

Fisher had strung Wilburn along on this score. He'd hated school and would never seriously consider going back. "I'm still looking at options," he said, not ready yet to kill Wilburn's dream.

"You're too smart to be a dishwasher in some dive restaurant."

Wilburn's eyes were hard to hide from. Fisher knew a response was expected. "Maybe."

"No maybe about it. What would you do if you had your choice?"

"That's an odd question." Fisher wondered where all this navel-gazing was coming from. Usually Wilburn checked off boxes and sent him on his way. But Fisher decided to play along. "Like, anything in the world?"

"Yeah, like that."

"I dunno. Get a piece of land in the bush, build a lodge, and run fishing tours. Never going to happen though."

"Why not?"

"No money. No land. That's just for starters."

Wilburn grunted, rolled his chair forward, and picked up the pen lying next to Fisher's file. "Never say never, Mr. Dumont." He pulled out the form page and began checking off boxes. "Sign here and that's it for another week. I'm away next Friday so I've moved your appointment to the following Tuesday. I'm trusting you to stay out of trouble."

Four extra days. Almost as if the Creator was handing him a gift.

"Don't worry about me." Fisher reached for the pen and smiled. "I gave up on trouble a long time ago."

Five minutes later, he stepped outside the office tower onto Yonge Street. He'd brought his knapsack with a change of clothes, and his month's pay, such as it was, was zipped inside the front pouch. The thought of running into Loot made him cautious so he stopped, took out the money, and divided it between his shoes before turning south on Yonge. The bills felt uncomfortable under the soles of his feet, but he felt reassured knowing they were relatively safe.

He hadn't made it a block when his stomach took a nosedive. Loot and Ronnie were beelining toward him, Loot's face as angry and determined as a mastiff chasing down a rabbit. Fisher figured he had two choices: try to outrun them or try to out-talk them. Since they were less than a block away and gaining fast, he plastered a smile on his face and stood his ground. Hopefully, all the people walking past would keep him safe.

"Guys," he said as they positioned themselves on either side of him. "I was hoping I'd run into you."

They each took one of his arms without saying a word and frogmarched him back the way he'd come. They crossed the street at the lights and he didn't struggle until he saw the alleyway leading to a parking garage. They'd obviously scoped out the neighbourhood, probably when Loot checked in with his own parole officer. Somehow Loot had weaseled out the date and time that Fisher would be meeting his counsellor.

They waited until they were in the shadows before shoving him against the brick wall.

"You got my money?" Loot asked.

"Not yet, but I'm working on it." Fisher buckled when Loot's fist connected with his stomach. He would have fallen over if Ronnie didn't have a firm hand pinning him to the wall.

"I gave you your final warning." Loot hit him again.

Fisher gagged and only just managed to keep down his lunch. "I told you, man, I'm working on it," he gasped. He didn't like hearing himself beg but couldn't help the whine in his voice. "Please stop."

"What do you think, Ronnie?" Loot was toying with him now. "Should we give this bag of shit one more week?"

"I dunno," said Ronnie. "You've been more than generous as far as I can see, Loot." Ronnie got a hand under the strap of Fisher's knapsack and ripped it from his shoulders. "Let's make sure he isn't holding out on us."

Fisher watched in growing rage as Ronnie pulled every piece of clothing from the bag one by one and tossed it onto the pavement. He pocketed Fisher's smokes. "Nothing, boss," he said once he'd dumped out the last of Fisher's possessions. He kicked the bag several feet away.

"I'm not sure you deserve it, but I'll give you one more week to put the ten thousand in my hand or you're going to be dinner for the fish in Lake Ontario. Got it, Dumont? And you better not duck out on us again when we show up at your place of work."

Fisher nodded, then Loot's fist smashed into his kidneys. This time Ronnie's hand wasn't holding him up. He dropped onto his knees, vomiting bile and half-digested taco onto the asphalt.

"You're disgusting, Injun," said Ronnie, kicking him in the ribs. "If it was me, you'd already be fish food for making us chase you halfway around Toronto."

"I know. I'm a soft touch," said Loot. "But even a nice guy like me has limits." He laughed and Ronnie joined in.

Ronnie aimed one final kick at the side of Fisher's face. Fisher heard Loot say that was enough. He watched their legs retreat up the alley from where he lay on his side. After what seemed like a lifetime, he inched his way backward until he was lying in the deepest shadows against the brick wall. When he was certain they weren't coming back, he closed his eyes and let the pain and darkness carry him away.

Dawn watched Vanessa discreetly in English class, trying to figure out if something was bothering her. Not that they'd ever been friends, but Emily's description of Vanessa's home life had piqued Dawn's interest. To discover that not everyone blond and privileged was leading the perfect life shouldn't have come as a surprise. She knew that Emily's parents had given her brother a hard time when they found out he was gay, and that Emily used to cut herself and had been seeing a shrink. She seemed better now but Dawn still watched for signs that she might be back to cutting. Dawn had once believed that if she'd been born white, all the awful things in her family would never have happened and she'd be happy. Knowing that this might not be the case was disconcerting.

Dawn had only ever known Vanessa as part of the blond brigade tagging behind Emily. Snobby with a bitchy edge and no ideas of her own. Today, she looked haunted, as if she'd been crying and was trying to hold it together. Dawn waited until class ended to catch up with her on the way to their lockers.

"You seem upset about something," she said. "Can I help at all?"

Vanessa gave her a strange stare before shaking her head. "What makes you think something is wrong?"

"I don't know. You don't seem like your normal self."

"I'm getting a cold."

"That sucks."

"Yeah."

Dawn could have taken the hint and let it go, but she knew something was off with Vanessa and felt obliged to try one more time. They'd reached Dawn's locker but she kept walking with Vanessa. "The thing is," she said, "you seem to have something on your mind and I thought you might like to talk about it — if not with me, then maybe with Emily or Chelsea. I've found that it helps to talk."

Vanessa stopped in front of her locker and turned her back on Dawn. She reached up a hand to open the lock with her head lowered. "I'm okay," she said after a pause. She looked at Dawn and opened her mouth to say something else, but instead squeezed her lips together and shook her head. Finally, she said, "I'll see you around."

"See you around." Dawn didn't know what else to say but figured she'd provided an opening and Vanessa could choose to take her up on it later if she wanted to talk.

She returned to her own locker and put the books she'd need into her knapsack. By the time she'd put on her jacket, Vanessa was gone. Everyone she knew had plans for Friday night but Dawn didn't mind going home alone. Kala would be working late tonight and all weekend but Taiku was all the company she needed. She would have offered to walk Gundersund's dog, Minnie, if his wife wasn't living there again.

She left the school by the front entrance and was glad to find that it wasn't raining. She was tired of getting soaked every time she walked to the bus stop. Soaked and chilled. Vanessa wasn't the only one who felt a cold coming on. As Dawn started down the steps, she saw a black car with tinted windows pulling up to the curb and watched as Vanessa hurried across the sidewalk. Her jacket was open and she was wearing a tight blue top and ripped jeans. Had she been wearing that in English class? Dawn tried to picture her but couldn't remember. The side window of the car opened slowly and Vanessa leaned in to talk to somebody before she pulled on the door handle and climbed inside. The door slammed and the car pulled away, picking up speed as it went. Dawn raised her arm to wave as she ran down the stairs. The red tail lights were disappearing around the corner when she reached the sidewalk.

Emily had said that Vanessa's boyfriend picked her up every day after school. Dawn wondered what that felt like … to have someone care about you enough to drive to wherever you were, every single day. She zipped up her coat and readjusted her knapsack before crossing the street. The sun was warm on her skin even with the coolness in the air. She could see the buds on the bushes and trees; they were greener than the day before. Blue spring flowers dotted the lawn in front of a house and vivid red tulips lined the walkway. As she watched two robins hop across the lawn, she thought after all that she might not like having someone pick her up every day. The very idea was suffocating. She liked being alone with her thoughts. Doing what she wanted.

That was what people didn't get.

She wasn't upset about being an outsider. She liked Emily but could just as easily never hang out with her again. She didn't need anybody else to make her world complete. As long as she had Kala and Taiku to go home to, she could handle the rest. The thought of being taken from them again was the only thing that terrified her in the middle of the night.

They were the only ones she couldn't bear to lose.

CHAPTER TWELVE

Marci Stokes looked up from her computer as Rick dropped into the seat across from her desk. "Such a long day," he said, stretching his arms over his head. The entertainment beat is heating up lately and I've been out every night this week covering events. "You still working on the suicide?"

"Not a suicide any longer. Police are thinking murder. And the girl has a name. Nadia Armstrong."

"I guess you have the inside track."

"What do you mean?"

"My sources tell me you're in thick with the head of Major Crimes."

Marci didn't like the direction this conversation was taking. Not for the first time, she considered the fallout of dating Rouleau. She didn't see the relationship impacting her work much but he'd be under scrutiny. "He doesn't share information about cases," she said. "Tell your sources that." She wouldn't reveal even to Rick that her info was coming from Woodhouse.

Rick waved a dismissive hand. "They wouldn't believe me. Everyone likes to think the worst of others.

Makes life just that much more delicious. Does Scotty know who you're climbing into bed with?"

"Do you honestly think he'd care?"

"Well, he is running the paper and he hates getting blindsided."

"For God's sake, Rick. It's not as if I'm doing anything illegal."

"Girl, we'll leave that talk for another day." Rick gave what passed as a lecherous leer and stood, smoothing down his blue velvet jacket. "Well, I'm off to cover the spring fashion show at the mall. Catch you later."

"Yeah, later. I'll be avidly awaiting your report on the must-haves for my spring wardrobe."

"As if." Rick shook his head and feigned sadness before walking away.

Marci looked down at the clothes she'd put on that morning, actually inspecting them for the first time. Perhaps she should have ironed the striped blue shirt. Her black pants had definitely needed an iron but she'd been running late. She promised herself a trip to the mall to replace the scuffed leather boots that she'd worn for the past decade, turning her attention back to the document she'd been typing before Rick's interruption.

A half hour later, she was woefully aware of the gaps in her story about Nadia Armstrong. She had nothing about the woman's life in Kingston or her past except that she'd grown up in Ottawa. It was as if Nadia had avoided social media; she didn't even have a Facebook account that Marci could find. She thought for a moment. Scotty would have to approve a trip to the nation's capital to dig into Nadia's background. Marci figured she could talk him into covering expenses for at least a day. Maybe he'd even spring for a night in a motel so she could spend two days tracking down sources.

Rather than try to see him in person, she dashed off a note outlining her reasons for going to Ottawa and asking for his approval for the trip — Scotty had been hard to pin down lately, always in meetings. She reached for her coat slung over the back of the chair. She'd take a run past the apartment building where Nadia had lived and see if she could meet with any of the tenants. Then she hesitated, her arm halfway into her sleeve, and sat back down. She had the name of the woman who'd reported Nadia missing somewhere in her notes. It would take a minute to find but would be the perfect place to start her inquiries. Marci had a couple of hours before Rouleau would be stopping by her place for supper — plenty of time to check out the apartment building and then pick up something premade on her way home.

Twenty minutes later, she cruised past Bellevue Towers, craning her neck to get a closer look at the four-storey building. The houses on either side of it looked tired and worn, resigned to life in the shadow of the badly maintained low-rise. The roof of the two-storey grey-brick house on the left was black in places, its eavestrough hanging at a drunken angle. The homeowner on the other side hadn't bothered to wheel their garbage bins back from the curb and chunks of decaying food and soggy newspapers were strewn across the sparse brown grass. The sun was on the decline and it sparkled off the jagged pieces of a broken bottle scattered across the road.

Lovely, thought Marci, as she drove around the smashed bottle and farther up the street, looking for a safe place to park her car. She doubled back on foot and walked up the concrete walkway to the front door. The intercom appeared to be working; she rang Teagan McPherson's apartment. A moment later, a woman's voice with a lovely Irish lilt answered and agreed to buzz her in. Marci took the stairs to the second floor, covering her nose to keep out the pungent aroma of cooking grease, dank mould, and unwashed bodies — although she might have been imagining that last smell.

A woman with carrot-coloured hair answered the door. She was holding a wooden spoon and her white sweatshirt was stained with splotches of something brown. "Come back to the kitchen," she said.

Marci followed the woman and the scent of cooking meat and onions down the hallway, stepping around children's shoes and bookbags. "Whatever you're cooking smells delicious," she said, sitting on the stool that Teagan cleared off and pulled out for her.

"The kitchen's a bit of a tip, but I've been baking and freezing apple pies and I'm now working on a lamb stew. My mother's recipe. I have to pick up the kids from an after-school program in twenty minutes so I'll finish this up as we talk."

Marci took a subtle look around before fishing in her bag for her notebook. The kitchen was more than "tipped"; it had been upended and coated in flour and lord knows what else. Marci's fingers landed on a pen. "When did you move here from Ireland?"

"I immigrated with my parents when I was ten. The accent should have worn off by now but I can't seem to shake it. My parents' influence, I guess." She laughed before turning back to the stove. "You want to know about Nadia. I haven't much to tell."

"You were looking after her baby. She must have trusted you."

"I suppose because I have two bairns myself, she felt I was as good a choice as any. She wasn't overly friendly. Kept to herself."

"Did she say anything about how she'd ended up in this apartment building?"

"She told me that she saw an ad for a vacant apartment and met with the owner. This place isn't much, but it's a safe area and there is a super on hand to fix things. Jeff Simmons is a bit of a mog, but handy."

"Mog?"

"Sorry. A simple bloke. As far as I can tell, he's only here because his brother Murray owns the building, although I must say Jeff's a hard-working lad and tries his best."

"Got it." Marci made a note of their names.

Teagan set the wooden spoon down next to the stove and spun back to look at her. "Nadia did mention that she'd been living with her sister in Brockville but thought it was time to leave. She said that she planned to finish high school and then go to college. I'd have thought she'd have an easier time finishing high school courses while living with family to help out with baby Hugo, but I didn't voice my opinion since it was none of my business."

"Understood. Do you have the sister's name?"

"No, sorry." Teagan reached across the counter for the pot lid and turned down the heat on her stew. She half turned. "Lorraine? Yeah, she called her sister Lorraine."

Marci knew Teagan was preparing to leave to pick up her kids. She felt the interview slipping away. "How long had Nadia been living in this building?"

"Five, no, six months. She moved in late November, I know that much. Sorry, but I really must be going. The staff get huffy if we arrive late to get the kids."

Marci stood and reached into her pocket for a business card. "Please call this number anytime if you remember something else."

Teagan took the card and set it on top of a stack of takeout flyers on the counter. "I feel bad about Nadia. I wish now that I had gotten to know her better. We're both single moms and it's a tough slog, especially on minimum wage — or welfare, in my case."

Marci nodded in what she hoped looked like commiseration and started down the hallway, followed by Teagan. "It's never easy when somebody you know dies, no matter how slim the connection."

"She didn't deserve what happened to her. Not even if she *was* messing in something she shouldn't have been."

Marci, at the front door now, turned to ask what Teagan meant by that, but a phone rang from deep in the apartment. Teagan said, "See yourself out. I have to take this." With that, she disappeared into what Marci assumed was a back bedroom, and Marci had no choice but to exit the apartment. She stood in the outer hallway, wondering if she should wait for Teagan to come out, but as the seconds stretched into minutes, Marci decided to leave it for the time being.

For someone racing to pick up your kids, you seem to have gotten sidetracked very easily, she thought as she pushed open the door to the stairwell. She took one last look down the empty hallway before letting the door slam behind her. Once she reached the lobby, she searched for Jeff the super but he was nowhere to be found. She exited the building with more questions than answers but at least she had a new avenue of inquiry to pursue. She'd track down the sister's name and address and be on the road to Brockville first thing in the morning. No need to run the one-hour trip up the highway past Scotty, since it wasn't an overnighter. If he approved her request for money to visit Ottawa, she'd do the entire circuit.

"That your friend?" asked Leo, leaning sideways to see past Vanessa out her passenger window. She imagined his eyes all lit up with possibilities behind the dark sunglasses and didn't know what to do about the emotions rippling through her. The first was jealousy that he was sizing up another girl followed by unease as to where his interest could lead.

"I don't know her that well."

"What's her name?"

"Dawn."

"Dawn what?"

"I don't know." She wasn't about to make it easy for him.

"What's her story?"

Vanessa sighed and looked out the window. She jumped when Leo slammed the steering wheel with the flat of his hand, then began talking fast. "She lives with her aunt. I have no idea where her parents are but she was in foster care last summer for a while. I really don't know anything else about her except she's smart in school."

Leo showed his teeth in his idea of a smile. "Now was that so hard?" He turned his face sideways and said over his shoulder, "Whaddaya think, Shawn B.? Your next girlfriend?"

"I dunno. Wasn't looking." The man with the black beard, stretched out in the back seat, lifted the baseball cap covering his face, opened his eyes, and shut them again.

Vanessa kept her gaze forward. She focused on a mother pushing a stroller on the next block. Leo turned right at the stop sign, and she was sorry not to get a closer look at the woman's face. For one second, she'd reminded Vanessa of her own mother when she was younger. It took her a moment to return to herself and feel Leo's hand on her thigh, sliding up under her jacket. His voice was playful and she was immediately on guard.

"I thought Shawn B. would come with us today. We can fool around a while and then I have a couple of paying customers lined up."

"I told you I don't want to do that anymore. You said I could stop."

"Yeah, well, we need the money."

"It makes me feel bad."

"You know I love you, baby. I'm always going to look after you." His hand was rubbing her stomach above the belt of her jeans. "I just need you to do this for me. For a while until I'm back on my feet."

He didn't need to mention the video and the photos he'd taken of her. He'd only had to threaten her once with putting them out on social media, sending them to her parents and teachers. She felt her resolve crumbling but she wouldn't cry. Not this time. Her tears only made him colder. She shivered, thinking about having the man in the back seat's hands all over her.

She wondered how her life had turned into this. What would Emily and Chelsea think of her if they knew? Would her parents disown her?

"I have to be home by six," she said. "My mother's been asking where I go after school."

"I thought you said that she doesn't care where you are."

"She didn't, but she's starting to notice I'm never around."

Leo was silent. He removed his hand from her stomach and turned the volume up on the radio.

"All right. My man Drake," said Shawn B. from the back seat.

They travelled out of the downtown area and farther north, and Vanessa's stomach clenched tighter with every kilometre. Leo turned the car into the

Blue Nights Motel, then reached over and rubbed the side of her face with his knuckles. She flinched before making herself hold very still. He'd hurt her a couple of times where nobody could see and she knew better than to make him angry. Resisting made him angriest of all.

"I've been thinking all day about what I'm going to do to you," he said above the music. "There's nobody I'd rather be with — you know that, right, baby?"

"Yeah, I know."

She looked over to the far end of the parking lot. There was another girl here the week before. She'd been walking with a tall man in a grey suit toward a room at the other end of the building, hanging on to his arm, her head thrown back, laughing. Her face had turned and their eyes had met for a split second before the girl looked away. *Help me*, Vanessa had wanted to say, but she hadn't, and she knew now that the other girl was in no position to help her or anybody else.

Vanessa had told Leo once that she loved him. Before he made her have sex with the other men. She couldn't bear to think about how naive and gullible she'd been at the start. She'd thought Leo was going to be her saviour. He must have been laughing at her the entire time, thinking about how easy she'd been to reel in. About what he planned to do to her.

"Might be time you brought me home for supper," Leo said after he turned off the engine. She could make out the round orbs of his eyes behind the glasses. "I could soften up your mom, then we can spend more time together."

Vanessa tried to keep the panic from showing in her eyes. She nodded, letting her hair swing forward to hide her face. He had to be teasing her. He'd never want her family to meet him. Tears welled up in her eyes and she reached blindly for the door handle. As she stepped out of the car, she blinked hard and glanced again toward the room that the other girl had entered with the man, but she knew already that the girl wouldn't be there.

The girl would never be there ever again.

Because Vanessa had seen the girl's picture on the news that very morning as she was eating breakfast. A smiling version of the girl she'd seen walking and laughing with the man in the grey suit. The girl in the photo onscreen was a bit younger, and her hair was brown, not coal black, but there was no mistaking the eyes or the diamond glinting above her lip. Vanessa had listened to the reporter laying out the facts with growing horror. The girl she'd seen across the parking lot had been found dead not far from this very motel. The girl with the piercing eyes that had locked with hers in a moment of shared connection. Splattered on the pavement after falling several storeys from a half-built hotel.

Vanessa waited for Leo to unlock the door to their room, and all thoughts of running away vanished. Where would she even run with all that Leo had on her — and this place in the middle of nowhere? *Had the other girl tried to run away?*

"Check it out. I bought you a present," said Leo, pointing to a package on the bed. "Some sexy red underwear ought to keep our customers coming back for more." He laid his arm across her shoulders before giving her a playful push. "Go put it on and Shawn B. and I will get the party started."

Vanessa watched herself walk over to the bed and pick up the package. Fear kept her moving, her desire to please Leo long dead. With every after-school trip to this motel, she felt herself disappearing.

When she'd met him, she thought that Leo was going to be the one — the person to make her forget that her parents hated each other, to calm the rage she felt every time they screamed in front of her like a couple of five-year-olds. The one to make her feel like she was somebody worth loving.

What she wouldn't give to feel that rage again instead of this deadness inside. What she wouldn't give to be home right now with her dysfunctional family, not knowing now what she didn't know then.

If only she'd never accepted Leo's friend request on Facebook.

CHAPTER THIRTEEN

"What are you going to do today?" asked Kala as she placed a bowl of oatmeal and blueberries in front of Dawn. She'd gotten up early to prepare breakfast and spend a bit of time with Dawn before she left for the day. "I'm sorry about having to cancel the visit to your mom."

Dawn looked up from her iPad. "I'm going to art class downtown. Emily asked me if I wanted to catch a movie a few days ago. Maybe I'll see if she still wants to."

"That would be good. I don't like to think of you alone here all day."

Dawn smiled. "I like being alone, Aunt Kala. I'm your clone."

"Goodness, not something to aim for." Kala grimaced, but she was secretly relieved that Dawn was so self-sufficient. At the same time, she worried that Dawn was turning into a loner. At least she had friends who invited her to movies. That had to be something positive. "I'm hoping we'll get far enough along in the investigation today that I can take tomorrow afternoon off."

"Don't worry if you can't."

Twenty minutes later Kala stepped outside, juggling a mug of coffee, her handbag, and the truck keys. She stood for a moment on the top step and surveyed the sparkling spring morning. Breathed in the sweetness. Wispy white clouds hung far away on the horizon — not enough to threaten rain — and the sky reflected icy blue on the rippling waters of Lake Ontario. The grass was greening up nicely, nourished by days of rain and today warmed by the sun.

In October she and Dawn had dug up a large rectangle of lawn to the right of the deck and hauled in half a truckload of black earth and compost. A few weeks ago Dawn had planted carrot and radish seeds, and already sprouts were showing through the thick loam. They planned to grow lettuce, tomatoes, and beans when the weather warmed enough to plant a summer harvest. They were both new to gardening but Dawn was becoming an encyclopedia of information, spending hours reading up on the internet about best growing practices. Kala saw this new pastime as them putting down roots — both physically and metaphorically.

Gundersund was in his driveway when she drove by. He spotted her and waved before opening the door to his Mustang. She slowed and he soon caught up in her rear-view mirror. He followed her along the waterfront and north to Division, which took them to headquarters. The parking lot was half-empty and they found spaces side by side.

"Thanks for the police escort," she said when she joined him behind their vehicles.

"Just making sure you arrive safely. Don't want you slipping off and having a good time when the rest of us are stuck working." His blond hair was combed straight back from his forehead, wet from a recent shower. He hadn't shaved the beard and moustache that he'd grown on his time off. Not for the first time, Kala imagined him wearing Viking armour and brandishing a sword instead of the coffee thermos dangling from his hand.

"Isn't working considered a good time?" she asked, falling into step with him.

"Only if you're in the circus. And a monkey riding a bicycle at that." He shot her a sideways glance with his intense blue eyes. "I thought I'd take you up on that meal offer, if it's still open."

She tried not to act surprised. "When we get an early night, I can pick up some steaks. Dawn will be happy to see you. Do you think … would Fiona like to join us?"

"She might if I ask her but I'd rather it be just the three of us. Like it used to be."

She was curious about his response but relieved not to have to entertain Fiona for an evening. Making small talk with her would have been more awkwardness than she was prepared to handle.

Bennett called to them from where he stood waiting with the main door open. "Looks like we're all making it in under the wire," he said when they reached him. He lifted a box of doughnuts from where he'd been holding it at his side. "I brought breakfast."

"I didn't have time to eat so I owe you one," said Gundersund. "Don't all champions start the day with a maple-glazed?"

"Only the plump ones," said Kala.

Rouleau was already in the office, and he called them into the meeting space as soon as they hung up their coats. Bennett slid in next to Kala, Morrison on her other side. Woodhouse and Bedouin were directly behind them. Gundersund joined Rouleau standing at the front.

"The gang's all here," said Bedouin. "Ready for another day in the trenches."

"For which I thank each one of you," said Rouleau. "Let's get started so we can be home with our loved ones at a decent hour. Woodhouse, you're up first. Anything come out of the door-to-door?"

"The super, Jeff Simmons, has a cot in the furnace room that I checked out just because it seemed creepy. Nothing there but turns out he's a bit light in the front-end loader, if you get my drift. I'd put his name on the suspect list until we know more about him. His brother Murray Simmons owns the building. He should be checked out too."

Gundersund wrote their names on the whiteboard.

Morrison said, "I spoke to one of the first-floor tenants, who said that the owner usually visits the building for an hour, two nights a week. She figures he's checking on his brother." She looked at her notebook. "She thought he was there Monday, not sure about Friday because he also comes during the day sometimes. The tenant's name is Hilda Schwartz."

"Sounds like one of those nosy old women sitting at her living room window with a telescope aimed at the neighbours," said Woodhouse. "Let me guess. She was wearing curlers and a housecoat."

"Not too hard to guess she's a bit down and out, living in that building," said Morrison. "But no curlers or housecoat anywhere in sight."

"Give her time."

"Anything else on point, Woodhouse?" asked Rouleau.

"We canvassed the neighbourhood and nobody remembers seeing the vic that night."

"Surely someone saw her getting into a car or walking to the bus."

"Not that we found."

"Do a second door-to-door today. People will be home from work or school. Did you go to the local bars and stores?"

"We did. Nobody has any recollection of seeing her."

"A second go-around might pick up those who were off shift yesterday."

"We'll get on it. I know for a fact the woman living across the hall from Nadia was home, but not answering. We'll be more insistent this time." Woodhouse rested his gaze briefly on each member of the team, asserting his control.

Kala saw Rouleau intercept the look before he said, "You can have Bennett and Bedouin. I'd like

Stonechild and Morrison to return to Ottawa to follow up with Nadia's parents and attempt to track down this fellow Danny and his friends. Find out what school Nadia attended when she actually went, where she hung out. I've cleared this with the Ottawa force and they'll offer assistance as required."

Kala met Morrison's eyes. Morrison looked back at Rouleau and said, "Sir, I believe I can make this reconnaissance trip alone today. Stonechild might be better placed to look into the Simmons brothers and get their stories. If I need any backup, I can recruit an Ottawa cop."

"I'd also like another run out to the construction site," said Kala. She turned toward Rouleau. "That is, if you agree." She didn't know what was written on her face that Morrison had picked up on but she hadn't relished the idea of a trip to Ottawa that would have her getting home late again to Dawn. Rose's panic about Fisher might be unfounded, but it was enough to make Kala cautious.

"Works." Rouleau nodded.

"What would you like me to focus on today?" asked Gundersund.

"Check out the restaurant where Nadia worked part-time and interview her co-workers. At this point, we're trying to find out her patterns and the people she interacted with, even occasionally. I've got the tech team taking apart her laptop and phone to get more leads. However, she only bought the laptop a few months ago so there's not much on it yet. But the phone is an older model that she's used for a few years." Rouleau pointed at the whiteboard.

"We have very few leads or suspects. We need to fill in the gaps and find out who Nadia Armstrong was and what brought her to the construction site."

After the team had dispersed to get on with things, Rouleau returned to his office. He checked his messages. Ellington had lined up Vera to organize a press briefing for 2:00 p.m. A text from Vera followed: a request for Rouleau to call her at home as soon as he had a chance. He sat down at his desk and dialled her number. She answered so quickly he thought she might have been in the process of making another call.

"Happy Saturday morning, Vera. What's going on?"

"His highness wants you to send him the latest information about the Armstrong case by noon. He's decided to make a plea on television for public assistance in tracking down her killer."

"And why didn't Ellington tell me this himself?"

"My sense is that he was told from above to get in front of the story. He's going to meet us at City Hall at quarter to twelve."

"He's calling you in?"

"I have the command in writing."

They were both silent while Rouleau considered what Ellington was up to. Vera was an executive admin assistant and never attended news briefings.

He knew her enough to read the outrage in her clipped explanation. "I'm to wear a tight-fitting navy suit and full makeup. Paint my lips a cherry red. He said something about branding the department."

"I'm sorry, Vera. Are you going to HR?"

"I'm keeping records and biding my time."

"I'd be happy to set him straight."

"What, and save a damsel in distress? No thanks, Rouleau. I'm a big girl and can fight my own battles."

"It's hardly a fair fight, with him being your boss."

"I'll let you know if I need your help. I'd appreciate you staying out of this."

Her voice had a steely quality that was meant to shut down the conversation but he added anyway, "Just know that I'm prepared to unleash whatever is necessary whenever you give the word."

"I don't expect it will come to that. Look, I need to go. I'm still calling news outlets, among other things."

"And I have a report to get ready."

She said a terse goodbye and ended the call.

Rouleau sat for a moment staring out the window, imagining himself stretched out in a lawn chair with the sun warming his face instead of stuck inside typing another report. At least he was back in Major Crimes and closer to the action. Closer to his team. Vera was the only casualty in his decision to turn down acting chief and she weighed heavily on his conscience. He was going to have to think of a way to help without her knowing. The trick would be not to make things worse for her when he confronted Ellington.

"Do you have a moment, sir?"

He swivelled his chair around. Stonechild was standing in the doorway, her hand raised to knock. "Of course. Come in and take a seat." He shoved the report to one side.

"Thank you. I'm on my way to the construction site but wanted to run something by you first."

She crossed the space and sat, letting her breath out in a long sigh as she settled on the edge of the seat. She looked as if she was having trouble broaching whatever it was she wanted to say. He was surprised to see her so hesitant. "Does this concern the case?" he asked.

"Yes and no." She seemed to reach a decision. "I don't normally get involved in office politics," she began.

"I think we can safely agree on that." He smiled but she didn't smile back.

Her brow furrowed. "Certain evidence has come forward to suggest that we might have a lead on the person in the force who's been leaking information to the media."

"Oh?"

"The proof is slim but compelling, and I wanted to warn you so that you can take steps to … protect yourself if it ever comes to light. What most concerns me is that if one person knows …"

"Word will get around."

"Exactly."

"Do you have a name?"

"I'd like to know for certain before saying. However, the reporter with whom this officer was seen sharing information — that is, potentially

sharing information since even this is unproven —
was Marci Stokes."

"I see."

And he did see. Marci was a reporter first and
foremost and would do anything to get a story. Of
course she'd line up an informant if it meant getting
the inside scoop before anyone else. It was how she
was wired. He'd long suspected she was being fed
info but he knew she'd never reveal her source.

Stonechild's eyes were black pools of regret.
"I'm concerned that your relationship with her will
be blamed for any future leaks."

"Any suggestions as to how to stop that from
happening?"

She shook her head. "I don't have an answer,
sir."

He ran a hand across his shaved head and let it
rest on the nape of his neck. "Let me think on it."

"When I get concrete evidence, I'll bring it to
you."

"I'd appreciate that. Thank you for coming forward Kala. I know this wasn't an easy conversation."

"No problem." She got to her feet. "I'll be
keeping an eye out. Hopefully, I'm worrying for no
reason."

"That would be the best outcome."

He watched her leave. Stonechild wouldn't have
approached him without solid evidence, although
it must not be ironclad if she wouldn't name the
informant ... yet. He'd suspected Woodhouse but
given the man's previous HR complaint against him,
he had to tread carefully. If Stonechild could get the

evidence, they could finally remove the thorn from the team.

Rouleau wished things were as straightforward when it came to his relationship with Marci. Did her methods for getting a story matter? Should they even be an issue, or were they a sign of trouble between them down the road? He took one long last look out the window and forced himself to set aside these worries for now. He had a report to write, and the clock was ticking.

CHAPTER FOURTEEN

Kala parked under a pine at the opening to the construction site and brought up Google Earth on her phone, zooming in on the site and the surrounding area. The new hotel location was immediately south of the 401 in a wooded parcel of land that stretched northwest of the juncture of Gardiners and Creekford Roads. East of Gardiners was a commercial area with a couple of fast-food chain restaurants and motels. Warehouses and sports facilities spanned southward at the same latitude as a new subdivision and a large animal hospital. The St. Louis Bar and Grill was the closest pub on the map. Could Nadia have met her killer there?

Kala got out of her truck and looked down the road toward the sound of heavy equipment and men yelling over the hum of machinery. In her immediate sightline, directly in front of the half-built hotel, she recognized the site foreman, Bill Lapointe. He was talking to two men — one in a black overcoat, the other in a blue suit, both wearing white hard hats — standing next to a Mortimer Construction truck. They'd spread out what looked like architectural drawings over the hood of the truck. Kala realized as she approached that they hadn't noticed her arrival. She stopped walking and listened to their raised voices.

"Bottom line, you have to scale it back." The blue-suited man, who was the tallest and youngest of the three, was tapping his index finger on the plans. "This will never get through council."

Lapointe glanced up and said something to the others. His two companions lifted their heads and turned to look in her direction. Lapointe rounded the truck and began walking toward her. The man in the black overcoat removed his hard hat, revealing a balding head. He folded up the drawings and waited along with the other man.

"Can I help you, officer?" asked Lapointe. "I thought you were done here."

"I came to have another look. Who are those two men you're talking with?"

Lapointe glanced back at them, then directly at her. "The man in the black coat is the owner, Harold Mortimer. The other one is a city planner."

"His name?"

"Mark Richardson."

"Looks like you're having a debate about the site."

Lapointe shrugged. "Construction. Goes on all the time."

Kala made a beeline toward the two men, even though she got the feeling Lapointe was angling to block her way. He finally fell into step and then hurried past her to reach the others first.

"This is Officer Stonechild," said Lapointe. He introduced Harold Mortimer but ignored Mark Richardson.

"The girl's death was a tragedy," said Mortimer. "Have you really ruled out suicide?"

"At this point, we believe someone staged it to look like suicide. Did you know her?"

"No. I have no idea why she'd be at this site." Mortimer's stare showed measured intelligence. His mouth settled naturally into a hard line, and Kala sensed he'd be a tough boss, used to getting what he wanted. Early fifties and fit — he'd be attractive to those who were turned on by a man's man.

Kala looked at Richardson and said, "I understand you're the city planner. Is there a problem with the building?"

"Not at all. I was simply going over a few proposed changes." Sweat beaded on Richardson's forehead and his eyes slid past hers. His discomfort made her curious. She couldn't probe deeper, however, since the site plans had nothing to do with the case. He had to be taller than Gundersund, maybe six four, and his blue suit hung loosely on his skinny frame. Tight brown curls covered his pate like so many haphazard corkscrews. A nerd in school, she'd bet.

She turned back to Mortimer. "Do you visit the site often?"

"Whenever necessary. We're behind now since you shut us down for three days."

She ignored the resentment in his tone. "Did you know Nadia Armstrong?" she asked Richardson.

A look passed between Richardson and Mortimer. Kala might have missed it if she hadn't been studying Richardson closely. "No," he said. "I never met her."

The three men were closing ranks against her. She could see the stubborn solidarity on their faces. *What are you hiding?* she thought, but she kept her face deliberately blank. The best way to lull someone into sharing a confidence was to make them feel that they were above suspicion. Make them think they were smarter than the police.

"Do you have many projects on the go, Mr. Mortimer?" she asked.

"We're gearing up to do a renovation on the hospital, and we're building a new school in the east end this summer. A few other minor projects as well."

"You're busy."

"Can never have enough work in the construction business. You need to get ahead so you'll be able to make it through leaner times. Everything slows down in the winter, as you can imagine."

"Well, I won't keep you." She started walking past them to get a better look at the site, but Lapointe called to her.

"You'll need someone to accompany you, and you'll have to wear a hard hat, vest, and workboots if you plan to go any farther."

She stopped and reconsidered. "I've got what I came for," she said, taking a last look at the shell of the hotel, now alive with construction workers moving around like ants inside on the slab. She wasn't sure why she'd been drawn back, except that she wanted to fix the location in her mind and to drive around the surrounding area.

Nadia might have come willingly to this location with someone. She would have believed she was safe as she'd climbed the concrete steps. It might have been a moonlit lark or a dare. Kala imagined them crawling through the opening in the back fence, swinging a bottle of wine and laughing their way through the darkness. The overdose might have been an accident, and whoever she was with might have panicked and rolled her off the ledge.

Kala imagined a darker scenario; that Nadia was brought here by force. Led up the stairs in the dark, frightened out of her mind — someone's rough hands pushing her forward. Had she spent her last moments begging for her life before being held down and forced to ingest a large amount of drugs? Or had her lifeless body been carried up the stairs and thrown over the edge to hide evidence of murder? In every scenario, somebody removed all her identification and tried to cover up what had happened.

Kala turned from the site and started back toward her truck. She knew the three men were watching her go and she didn't hurry. They were hiding something, she could feel it. Whatever it was might not have anything to do with Nadia's death, but then again, it just might. She reached her truck and looked over her shoulder. They were still staring in her direction. She lifted her hand in a wave before climbing into the driver's seat. She took her time backing down the driveway, hoping her slow exit onto the highway would give them pause.

At the station, she picked up a coffee and a cheese sandwich from the cafeteria to eat at her desk. Before sitting down, she wrote the names of the three men on the whiteboard for further consideration when the team next gathered, although she had to admit that it was counterintuitive to believe that Harold Mortimer would carry out a murder on his own construction site. She removed their names from the suspect list and rewrote them under the category *Possible Witnesses.* A stretch, perhaps, but she couldn't ignore the feeling she got around these three; it was a cross between dislike and distrust.

She was alone in the office and remembered that Rouleau was at City Hall for the media briefing. The others were carrying out their investigations. She opened the police search engine and typed in *Murray Simmons.* Two hits. Six years earlier, he'd been arrested and charged with assault. He'd gotten a suspended sentence and been ordered to attend anger management classes. Two years ago, he'd been pulled over for drunk driving and had his driver's licence lifted for six months. The second offence had netted him three months' worth of weekends in detention. Another search of his business assets revealed that he owned two low-rise apartment buildings and worked for Mortimer Construction. Kala raised her head and considered the significance.

She typed in *Jeff Simmons.* No social media presence. She returned to the police database and typed in his name and his mother's address. They lived in a home on McDonald Avenue. She brought the property up on Google Maps. The house was an older two-storey on a corner lot with a detached garage. Elm trees encircled the house. The second floor was an addition, taller than the main floor, giving the white-sided house a top-heavy appearance. She did a final check of news articles dating back five years. One hit. She opened the article and scanned the story before going back to reread it carefully.

Jeff Simmons had been charged for stalking a fourteen-year-old girl and touching her inappropriately at the city pool. Never convicted because the girl had withdrawn the charges. A slightly blurry photo of Jeff had been taken from a distance. A quote from his mother: "My boy would never have hurt her. He just doesn't know how to go about asking for a date."

Kala copied the link and forwarded the story to Rouleau and the team.

There'll be no living with Woodhouse, she thought, *once he finds out there was something behind his snap judgment.*

Marci was on her way to Brockville when she got word of the press conference at noon. She checked the clock on the dashboard and pulled into the show-off lane. If she hurried, she'd have an hour to track down and interview Lorraine and Peter Billings. Scotty hadn't signed off on the overnight in Ottawa so her plans wouldn't have to change much. It was early enough that the church crowd were safely in their pews and not on the highway. The transport trucks were another story but they stayed in the slower lanes. She arrived at the off-ramp at 9:10. Her GPS guided her to a residential street with bungalows set back on inclines and long grassy lots stretching down to the road. A property like this would go for a few million in Toronto, more in Manhattan but under three hundred thousand here. It truly was all about location, location, location.

She parked behind the car angled halfway up the driveway and got out, filling her lungs with country-fresh air — the intangible that money couldn't buy, no matter the size of the mortgage. The sky went on forever here outside the city. The early morning haze had cleared and the blue sky overhead, along with the sunshine warming her face, gave her a rare sense of contentment. Knowing Rouleau was stopping by for supper tonight didn't hurt her mood either. They hadn't spoken in a few days but he'd accepted her texted invitation the night before. She hadn't planned to want him around as much as she did. The idea of needing him in her life scared her, but she liked the happy flutter in her chest when she thought of him.

She saw a curtain twitch in the front window and started walking toward the house. She'd found that the best approach with victims' families was empathy with a shared outrage for the life lost. She didn't have to feign either of these but still found her own calculated approach to these interviews distasteful.

Simply having an agenda meant that she was playing with their emotions.

The man who answered the door had espresso-brown eyes soft as velvet. Marci's breath caught in her throat for an instant. She forced herself to look past him at the woman in the hallway. "Sorry to bother you so early this morning. My name is Marci Stokes and I'm a reporter with the *Whig-Standard*. I'm working on a story about Nadia and I want to make sure I portray her the way her family would want her to be remembered. I called yesterday and left a message." *That nobody returned.*

"You want to talk to this lady?" the man asked the woman behind him without taking his eyes off Marci. His peepers should be registered as weapons. A girl could drown in them without giving a thought to her own survival.

"Let her in." The voice was resigned rather than welcoming but Marci was happy to get a foot in the door anyway.

They led her into a back sunroom filled with light and hanging plants. Marci chose the seat facing the couch, which the couple sat on together. She pulled a small tape recorder out of her handbag. "With your permission, I'll record the conversation to ensure accuracy later." Lorraine nodded, so Marci turned it on and set it beside her on the chair where they'd forget it was running.

"Lorraine, tell me about your sister," she said. "How would you want people to remember Nadia?"

"Not as a victim, that's for sure," said Lorraine.

"Nadia loved her little boy and was turning her life around to care for him. That's what I want people to know about her. She had rough teen years but had a good life ahead."

"Can you tell me about her teen years? I won't include the information in my story, but I should know everything about her life so that I don't make any false references by accident." Marci winced inwardly at the lame explanation but Lorraine seemed to buy it.

"Nadia had a lot of spirit. She was rebellious and hated being told what to do. She moved out of my parents' house when she was fifteen and took care of herself."

"She lived on the street?"

"With friends."

"Do you have the names of any friends I could follow up with?"

"No. I never met them. She'd broken away from all those people before she had her son, Hugo. She doted on him."

"I hate to ask this, but there are rumours that your sister was involved in something that might have gone bad. Do you know anything about what that could be?"

Lorraine looked puzzled. "You mean when she lived in Ottawa? I know she was into drugs a bit but she stopped all that when she got pregnant. Do you really have to write about that in your article?"

"It won't be the focus. Her relationship with her son is the angle I see as the lead ... and how she'd turned her life around."

"I have a nice photo of Nadia with Hugo that you can use. I can send it to you."

"Perfect." Marci glanced at Peter, who was slumped back into the couch, staring past her out the window. So far, he hadn't uttered a word. Marci looked back at Lorraine. "Why did Nadia move to Kingston?"

"My sister decided it was time to stand on her own two feet. She got a waitressing job and was getting ready to go back to school. She was excited about the future."

"What did she intend to study?"

"Well, first she had to graduate high school. She mentioned getting a business diploma. Did she say anything to you, Peter?"

"Nope."

Lorraine shifted in her seat to look at him. "Why don't I go find that photo and send it to you now?" she asked, turning back to Marci. "Otherwise, I'll forget."

"Here's a card with my email address," said Marci. "I hope it's not too much trouble."

"No trouble."

Marci waited until she heard Lorraine's footsteps going upstairs. She leaned forward and after a few moments Peter's eyes focused in on her gaze. "Do you have any stories to tell me about Nadia?"

"None that you can use in your article."

"You don't seem as convinced as your wife about Nadia's rebirth."

"I have no comment."

"Was it difficult having her and Hugo live with you?"

An odd look crossed his face and he abruptly stood up. "I have nothing to add to your article. I've got work to do in the garage."

No one had been this eager to get away from her in quite some time. "Where's the fire, Mr. Billings?" she said under her breath, but she refrained from chasing after him. A few seconds passed. She could hear the angry timbre of his voice mixing with Lorraine's placating one in the other room and knew her time had run out.

Lorraine reappeared, face flushed and eyes apologetic. "I'm sorry, but I have to ask you to leave, Ms. Stokes. I forgot that we're meeting with the pastor about Nadia's funeral in fifteen minutes. Peter just reminded me."

"No problem. I have enough to get started on the story."

"I told Peter you'd understand."

Marci gathered up her things and left the Billings house with the photo emailed to her phone and Lorraine's glowing portrayal of her sister. This wasn't enough to counter her deep curiosity about the truths Peter was hiding about his sister-in-law. She knew there was no way he'd spill them to her since her job was to share them with the public, but she had a good idea who might be able to pull the information out of him.

She got into her car and tapped on her phone.

May as well get the follow-up ball rolling, she thought. *Plus, it never hurts to keep on the good side of Kala Stonechild.*

CHAPTER FIFTEEN

Woodhouse squinted at Bennett's pretty-boy face and scowled. He didn't know why the guy bothered him so much, except that men like Bennett had it soft, using their good looks and charm to get through life. They didn't know what it was like to be bullied at school or at home. Bennett was everything Woodhouse had envied throughout his miserable childhood. Every time he looked at Bennett's face, he relived his anger and resentment. But he was in charge now.

"What do you mean she wouldn't answer? You heard her in there, right?"

"I *thought* I heard her moving around but she never came to the door."

"Well, we need to interview her so think of something." Woodhouse ran a silent play-by-play through his head and let his eyes travel around the Bellevue Towers lobby.

Pretty-boy brow's all wrinkled in concentration. Do we have an idea? Going once ... going twice ..."

"Maybe the super could get her to open up."

And we have a winner.

"Now you're using the brain God gave you. Go get him and I'll meet you on the third."

That sullen look returned to Bennett's face. "I can interview her alone. My only issue is getting inside."

"Let's say her reluctance to answer the door has me curious. It might take two of us to persuade her to talk." He only just kept himself from saying, *in case your pretty-boy face doesn't do it for her.* Luckily, his brain took a few seconds to operate his mouth.

Woodhouse took the elevator to the third floor and checked his phone messages while he waited in the hall. Two from Marci Stokes that he deleted after reading. She was tight with Rouleau and could be setting him up now that she was sleeping with an even better source of information. Maybe she'd screw him over by letting Rouleau read his message to her "by accident." He wouldn't put it past her.

The elevator rumbled to a stop and Bennett got off with a reluctant-looking Jeff Simmons trailing a few steps behind. They met outside the door across the hall from the victim's apartment.

"I can't let you into her apartment. Murray told me under no circumstances could I go into someone's apartment when they're home unless they invite me." Jeff had his head down, bangs in his eyes, looking at the floor.

Woodhouse asked, "Did your brother tell you to listen to the police too?"

Jeff nodded and kicked the toe of his boot into the carpet.

"Well, I'm telling you to knock at her door and

call her name. Maybe she'll answer to you and we won't have to use the key to get in."

"I'm not supposed —"

"Let's try knocking," Bennett interrupted, putting himself between Jeff and Woodhouse. He rested his hand on Jeff's forearm. "She might come to the door for you."

Jeff lifted his head. "I won't get into trouble?"

"I'll make sure you don't."

"Okay," Jeff said, and shuffled over to the door. He knocked and called, "Mrs. Greenboro. It's Jeff Simmons. I need to talk to you. Can you open the door, Mrs. Greenboro?"

"Louder," barked Woodhouse.

Jeff's head jerked back but he called out her name again, louder this time.

Bennett knocked on the door and stood still, listening. He motioned for Woodhouse to step back out of view of the peephole. "I hear her coming down the hall."

The chain rattled and the door finally swung open. Woodhouse and Bennett both dropped their eyes. The woman in front of them had to be at least ninety and she stood about four foot ten. Strands of snow-white hair partially hid a pink scalp and her face was blotched with brown age spots. Her blackcurrant eyes looked them over and appeared unimpressed with what she saw.

"You can't come in. Only reason I opened the door was so you'd leave this poor young man alone. You should be ashamed of yourselves, using him like this to get to me."

Woodhouse wanted to reach down and throttle the woman but Bennett was intent on handling the interview.

"We apologize," Bennett said, "but we're investigating the death of your neighbour Nadia Armstrong. Did you interact with her at all, ma'am?"

"I saw her coming and going with her baby. Called him Hugo."

"Did you speak with her?"

"Now what in blazes would we have to talk about?" Her fingers grabbed onto the door frame and the door began to swing shut.

Bennett spoke quickly. "Did you see her Tuesday evening?"

The door stopped moving. "The girl went out after I ate my supper at five o'clock. I never saw her come home."

"Was she alone?"

"That I couldn't tell you."

The door slammed shut and the chain scraped into place.

Jeff said, "Mrs. Greenboro's not much for talking."

Woodhouse snorted, but before he could say anything, Bennett cut in. "Have you remembered anything that could help us find out what happened to Nadia, Jeff?"

"No."

"Well, thanks for your help," said Woodhouse. He was quite certain Simmons wouldn't catch the sarcasm, and the expression on his face bore this out. He watched Jeff hightail it over to the stairwell and disappear through the door. Woodhouse glared at Bennett. "I feel like we've entered the loony bin. This has been one wasted Sunday we'll never get back."

Bennett said, "I don't know. I thought she was kind of cute."

"Nothing cute about that wizened bag of bones. Jeff Simmons ought to have his head examined too."

Bennett's face reddened. "You're one foul piece of work, you know that, Woodhouse? Some day, all the nastiness you send out into the world is going to come back to you in spades. I guarantee it."

Woodhouse laughed. "Don't hold your breath, little grasshopper. I've been in this game a lot longer than you, Bennett, and I can assure you that nice guys do not finish first. You might want to think about that next time you bend over to take a poker in the ass."

"At least I'll be able to look at myself in the mirror and not shudder in disgust."

"You believe that now. Come see me in a few years when everyone and his dog has stepped over you on the way to the top. Then you'll know what I'm talking about."

Bennett shook his head, but Woodhouse had had enough of sharing his wisdom. He started walking toward the elevator. "You can call it a day. I'll send in the report to Rouleau. See you tomorrow, Bennett. My turn to spring for the doughnuts."

Dawn blinked in the bright sunshine as she and Emily walked out of the Landmark Cinema.

"I don't think those action hero movies are my thing," said Emily. "I like romantic comedies."

"Why did you pick that movie again?" asked Dawn. "I'm not a fan of action hero movies either."

"Blame it on Chelsea. She saw it last week and told me it was great. I shouldn't have listened to her."

They'd crossed the parking lot and reached Emily's car when her phone rang in her purse. She fished it out and carried on a conversation while unlocking and opening the door. She slid into the driver's seat after tucking the phone into her pocket.

"That was Vanessa. She and Chelsea want to meet up. Are you sure you don't want to sleep over?"

"I'm sure."

"Do you have time for a bite to eat and then I can drive you home?"

"I'll eat but I can make it home on the bus afterward."

"I'm going to start thinking you're running a grow op or something else you don't want us to know about. You've refused every ride home I've ever offered."

"Yeah, my cop aunt is growing pot. You have one overactive imagination."

Emily started the car. "I'm just saying … you've never had anybody to your house."

Dawn didn't answer. How to explain that the house on Old Front Road was her sanctuary — hers, Kala's, and Taiku's — and she didn't want to let the outside world in, especially anyone from school. Not even Emily. Instead, she asked, "Where're we meeting them?"

"Tim Hortons on Princess."

Vanessa and Chelsea were already sitting at a table with cups of coffee and doughnuts when Emily and Dawn entered. They got mugs of tea and sandwiches before joining the other two girls.

"So, did you love the movie?" asked Chelsea. "Wasn't Chris Hemsworth dreamy?"

"Dreamy? *Really?*" asked Emily.

"Well, someone you'd want to hop into bed with, anyway. Right, Van? Back me up here."

Dawn was the only one looking at Vanessa and she was shocked at the sight of all the colour draining from her face. For a split second, Dawn thought Vanessa was going to keel over. Dawn started to get up to help her but Vanessa glared her down.

"Yeah, he's definitely top of my list," Vanessa said before picking up her doughnut and taking a big bite.

"But maybe your boyfriend will have something to say about that," laughed Chelsea. "Where is he tonight, by the way?"

How clueless are you? thought Dawn, taking another glance at Vanessa under half-lowered eyelids. How could anyone not see that she was distressed about something? Vanessa's voice came out lighter than the unhappy expression on her face.

"He's out with his friends. Speaking of which, he'd like to meet you, Dawn. He saw you the other day at school and thought you looked nice."

All three girls stared at her and a rush of embarrassment made Dawn's face warm. "Does he need an eye test?" she joked to deflect whatever they were thinking but not saying.

Emily said, "I'm sure his eyesight is excellent."

She smiled at Dawn and Dawn gave a sideways smile back. She wondered why nobody asked the obvious: what was Vanessa's boyfriend doing looking at another girl?

Vanessa tossed her hair back over her shoulder. "Leo has a friend he thinks you might like, Dawn. It'd be fun to double date."

Again, Emily and Chelsea stared at Dawn, the expressions on their faces as curious as Dawn felt. Where was this coming from? Vanessa had never treated Dawn like anything more than a tagalong before. "Maybe," she finally managed to say.

"Next week, then."

Vanessa's eyes were smug, shadowed in secrets. She smiled at Dawn for the first time and a tinge of pink returned to her face.

Dawn wanted to tell her that she had no intention of dating anybody. She'd give it the weekend and break it to Vanessa on Monday morning when they were back in school. That ought to give her enough time to come up with a believable excuse. She might not need one, though. Vanessa probably wouldn't even remember making the offer by then.

CHAPTER SIXTEEN

Kala looked up from her computer screen and was surprised to see that everybody had left for the day. A light was on in Rouleau's office. She checked the time. Quarter past six. Where had the hours gone? She reread her notes before shutting down the computer and texting Dawn to say she was leaving the office now. She'd pick up some supper on her way. As she was putting on her jacket, she glanced again at Rouleau's office. He should be calling it a day too. She crossed the room and tapped lightly on his door. He was standing at the window looking out and spun around to face her.

"Ah, Stonechild. I thought everyone had gone."

"I should have by now, and you should go home as well."

"You're right."

She glimpsed anger in his eyes before he smiled at her. "News briefing go okay?" she asked.

"As far as those things go. We haven't gotten many calls yet, but that should pick up tomorrow when the papers and the radio run the story."

"So, nothing else?"

"Only that you'll be seeing Vera front and centre in the media photos."

Kala took a second to understand what he was saying. "Is Ellington parading her out to be the face of the police force?"

"That appears to be his plan."

"I'm surprised Vera agreed to it." Kala could understand the pressure to comply, though. There was a time when she had been put in the same position and she hadn't liked it.

"She says that she's biding her time. I wonder if you could be on the watch for any incidents of questionable judgment and keep a record in case Vera ever needs backup."

"Of course. I'm guessing she won't let you intervene?"

"Not yet." The anger returned to his eyes.

She wondered if he was aware of Vera's feelings for him and the blow to her pride when he began dating Marci Stokes. There was no way Vera would accept his help with this. His next words went a long way to explaining his apparent lack of interest in having a relationship with Vera.

"No person in a position of authority should be exploiting an employee. Even dating a subordinate shows questionable judgment at best."

"Not all bosses hold themselves to the same high standard."

"Then it's time things changed." He walked over to his desk and began putting documents in his briefcase. "You should get moving. Dawn will be waiting for you."

Kala turned to leave before remembering what she'd wanted to tell him. "I'll be driving to Brockville tomorrow to speak with Nadia Armstrong's brother-in-law, Peter Billings. Marci was there today and she phoned to say she thinks Peter is holding something back. Morrison is spending the night in Ottawa looking for this mysterious Danny and I thought I could swing up there afterward to give her a hand in the search."

"Sounds like a plan. We'll have an early-morning team meeting to start the day. I already spoke to Morrison and she'll be phoning in."

"Then I'll come here first thing and leave for Brockville after the debrief. I entered a report about the Simmons brothers that you might want to read beforehand. They're an interesting pair."

"Possible killers?"

"I wouldn't rule them out. Woodhouse's hunch could be right this time."

Rouleau smiled but didn't say anything.

Kala unrolled her truck window and drove slowly through the gathering dusk down Old Front Road. She breathed in the new spring smells of damp earth and trees starting to flower — lilac, cherry, crab apple, magnolia. A breeze from the east scudded across the lake, rippling the water and whipping up waves that struck the shore in fitful bursts. In the distance, a low rumble of thunder announced the arrival of a cold front that would bring stronger winds and rain overnight. For this moment in time, Kala savoured the leftover warmth from the day and tried not to think of the unsettled weather that lay ahead.

Gundersund's car was in his driveway and she could see a light on in the living room. He'd be settling in to watch some sports game on television while Fiona prepared him a late meal ... or, more likely, Gundersund was cooking for her. Kala had heard through the work grapevine that Fiona had decided not to return to her teaching position at the university. She was home for good. Back to reclaim her old job and her husband, or that's what she'd been telling people. Her words had sifted down to Kala, which Kala knew was Fiona's intent.

She parked halfway up the driveway, relieved to see the lights on. Dawn hadn't returned her last text and uneasiness had travelled home with Kala. She trusted Dawn but worrying about her went with the territory. She supposed that she was lucky not to have had this responsibility for the entirety of Dawn's life. The last few years had been stressful enough.

Kala took a moment to stand in the shadows of the backyard and listen to the waves crashing and the wind soughing through the conifers. The clouds were already filling in the sky, blotting out stars so that she could barely see across the yard. For a moment, the moon was freed from the cloud that blocked it from sight and the ground was swathed in shimmering golden light. The beauty of this place made her heart ache. There were still times she couldn't believe she owned this bit of land. She turned toward the porch light streaming across the back deck and climbed the steps, eager to open the door and see Dawn and Taiku.

A man's voice and Dawn's laughter filled the kitchen and spilled into the hallway along with the smell of beef, onions, and garlic sizzling in a frying pan. Kala kicked off her boots and gave in to the moment's happiness. She entered the kitchen to find Gundersund standing with his back to her at the stove and Dawn setting the table. They didn't notice her at first and she stood silently in the doorway, listening to their banter. Dawn was trying to convince Gundersund to give her generation's music a chance while he kept insisting that with only a few exceptions, nothing good had been recorded since the seventies. Gundersund was the first to spot her.

"Home at last, woman. I was beginning to think we'd have to issue a missing person bulletin."

"You look mighty dashing in my apron," said Kala, plucking a slice of carrot from the counter.

"Aunt Kala," said Dawn, "Gundersund is cooking pepper steak. Have you ever eaten that before?"

"If she has, it wouldn't even come close to this tasty masterpiece," said Gundersund. "A family recipe handed down for generations on the internet."

"I *thought* you bore a strong resemblance to Betty Crocker." Kala tilted her head as if considering a painting.

Gundersund wiped his hands on a towel and escorted Kala to the table. He pulled out the chair with a flourish and leaned close as she sat down. "We call her dear Aunt Bet. Now, get ready to be wined and dined ... so to speak. Cue the music, Dawn."

Dawn danced over to the counter and clicked on the radio, which was pretuned to a jazz station. Then she poured glasses of ice water while Gundersund dished out the food. Dawn had made a salad to go with the steak and rice, and they dug in with little talking. Kala hadn't realized how hungry she was. "So good," she said between forkfuls. She raised her eyes to find Gundersund watching her. "What?" she asked, embarrassed to be caught eating with such gusto.

"Nothing. I just like seeing you enjoy my cooking."

"Well, I skipped lunch so I might be eating a bit fast." She looked over at Dawn. "How was your day? Did you go to a movie with Emily?"

"I did, after art class. Then we met Chelsea and Vanessa at Tim Hortons before I caught the bus home."

"To be greeted by me and a shopping bag full of food sitting on the back steps," said Gundersund.

Kala set down her knife and fork and patted her stomach. "The two of you have outdone yourselves. But I was supposed to cook for you, Gundersund."

"There'll be other opportunities." His eyes warmed her with their intensity and she had trouble looking away.

Dawn stood and began stacking their plates. "I have homework to do, so I'll leave you to entertain each other after I put the kettle on," she said. She gave them a mischievous grin.

"We'll try to get along without you," said Gundersund.

"I'll bring you up a cup of tea when it's ready," said Kala.

Taiku followed Dawn out of the kitchen and Kala listened to their footsteps clatter up the stairs and across the landing.

"She's doing better," Gundersund said, resting his elbows on the table.

Kala wanted to believe him but couldn't let go of her unease. Dawn often wandered the house in the middle of the night when she couldn't sleep. "She still keeps so much to herself."

"Isn't that normal for girls this age?"

"I really have no yardstick. My teen years weren't anything to go by."

"You never talk about those years."

"No." She knew that he wanted something more. She said, "I moved foster homes six times between the ages of ten and fifteen. That's when I decided living on the street was better than trying to fit into somebody's idea of who I should be."

"I'm sorry."

"I don't need your sympathy."

"It's not sympathy I feel."

"Well it sure sounded like it."

Gundersund stood and pulled Kala to her feet along with him. "What I feel for you has nothing to do with pity. I'm sad for the girl you were and all that was taken from you. But more than anything, I admire the person you've become."

His face bent over her and she felt his lips, soft at first and then opening hers so that they stood locked together for what felt like a long time. His hands cupped the sides of her face and she grabbed onto his shoulders. She was drowning in the strength of her feelings for him and her need to feel his body pressed against hers. She returned his kiss with equal passion and they stumbled back against the table. A ringing phone startled her and she pulled abruptly away from him.

"Let it ring," he said gruffly.

"What if it's about the case?"

"They'll leave a message."

She took another step away. "You need to answer."

He kept his eyes on hers but reached behind him to pick up his cellphone from the table where he'd left it. He held the phone to his ear and listened. After a pause, he said, "Okay. I'll be there in a few minutes."

"What is it?" Kala asked.

"Fiona's fallen and thinks she sprained her ankle. She wants me to run her over to the hospital."

Kala's first unkind thought was that Fiona had injured herself on purpose, but that seemed beyond the pale, even for her. "What would she do if you weren't around?"

"Good question." Gundersund picked up his jacket. "Hopefully she'll be in her own place soon and we'll find out."

"Is it true she's home for good?"

"So she says. I've yet to get the full story but more than likely it concerns a married man. She's attracted to them like a bee to honey and only runs back to me when things turn ugly."

"That's awful. It's sad that you would even think that of her."

"She's not a woman who likes to be alone."

He was almost at the door when he turned and strode back across the room. He grabbed Kala around the waist and pulled her to him in a tight hug. "Give me a little more time," he said, pressing his cheek against hers. "Fiona's agreed to the separation and knows she can't stay with me much longer." He kissed Kala's forehead before he left her.

She stood rooted in place, imagining a future with Gundersund. Waking up next to him in her bed. Seeing his smile every morning and feeling the warmth of his hands on her body. Eating breakfast together with Dawn and taking the dogs for walks by the water. For the first time in her life, she'd have someone she could count on. She'd have a real home.

The boiling kettle broke her reverie and dropped her back to earth.

People like her didn't get to live the fairy-tale life. She could never escape her childhood or the terrible things she'd done. She'd spent twenty years blocking out the part she'd played in getting rid of that man's body after Rose had beaten his head in with a rock, but the knowledge of it was always with her. His death haunted Rose. It haunted her. Their secret crime was an invisible knot, tying them together in guilt and strangling their happiness.

Gundersund would learn soon enough that she wasn't good at long-term relationships. He'd find that she and Dawn were too much work and move on to a less complicated woman. If not another woman, then he'd go back to Fiona as everyone expected. Gundersund must still have feelings for his wife or he'd have extricated his life from hers long before now. He'd learned to forgive her infidelities.

Kala crossed to the stove and turned off the element, lifting the kettle and filling the waiting teapot. While the tea steeped, she closed her eyes and traced a finger over her lips.

Let yourself have this moment, she thought. *He loves you tonight and wants to make this something more. Don't fret about tomorrow. Let yourself have this.*

CHAPTER SEVENTEEN

The morning meeting lasted half an hour. Everyone was present except Morrison, who phoned in to report that she had a lead on Danny and had traced him to a business in the ByWard Market and would be going there after the call to interview him.

"Do you want to wait for me to join you?" Kala asked her. "I can be there by lunchtime after a stop in Brockville."

Rouleau said, "I think that's a good idea. Why don't you relax for the morning and get a good breakfast, Morrison? The two of you can meet up and interview this Danny fellow together."

"Well, twist my arm."

Gundersund was waiting for Kala at her desk after the meeting broke up. "Do you want me to check in on Dawn later?" he asked.

"If you've time."

"I'll make time."

She shut down her computer and picked up her handbag. "How's Fiona?"

"Home with her foot up. She twisted her ankle but it's not a serious injury."

"That's lucky. How did she do it?"

"Fell on the bottom step going into the backyard."

Fell on a step at the same time Gundersund was making supper for her and Dawn. Kala wondered if Gundersund had put two and two together. She decided not to pursue it. He was too nice a man for his own good and she didn't want him questioning his sense of duty. "Are you staying in the office or going on interviews?" she asked.

"Haven't decided."

"I'll see you later, then?"

"Yes, but call in after Brockville."

"I will."

He lowered his voice. "Are we good, Stonechild?"

She wanted to take away the uncertainty she saw in his eyes. She checked that no one was watching and reached over to touch the back of his hand. "We're good. I'll call when I'm on my way to Ottawa."

Marci had suggested getting Peter alone, so when Kala arrived in Brockville at quarter to ten, she drove straight to the Jiffy Lube. She was in luck. Peter was behind the counter with a fresh pot of coffee in his hand. He held it up in her direction when she entered the shop and she nodded. They took their cups to the two chairs in the waiting area and settled in.

"I figured you wouldn't stay away," he said by way of an opening. His puppy-dog brown eyes flickered over her and looked out the window. "That reporter, I'm guessing?"

"She called me, yes."

"I shouldn't have sat in on her interview with Lorraine."

"Why not?"

"The way she stared at me. Like a bug under a microscope." He pulled his eyes away from the window to look at her.

"She thought you had more to tell about Nadia but was intuitive enough to know that you'd never talk to a reporter."

"Damn straight."

"About which part?"

"Both. No way I'd air dirty laundry in public. Nadia ... well, let's say my wife has rose-coloured glasses when it comes to her sister. She wanted her to be good so she bought into the illusion."

"Whatever you tell me won't be shared with the media. I promise you that."

"Nadia was hooking before she came to live with us."

"You know that for a fact?"

"I do, because Nadia told me."

"When?"

"Right before she dropped her nightgown on the floor and propositioned me. I told her to put it back on. Lorraine doesn't know and I don't want her to find out."

"How did Nadia react when you rebuffed her?"

"She said that she saw the way I looked at her when Lorraine wasn't watching. But she only imagined my interest because I had none. I told her she was going to have to move out or I'd tell Lorraine what kind of two-faced bitch of a sister she was letting stay in our house. She left a week later."

Kala believed the disgust on his face. "Do you know if Nadia went back to soliciting in Kingston?"

"I don't know but I could make a guess." He sighed. "Maybe she didn't. Nadia was trying to start a new life for her son. The only time I was alone with her after that incident, she said she was sorry and hadn't meant anything by it. She'd had a few drinks and was lonely. She said she was planning to make a go of it in Kingston and we should let bygones be bygones."

"And that's how you left it?"

"I told her not to let her sister down again."

"Is there anything else you can tell me about Nadia that would help me to understand her?"

"I only know her from what Lorraine told me about her and from those months she lived with us. Nadia loved her kid. She may have only tolerated Lorraine and pretended to be a decent sister, but Hugo meant everything to her. Maybe Hugo was enough to make her want to pull herself together but I believe the addict in her wasn't far from the surface. She was like this streetwise, tough chick pretending to fit into the civilized world of diaper bags and soccer moms. I hoped the straight life would win for her kid's sake. I had trouble believing it would, though." He shrugged. "Looks like we'll never know now."

"Well, thanks for being so candid. I'll see where this fits in to what we uncover in Kingston." His eyes were focused back on hers and she wondered if he knew their effect.

"I'd like Lorraine to keep her good thoughts about Nadia, if that's possible. She's been through enough hell where her sister's concerned."

'I'll do what I can but if this information has something to do with her death ..."

"I know. It'll be tough to keep secret."

"But hopefully not impossible."

Back in her truck, Kala sat for a second, leaning on the steering wheel and staring through the Jiffy Lube front window. Peter had gone deeper into the shop and was nowhere to be seen. She couldn't decide if he was the faithful husband he professed to be or if he'd gone further with Nadia than he'd ever admit. They'd never determined who had fathered Hugo. Ottawa was about an hour from Brockville and he could have met Nadia there easily enough before she got pregnant. It might not be a coincidence that he and Lorraine were now trying to get custody.

Kala took out her phone and texted Morrison that she was leaving Brockville. She sincerely hoped this Danny friend would have some answers about Nadia's state of mind before she died. She followed up with a quick text to Gundersund before pointing the truck toward the highway leading to Ottawa.

Rouleau called Gundersund into his office in the late morning. They settled in with strong cups of office coffee brewed sometime around 7:30, if Gundersund calculated correctly. Anybody drinking it would be wide awake for the afternoon. Rouleau didn't take long to get to the case.

"Woodhouse's team has not managed to track Nadia Armstrong's movements the day she died. In fact, nobody's given us much to go on concerning her lifestyle or the people she associated with. The public appeal hasn't generated anything either."

"Hopefully Stonechild and Morrison will come up with more in Ottawa."

"Heard from them yet this morning?"

"Stonechild texted she was leaving Brockville around ten-thirty. She didn't say anything about her interview with Peter Billings." Gundersund hoped his voice didn't give away his longing to hear from her. The thought that she might regret yesterday's physical contact had him nervous as a cat.

Rouleau was silent for a moment, twirling the coffee mug on his desk. "I've received a confidence that someone could be feeding information about our cases to Marci. Woodhouse would be my first guess, but it's only a guess at this point."

"Who told you?"

"Not important, although I've asked them to bring me definitive proof."

"Would Marci confirm —"

Rouleau didn't let him finish his thought. "No. It would go against everything a journalist stands for. I wouldn't ask her to break her code by revealing the identity of her source."

"Too bad. Would have simplified our lives. What do you plan to do if Woodhouse turns out to be the leak? I might add that I wouldn't be surprised either."

"I haven't decided how to deal with him yet."

"But you'll do something?"

"*That* I can promise you."

Andrew Bennett looked across at his partner, Woodhouse, and wondered how much longer he'd tough it out on the Kingston force. He'd jumped at the chance to transfer from Ottawa to work with Stonechild and Rouleau again but the cons were starting to outweigh the pros — and by cons, he meant Woodhouse. Even the sound of Woodhouse's name had become grating. *Self-righteous, condescending, self-serving bastard.* Bennett's desk phone rang, interrupting his therapeutic search for adjectives. He picked up.

"Officer Bennett."

"Yeah, it's Fred Taylor. I got a woman asking to speak to you about the Armstrong case. Could be a nutbar. You want to take it?"

"Sure. Make my day."

"Happy to let you deal with her."

Bennett didn't recognize the woman's voice right away until she asked, "You the young man who came to my door yesterday? The good-looking one?"

"Mrs. Greenboro?" He took a quick look at Woodhouse to see if he was listening. Happily, he was texting away on his cellphone, oblivious to Bennett's call.

"Of course it's me, young man. I told your gatekeeper about six times. I think he might need a hearing aid. You should look into it."

"Thanks for the tip. How can I help you today?"

"I have something more to tell you about Nadia Armstrong but I want to do it in person."

Bennett checked his watch. "I could come by around four o'clock. Would that work for you?"

"Do you imbibe?"

"Excuse me?"

"Four o'clock is martini hour. Do you like them shaken or stirred?"

Is this a test?

"I'm not fussy."

"Well, if you come by at four o'clock, you'll have to partake. I insist. While your answer was diplomatic, stirred is the right response. Bond had it wrong. I can see you're going to need a lesson in the finer points of life. Don't bring that overweight partner of yours. If you do, I won't let you in."

"Understood."

Bennett hung up and glanced again at Woodhouse. He was still engrossed in his phone and still unaware of Bennett's phone call. Bennett could share the information with Woodhouse — probably the wisest path forward — but every fibre of his being rebelled against the idea. What would be the harm in meeting with Mrs. Greenboro on his own time? She probably had nothing much of interest to share, anyhow. What could it hurt to make the old lady's day?

CHAPTER EIGHTEEN

Kala took the Queensway across the west end of the city and exited by the Nicholas off-ramp into downtown Ottawa. It was too early for rush hour but traffic was backed up at the lights anyway. Rather than waste time circling the streets to find a parking spot in the ByWard Market, she drove into the city parking garage on Clarence and paid the inflated downtown fee. She walked to the Heart and Crown pub at the other end of Clarence, taking a moment to enjoy the spring breeze and the chance to stretch her legs. Tanya Morrison was waiting for her at a table for two in front of the bar. A half-drunk glass of Guinness sat on the table in front of an open menu.

"Sorry I'm late," said Kala, shrugging out of her leather jacket. "Have you been here long?"

"Forty minutes. No problem. I knew you'd get here eventually."

The waiter appeared and they ordered cheeseburgers and fries.

"The hell with the diet," said Morrison as the server set a soda and cranberry on the table in front of Kala. "I need a good dose of grease and carbs."

"That rough?"

"This morning was. I spent it with Nadia's parents and the mother is a wreck. She blames her husband so you can imagine the tension."

"Why does she blame him?"

"For the last fight with Nadia and for not making up. She thinks his actions pushed her to move to Kingston rather than come home with the baby."

"Many marriages never recover from a child's death."

"You'd think such a tragedy would bring a couple closer, but I guess I can understand how it does the opposite. The upshot is that I got nothing more out of them that would help us find her killer."

"But you found Danny?"

"I did. He's working at a tattoo parlour on Rideau Street not far from here. His full name is Danny Fazendeiro but he's known as Faz to all his friends. He was basically a street kid but seems to be doing better. Apparently, he's a rock star in the tattoo business."

"How did you ever track him down?"

"I visited all the shelters and soup kitchens and talked to a lot of street people. On my second trip to one of the shelters, a volunteer who'd been working there for several years remembered Nadia and somehow realized that Faz was the Danny that I was looking for. Lucky for us Nadia had called him Danny once in her hearing. She said they both used to come in together sporadically but she hadn't see either for a couple of years. Faz was off work yesterday when I went in. He starts today at one."

Kala checked the time on her cellphone. "He should be arriving about now. Let's hope the food comes quickly so we can get over there. It's past time we figured out what was going on with Nadia. I'm hoping this Faz kid holds the key."

At 1:30, they were opening the door to Tat's Ass Tattoo Parlour, a brightly lit space with photos of previous customers' art projects plastering the walls. A girl with green tattooed sleeves adorning both arms and pink roses colouring her upper chest greeted them with more bubbliness than Kala thought was warranted. The girl introduced herself as Skyla and invited them to sit and go through the tattoo books. "Although our artists can do pretty much whatever you want, even if you just describe your idea," she said. "You're so in luck today. Faz is with a customer right now but he'll be free to meet you soon. He's the one everybody asks for." Her face was radiant with either delight at his craftsmanship or lust — Kala couldn't tell which.

"How long until we can see him?" she asked.

Skyla checked her book. "Ten minutes?"

Kala looked at Tanya, who nodded. "Okay, we'll wait."

They could hear voices in the next room rising and falling. A woman shrieked once and then laughed.

"Wild horses ..." muttered Morrison, flipping through one of the books and wincing at every photo. "I pray to God this fad is over by the time

Sara and Jack are old enough to sneak to one of these places behind my back."

"It's been more than ten minutes," said Kala. "We should have shown our warrant cards and gotten this going."

Fifteen more minutes and Faz appeared from the back room with the woman who'd been recently inked. "How would you like to pay for that?" Skyla asked the woman as she stepped over to the counter.

Faz was a skinny kid with dirty-blond hair that hung straight past his shoulders. A scruffy goatee and moustache added to the hippy look along with loose faded jeans, an untucked black T-shirt, and a red-and-blue beaded necklace. Kala counted only two tattoos on him: an eagle on his right shoulder and green script on his forearm whose words she couldn't make out. His grey eyes were constantly moving, like those of a crack addict who couldn't focus. His smile was shy but sweet, reminding Kala of a much younger boy.

"We're not here for tattoos," said Kala. She and Morrison pulled out their IDs. She watched his eyes pass over the badges and back up to her face. His expression had sharpened, the smile now a straight line. "Come in the back," he said. "I don't need Skyla overhearing whatever it is you're here about." He led them into his workspace and they took positions facing each other on either side of the reclining chair. Faz crossed his arms across his chest and waited.

"We're here about your friend Nadia Armstrong," said Kala, pulling her eyes away from the photos of tattoos that covered the wall behind him. The one of a man's face covered in green ink made her queasy. She focused on Faz's face instead. "We're very sorry to tell you that she died a few days ago."

Faz stared at her. "I don't believe you."

"Nadia's family has identified her. I'm sorry, but there is no doubt."

Faz lifted a hand to cover his mouth. His eyes reddened and filled with tears, but he didn't make a sound. He swallowed several times and blinked rapidly until his eyes cleared. Kala waited, giving him time to absorb Nadia's death.

His voice was husky. "Did she OD?"

"Possibly, but we believe someone was with her who killed her, or at least tried to cover up her death. We're working to find out who did this and why."

Faz turned away from them and punched his fist into the wall. The sound of smashing plaster filled the room. Kala rounded the table and put a hand on his back. She could feel his shoulder blade jutting through his shirt and his entire body seemed to be vibrating. She got an arm around his waist as his knees began to buckle and manoeuvred him onto the chair. She nodded to Morrison, who was already on her way to get a glass of water from the cooler in the waiting room.

"This is shock," she said. "Your body is reacting."

Morrison returned with the water and Faz drank before leaning back in the chair and closing his eyes. "Man, I thought I was going to pass out." His voice was achingly sad when he said, "I can't believe Nadia's dead."

Kala waited until some colour returned to his cheeks. "Is your hand okay?"

He looked down and shook it out. "Knuckles hurt but it's fine. Guess that wasn't the smartest move for a tattoo artist."

"It's going to throb."

"Don't worry. I'm tough." He gave her a half smile.

She waited until he'd finished the glass of water. "We don't know much about Nadia and we're hoping you can enlighten us. Were you her boyfriend?"

"Not exactly. We were together for a while but not recently." He rubbed his forehead slowly and looked up at Kala. "Could we get out of here? I could use a drink and this isn't the best place to reminisce about her."

"Of course. Where would you like to go?"

"There's a quiet place called the Albion Room not far from Rideau Centre. It's a short walk from here."

"Sounds good."

They filed out of the room, and Faz told Skyla he'd be gone a while and to keep an eye on the place. They walked to the Albion without saying much and entered the bar, which fed into a restaurant. Kala could tell that Morrison was as surprised as she was at the sophisticated feel of the space: dark leather couches and white leather chairs, round wooden tables, black hanging lamps of various shapes and sizes, and a floor-to-ceiling window facing a red brick wall. The bar running across the end of the room had a stained wooden top with shiny white tile as its base. Teak panels lined the wall behind the bar topped with wine bottles lying on their sides in a criss-cross of wooden slots. Pleasant jazz floated through the room from speakers hidden in the ceiling. This didn't seem like the kind of place Faz would hang out but he waved at the bartender and sank into one of the couches as if he'd been here many times before.

"Seems like a nice spot," Kala said.

"Yeah, I like it. Food's decent too."

A server dressed in black with a bouncy ponytail took their order. Faz asked for a low-alcohol beer while Kala and Tanya went with coffee.

Kala could see that he was still extremely upset. She softened her voice. "I know it will take a lot longer than a few minutes to come to terms with Nadia's death, but are you up to sharing with us what you know about her?"

"Yeah, why not. I met Nadia after she'd left home. I guess she was nearly sixteen."

"You weren't living at home either?"

"No."

He made a face but didn't elaborate, and Kala thought that now wasn't the time to push him on it. She asked, "What was Nadia like when you met her?"

"She was this hurt kid filled with anger when I met her at the shelter. She'd only recently found out that she was adopted and she felt betrayed."

"She'd had no idea?"

"No, and it came as a shock. They took her in when she was four and she didn't remember anything before then. Blocked it, I guess. She didn't take the news well but said it explained a lot. Like why she always felt like the odd person out and why her sister always came off as the favourite. I'd say the anger never went away the entire five years I knew her. Her father came down here to try to get her back home almost every week in the beginning. I don't think her mother knew. I almost felt bad for the guy. Nadia was stubborn and unreasonable but that was because she was so hurt and angry. She was a lot like her old man even if they didn't have a biological connection."

"Where did the two of you live? How did you get by?"

"We crashed different places. The shelters sometimes. I had friends with a bachelor apartment not far from here and we'd land there a few nights a week. I also had a friend who dealt and he'd pay me to deliver to clients. We'd panhandle when we really needed money." Faz shrugged. "Life was simple."

"Were you both using?"

"We smoked a lot of pot. Snorted coke when we had money. Drank beer. Not much else because we couldn't afford it, usually. Nadia always said she didn't want to get hooked on anything heavy because she planned to get out of the street life and live somewhere decent."

"She got pregnant. Was that in her plans?"

"I don't know. We'd stopped spending much time together by then. She'd met somebody."

Kala tried to keep the urgency from her voice. "Do you know his name?"

Faz shook his head. "She wouldn't tell me but I know he was older and had money."

A common story. Kala never identified with girls who tried to use men to get to easy street, although she didn't judge. "Was he the father of her baby?"

"I guess. She'd stopped seeing other guys ... including me."

"Was she hooking, Faz?"

He evaded her eyes and took his time answering. "Sometimes we needed money. She said it wasn't who she was. She dreamed big." His laugh came out a choking sound. "Look where that got her."

"What did Nadia think of her sister, Lorraine, and Lorraine's husband, Peter?"

"She thought her sister was a goody two-shoes and didn't have much use for her. I don't know about this Peter guy. She never mentioned him."

Kala looked over at Morrison. "Any questions to add?"

Morrison stopped writing in her notebook. "What kind of friend was Nadia?"

Faz's eyes welled up again. "Loyal. Complicated. Beautiful. I would have done anything for her, but I wasn't enough. She's the reason I cleaned myself up and got this job. I was hoping to win her back." He looked down at his hand gripping the beer glass and sat motionless for several heartbeats before draining the last of his drink.

Bennett had a feeling he'd better not be late so he told Woodhouse he had a doctor's appointment and hightailed it over to Bellevue Towers at quarter to four. He arrived with two minutes to spare and Mrs. Greenboro buzzed him in. Her apartment door swung open as the elevator let him out on the third floor.

She was as tiny as he remembered, but the rest of her was startlingly different. Her flowered silk dress, likely kept in her wardrobe since the fifties, hung in loose folds on her tiny frame and gathered lower than it should under the bodice. She'd dyed her hair an off-orange colour since his last visit and matched its garish hue with bright-blue eyeshadow, rouge, and a pumpkiny shade of lipstick that bled into the creases around her mouth.

Finding her efforts more endearing than she'd appreciate, Bennett bowed slightly at the waist. "You're looking lovely this evening," he said.

"I don't usually have company for martini hour." Her voice was harsh but her eyes twinkled, and Bennett was reminded of his grandmother, now in an old-age home. "Come in before the ice melts and dilutes the gin," she commanded and led the way on arthritic legs down the short hallway into a living room that smelled of Glade air freshener and furniture polish. Nat King Cole was singing from the record player under an open window with a view into the parking lot behind the building. Her chair and footstool were arranged so that she could look outside, and he wondered how many hours she'd spent watching the world go by from her lonely perch in the sky, listening to music from a bygone era.

She pointed to the couch. He sat at one end while she poured glasses of iced gin through a strainer into tall glasses. She already had olives skewered on toothpicks and she dropped them into the drinks. He rose and took the glasses from her as she settled onto the other end of the couch. Then she took hers back and raised it in a toast.

"To the bountiful God who was thoughtful enough to give us forty proof," she said, clinking her glass against his and taking a sip. She set her glass on the table and lifted up the plate with cheese slices cut into circles and placed on Ritz crackers that she'd also prepared ahead of his visit. He accepted two, thankful to have something to eat once he tasted the straight gin. He'd have to take it slow or he wouldn't be able to drive home. He understood that Mrs. Greenboro would not be sharing what she knew about Nadia Armstrong until she was good and ready. By the time he was halfway through the first martini, he realized that he didn't care how long she took to get to the point.

"I was a postwar mail-order bride," she said. "Came here from England and met my husband for the first time. He needed a wife and I wanted a family. Went from the boat to City Hall and tied the knot. We were married forty-six years before he died of a heart attack."

"You must miss him."

"I miss the routine of looking after him. Cooking meals, cleaning the house, growing my garden. I stayed home and raised our two sons, which is something women did in those days. Not like the new generation."

"Where are your sons now?"

"Gordon is living in Australia with his partner John. Alvin lives in Vancouver with his wife and four kids. I've stopped flying now that I'm eighty-eight. The seats are too uncomfortable. Alvin comes to visit twice a year." She reached over and took his empty glass. "I see a top-up is in order."

He knew he should refuse, but she was eighty-eight and alone, and the long hours and the alcohol were making him sink deeper into the couch. He accepted the full glass and scarfed down more soggy cheese and crackers while she returned to reminiscing. At a break in her monologue, he asked, "Is this a quiet building?"

Her eyes swung over to pin him into stillness. He was certain she knew he was leading her back to spilling what she knew and hoped he hadn't pushed too early. He took another sip of his drink and smiled to let her know that he was enjoying the martini. Her button eyes appeared to relent.

"Let me put on another record and we can get down to business." She rose slowly from the couch and set a fresh disc on the player. "Are you a Perry Como fan?" she asked as a swirl of violins filled the room.

"I like this music," he said, unsure of who she was speaking about but knowing the singer was likely long gone. He felt as if they were on a movie set and he should be putting on tap shoes and dancing her across the stage.

"I met him once, you know," she said, settling back into her seat. "I saved up my household money and took a plane to Vegas with two girlfriends.

Nineteen-sixty-one. I was a looker then. Betty Grable had nothing on me. Perry Como was performing at the Sands and the girls and I got gussied up and nabbed a table near the stage. Como caught my eye and had me up on stage to sing 'Catch a Falling Star.' Not to be immodest, but we brought down the house."

"I wish I'd been there," Bennett said, surprised that he meant it. Mrs. Greenboro's acerbic charm was getting to him.

She took a sip and put down the glass. "I normally stop at one, but tonight is a special occasion. How long have you been working with that boor of a partner?"

"Almost two years."

"Two years too long. Surely, you could ask to be with someone who appreciates you. Is your superior officer that good-looking sergeant John Rouleau that I see on the news?"

"His name is Jacques Rouleau and yes, he's my staff sergeant."

"Well, I could put in a word."

"No, Mrs. Greenboro. I'd rather you didn't."

She squinted at him and frowned. "You remind me of my late husband. Always putting up a brave front while he swallowed other people's abuse. Mark my words, young man. Not taking a stand against the venom will make you sick." She picked up her glass. "The super's brother used to visit Nadia two nights a week. Tuesdays and Thursdays. In and out in under an hour, if you get my drift."

"They were having sex?"

"Well, I'm quite certain that he wasn't fixing her leaky faucet twice a week for six months."

"Just to be clear, you're talking about Murray Simmons and Nadia Armstrong?"

"The very same."

Bennett looked at her chair by the window and back at her. "Did other ... men visit Nadia in her apartment?"

"None that I saw." Mrs. Greenboro stood and refilled their glasses. "Girl was good with the baby. She took him to a sitter a few afternoons a week and they'd be home around suppertime. Sometimes she appeared to leave him overnight. I didn't really keep track."

"How do you know the baby spent the time with a sitter?"

"She told me once when we rode the elevator together. Sitter was close by and her name was Holly Tremaine. I remember because Nadia was going there for the first time and asked if I happened to know her. Nadia was nervous about leaving Hugo with a stranger."

"Did you know Holly Tremaine?"

"No."

"Is there anything else you can tell me about Nadia or anyone else she associated with?"

"No. That's all I've got. The girl might have had a troubled life but she had backbone. Reminded me of myself."

Bennett pulled his notebook out of his pocket and jotted down the sitter's name. Perry Como's voice faded into silence and the record needle lifted and swung back into its holder. Mrs. Greenboro's head sank back against the couch and her eyes started to close.

Bennett left the last of his drink on the table and stood. A wave of vertigo passed after a few deep breaths. "I'll let myself out. Thank you again for a lovely visit and for sharing this information."

"I expect the child deserves to know who killed his mother. He'll want to know when he gets older. I'll have a rest now. Take care, young man." She looked up at him, her deep-set black eyes surrounded in blue shadow, and winked before they closed fully. She was snoring softly when Bennett closed her apartment door.

CHAPTER NINETEEN

Dawn walked alone down the hall to her locker. She'd been avoiding Vanessa and had waited in the washroom after class ended for the day until she was certain Vanessa was gone. She had no intention of double dating but didn't want to have to explain why to Vanessa. For now, staying away from her seemed better than a confrontation.

Dawn shifted her books and pulled her phone out of her bag, stopping in front of her locker to check for messages. She'd been expecting Fisher to show up on the weekend but wasn't surprised when he hadn't. It would have been nice to get a text from him, though. She read one from Kala telling her that she was on her way back from Ottawa and would be home around seven o'clock if traffic co-operated. She scrolled down the list of messages in case she'd missed one. Still nothing from her father.

She collected the books she'd need for an assignment due the next day and exited the school by the front door. The sun was still shining and the air had warmed since she'd gone for a walk at lunchtime. She took a deep, cleansing breath and started down the stairs. Emily and Chelsea were at volleyball practice but Vanessa had quit the team after Christmas. She said she'd rather spend time with her boyfriend. Leo. She'd finally shared his name with her and Chelsea, although nobody had met him yet. Emily said Vanessa obviously wanted to keep him all to herself. Dawn thought that maybe Vanessa was worried about Leo falling for Emily. Not outside the realm of possibility.

Dawn was on the last step when she spotted Leo's black car idling at the curb. *Oh, no,* she thought. *How can you still be here?* The urge to run the other way surged through her. *Please don't let them see me.* Her foot hit the sidewalk at the same time as the front passenger door of the car swung open and Vanessa stepped out.

"Hey, Dawn! Over here!" Vanessa was waving like a crazy person. There was no polite way to ignore her.

Dawn walked slowly toward the car, stopping several feet from Vanessa. "Hey, Vanessa. I have to get home."

Vanessa leapt closer and grabbed her by the arm. "Leo can drive you. He wants to meet you."

Vanessa was smiling, but her eyes were saying something different. Dawn couldn't figure out what it was about Vanessa that worried her but couldn't shake the feeling. "That's okay," she said. "I have to go to the library first."

"We'll drop you off. Get in the front and I'll take the back. Too bad Shawn isn't with us today to meet you."

She gave Dawn a little push toward the open door and got into the back seat. Leo was leaning across the passenger seat saying hello, a big grin on his face, his eyes hidden behind dark sunglasses. Dawn hesitated a moment more but she couldn't think of any reason not to take them up on the ride. She glanced up and down the street one last time before climbing in the front seat and pulling the door shut behind her.

Leo looked over at her as he slid the car into traffic. "Van's told me all about you," he said. "Good to finally meet."

"She wants to go to the library," said Vanessa from behind Dawn's left shoulder. She'd manoeuvred into the centre of the back seat so that she was between them. Dawn could see Vanessa in her peripheral vision when she turned her head.

"Yes, the one downtown at Johnson and Bagot."

"You kidding me?" asked Leo. "You must be ready for some fun after school all day. Why don't you drive around for a while with me and Van? We could stop for a drink or something."

"No, my aunt is picking me up at the library in half an hour."

"Text her and tell her you have a ride home."

He was still smiling, but his suggestions were beginning to sound more like commands, and Dawn was becoming even more uneasy. Leo was older than them, probably in his twenties. She felt out of her depth and wondered what he was doing dating Vanessa.

"Her aunt's a cop," said Vanessa behind them.

"She's already on her way to meet me," said Dawn. "Thanks, anyway."

"Another time then."

Leo drove with one hand resting casually on the wheel and the other trailing out the open window. He half turned his head and said to Vanessa, "Think we should set up a date with Shawn B. and Dawn? I have a feeling they'll like each other." His voice was playful, the demanding intonation gone.

"Sure, if you want to." Vanessa sounded distant, as if she wasn't thinking about her answer.

Dawn glanced back. Vanessa was looking out the side window with the same vacant look on her face that she'd had in math class. Dawn straightened and looked at Leo. "I'm not really looking for a boyfriend," she said.

"Shawn B.'s cool, isn't that right, Vanessa?"

"Yeah."

"He likes books so you have a lot in common."

"There's the library," said Dawn, pointing. Leo had stopped at a light and Dawn undid her seatbelt. "Thanks for the ride. I'll get out here." She opened the door and looked at Vanessa as she jumped onto the road. "See you in class tomorrow, Van."

Vanessa lifted a hand in a wave but made no move to get into the front seat. Dawn waited for the car to pull away before she crossed the street and entered the library. She stayed inside the door watching for a good ten minutes before she felt safe enough to go back outside to search for a bus stop.

Vanessa got into the front seat when they were in line at the Tim Hortons drive-through. Leo was being especially nice today and hadn't mentioned going to the motel at all. She was relieved that he wasn't talking about meeting up with Shawn B., someone she'd just as soon forget existed.

He ordered for her without asking. A small coffee with cream but no sugar. A toasted bagel with cream cheese and a large coke for himself. "You need to lose a few pounds," he said when he saw her eying his bagel. "I'm teaching you self-restraint."

He drove the car to the far end of the parking lot and turned off the engine. He pushed his seat back. She sipped her coffee and looked out the side window, listening to him chewing and trying not to think about how hungry she was. She hated coffee without sugar but at least the liquid was filling her up a bit.

"Your friend doesn't seem so friendly," he said, scrunching up the wrapper after he'd finished eating. "Is her aunt really a cop?"

"Yes, but Dawn doesn't talk about her much. I don't think her aunt is very strict if that's what you're worried about. She's always at work." Vanessa supposed what she was doing was throwing Dawn under the bus but going along with Leo was easier than arguing with him. Leo had noticed Dawn on his own so she wasn't responsible for that, at least. Anyway, it wasn't like she and Dawn were even friends. She was just someone Emily felt sorry for and should never have let into their group. Chelsea had said the same thing.

"Where do they live?"

"I'm not sure. West end somewhere, on the lakefront," said Vanessa.

"What's her aunt's last name?"

"Stonechild." Vanessa remembered only because the name was so weird and she and Chelsea had had a good laugh about it. She felt Leo's fingers running up and down her arm.

"You're not jealous, are you, baby?"

"No, why would I be?"

"You know you'll always be my number-one girl."

She pursed her lips and nodded, letting her hair cover her face.

He leaned closer, wrapping his arm around her shoulders and pulling her toward him. His mouth was on hers and his tongue pushed her lips apart. She wondered if anyone could see them but knew Leo wouldn't care if they did. After what felt like forever, but was more like ten minutes of his mouth on hers, he pulled away.

"Get in the back," he said, "and take off your pants."

"I don't want —"

The slap across her face came out of nowhere and cut off the rest of her protest. "It doesn't matter what you want or don't want," he said. "The sooner you figure that out the better. Tomorrow, I have a special surprise for you so let your mother know you'll be home late for supper. Consider tonight the appetizer."

Vanessa whimpered and pushed herself against the door as far away from him as she could get. Tears dripped onto the backs of her hands. Leo's hand was once again on her arm, rubbing up and down.

"You have to do what I say, Vanessa. You're my girl and that's the way it's going to be. I don't want to hurt you, baby, but I'll do what I need to do. Do you understand?"

She nodded.

"That's my girl. Now, move into the back and get yourself ready for some fun."

This time, she did what she was told without putting up a fight. She'd learned it was easier that way.

CHAPTER TWENTY

Kala poured coffee into her travel mug while chewing on a piece of toast. She could hear Dawn moving around upstairs and Taiku padding back and forth along with her between her bedroom and the bathroom. Kala smiled at the image and toasted another slice of bread while she waited for the two of them to come downstairs. She'd heard Dawn pacing in her room at 3:00 a.m. and needed to make sure she was okay before leaving for work.

"I thought you'd be gone by now," said Dawn when she entered the kitchen.

Kala looked her over carefully. Dawn's face was tired, with dark circles under her eyes. "Rough night?" Kala asked.

"I woke up and couldn't get back to sleep."

"Something on your mind?"

"Just school. I'll be okay."

"I'm here if you want to talk about anything."

"I know." Dawn walked over to the cupboard and pulled out the box of granola. "Aren't you going to be late for work? You've usually left by now when you're working on a serious case."

"I wanted to see you since I made it home so late last night. I was with another officer and we got called to speak to a woman about an assault when we'd only just gotten into Ottawa. We ended up taking her to the hospital."

"I got your text. No problem, Aunt Kala. Gundersund came by with Minnie after supper and we went for a long walk. He left after I got your message."

"Well, I'm glad you weren't alone all evening. I'm going to try to get home early today. All these overtime hours are wearing me out."

"I don't know how you do it. Have you made progress on the case?"

"Some. We're piecing together the dead girl's life and looking for a motive."

"Well, I know you'll find whoever did it. They should be locked away for a long, long time."

"We have some way to go yet. I'll see you after school. The weather forecast calls for sun and eighteen degrees today. Maybe we can get a fire going in the pit and cook supper à la Old West. Welcome in the first good spring day."

"That'd be great." Dawn's phone pinged in her pocket.

"Expecting a message?" asked Kala.

"It's probably Emily. She's worried about a math test today."

Kala spread peanut butter on her toast and held it in one hand while she grabbed her coffee. She stopped at the door and said, "Don't forget to let Taiku out before you leave. I've already filled his bowls."

Dawn gave her a thumbs-up. "Don't worry. I'll look after him."

Kala smiled at her. "I know you will. I never worry about you having my back."

Dawn sat down at the table with her bowl of cereal and opened her phone message.

I'm outside.

She leapt up and leaned on the counter to look out the window. Her heart quickened as she scanned the back deck and lawn but she couldn't see anyone. Pushing herself back from the counter, she thought for a moment about what she should do. Carry on to school as if she hadn't read the message or go in search of him? Putting off the inevitable would only make the situation worse. Maybe she could get Fisher to leave before Kala found out. Decision made, she crossed the kitchen to the back door. "Come, Taiku. Let's go for a walk."

The sun was up, but the lawn and deck were wet with dew and the air held the overnight chill. She'd have to dress in layers if the day was going to warm up as Kala had said. Right now, she was happy for her heavy sweater. Taiku was sniffing around the deck and he growled low in his throat. He lifted his head and looked toward the back of the property before taking off toward the lake. She called his name and raced after him, worried about what he'd do.

Scrambling down the incline to the water, she found Taiku standing with his fur on end and growling. He was several feet from her dad, who was sitting on the rocks looking out at the lake. She scrambled across the rocky beach to Taiku and grabbed him by the collar. "Good boy," she said and petted his side until she felt him relax under her hand. She walked closer to Fisher, all the while keeping a grasp on Taiku's collar. "What are you doing here, Dad?" she asked, then stopped short when he finally turned and she caught sight of his face. She raised the side of her fist to her mouth. "What happened to you?"

"I got into a slight altercation."

"Why?"

"I owe a bit of money to some unforgiving men. They decided to let me know how much they want it back." His smile disappeared into the folds of his swollen cheek.

"How much do you owe them?"

"Don't worry about it. I'm handling the problem."

She climbed the last distance between them and sat down a few feet away. Taiku sniffed Fisher's open hand and let him rub the ruff around his neck before going off to explore the shoreline.

"Have you been to a doctor?"

"I'm fine, Dawn. Don't worry yourself."

She picked up a stone and used the sharp edge of it to scrape across a larger rock. "Where did you sleep last night?"

He waved toward the woods. "I've got a nice spot set up. I brought my sleeping bag, and the weather is turning. It's good to sleep outside again. The stars were brilliant last night. Haven't seen them so clear in a long time. Say, I wonder if you could fill my water bottle before you go to school."

She nodded and took it from him. "I could get you some food too."

"No need … but I wouldn't say no."

"How long will you be staying? The thing is, Kala doesn't know that we've been in touch, and I'm pretty sure she won't be happy if she finds out. Mom doesn't want me near you."

"Yeah, I get it." He looked back out across the lake. "I feel like I can breathe here. I'll be glad to think of you in this place when I'm gone."

He looked at her and she tried not to wince at his black-and-blue face. She asked again, "How long are you staying?"

"A few days. Just until I don't look so beat-up. I'm going to catch a bus east and try my luck on the coast. Maybe find a place near the water and get hired onto a fishing boat."

"That would be good." He'd put distance between himself and whoever had hurt him so badly. Kala and her mom wouldn't have to know.

"Yeah." He pulled a pack of cigarettes out of his pocket. "Been smoking since I was twelve. Might die with one of these cancer sticks in my mouth."

"Have you tried to quit?"

"Not while I was inside. Would you like me more if I did?"

"You'd feel better."

"Maybe. Maybe not. They're like my security blanket." He struck a match across a rock and lit the cigarette hanging from his bottom lip. "Don't you start, though," he added.

"I don't intend to." She wanted him to leave but couldn't ask with him looking the way he did. Instead she said, "I'll get the water but I have to go right afterward to catch my bus."

"I'd come with you to the house but it hurts to walk. Couple of busted ribs and something not right with one of my legs."

"You should rest." She got to her feet. "Promise me you'll stay out of sight."

"Nobody else will know I'm here. Does Kala own this place?"

Something in his voice made her wary. "I'm not sure but I know she was renting."

"Well, she seems to be doing okay for herself."

Taiku raced ahead of Dawn to the house. She filled the water bottle, made two sandwiches with leftover chicken, and put them into a bag with an apple and a banana. She went up to the bathroom and wrapped a couple of aspirin inside a tissue before grabbing a washcloth, soap, and a towel. She'd find out what else he needed and bring it to him after school.

Gundersund watched Kala walk into the makeshift meeting room at the back of the main office and take a seat next to Bennett. He enjoyed watching her confident, long-legged strides as she crossed a room. He knew that he wasn't alone by the heads lifting and faces turning to watch her make her way. She attracted their eyes like moths to a flame. He wasn't a spiritual man, but since he'd met her, he could acknowledge the existence of another plane.

An intuitive, otherworldly layer that couldn't be seen or explained — a sixth sense that hinted at more than their physical reality. Judging by the reaction of people in crisis when she spoke with them, they felt it too. He pulled his gaze away from her and surveyed the others. Fatigue lined their faces, but not despair. Not yet. They were still working on the initial hit of adrenaline, confident they would find the puzzle piece that would set them on course to discovering why and how Nadia Armstrong had died — and in his bones, he believed Stonechild was right. This wasn't a simple suicide. Somebody was covering up their part in her death.

Rouleau entered the space and joined Gundersund at the front of the room. "Sorry I'm late."

"Everything okay?"

"Ellington wanted an update."

"Wouldn't it have been better to update him after our debrief?"

"It was the only opening he had until four o'clock, when we're meeting up again." Rouleau shot him a quick grin before turning to face the team. "Good morning, everyone. I'm hoping you made some progress yesterday. Who wants to go first?"

Morrison raised her hand and filled them in on her trip to Ottawa and the meeting with Faz. "So Nadia wasn't averse to raising money through soliciting when required, but apparently she gave it up when she met an older man, whom Faz believes could be Hugo's father." She looked at Kala. "Did I leave anything out?"

"We don't think Faz was involved in her death. He was genuinely shocked to learn she'd died."

"He could have been acting," said Woodhouse.

"Then he deserved an Academy Award," said Morrison. "If you'd been with us, you'd have seen how genuinely distressed he was. He almost passed out."

"Maybe it was because you tracked him down and he was worried about getting caught." Woodhouse held up both hands. "I'm not saying he killed her but I don't think we should cross anyone off based on a feeling. Especially not this Faz guy, who did drugs with her in the past and then was replaced. You just said he was still trying to get back with her."

"Agreed we shouldn't be too hasty," Stonechild conceded. She glanced at Morrison as if to say, *let it go*. "I also found out from Nadia's brother-in-law, Peter Billings, that the reason she moved to Kingston was that she took her clothes off and propositioned him and he told her to leave. He doesn't believe her sister Lorraine knew."

"But she might have?" asked Rouleau.

"It's possible. Women have a way of finding these things out."

"Tell me about it," said Woodhouse.

"What, one of your blow-up dolls discover she has a rival?" asked Bedouin.

"Very funny. I notice you never mention a significant other." Woodhouse's voice rose above the laughter. "In fact, it looks like none of you can keep a relationship together."

The laughter died. Gundersund thought Woodhouse had landed on a truth that hit painfully close to home for most, if not all of them. Himself, for certain.

"My wife might be offended by that statement," said Bedouin. "Twenty-six years of wedded bliss and counting."

"Twenty-six years of the old ball and chain more like."

Rouleau sighed and said, "Okay, let's get back to work. Woodhouse, what did you find out from the latest door-to-door?"

"Nothing of consequence."

"I have something," said Bennett, ignoring the look Woodhouse shot him. "I got a call late yesterday from Mrs. Greenboro."

"The old woman across the hall from Nadia's apartment?" asked Woodhouse.

"Yeah. I'd have asked you to come along but thought it might be a waste of time after our first encounter." He looked at Rouleau. "Mrs. Greenboro refused to say much of anything when we first got her to open her door."

Woodhouse tapped his temple with two fingers. "Loony-tunes."

"She was lucid and more forthcoming the second time around. She told me that the building's owner, Murray Simmons, was dropping by two nights a week and spending half an hour to an hour in Nadia's apartment each visit."

All eyes were on him now. "What did Mrs. Greenboro think was going on?"

"She seemed certain that they were having sex. I checked and Murray Simmons is married with three young kids. A good reason to want Nadia silenced if they had a falling out."

Rouleau said, "Combined with her previous soliciting, a sexual relationship with a married man isn't too big a stretch. He might even be the older man she was seeing in Ottawa. Woodhouse, bring Murray Simmons in for an interview. Gundersund, arrange to have Jeff brought in at the same time and make Murray aware of his brother's presence in the station. Maybe we can shake the pair of them enough to get at the truth."

CHAPTER TWENTY-ONE

"You should have told me that you were going back to speak to the old lady," Woodhouse said as he pulled into the Mortimer Construction parking lot. It figured Simmons was in construction in addition to being a slumlord.

"I thought of calling you," said Bennett, "but you were already on your way home for the day and I had no idea if she'd have anything of value to share. I didn't want to kill your evening if it was a wild goose chase."

Woodhouse glanced at him, trying to determine whether he was blowing smoke. Bennett was staring straight ahead. If Bennett was telling the truth, Woodhouse was sure he'd have met his eyes squarely. "You better not be working to raise your profile at the expense of mine."

"Now why would I do that?" Bennett finally turned his head to stare at him.

"Because you're a dumb fuck." Woodhouse got out of the car and didn't wait for Bennett before walking into Mortimer Construction's headquarters. If there was one thing he couldn't stand, it was disloyalty in uniform. He'd been given a worse time than he was giving Bennett, but he'd always toed the line. Well, except for feeding information to Marci Stokes, but that was a long game that his old partner, Ed Chalmers, had condoned. *Senior management likes us to make use of the press but they can't very well come out and say so, now can they, Woody?* Chalmers's words replayed in his head, giving him absolution.

Murray Simmons was standing behind the counter talking to a woman. Woodhouse called him over and held up his badge. He heard Bennett open the door behind him. "We're here to take you to the station for a chat about Nadia Armstrong. We need you to elaborate on your initial statement."

"I'm busy. Can't it wait?"

"No. No, it can't."

Simmons looked at the woman, exasperation written all over his face. He was about to say something but thought better of it. "Tell Harold I'll be gone for a few hours. Reschedule my eleven o'clock for after lunch."

He followed them at a distance to the car. Woodhouse stopped and looked at Bennett and made sure he was staring back before tossing him the car keys. "You can drive. I've got some texts to answer on our way in." He opened the back door and asked as Simmons ducked his head to slip past, "So, what is it you do in the office, exactly?"

Simmons paused, one foot on the ground and the other on the floor of the vehicle. "I'm the paperwork guy. Contracts, zoning applications, feasibility studies. That kind of thing."

"Is that how you got your hands on two apartment buildings?"

Simmons finished sliding into his seat and reached for the seat belt. His voice was indignant. "I didn't get them illegally if that's what you're implying. I purchased them above board in a fully transparent manner. You can check the records."

"Oh, I intend to. You can rest assured about that." Woodhouse slammed the door shut and tapped the roof of the car sharply two times.

They entered the station twenty minutes later. Woodhouse told Bennett to stay in the hall with Simmons while he spoke with the desk sergeant about booking a room. He waited until Stonechild and Gundersund arrived with Jeff Simmons and told them to hold up at the end of the hallway where Murray Simmons could see his brother.

"All set," Woodhouse said, sauntering down the hallway toward Murray Simmons and acting as if all were right with the world.

"What the hell is going on?" Murray's face flushed beet red and his hands bunched into fists. He craned his neck to look around Woodhouse at his brother standing next to Stonechild. Bennett grabbed Murray's arm and hustled him into the meeting room as if trying to prevent him from seeing Jeff. Murray shook him off. "What is my brother doing here?"

"We're interviewing everyone who knew Ms. Armstrong," said Woodhouse, entering and shutting the door. He kicked out a chair. "Sit down and make yourself comfortable, *Mr.* Simmons."

Murray looked like a fire pot ready to explode but he dropped onto the seat as asked. He pounded his fist on the table. "My brother didn't do nothing. He doesn't know squat about anything."

"Then neither of you have anything to worry about, do you?" Woodhouse took the seat directly across from Simmons and turned on the tape recorder. He recited date, time, and those present before settling against the back of the chair and folding his hands across his belly. "So tell me all about your relationship with Nadia Armstrong."

Simmons crossed his own arms. "She was a tenant in my apartment building."

"How long did she live there?"

"Five, six months? I'd have to check my records to verify."

"Did you know her before she moved into the apartment?"

"Nope."

"You might want to think about your answer. Did you know her when she lived in Ottawa?"

"Never met her before she came in and decided to rent apartment 302."

"We have a witness who says that you visited Nadia twice a week in the evenings and stayed inside her apartment half an hour to an hour each time. What were the two of you doing?"

Murray's face whitened. "I might have dropped in a few times to fix the appliances. The last tenant hadn't let me know they were breaking down. Who told you, anyway? If it was Mrs. Greenboro across the hall, that old woman has a few screws loose."

Woodhouse ignored Murray's stab at identifying the source, though he was satisfied to have his own assessment of Mrs. Greenboro confirmed. "Isn't that what your brother is there for? To fix things for tenants?"

"Jeff looks after the building and general maintenance but fixing appliances is beyond his capabilities. I didn't mind stopping in to get them in working order, seeing as it saved me a lot of money. Yeah, I'd spend a bit of time in her apartment on my way home. What of it?"

Woodhouse could see his point but the explanation didn't negate the obvious. He sweetened the sarcasm. "She must have had a lot of broken appliances if you were there twice a week for six months. What, were you working on her internal plumbing too?"

Simmons laughed. "Is that what the old lady told you? Man, I think I was by maybe four times in total. I never jumped her bones, nor would I. I'm happily married with three kids, thank you very much. I get more than enough at home. Sorry. Should I have said that on tape?"

"Only if you want bragging about your sex life on police record for posterity."

"I got nothing to hide."

Bennett spoke for the first time. "What about your brother? He was charged with inappropriate behavior. Stalking and sexual touching, wasn't it?"

The vein in Murray's temple pulsed but he kept his voice level. "Jeffy has a simpler view of the world. He took a shine to a girl and didn't know the first thing about how to go about asking her out. Not that she would have agreed ... but he didn't know that. He started following her around like a lovesick puppy and he tried to get her attention. She took it all wrong and called in the cops."

"Maybe he tried something with Nadia Armstrong."

"Nah, he learned his lesson. We sent him to live with relatives on a farm in the U.S. and he hated that. He wouldn't do anything to get sent back there. I told him to never go into a tenant's apartment alone and he hasn't. My brother had nothing to do with what happened to Nadia. I guarantee you that."

Woodhouse cut in before Bennett could form another question. "We'll need a list of dates and times you visited Ms. Armstrong's apartment and a signed statement as to where you were the evening she went missing."

"Yeah, I can get you that, although the dates I stopped by her place will be a guess. My visits would have been on a Monday or Thursday, though, because those are the days I pick up my daughter at ballet and have some time to kill between work and the end of her class."

Woodhouse stretched. He'd done enough of these interviews to know Simmons wasn't going to give him anything. "Officer Bennett will take your statement and then you're free to leave."

"What about Jeff?"

"You can wait in the lobby. If he's as innocent as you say, he'll be joining you shortly. If not ..." Woodhouse raised his hands and flipped them over so that the palms faced the ceiling.

Simmons stood and glared down at him before the bluster returned to his voice. "Then you'll be releasing him right after me, because neither of us had anything to do with that girl's death."

In the second interview room, Kala tried to think of how to approach Jeff Simmons after Gundersund's efforts had fallen flat. He'd wrapped up his tough-guy approach and was looking at her as if to say, *what now?* She couldn't tell if Jeff had been deliberately obtuse or if the person they saw was all there was. She glanced at her page of doodles and raised her head.

"Jeff, you said that you never went into Nadia Armstrong's apartment alone; is that correct?"

His disconcerting stare, wide and unblinking as a garter snake's, swung over to her. "I never went in alone."

She tried to think of what he wasn't telling her. "Did you go in with anybody else, maybe when Nadia and the baby were there?"

He was silent, his eyes darting between her and the wall behind her head. "You won't tell my brother?"

"No. This is between you and me. For the purposes of our files only."

He wiped a hand across his nose. "She asked me in sometimes."

She had to strain forward in her seat to hear him. "Could you repeat that a little louder, please, Jeff?"

"Some afternoons after my work was done, she'd ask me in for a Coke. I said no at first, but she said it was our secret."

"Nadia was kind to you."

"I didn't mind watching her baby when she went out. Hugo. He only woke up once and I sang to him like she told me until she got back."

"You'll miss her friendship."

"I liked spending time with her."

"Do you know where she went those afternoons when she left you with Hugo?"

"She said that she was working on a project."

"What kind of project?"

"One to bring in money for her and Hugo. She said they wouldn't be living at Bellevue Towers much longer."

"Did she say who she was working with on her project?"

"I don't remember." His face drooped sullenly, a stubbornness in his eyes.

"That's fine," said Kala. She kept her voice low and smiled whenever his stare crossed hers. "How about Murray? Did he like to visit Nadia too?"

"I dunno."

"You never saw him enter her apartment, say on a Monday evening?"

"I dunno."

She leaned back in her chair and studied him. "I'm going to give you my card, Jeff, and if you ever remember, you can call me. Would you do that, Jeff?"

"I guess."

"I have one more question for you." She hesitated and forced her body and face to relax, leaning forward as if they were friends having a chat. "You were charged with assaulting a girl a few years ago. Can you tell me what happened?"

She jerked back reflexively as his face contorted. If panic had a human name, it would have been Jeff Simmons.

"I didn't do nothing wrong. She lied and said I was trying to do something bad to her. I wouldn't! I wouldn't!" He was pushing himself out of the chair, yelling as he got to his feet. "She set me up. Murray said she was nothing but a lying whore!"

He bolted for the door, but Gundersund was there first, blocking the way. "Sit down, Jeff," he ordered, but followed up with a gentler voice, "Officer Stonechild only wants to hear your side."

Kala stood and moved closer to Jeff, who again wouldn't meet her eyes. She reached out and touched his arm. "I think we have all we need for now. You're free to go home, and don't forget to call me if you remember anything to help us. Will you do that, Jeff?"

He dropped his head and nodded once before Gundersund opened the door and ushered him out.

"He's one scared rabbit," said Gundersund after Jeff's footsteps disappeared down the hall. He turned and looked at Kala. "Good work getting him to talk. All I managed to do was intimidate him."

"Well, you are twice his size."

Gundersund took a step closer to her. She could smell his scent. Citrusy cologne and musky soap that made her knees weaken. "Are *you* intimidated?" he asked, and she saw amusement in his crystal-blue eyes. She thought he might bend and kiss her; she looked up at the camera suspended from the ceiling. He followed the direction of her eyes and stepped back, turning so that his back was to the lens. "Your response will have to wait until later," he said. His grin made her bite her bottom lip to keep from smiling back in case the camera operator was recording their exchange on tape.

They were halfway down the hallway when Gundersund said, "Woodhouse told me that he got to Murray through his brother. What do you think?"

"Woodhouse has been dealing with them both, so maybe he can. Let's track him down and find out what happened in his interview. I'm not convinced that either of them is in the clear yet."

"Yeah, there's something about the pair of them that doesn't ring true."

CHAPTER TWENTY-TWO

Rouleau walked down the windowed hallway through the fading daylight toward Ellington's office. He was tired and this was his last obligation before he could leave for the day. His father had been working on a beef stew, which he promised would only get better the later the hour. Rouleau was relieved that Henri was perceptive enough not to ask why he hadn't been spending evenings with Marci. He didn't want to have to explain that she was being fed information by somebody in his team. Until he knew more about her relationship with the leak, he had to keep his distance. He was using this investigation to buy time.

Ellington appeared ill-tempered when he looked up from the paper he was reading. Rouleau took the seat across from him. "What have you got?" Ellington asked without preamble. He turned the page face down on his desk.

"Nadia Armstrong had occasionally worked as a prostitute in Ottawa until she started seeing an older man — who is likely the father of her baby."

"She was turning tricks?"

"Looks that way. She might have been having sex with Murray Simmons, the owner of the apartment building where she was living. The team is pursuing the lead. Nobody has come forward yet to say they saw her the day she went missing. We'll be making another public plea."

"You can handle the media?"

"If you like."

Ellington picked up the paper again and pursed his lips before saying, "It's beginning to sound like her murder was a one-off — if it even was a murder. Sure, somebody moved her body, but maybe they didn't kill her. She might simply have OD'd. Can you follow up with the coroner and see if he can run more tests? We'll soon be able to stand down from news briefings, and the public will lose interest."

"We can't know that yet." Rouleau hoped he was misreading the indifference Ellington started to show ever since he'd said the word "prostitute."

"Once the media finds out she was involved in a high-risk lifestyle, this story won't be front-page news anymore. People will think it's too bad but maybe she shouldn't have engaged in such dangerous activities. I've seen this scenario play out over and over."

"Or the media could give the story a higher profile."

"I wouldn't bet on it. The emotional investment will end once the public hears that the deceased came from the underbelly of society. They'll feel safe in their ivory towers, high above the ugliness. Trust me on this. Nobody wants to think too deeply about what really goes on in the back alleys while they're tucked up warm and snug in their beds at night. Anything else?"

"No, I'd say that about wraps it up." Rouleau stood. His weariness at being part of a system that would allow a political player such as Ellington to rise to a position of authority weighted his footsteps across the plush carpet ... and Ellington was only one in a long string. Still, say what you might about the absent police chief Malcolm T. Heath but he wouldn't have lost interest in bringing a killer to justice just because the victim was a prostitute. Rouleau hoped that his decision to return to Major Crimes wouldn't result in irreparable harm to the force. But he wasn't the one who'd picked this replacement. The police board could have chosen better. Ellington's voice stopped him at the door.

"I'm off-site tomorrow, but available by text if something comes up. Shut the door on your way out, if you would. I have a call to make. And Rouleau?"

"Yes?"

"Keep me in the loop. The public might lose interest, but I still need to report up. Let me know about the new test results."

"Of course."

Rouleau almost collided with Vera, who was rushing to her desk, coat on, purse swinging over her shoulder. He reached out a hand to steady her but she brushed him away.

"Sorry," she said. "I forgot something in my desk." She skirted past him and rummaged in the top drawer. Rouleau stood watching her, uncertain of her mood.

"That was a quick meeting," she said at last, looking up as she slammed the drawer shut. She straightened. "Did his majesty tell you that I handed in my resignation letter this afternoon? I imagine he found it on his desk before you arrived."

"No, I had no idea. Vera, surely this is premature. Ellington won't be in the job for long. He's merely a placeholder."

"You have no way of knowing that. I heard from Laney and she says that she and Heath won't be back in Canada for a few months at least. They're sunning themselves on the Riviera and planning a jaunt to Tuscany in May. She thanked me for holding down the fort. The damn irresponsibility of both of them."

"Did something else happen with Ellington?"

"Isn't what's already happened enough? I won't be objectified and paraded in front of the media like … like a brainless mannequin with cleavage."

They were speaking in hushed voices, hers becoming angrier with every word. Rouleau was finding it difficult to accept what was unfolding. Guilt coursed through him over his inaction. He should have ignored her request to stay out of it and confronted Ellington. He'd certainly planned to, once he got the chance. He asked, "Have you got another job offer?"

"I will have. No need to concern yourself."

"Let me take you for a drink. We can talk this through, Vera."

"What, so you can change my mind?"

"If I can."

She stepped closer, and he became aware of her light lavender scent. "That's not going to happen, Jacques. I've been thinking of leaving for a while. This latest addition to the team was just the push I needed." She smiled and tilted her head while keeping her tawny eyes on his. "I'm here another week so there's still time for that drink. But it'll be to toast my departure. I've made up my mind and there's no turning back."

School was over for the day, and the hours Vanessa had grown to dread had once again arrived. Leo had said to bring Dawn with her this time to meet Shawn B. but Dawn was nowhere to be found — not that Vanessa had looked too hard. She suspected Dawn was tutoring Emily in the library but decided not to look there. Then, when Leo asked her if she'd seen Dawn in the school, she could honestly say no. She wouldn't flinch under his evil-eyed scrutiny.

She felt bad about involving Dawn when she let herself think about it, even if the choice wasn't hers. Leo was a creep and Shawn B. was hard to figure out. She still had welts on her stomach where Leo slapped her for saying she didn't want to go with Shawn ever again. How could she bring Dawn into this, even if they weren't really friends? Vanessa wouldn't wish Shawn or Leo on her worst enemy. But what would they do to her if they thought she'd gone behind their backs to warn Dawn? She shivered even though the late afternoon sun was warm on her face and arms.

They'll post the naked photos and video of me on the internet and email them to my parents, friends, and teachers. That's what they'll do. They'll humiliate me and wreck my life.

Her feet were lead weights carrying her down the sidewalk.

Leo was waiting for her partway along the street, sitting behind the tinted windshield of his black car. In the school washroom, she'd changed into the clothes he'd given her to put on. Black lacy underwear, short skirt, and striped red T-shirt. He'd told her to wear her running shoes and tie her hair in pigtails; the total ensemble made her look about twelve years old unless you saw the bra and panties. They scratched uncomfortably as she walked down the sidewalk.

"You're late," he said when she slipped into the front seat. He'd parked under an oak tree and his face was half in shadow. He turned his head slowly to stare at her and sunlight reflected off his black sunglasses.

"I was looking everywhere for Dawn. She must have left for the day."

"Shame," said Shawn B. from the back seat. "But we'll catch up with her later."

Vanessa gave Leo a nervous smile before looking straight ahead. She couldn't make herself turn around to look at Shawn B. Knowing he was behind her was horrible enough.

"Might be better anyway," said Leo, and Shawn grunted what sounded like agreement.

"Are we going back to the motel?" Vanessa asked. She wanted to make sure she had enough time to disappear inside herself.

"Not today," said Leo. "Remember that surprise I promised?"

"Yes."

"We have a client who's asked for a house call, or in this case, an office call. He pays out big time in exchange for discretion. You'll do real well if you become his new favourite."

"What happened to his old favourite?"

"She's not around anymore."

Vanessa thought about the girl she'd seen in the motel parking lot who'd gotten herself killed. She said without thinking, "I saw that girl who died ... at the hotel construction site down the road from the motel."

Leo had been about to pull out of the parking spot, but he stopped and looked at her. She could hear the squeal of leather as Shawn B. sat up in the back seat. "Where did you see her?" Leo asked. He acted casual, pulling a cigarette out of his pocket with one hand and glancing at her, but Vanessa felt her body tense. *Why did I say that?*

"At the Blue Nights. Going into one of the rooms."

"How do you know it was her?"

"I saw her photo in the news. I recognized her." And now, why was she being so stubborn? She wanted to let the matter drop but Leo kept staring at her with a strange look on his face.

"Was she with anybody?" asked Shawn beside her ear.

She recoiled at his hot breath on her neck and banged her head against the headrest. The girl had been with that man but Vanessa had a feeling that saying so might get her into more trouble. She began to find the silence in the car threatening. She swallowed hard and said, "She must have been with a guy but I don't remember seeing him." Her voice wavered and she wasn't certain they believed her.

Leo sucked on the end of the cigarette and took a look behind him. "Whaddaya think, Shawn? Should we proceed as planned?"

"Don't see why not. Turn up the tunes, will you? I need some wailing electric guitar to block out this shit."

Dawn collected her books at her locker and left school a few minutes before the halls became clogged with students done for the day. She'd slipped out of class a few minutes early on the pretext of going to the washroom. The bus came a moment after she'd reached the stop, her hair loosened from its braid in her mad dash down the sidewalk.

She'd gone out at lunchtime to a corner store and bought some snacks she thought her father might like. Chips and chocolate bars. Gum and peanuts. Aspirin. She'd had trouble concentrating in her classes, thinking of him lying in the woods, injured and in pain.

She usually enjoyed the walk up Old Front Road at the end of her day. She could see the sparkling water through the trees from different spots. Most people grew thickets of trees on their property, making the road feel like it cut through the woods.

Sun and shadows mingled in front of her as the tree branches swayed like feathery fans in the wind off the lake. She waited for the sense of calm that usually filled her as she got closer to home but today the feeling didn't come. Instead, a growing anxiety buzzed in her stomach like a swarm of bees. She reached Gundersund's house, set back from the road and less welcoming now that his wife was back. Before her arrival, Dawn would have used her key to get Minnie and bring her home to play with Taiku. Now, she walked on by.

Taiku was waiting at the back door for her and they started off together toward the lake. Taiku found Fisher first, cutting off the stretch of rocky beach into the woods near the edge of their land. He was sitting on his sleeping bag, which he'd set on a layer of freshly cut cedar boughs. The tree branches overhead protected him from rain. He'd tied his food in a piece of cloth up a tree to keep the animals from getting at it. His face wasn't as purple and puffy as it had been when she'd left for school. She handed him the bag of stuff she'd bought at lunchtime and he thanked her before setting it within reach.

"We could sit at the edge of the beach, in the sun," she said. "Kala texted me that she won't be home for another hour at least and nobody else comes down this way."

They chose a flat rock warmed by the spring sun. Dawn rested her hands on its smooth surface and let the heat travel up her arms. Fisher moved carefully and lowered himself gingerly into place, but he said he wasn't as stiff as he had been. He'd slept away the morning and afternoon. Another few days and he'd be ready to dance a jig.

"How long will you stay?" she asked.

"I'll leave when my face heals a bit more. Don't want to scare anybody." He looked across the water and breathed deeply in and out. "You could come with me. I'll get a job on a boat and rent a cottage near the ocean. When your mom gets out of prison, she can stay until she gets back on her feet. Longer if she wants."

Dawn didn't know why she felt like crying. She wished with her whole heart that their lives had been different. That he wasn't so all alone. "I don't know, Dad," she said finally. "I'll have to think about it."

"I know. Just thought I'd put it out there."

They sat without talking and Taiku ran in and out of the water. He shook himself off and they laughed as the water sprayed across their legs.

"He's a good dog," said Fisher. "I had a hound dog named Shamus before I went in the pen."

"Can you get him back?"

"He died two years after I went in. He was ten years old and sickly when I left him."

"You can get another dog when you move to Nova Scotia."

"I could."

A dog would keep him from being lonely. Dawn's spirit lightened at the thought.

Fisher patted his pockets and pulled out the crumpled pack of cigarettes. He removed a half-smoked one and lit it, squinting at her through the smoke.

"How's school going?"

"Fine. I like school."

"I never did." He laughed. "You got all the brains in the family."

Dawn looked above the lake to the horizon. The sun was losing strength, and the light had changed. "I need to go in. I get supper going for Kala."

"Run on home, then. I'll be fine here."

"Are you warm enough?"

"I enjoy sleeping outside. I feel safe in the woods and I like knowing you're nearby."

"I'll bring you more water in the morning."

"And a cup of coffee would be good if you can manage it."

"Okay."

She called to Taiku and scrambled across the rocks with him bounding ahead, crisscrossing into the bushes and back. She looked behind her once to wave but her father was gone, returned to his sleeping bag with the bag of snacks.

Dawn had been cautious several months earlier when she'd first realized who it was standing across the street from her school. She'd worried that he wanted something from her. He hadn't, though. Everything she'd given him had been without him asking. He'd never touched her. He'd respected her space and she relaxed in the unpressured ease of their meetings. He was her father but he would never be her parent. He was a stranger whom she would have helped even if he wasn't her dad.

It wasn't that she needed him. She wanted him to disappear without anybody knowing that he had been here. Yet she needed to understand why she felt this invisible tie to him. Why she wondered what it would feel like to hold his hand in hers.

CHAPTER TWENTY-THREE

Marci was at her desk by 7:00 a.m. She'd brewed a pot of coffee and was on her second cup when the other reporters straggled in just before 9:00. The urge for a cigarette made her fingers twitch but she refused to give in. She wanted to call Rouleau but she wouldn't give in to that craving, either. He'd sent her a text the evening before, around eight, saying that he wouldn't be over and she'd been disappointed, even though she'd already guessed that he wasn't going to show. Waiting around for him to call was so high school. The very idea of letting a man do this to her again filled her with disgust. The question was, what was she prepared to do about it?

She looked out the window at the morning haze blotting out the view of the sky. Her drive to work had been done in darkness; the sun started peeking over the distant treeline when she pulled into the parking lot. A ribbon of pink-and-violet sky broke the line of indigo by the time she'd locked her car and entered the front door. She'd had the radio tuned to CBC and sighed at the forecast. *Unsettled weather. Periods of sun but mainly cloudy. Carry an umbrella to be on the safe side.* Another day of crazy weather north of the forty-ninth parallel.

Screw this, she thought, reaching for the phone on her desk. *Better to know if Rouleau's dumped me than wait around like a Jane Austen bimbo.*

Rick breezed into her office and she pulled her hand back. He plopped down in the visitor chair, dunking a tea bag into a bright-yellow mug while he looked her over. "Is that a new sweater?"

"I do have some half-decent pieces in my closet."

"Well, pull them out more often, girl. It's refreshing to see you in something from this decade. The green goes well with your coppery hair."

"Stop. You'll have me blushing."

"I doubt that. How's it coming with the murder case? Still making meaningful music with the delish sergeant in arms?"

"None of your business." She smiled and batted her eyelashes.

"Coy becomes you."

"Goes with the sweater." The phone rang and her heart jumped until she saw Scotty's name on the screen. She picked up and listened to him tell her to make the trek to his office before the phone went dead. She stood and grabbed her iPad. "Duty calls," she said with false gaiety.

"Give my best to Scotty," Rick said. "I know I'd sure like to."

She was still running Rick's sexual innuendo around in her mind as she took the seat across from her boss. She'd wondered about Scotty's personal life since she started at the paper. The thing was, Rick said that same suggestive line about every man around, regardless of his orientation. She suspected Scotty preferred women but couldn't pinpoint why. He was unmarried, forty-something, and short. The jury could swing either way.

Scotty looked at her over his computer screen. "I got your piece on the Nadia Armstrong killing. It's thin. Doesn't add anything new since your previous posts."

"Nothing new has happened. I thought her sister's interview gave context."

Scotty's voice rose higher to a singsong key. "Nadia grew up in Ottawa, lived on the street, got pregnant, and moved here to start a new life." His lips lifted sideways. "You said that in yesterday's scoop, and I use the word 'scoop' lightly. Rearranging the sentences doesn't make the rehash news. Get me something newsworthy. That's what we're paying you for."

She accepted the implied reprimand without comment, knowing that the story hadn't been her best effort. She pushed herself out of the chair. Scotty was already typing on his keyboard, eyes focused on the screen, his charming way of telling her that he'd said all he planned to say. Short and sweet. Just like him. Well, short, anyway.

She walked back to her desk to get her jacket and log off her computer. She hadn't wanted to go this route since it felt disloyal to Rouleau. Silly, really, since one had nothing to do with the other. She had a right to milk her sources.

Rouleau could have called me.

Rick was busy on the phone as she walked past but he saw her and gave a thumbs-up. She saluted him before reaching into her pocket for her cellphone. She hesitated as she ran through other possibilities. Every one of them led back to this. She was a journalist. She had to set all qualms aside and do whatever it took to get her story.

It was time to give Woodhouse a call.

Dawn was late for school. She'd spent half an hour on the beach with her dad and Taiku that she shouldn't have. She'd missed her usual bus and had to catch the next one, which put her twenty minutes behind. The halls were nearly empty when she ran to her locker and anxiety made her fingers fumble with her lock. She got it open on the third try.

Her first class had started and she tried to slip in unnoticed. She would have made it if one of the class clowns hadn't yelled, "Look who's late!" Mrs. Barnes turned from the chalkboard and saw Dawn slinking over to her desk at the back of the room, but didn't comment.

Dawn slumped low in her chair and opened her notebook as Mrs. Barnes began talking about the history unit test on Friday. Dawn listened while copying the points from the board. Emily turned around when a boy at the front asked a question. Her voice was a cross between a hiss and a whisper. "Did Vanessa's mother call you?"

Dawn shook her head. "No, why would she? I doubt she even knows my name."

"Vanessa missed supper and it was nearly nine o'clock when her mom called to see if she was at my house. Vanessa hadn't even checked in."

"Girls!" Mrs. Barnes was staring at them. Emily straightened around.

Two strikes, Dawn thought, relieved not to have been given a detention. Mrs. Barnes was known to hand them out freely for the smallest of reasons.

Dawn tried to concentrate on the unit review but her mind kept returning to Vanessa. She hadn't seemed like herself the last few weeks. Was she that unhappy at home? Maybe staying out with Leo was her way of rebelling — or it could be a cry for attention. Either way, Dawn thought Vanessa was getting herself into trouble. There were better ways to make people notice you. Had she been with him all night?

Emily grabbed her arm on the way out of the classroom after the lesson ended. "Vanessa's in biology. Let's wait for her at the lockers. I want to find out what happened when she finally got home."

"She made it home then?"

"Yeah, I didn't get a chance to tell you that she sent me a text around eleven. Her mom told her to let me know everything was okay."

"Where was she?"

"She never said so I guess we'll find out."

They waited in the hall at Vanessa's locker, getting jostled by students on their way past. The corridor echoed with loud voices and a herd of footsteps tromping in either direction. Finally, Dawn spotted Vanessa coming toward them. She had that vacant look on her face which looked waxy under the fluorescent hall lighting. She was wearing a red sweatshirt with the school crest centred over her chest, tight jeans ripped at the knees, and yellow runners. She gave a limp half wave as she approached.

"Did you get in trouble last night?" asked Emily.

"A bit. I'm grounded for a month." Vanessa turned her back on them and began spinning the dial on her lock. She tossed back her hair and shot Emily a grin. "My mom is picking me up after school for the rest of the week so I 'can't get up to no good.'"

"You don't seem all that upset." Emily looked skeptical. "Where were you, anyhow?"

"Out with Leo. I lost track of time." Vanessa stooped to pick up a book and threw some others onto the pile. "Aren't you going to be late for class?"

"I have a few more minutes," said Emily. She looked at Dawn. "What about you?"

"Spare. I've got to get to the library, though."

Vanessa slammed her locker door. "I wanted to break up with Leo. If I'm not around, maybe he'll find somebody else." She turned her head sideways and looked at Dawn. "He likes you."

"Well, I'm not interested in a boyfriend. Especially not one you're dating." Dawn couldn't believe Vanessa would think it, much less suggest it.

Vanessa gave a quick smile. "Having a boyfriend wasn't as much fun as I'd imagined." She started walking away from them. "See you at lunch, Em," she said.

Emily grabbed Dawn by the arm. "Her mother must have found out about Leo, and now she's in bigger shit than she's letting on. I never did get to meet him. We'll have to work on her to find out the truth. See you at lunch?"

"Maybe. I might go for a walk." Dawn should have told Emily earlier about meeting Leo. She wasn't sure what kept her from telling Emily now.

"Later, then."

Emily let go of her arm and started a half jog toward the far end of the building. Dawn turned in the other direction and hurried toward the library. Was she the only one who thought something was off with Vanessa? She didn't know Vanessa well but there'd been a big change in her appearance, and she was always staring at nothing until somebody pulled her back to the present. Dawn's mother had had that same beaten-down look after the first year living with Gil Valiquette. Drifting in and out of conversations. Startling like a deer does when you come across it unexpectedly in the woods. But Vanessa had been dating Leo only a few months and she could dump him anytime she wanted. He wasn't living with her, controlling who she spoke to and counting every dollar she spent. He wasn't manoeuvring her out of the way so he could be alone with her twelve-year-old daughter.

Dawn reached the library door and almost collided with two boys on their way out. She had half an hour before English class to study for the history test and then she'd rush to the store to buy more supplies for Fisher. When she'd found him sitting on the beach this morning, he was eating the last of the chocolate bars. His face was slightly less swollen and some of the purple had changed to a dull yellow. He could open his right eye wider than a slit. She was using the money she'd earned doing research for Mr. Rouleau at the university to buy Fisher's supplies. If he left soon, she might still have enough to get the bike she had her eye on. Kala would never have to know that she'd used her savings to take care of the father she was forbidden to see.

"Not that I'm disbelieving by nature," said Morrison, hanging up the phone, "but the latest caller asked if he'd get a reward for telling me where the dead girl spent her last hours."

"*No* — you think he's only in it for the money?" asked Bedouin, pretending to be shocked.

"Well, he couldn't describe her *and* he was calling from a bar."

Kala straightened from typing on her keyboard. "He might not be lying. Nadia could have spent time in a bar that day."

"That crossed my mind too," said Morrison. She sighed and stood up. "So I'm going to meet him now. I'd drag one of you along but this is likely nothing. The gentleman caller lost interest when I told him there was no reward. However, he agreed to wait for me to arrive. Likely, he'll be there until closing anyhow. You're on tap for the next call-ins while I'm off on this goose chase, Bedouin."

"Then hurry back."

Kala glanced across at Rouleau's closed office door. He'd seemed distracted during the morning update and had shut his door as soon as the meeting broke up. Gundersund had been in and out a few times but hadn't shared any information. She would have gone in herself to see if she could help with whatever was troubling Rouleau if not for the closed door. It felt like a warning to leave him alone with his thoughts.

She was waiting for a document but at 1:30 decided to get some lunch. She put on her leather jacket and hesitated, staring at Rouleau's door. *Damn it all, the man has to eat.* She started purposefully across the space when Gundersund got there ahead of her with coffee and sandwiches on a tray. He had his back to her and rapped on the door, disappeared inside and shut the door behind him. Kala waited a moment to see if he'd come out, but when he didn't, she returned to her desk to get her handbag. Turning to leave, she glanced over at Woodhouse. He was on his cellphone with his back to the room. She took a few silent steps toward him and strained her ears to hear what he was saying, managing to catch the last of his conversation even though he was speaking quietly.

"Today won't work. Tomorrow. End of day. Usual place."

He clicked off and she slid back to her desk as he turned around. His eyes swept the room and landed on her. "I thought you'd gone for lunch."

"I'm about to. Can I bring you back anything?"

"No, that's okay. I'll grab something later." He waited a beat. "Thanks."

"Any time."

After a quick bowl of soup in the cafeteria, Kala returned to her desk. The document she'd been waiting for was in her inbox. She scanned it quickly at first, then more carefully and experienced a surge of satisfaction that her hunch had borne out. Neither Morrison nor Gundersund was at their desk, and Bennett was discussing something with Woodhouse. She could wait for Bennett to be free but that would mean explaining to Woodhouse why she wanted Bennett to accompany her and she was loath to do that. Knowing Woodhouse, he'd either give her a hard time or insist on following up her idea himself. She chided herself. This wasn't about her — so what if Woodhouse took the credit?

She printed out the pages and walked over to his desk. Woodhouse and Bennett broke off their conversation and stared at her.

Hey Kala," said Bennett. "What have you got?"

"Have a look at this." She handed the pages to Woodhouse.

He read them much as she had: quickly at first and then more closely. He looked up at her and handed the pages to Bennett. "This could nail him. Didn't you need a court permit to get the bank to release this information?"

"I asked Rouleau to add the bank request in the search warrant and the judge signed off."

"Forward-thinking of you, but you should have cleared it with me, since I'm heading up the search."

"I know. I only thought of it last minute and meant to tell you. I'm digging to see if he had this arrangement with any other tenants."

"Well, no harm done as it turns out." Woodhouse grinned and tapped the desk in front of Bennett.

"Looks like we'll be taking a ride to pick up Murray Simmons. He has some more 'splaining to do."

"Are you sure? I'm waiting for more paperwork on his other rental building," said Kala doubtfully. "There could be more victims."

"This ought to be enough to shake the truth out of him."

"I'll let Rouleau know that you're bringing him in," said Kala. "He'll probably want to listen in on the interview."

She waited until Woodhouse and Bennett were gone before knocking on Rouleau's door. Gundersund smiled when he saw her and Rouleau invited her in. The remains of their lunch was on the table and each man held a cup of coffee. They were sitting back, relaxed in their chairs by the window. She took a step into the room but no farther, regretting that she had to interrupt.

"Woodhouse and Bennett are picking up Murray Simmons and bringing him in for more questioning," she said. "You might want to watch through the two-way."

"Did something come to light?" asked Rouleau.

"He was charging Nadia Armstrong three hundred dollars a month in rent. The other tenants in the building averaged eleven hundred. Nobody else's rent comes close to the small amount he was charging her." She didn't add that she was still waiting for the paperwork from Simmons's other apartment building. There'd be no point now.

Gundersund whistled. "Seems like the smoking gun."

"When you combine this with his twice-weekly visits, I'd say so," said Rouleau. "Let us know when he arrives." He looked over at Kala. "You're right. I'd like to watch him being interviewed. This should have him squirming."

She bit her lip and nodded. Gundersund was watching her with a quizzical expression, but he remained silent.

The interview took place in the late afternoon. Simmons insisted on having his lawyer present this time and she was in court until four o'clock. Bennett accompanied Woodhouse, making a quartet in the small meeting room. The lawyer was Carol Jennings, well known for taking on construction cases. She was in her late fifties, experienced, and tough. She'd gotten more than one client off fraud and bribery charges, price-fixing, and broken contracts.

Woodhouse opened by going step by step through Simmons's previous statement for half an hour. He waited until Simmons had settled back in the chair with a bored look on his face before slapping down the bank statements with printouts of the tenants' cheques going back a year. Simmons's face went from relaxed to pale and uneasy as he grasped where the questions were headed.

"Do you have a warrant for those?"

"We do."

"I want to talk to my lawyer."

"Turn off the tape," said Carol. "We'll have a private moment."

From her vantage point behind the two-way mirror, Kala thought the request was to buy time.

Woodhouse had no choice but to shut off the recorder and leave the room with Bennett.

"Not what Simmons was expecting," said Gundersund.

He was standing next to Kala, and she felt his arm press against hers when he shifted positions. Rouleau was sitting in a chair on the other side of Gundersund, his focus still on the two in the room even though he couldn't hear them. The urge to turn and wrap herself in Gundersund's arms was strong. She forced herself to take a sideways step away from him. If he minded, he didn't give anything away.

Carol got up after a few minutes and tapped on the door. She was back in place when Woodhouse and Bennett entered. As they took their seats, she grimaced at Woodhouse and rested her arms on the table. "Murray will make a statement, and you'll see that you're barking up the wrong tree. She kept her eyes on Woodhouse and said, "Go ahead, Murray."

"Yeah, I gave Nadia a cut in rent but only because she was trying to get on her feet. I felt sorry for her." He raised his hands, pretending to give in to their accusations. "My crime was being a good Samaritan. So cuff me."

Carol put a restraining hand on his arm. "Murray should be lauded for his philanthropy, not accused of something heinous."

"Was this the only woman you ever gave a discount to so that she could" — Woodhouse read theatrically from his notepad — "get on her feet?"

"Yeah."

"Just this one woman, whom you visited twice a week for half an hour to an hour each time for six months running, after giving her a huge break on her rent?"

Carol stopped Simmons from answering. "You already know that Murray was fixing appliances on his way home. Is there anything else, Detective?"

Woodhouse's snort could be heard by everyone behind the glass. "You can't honestly think we believe Murray here had nothing going on with the victim? Nobody has *that* many appliances. What he was doing with his tenant was, in effect, prostitution."

Carol began packing up her papers, putting them into a briefcase at her feet. She glanced up at him. "Oh, but I do expect you to believe it, Officer Woodhouse, because Murray has explained to you exactly what happened. So unless you have proof to the contrary and can back up your slanderous statement, I'd say this interview is over."

Woodhouse looked toward the two-way and held the palms of his hands skyward. She had called his bluff.

"Might have been premature getting Simmons in this early," said Gundersund.

Rouleau stood. "I agree, although we have got his statements on tape. That could be helpful later. Tell Woodhouse to keep digging."

"I'll let him know," said Kala.

She left ahead of them and returned to her desk, checking her emails while still standing. Scanning the list, she stopped at a second message with an attachment from the financial contact. She opened the document and slowly lowered herself into her chair while reading the list of names and rent payments. One name stood out — and that was all she needed. Simmons had lied. She printed the document and waited by the printer to ensure nobody else saw the information. She collected the pages and shoved them into her handbag before putting on her jacket and shutting down her computer.

This time, she'd complete the research herself before bringing Woodhouse into the loop. He'd be pissed off at her when he found out but the way she saw it, she didn't owe him a thing. Not after he'd ignored her warning to wait for all the tenant information to come in and made a mess of the last interview.

CHAPTER TWENTY-FOUR

Murray Simmons's second apartment building was farther north, tucked into the neighbourhood off Princess on Portsmouth. Dull brown brick, six storeys, with four units on each floor. The building looked to be the same vintage as Bellevue Towers but better maintained. Kala parked in the only available space in visitor parking and walked through the main door into the compact entryway. She found Abby Green's name on the directory and typed in her number. A woman's voice came over the intercom and Kala identified herself. A moment later, the door buzzed open and Kala jumped to grab the handle before it locked.

Abby lived on the second floor. Kala took the stairs and rapped on her door, all the while considering how to approach the interview. She was unsure how she'd be received once Abby knew the reason she was here. *How can I bring up the subject of prostitution without appearing threatening and judgmental?*

The woman who opened the door was in her early twenties like Nadia Armstrong: fresh-faced with long blond hair and protruding collarbones visible under a baggy grey sweater. She wore black leggings cut above her ankles and her bright-red running shoes drew the eye downward. She peered out from behind the chain lock, holding the door open a foot. "I'd like to see your ID," she said.

Kala fished out her badge and held it at eye level. "I have a few questions about Murray Simmons."

The door closed and Kala heard the chain scraping out of its lock. Abby led her into a small living room sparsely decorated with furnishings that looked to be second-hand. The room smelled of sandalwood incense. Psychology textbooks and crime paperbacks were stacked on an Ikea bookshelf. Kala sat on a green-metal fold-up chair that would have been better suited to a back deck. Abby tucked her legs under herself on the brown-and-beige striped couch. "What's this about?"

"I'm looking into the death of a woman who lived in another apartment building owned by Murray Simmons. Her name is Nadia Armstrong. Have you ever met her?"

"No, should I have?"

"She moved in about six months ago, close to your age."

"I really don't —"

"What are you studying, Abby?"

"Psychology. I took the last exam for my bachelor's degree a few days ago."

"Did you grow up in this area?"

"No. I'm from a small town in northwestern Ontario, Geraldton. Do you know it?"

"I do. I worked in Nipigon for a while. A bit farther south than Geraldton, closer to Lake Superior."

"Are you as happy as I am to be away from the small towns?"

Kala felt a toehold. "It was difficult for you, growing up?"

A spectrum of emotions from bitter to wistful crossed Abby's face. "My mother died in a car accident when I was eight. My father was driving and he'd been drinking. My brother, Tony, and I were in the back seat. We survived, although Tony suffered a head injury. I came out of it unscathed."

"And your father?"

"He broke his arm and had internal damage but he lived. He had to quit his job and he collected disability and welfare. Being unemployed gave him more time to drink. The accident gave him a reason. We didn't have much, as you can imagine. Tony needed care." She changed positions on the couch. Ran a hand through her hair and smiled an apology. "I'm not sure why I told you all that. I've tried to put it behind me."

"You're allowed to feel whatever you feel, to take however long you need to work through it."

"I thought my shrink was just telling me that to keep my business. Luckily, my visits were covered by provincial health care. Otherwise, who knows what kind of crazy I'd be now?"

"Are you still seeing him?"

"No. I stopped." She turned her face away from Kala and stared out the window.

Kala gave Abby some time to collect herself while she thought about her next question. Abby felt fragile, and Kala knew she couldn't push too hard or too fast. "We've discovered that Nadia Armstrong, the girl who died, was paying only three hundred a month in rent. Everyone else, in both buildings, pays over a thousand a month … except you."

Abby slowly turned her face to meet Kala's gaze. Her own eyes were defensive and guarded. "So?"

"Did you have an arrangement with Murray Simmons?"

"I didn't have the money this year. My brother needed help and until Murray made his offer, I was planning to drop out of university."

"What was the offer?"

"It was between us."

"He had the same arrangement with Nadia Armstrong and now she's dead. I need to make certain Murray's offer had nothing to do with what happened to her. I need to make sure you're not in danger too."

Alarm filled Abby's eyes before she blinked it away. She sank against the back of the couch. "Why would I be in danger?"

"I'm sure Nadia thought she had everything under control too."

A longer silence this time. Kala let the room breathe its afternoon stillness, focusing on the pale lemony light streaming through the window, pooling on the faded hardwood. A clock ticked behind her on the Ikea bookcase. A car crunched gravel in the parking lot beneath the window and two car doors slammed, one after the other, like gunshots. Abby let her feet swing to the floor and crossed one leg over the other. She sighed deeply. "I had to promise him sex."

Kala knew if she said one wrong word, Abby would shut down. She kept her voice neutral. "Murray Simmons only charged you three hundred dollars a month rent but in return you had to agree to have sex with him. Is this correct?"

"It sounds so ugly when you put it into words. Yes, Murray came here once a week. Twice at the beginning. I figured he'd gotten another girl on the string a few months ago."

"Why?"

"He missed a week, which he'd never done since I took this place in August, and he seemed less interested when he was here. Quicker, if that was possible."

"How did you feel about him?"

"I could tolerate him. I thought of the sex as a business transaction."

"You knew he was married with three kids?"

"Yeah. That makes him a snake, but he never talked about them with me. It was easy to forget they existed." The defensive look was back. "Look, I would never do anything like this except I want that degree. I won a scholarship for next year and I'm in line for a teaching assistant job that'll pay me enough to move out of here. If sleeping with the landlord once or twice a week for a semester allowed me to step up in the world, I can swallow my morals. I made the choice with my eyes wide open."

"You're a strong young woman but I wish Murray Simmons hadn't taken advantage of your situation. He's the only one who acted dishonourably."

"Thank you for that," Abby said, casting her eyes down. "I talk tough but … sleeping with Murray for rent money hasn't been my proudest moment either. I've lived in fear that somebody would find out. It's kept me from dating."

"I understand … but I need to ask: have you ever done anything sexual with anybody else for money?"

"God no, and I don't intend to ever again."

"Did Murray ever pressure you or make you feel unsafe?"

"No. Our … arrangement … was very matter of fact."

"He didn't ask you to sleep with anybody else?"

The irises of Abby's eyes seemed to darken and her fingers curled into fists. She took a moment to answer. "No. I only slept with him, and that was to get a break on my rent. I'm not a prostitute. I'm not."

"I'll need to report what you've told me to my team," Kala said. "Would you be okay with signing a statement with these facts?"

"Will anybody else have to know?"

"I'll keep your name out of the media."

"Then I guess so." Abby met her eyes again. "We didn't do anything against the law. I've met other people with the same deal going on with their land-lords. I'm moving out in a few days, anyhow, and I'll never return to this apartment again. I could come to the station in the morning, if that's okay. I'm meeting friends for supper. It's my going-away party."

Kala wanted to tell her that Murray Simmons had definitely been taking advantage of her, but she didn't. Abby already knew it; rationalizing herself as complicit in the arrangement let her live with herself. "I could have someone pick you up in the morning in an unmarked car, if that's easier."

"Okay, how about nine?"

"The car will be waiting outside." Kala leaned closer and waited until she had Abby's full attention. "You need to be careful around Murray Simmons, Abby. Don't be alone with him. Keep the chain on your door and call 911 if you feel threatened at all. Here's my card with my cell number if you need to talk at any time."

"Do you really think he killed this other girl?"

"I don't know but he could have. Until we have proof one way or the other, you should take precautions."

They got up and Abby followed Kala to the door. "Good luck moving forward, Abby. Don't let this past year define you, even in moments of self-doubt."

Abby nodded but didn't say anything. She was still standing in the doorway watching as Kala opened the fire exit door to take the stairs to the lobby.

Fisher popped a couple of painkillers and slept a few hours more after Dawn had left for school. He awoke feeling slightly better than a man run over by a Mack truck. His ribs were healing and he could move without stabbing pain. He hobbled out of the woods and checked for any other people on the stretch of beach. Satisfied that he was alone, he made his way carefully to the water's edge and scooped water into his hands to wash his face. He cursed himself for leaving the soap and his diminishing pack of cigs back with his gear.

The daybreak's morning mist was gone; the lake was a leaden grey bleeding into the horizon so that he couldn't tell where the water ended and the sky began. Gulls swooped above his head, and the smell of rotting fish was strong. Fisher moved closer to the woods and sat down on a flat rock. He liked it here near the water, away from all the concrete. He wondered if Wilburn had alerted the police that he'd missed his appointment. Would they come after him in another province or let him be? He'd nearly finished with the court-mandated visits. Wilburn might decide that reporting him up the chain was more trouble than it was worth. Wilburn had nothing to gain by putting him back in the system. Before long, Fisher's head swivelled to look toward the path up to Kala's house. *What I'd give for a hot shower*, he thought, *or to lie in a soft bed*.

He had nothing better to do than retrieve his knapsack and ease his way across the rocks to the path. He gritted his teeth with each step, but felt some of his old resolve return, the same bullheadedness that had gotten him through the years inside. The grass in the backyard stretched out to a deck large enough to hold four chairs and a table, where he imagined Kala and Dawn ate dinner in the summertime. A small garden plot roped off from the woods needed tilling and planting. He'd have liked to stick around to give them a hand.

For a cop, Kala did little to secure the house while she was away. He quickly determined that there was no alarm system, no cameras. The doors were locked, but the kitchen window was open. He found a stepladder in the garden shed and dragged it to the house. He removed the screen, and with a bit of effort, he opened the window wide enough to crawl through. He almost blacked out from the pain but he bit down hard on his lip and kept going.

Taiku was waiting for him by the kitchen door, the ruff of his fur standing on end, his low growl the most menacing sound Fisher had heard in some time. He spoke softly to the dog and called him by name while resting his aching body across the sink on the counter. The growling stopped and Taiku nuzzled his hand where he rested it over the side. "That's a good dog," said Fisher, grunting with the effort to right himself and slide onto the floor. After giving Taiku a good rubdown and himself time to recover, he got a glass from the cupboard and let the water run cold before gulping down two glasses full. Ambrosia.

"Right. First things first," he said. He lowered the window sash to where it had been, then unlocked the back door and went outside. He replaced the screen and put the stepladder in the shed where he'd found it. He knew from past experience that he might have to leave quickly and these signs of entry would not go unnoticed. He re-entered by the back door and cased the downstairs, going from room to room and looking for escape routes. Taiku followed him upstairs and flopped on the mat next to a single bed which Fisher could tell was Dawn's. Her art was framed on the walls. He paused to study the watercolour paintings of the lake, some flowers, and Taiku. "Where did this talent come from?" he asked the dog, moved beyond words by what he was seeing. Her work could be in an art gallery.

Kala's room had a double bed and some of Dawn's framed sketches above the headboard, pen and ink drawings of the house and the garden, one of Kala staring out at the lake in profile. The picture was haunting, her sadness palpable. Rose hadn't shared much about their time on Birdtail rez, so he could only imagine how bad it had been. Rose had never outgrown the same hurt expression when he'd come up on her unawares. She and Kala had both been foster kids, he knew that. He sometimes wished he'd been one too. Growing up with his old man had been a fight for survival.

Fisher looked through the chest of drawers and the closet, finding Kala's stash of money in a box on the top shelf. He counted six hundred dollars before putting it back in its spot under the spare blankets. He sifted through her jewellery case — some of the turquoise pieces were of good quality. He left them in the case and went down the hall to the bathroom. His face in the mirror startled him. His right eye was blackened with shades of yellow and purple and an angry red bruise covered half his face. It was better than he'd looked when he left Toronto; a few more days would make him presentable enough to take a Greyhound bus east and maybe not stand out in the crowd. It had been tough enough hiding half his face on the way here, although he'd learned that most people avoided eye contact and didn't look too closely.

He'd be at his most vulnerable in the shower if someone came home but he was willing to chance it. He stripped and took out his spare T-shirt, underwear, and socks and used the liquid hand soap to scrub all his clothes down, rinsing them thoroughly before getting into the shower. He could have stood forever in the steaming water but he washed his hair and body quickly, not liking the idea of being caught naked. His ribs seemed to appreciate the heat and his back loosened from the stiffness of sleeping rough. Ugly bruises covered a good part of his torso but he found no trace of infection and the wounds appeared to be healing. He chanced using a towel from the cupboard, wrapping it around himself before gathering up his clothes and going downstairs where he'd seen a dryer in the mud room.

While his clothes and the towel dried, he returned upstairs, naked, to remove all traces of his cleanup in the bathroom. Then he padded downstairs to wait for his clothes to finish drying. He thought about making an instant coffee or tea but didn't want to chance leaving a hot kettle behind. The dryer was bad enough but wasn't likely to be used at midday. He'd been in the house almost two hours and had no idea whether Kala made trips home during her workday to check on Taiku. So instead, he drank another tumbler of cold water before washing out the glass and placing it back in the cupboard. He swiped a couple of candies from the bowl in the living room, certain that nobody would miss them.

Clothes on and spares tucked away in his knapsack, he folded the towel and climbed the stairs one last time to put it back where he'd gotten it. He was bending down to straighten the towels when he heard a noise behind him. He spun around. Taiku was standing at the head of the stairs, his body in attack mode, his growl a low warning directed at the black car — visible through the hall window — that was sliding to a stop at the far end of the driveway.

CHAPTER TWENTY-FIVE

Fisher froze in place but his mind was working a mile a minute, assessing the best way to escape unnoticed. His first thought was that Kala had hired a cleaner and they'd soon be entering the house. Front door or back door? The back entrance appeared to be the main point of entry but the front was easier if they were carrying a vacuum and other cleaning supplies. He squatted down and spoke softly to Taiku, petting his head to calm him. They descended the stairs together, Taiku in the lead, not growling now, but very much on alert. Through the five-inch gap in the open living room window, Fisher heard two car doors slamming and footsteps crunching in the gravel. Taiku stopped at the bottom of the stairs and stood motionless, eyes fixed on the front door. Fisher skirted past him and walked to the window, keeping off to the side in the shadow of the curtain.

Two men were talking in hushed voices not far from the front step. Fisher crawled under the window to get a sight angle but could only see the back of one of them. He was wearing a black jacket and jeans and had longish black hair. Fisher couldn't make out what they were saying. He looked toward the car. A black Audi with tinted windows. He squinted until he could read the licence plate. He'd always had good long-distance vision and a memory for numbers. This one was easy: BRAG 213. The 2 and 1 added up to 3 and the letters formed a word. He tucked the information away in the "possibly useful" folder in his brain.

The handle of the front door rattled and Taiku stepped farther into the foyer, his low growl a dangerous warning. Fisher scooted backwards across the polished hardwood floor and down the hall into the kitchen. If they came in the front, he'd go out the back. The rattling of the front door handle stopped and Fisher froze near the doorway to the mud room. He listened but couldn't hear the two men and waited motionless, not sure which way he should move. Taiku's paws clicked down the hallway at a trot and Fisher stepped aside to let the dog take up his watch in front of the back door. Footsteps climbed the deck. This time, Fisher could hear one of them speaking through the kitchen window.

"This door's locked too. Whaddaya wanna do?"

The other guy must have said to leave because their footsteps clumped off the deck. Still, Fisher waited. He could make it to the front door or the back if they tried to get in. He wondered if they'd noticed the partially opened kitchen window as he had. Time was suspended while he tuned his ear to the sounds outdoors. A crow cawed at the back of the property and then was silent. A hornet bumped against the kitchen window screen before flying away.

As the minutes ticked by, Taiku seemed to sense the danger was over and lay down, resting his head on his front paws. Fisher moved directly in front of the kitchen window and pulled himself up onto the counter to get a better look. He scanned the far end of the property and both sides of the deck. The backyard was empty except for the crow hopping across the grass. He jumped onto the floor and darted toward the front of the house, just making it in time to see the Audi backing onto the road. He watched it stop, then glide forward and disappear behind the trees. Taiku didn't stir from his place near the door.

Fisher made one final check of the house to make certain nobody would know he'd been inside and left through the back entrance. He was tired and his body was aching. His ribs were paying the price for the trip through the kitchen window. He cursed the final distance and the rocks that stood between him and his hiding spot. Once he reached the woods, he stretched out on top of the sleeping bag and slept away the afternoon. He awoke disoriented in the dying hour, the shadows in the woods long, gloomy fingers stretching onto the beach. The lake was calm as a pond and dark grey, almost black in the fading light. He'd missed Dawn's visit but a bag of food and new bottle of water were sitting a few feet from his sleeping bag. The gift was enough that the sadness didn't overwhelm him. He'd wanted to talk to her, to find out if she knew the two men in the black car, but that would have to wait. He didn't dare return to the house to find her and she wouldn't come down to the beach tonight if Kala was home.

On Wednesday morning, Kala lingered over a second cup of coffee while she waited for Dawn to get ready for school. "I feel like we haven't seen much of each other since this investigation started," she said. "I'll drive you in today." Dawn protested but Kala wouldn't be deterred. "It's the least I can do in case I have to work late again tonight."

Kala took Taiku for a walk around the property, expecting Dawn would be ready by the time she got back. She was surprised to find Dawn still in her room getting dressed. Kala drained the last of the coffee when she finally heard Dawn's feet on the stairs.

"Are you feeling okay?" she asked when Dawn entered the kitchen. She studied Dawn's face for signs of illness.

"I'm okay. Just tired." Dawn's shoulders slumped and she had her head down as she crossed to the counter.

Kala hadn't heard Dawn get up in the night but she must have done. Kala had been so exhausted when her head hit the pillow that fireworks could have gone off outside her window and she wouldn't have woken up. She didn't really have a choice but to work the long hours, but that didn't stop her feeling guilty about leaving Dawn on her own so much. "I packed you a lunch. Grab some fruit and a granola bar to eat in the truck. We're running late."

"Sorry."

"No, I'm the one who's sorry that work is getting in the way of our time together. I'm going to do my best to be home for supper tonight."

"I'm doing fine, Aunt Kala. Really. You don't need to change your schedule for me."

"I do need to, for both of us."

After she'd dropped Dawn off in front of the school, Kala crossed the city and arrived at headquarters as the morning meeting was due to get underway. She hurried into the office and tried to slip unnoticed into the cozy gathering area. Gundersund was speaking at the front of the room; he nodded to her but kept on with his update. She tried to thank him with her eyes for not making a big deal of her tardiness but he'd already turned his attention to Morrison, asking her to fill them in on her follow-up of the phone tip.

"The potential witness who called from Coppers Pub might have seen Nadia the day she went missing — or he might have seen her a few days before. Time apparently means nothing when you spend every night in your cups. He —" Morrison paused to check her notes "— that is, Otis Halton, identified Nadia from a photo."

"Did Halton say whether she was alone?" asked Rouleau.

"He said that she was with a man but couldn't recall anything about him. They were at the bar, the girl sitting and the man standing in front of her. Halton only remembered her because she tossed her drink at the guy's chest before slapping him across the face. The man had his back to Halton and stormed out without looking around. Nadia, if it was her, got up from the stool and ran after him."

Kala raised her hand. "Where's this pub located?"

Tanya half turned in her seat to face Kala. "Brock Street, near the waterfront. About three blocks south and then a couple of blocks west of the Leon Centre, which is still known as the K-Rock Centre by the locals." She turned back around. "I talked with the bartender and staff but they didn't remember any incident. I'm going back tonight to speak with the alternate staff."

"Great. Let's hope someone has a better memory of what went on," said Gundersund. His gaze fell on Kala. "Have you any update, Stonechild?"

Now was the moment. She could wait to tell Gundersund in private what she'd found out from Abby Green or let everyone know and suffer Woodhouse's ire. Delaying the inevitable backlash would not be helpful so she opted for openness. "Information came in late yesterday that a woman in Murray Simmons's other apartment building was also receiving a significant cut on her rent. I dropped by the building on my way home on the off chance she was there and got lucky. Abby Green told me that Simmons was having sex with her in exchange for low rent. She described it as a mutually agreed-upon business arrangement."

"The man is slime," breathed Morrison, loud enough for everyone to hear.

"Agreed," said Kala, "but the question is whether or not he's a killer too. Abby said she never felt threatened by him and he never asked her to have sex with anybody else. They both had their reputations to lose if word got out so he wasn't worried about her talking. I imagine it would have been the same case with Nadia. His motivation to kill her is slim."

"Except that Simmons has a wife and kids and these two women are single. He had a family to lose. That's a big fucking difference, Stonechild." Woodhouse glared at her.

Kala knew she had to give him his moment of anger at her subterfuge, but she said anyway, "Granted, but Abby sure didn't want her arrangement getting out. I doubt Nadia did either since she was trying to straighten up for her child."

"Nadia was already whoring around in Ottawa so she had everything to gain by blackmailing Simmons," Woodhouse said. "She could gamble that he'd pay up because her reputation was in the toilet, anyhow. Simmons needed to keep her quiet." Woodhouse's face was turning a shade of plum and Kala stopped responding.

Rouleau cut in before Woodhouse could escalate further. "He lied about giving another woman a cut in rent. Bring him in again, Woodhouse. Keep the heat on."

Woodhouse took this as confirmation that he was right. A smile replaced the glare. The colour in his face diffused. "I'll be happy to handle this for the team. We should have the slime behind bars by suppertime."

"You'll have to get something solid that we can use in court," said Rouleau. He glanced over at Kala before handing the rest of the meeting back to Gundersund. She knew that he'd let her off the hook for stepping into Woodhouse's wheelhouse by giving Woodhouse another crack at Simmons. She was both thankful and contrite for putting Rouleau in that position and she stayed silent for the rest of the meeting.

She met with Abby Green following the meeting and took her statement before retuning to her desk to input a report on their conversation into the team database. After she'd been working at her computer for about half an hour, Gundersund stopped by her desk to discuss her latest search for information and to ask her to meet him for lunch in the cafeteria at 1:30 after the noon-hour rush.

Morrison waited until Woodhouse and Bennett had gone to pick up Murray Simmons before she rolled her chair over to Kala's desk. "I thought Woodhouse was going to blow when he found out you'd interviewed that girl behind his back. Too bad Rouleau didn't let it happen."

"It wouldn't have been pretty. That was my second offence in Woodhouse's books this week."

"Blowing up might have been reason to reprimand him. That, along with him being disruptive and misogynistic. Why does he get away with that behaviour?"

"He knows which lines not to cross. He's also helped to solve cases and he conducts a good interview."

"Did anything come of what I told you about seeing him with Marci Stokes?"

"Not yet."

"That's a shame." Morrison was about to say something more but the door to Rouleau's office opened and she rolled her chair back to her own desk.

Kala resumed typing. When she raised her eyes from the screen sometime later, she was surprised to see it was going on two o'clock. Her stomach rumbled.

Gundersund!

She leapt up from her chair and grabbed her wallet before running down the hall. The cafeteria was empty except for Gundersund sitting by the window with a tray in front of him. She called to him that she was there before grabbing a roast beef sandwich and a coffee.

"I thought you'd gotten a better offer," said Gundersund as she sat down across from him.

"I lost track of time." She returned his smile before her eyes settled on the empty plate on his tray. "Guess you've been here a while."

"Don't worry about it." He waited until she'd taken a bite from her sandwich. "Vera's leaving. She got a job at the university."

"No way." Kala lowered the sandwich onto the plate. "Is it because of the new acting?"

"Between you and me, yeah. You may not have noticed, but the force has a ways to go on the equality front. We're evolving but we still have dinosaurs."

"You think? When is Vera's last day?"

"Friday. She managed to shave a week off her notice since the university asked for her to start immediately. She'll be heading up support services for the medical department."

"How's Rouleau taking it?"

Gundersund met her eyes. "Not well. I don't think he realized how much she meant to him until she said she was leaving."

"But he's dating Marci Stokes. They seem well-suited."

"Rouleau is an enigma. Most men would have jumped at the chance to date someone like Vera, especially since she's been so obviously interested."

"Are you saying looks are a man's main criterion for a relationship?"

A look of horror crossed Gundersund's face as he realized he'd put his foot in it. It gave Kala a measure of satisfaction and she worked to keep the amusement off her face.

"Not at all," he said.

"You could have dated her. Why didn't you?"

He opened his mouth and shut it again. Kala laughed. "Guess I wound you up a bit there, eh, Gundersund, exposing your male chauvinist side?"

He gave her a slow, wide grin. "I was hoping to keep that under wraps. As for why I didn't ask Vera out, I was married, as you recall. And since separating, I've had my eye on another fine specimen."

"Anyone I know?"

"I believe you know her extremely well."

"Why, are you flirting with me, Officer Gundersund?"

"I believe that I just might be, although not particularly well if you have to ask."

"I appreciate the effort." She was quiet a moment, not sure if she should say something about their odd relationship or avoid wading into these uncertain waters. They both started speaking at the same time and both stopped. Kala motioned for Gundersund to continue. He leaned in closer.

"Fiona's back at work today. Hobbling around but able to do some paperwork. She was climbing the walls in my house all day with no company except the dog."

"How long is she staying with you?"

"Her apartment is free this weekend so she'll be able to move back then. I thought you and I could go on a date Saturday night, if work allows. How do you feel about supper downtown and a stroll along the waterfront?"

"I'd like that very much."

"Then consider it a done deal. I'll book some-where swanky and pick you up around seven." He stood and picked up his tray. "I have to head back but I'll see you upstairs."

"See you later."

She watched him until he was out of sight. This would be their first outing without Dawn and a major step forward. Gundersund was finally ready to move on from Fiona. Kala wanted to give in to the happiness filling her and believe the worst was behind them. She tamped down her feelings of disquiet. Surely, she deserved to give this mutual attraction a chance to see where it could lead. She wouldn't listen to the internal voice telling her that getting involved with her still-married partner was a bad idea.

Just this once, she'd throw caution to the wind and see where the road took them.

CHAPTER TWENTY-SIX

Emily and Chelsea were waiting in the hall near Dawn's locker when she entered the school. She was thinking about Fisher and didn't see them at first. She'd wanted to get down to the beach to check on him that morning but couldn't get out of the house without Kala getting suspicious. At least she'd gotten the bag of food and the bottle of water to him after school the day before. He'd been sleeping when she reached his hiding place, snoring softly until he rolled onto his side. He moaned in his sleep but didn't wake up. She'd try to get home right after school to visit him.

"Have you seen Vanessa?" asked Emily. "We were working on an assignment together and she has the final version. It's due first class."

"No," Dawn said without focusing, her mind still on Fisher. "She must be running late. She's been late a lot lately."

Emily and Chelsea exchanged looks but didn't say anything. They waited for Dawn to open her locker and take out her books and they all walked down the hall together, Chelsea a few steps behind them like a bodyguard. Kala wondered if Emily found this behaviour annoying. Chelsea seemed to enjoy playing the subservient role. She copied Emily's clothes and her hairstyle, even down to the same golden shade of blond. Chelsea's natural colour was closer to sandy brown as far as Dawn could tell. When Chelsea talked, it was to Emily, her voice often dropping to a whisper so that Dawn was excluded.

They parted at the doorway to Dawn's first class. Advanced math. She found her seat and cleared her head to take in the new concept being taught, knowing she'd fall behind if she didn't. All her worries about Fisher gradually dropped away. After math came English. She didn't meet up with Emily and Chelsea again until lunch. They'd saved a place for her at their table but Vanessa wasn't with them. Dawn sat down next to Emily and opened the bag Kala had packed. A note rested on top of the plastic sandwich container. *Hope you're having a good day!* Kala had drawn a happy face and a heart. Dawn tucked the note into her pocket and smiled before taking out the salmon sandwich and opening the bottle of iced tea. She left the apple and the banana in the bag for later.

Emily was talking to Chelsea on her other side, and Dawn started eating. She would have liked to sit alone in her usual seat at the nerd table so she could eat quickly and skip out to pick up more snacks for Fisher, but she was learning that friendship wasn't always about what she wanted. It involved some give and take.

Emily drank from her milk carton and said to Dawn, "Vanessa's gone missing. Mrs. Jefferson phoned the police early this morning."

Dawn lowered her sandwich and set it in the container. "I thought Vanessa was grounded. How can she be missing?"

"Vanessa's mother picked her up after school and brought her home. Vanessa went up to her room to do homework while her mom went to buy groceries. Mrs. Jefferson didn't check on Vanessa when she got home and when she called Vanessa for supper, she was gone. Mr. and Mrs. Jefferson spent the night driving around looking for her. If Vanessa wanted to shake them up, she's succeeded. They phoned the police at around four a.m."

"How do you know all this?"

"Mrs. Jefferson called me last night looking for Vanessa. I thought she might just come home later, like she did the last time. That's why I was waiting for her to meet us at our lockers this morning. But I was wrong. Mrs. Jefferson called me after my first class to tell me Vanessa never came home and she'd notified the police. She was hoping I'd heard from Vanessa this morning, but I haven't."

"Her mother called me last night too," said Chelsea leaning across Emily's arm resting on the table. "Vanessa never even texted me after school, which was weird. I was kind of mad at her."

"I hope she's all right," said Dawn.

"I'll bet she's with Leo," said Chelsea. "Her mother can't ground her and not expect Vanessa to do something crazy."

"Didn't she want to break up with him?"

"I don't know. She might have said that so we wouldn't know she cared."

"The police told Mrs. Jefferson that Van's probably acting out and with her boyfriend," said Emily. "I have no idea where he lives. Do you know anything about him, Dawn?"

"Not really. I think Vanessa said he has a friend named Shawn." She remembered the sick feeling she'd had when she'd been in Leo's car. She must have been overreacting. After all, Leo had let her out without doing anything terrible. It would be hard to tell Emily after so much time had passed that she'd met Leo and taken a ride with him. She rationalized her decision. What good would it do when she had no useful information? She knew what he looked like but how would that help?

"Vanessa's mom was livid when she found out how old Leo is. He's almost ten years older than us!" said Emily. "I have to call her after my next class. I'm *so* looking forward to that."

"Vanessa never sent me any photos of him, like she promised," said Chelsea. "I checked my phone just in case I missed the text or something."

"Not to me either," said Emily. She took out her phone and scrolled through her messages. She looked up and shook her head. "Van acted like he was this big secret. I'll text her again and see if she answers."

Dawn finished her lunch, even though she'd lost her appetite. She hadn't liked Leo and didn't want to think about Vanessa being off somewhere with him.

Vanessa had seemed so unlike herself lately. Still, who was Dawn to judge? If Vanessa wanted to teach her parents a lesson, it was her life. Dawn had enough secrets of her own with Fisher sleeping outside the house and her having no idea when he'd be leaving. She didn't like lying to Kala, but she'd kept her contact with her father hidden for so long that she didn't know how to bring him into the open. Maybe Vanessa felt the same way about Leo. She and Vanessa might have more in common than she'd imagined.

Teagan McPherson shifted a bag of groceries from one arm to the other while she fished in her coat pocket for her keys. She could see Jeff inside the lobby talking on his cell but knew from experience that he wouldn't open the door for her. He was fearful of breaking whatever rules his brother had drilled into him. Finally her fingers landed on the keys and she fumbled to insert the correct one into the lock. She heard footsteps behind her and half turned as she pulled the door open.

"Do you mind letting me in?" said a voice as deep and attractive as its owner. Well, she thought the man was attractive but she liked the dark, intense ones. She also liked a man in tight blue jeans and cowboy boots. He checked all the boxes.

"I'm sorry …" she started to say, but he cut in.

"I'm Nadia Armstrong's brother-in-law, Peter. I'm here to pick up the baby's things. The police gave permission. My wife and I have been granted temporary custody."

She liked how he assumed that she'd be in the know about Nadia's death. The conversation felt intimate, as if they'd met before. "Of course," she said. "I'm Teagan. I was the one looking after Hugo when ... you know, when Nadia went missing. I could help you get his things together if you like."

"I think I can manage, but thank you."

His eyes were so dark ... Teagan found herself staring. It had been a long time since animal attraction had caught her in its glare. Not since she'd been fifty pounds lighter without two children. She liked the feeling, happy to know that lust hadn't deserted her altogether. "I'm so sorry about Nadia," she said. "Will there be a service?"

"Yes, but only for family, I'm afraid."

The bag of groceries was getting heavy and she felt it slipping from her grasp. Peter reached over and grabbed the bag before it hit the floor. "What've you got in here? Rocks?"

She laughed. "My son likes Alphagetti and there was a sale. Three cans for four dollars. I stocked up."

"I'll bring this to your apartment on my way to Nadia's. What floor are you on?"

"Second, but there's no need."

"It's no problem."

Jeff had disappeared from the lobby. Teagan asked, "How will you get into her apartment?"

"I have a key. Nadia gave us a duplicate in case of emergency. I don't have one for the front door though. She was able to buzz me into the building from her cellphone."

"I didn't think she had family in Kingston."

"We're an hour up the highway."

They rode the elevator to the second floor and he waited until she'd unlocked her apartment door before handing the grocery bag to her. His arm brushed against her chest — an accident, she knew, because of the way he jumped back. He hesitated before walking away. "This might sound forward, but would you like to get a coffee before I head back to Brockville? I could use the company."

She considered how wise it would be to accept. She had six loads of laundry to do and floors that needed scrubbing. Still, going through Nadia's things couldn't be easy for him. "I'll be here when you're ready," she said.

After he left, Teagan flew around the apartment tidying up before she changed out of her sweatshirt into her best blue sweater and put on mascara and lip gloss. Any more of an effort would make her look as if she was trying too hard. All she really wanted was to feel the bit of lust in her belly for a few more hours. It had been years since she'd been on a date or thought about a man in that way and she found the feeling invigorating. Not that this was even close to a date.

She tried to remember what Nadia had said about her family. Parents in Ottawa and a married sister in Brockville. She hadn't mentioned Peter by name. Teagan started in on the breakfast dishes. Should she have asked him into her apartment for coffee instead of going to a coffee shop? Normally she would have, but what with the way she was thinking about him, it seemed indecent. She finished washing and drying the dishes and still he hadn't arrived. Just when she was despairing of ever seeing him again, he knocked on the door.

"I took a few loads of stuff out to the car, and it took a while," he explained as they waited for the elevator. "I had to wait for somebody to let me back in."

"I should have come with you ... or lent you my key. I wasn't thinking."

"No worries. Everything worked out."

They walked to a coffee shop on Princess. Peter went to order two cappuccinos while she saved a table. There was a strange fluttering in her stomach whenever she looked at him standing in line and she wondered what it would be like to have a good-looking man like Peter actually interested in her. Clyde had been short and not particularly handsome, although he'd made her laugh at one time and she'd envisioned growing old with him. That all changed when he started drinking and hit her a few times. When he took a swing at Shelley, she threw him out and refused to take him back.

Peter took the seat kitty corner to her rather than across the table. Their hands were almost touching and their heads were only a few feet apart. "I love your accent," he said. "Irish, isn't it?"

"'Tis that. I've tried to shake it but can't seem to get the Canadian twang." She sipped her coffee and looked around, pretending that the awkward pause in conversation didn't bother her. That his nearness didn't bother her. He hunched over his own cup, both his hands wrapped around it. He had the longest eyelashes she'd ever seen on a man.

"How close were you to Nadia?" he asked, holding her gaze.

"We were friendly enough." For some reason, Teagan wanted him to think she'd made a connection with his sister-in-law. It might make him feel more comfortable with her. Perhaps she'd rise in his estimation. He didn't need to know how anti-social Nadia had been.

"She lived with us before and a little while after Hugo was born. Did she talk to you about her life before Hugo came along?"

"Not much."

His eyes now seemed to be evaluating her. "She never said who the father was?"

"Not to me. I never asked." She was already regretting letting him think she'd been closer to Nadia than she was. "Is it someone you know?"

"Nadia kept him a secret. My wife, Lorraine, and I are hoping there are no surprises when we go to adopt Hugo."

"The biological father couldn't gain custody now, could he?"

"We're not sure, but he'd have to prove paternity first. The longer we have Hugo, the less likely it is that will happen. We've grown very attached to him."

"Yes, he's a sweetie." Teagan laughed. "How is Hugo?"

Peter's smile was wide and genuine. "He's a strong little guy. He was whimpery at first but he's settling in now that we've had him for a night. I always wanted a son."

"Well, I bet Hugo will be very happy living with you." *I know I would be.*

They were nearly done their coffee when he said, "Lorraine thought Nadia had turned her life around. But I know for a fact she hadn't. Did you know anything about her ... vocation?"

"Vocation?"

"How she made her money."

"She waitressed and she was going back to school. Was there something else?" He was looking at her again, trying to see inside her head, or at least that was how it felt. Teagan tried not to squirm under his stare.

"Maybe not. She was industrious when it came to money." He smiled and lifted his cup to his lips.

They moved on to safer subjects and finished their coffee without mentioning Nadia again. Their half hour together was over much too soon. He walked her to the front of the apartment building before carrying on to his car. Maybe her imagination was working overtime, but he'd seemed to lose interest in their conversation once he realized she really didn't know all that much about Nadia. She had the sneaking suspicion that he'd only spent time with her to go on a fishing expedition. That was okay, though. She'd been using him for her own fantasies.

She met Jeff in the lobby staring out the plate-glass window. His face was beet red and his eyes were bloodshot — from crying, she thought. She stepped closer to him. "Is everything okay, Jeff?"

He couldn't be faking the agony in his eyes when he turned his head to look at her. "The police took Murray back into the station. They think he did something wrong. This's how it started last time."

"Last time?"

Jeff leaned his forehead against the window and closed his eyes. "When they said I touched that girl. They took Murray into the station and then they came for me."

CHAPTER TWENTY-SEVEN

Rouleau stood next to Willy Ellington and Kingston Mayor Tom Clement and scanned the foyer of City Hall. All the usual media suspects were on hand for the planned update on the Armstrong case and an announcement from the mayor. All, that is, except for Marci. Rouleau had texted her a few minutes earlier without getting a response. What could be holding her up?

Ellington had been subdued all morning, holding his cards close to his chest. Rouleau wanted to raise the topic of Vera's resignation but hadn't found the right opening. He'd bide his time until the car ride back to the station. Just as he thought about shooting another text to Marci to say he'd send her an update if she couldn't make the briefing, she entered the room, her coat flapping loose about her legs and her hair windblown. Her cheeks were flushed from the cool spring air and Rouleau pictured her dashing from her car to City Hall. He imagined the scent of her perfume and his hands tangled in her hair. It had been a while. She nodded in his direction before taking a seat in the second row. Her eyes seemed amused, as if she'd read his mind.

Mayor Clement took the mic first. He was in his late fifties but still youthful in appearance. Sandy-coloured hair with a cowlick on the top of his head made him appear boyish. Pleasant face and slim build. He wore a suit well and women voters had taken to him like a fish to water. Rouleau had met him numerous times before, along with his wife, Sally, who owned a high-end clothing boutique. They had two sons in their twenties, the elder at university studying political science, the younger living on his own in Kingston and taking time off from school to decide what he wanted to do with his life. Clement had told Rouleau that he too had taken awhile to find himself, although he'd done so while sowing his oats on a backpacking trip in Europe. Clement's councillors and chief of staff milled about, angling for the best spot to be captured by the television camera. A couple of men waited off to the side and Clement motioned for them to join him at the mic. Rouleau recognized Harold Mortimer from other social gatherings and, of course, their current investigation. He tuned in to what Clement was saying.

"I'm pleased to announce a major new project on the waterfront. The Kingston Casino will be breaking ground this fall with completion date set for two years from then. This will be a major tourism boon for the city and a win-win for all involved. Mortimer Construction has been awarded the contract and I'm thrilled to have Harold with us today to say a few words. Harold?" Clement shook hands with Mortimer before stepping back from the dais.

Harold Mortimer's thinning white hair was combed back with gel and he'd put on a charcoal-coloured suit for the occasion. His eyes met Rouleau's for a split second as he stepped toward the mic and Rouleau saw sharpness in their blue depths. "Thank you, Mr. Mayor. We're thrilled to have been awarded the contract for this landmark building that will have a lasting impact on Kingston's economy. Immediately following today's announcement, the architect Mick Jefferson's drawings will be set up for public viewing right here in the foyer. We invite all comments and compliments." He waited for the laughter to subside. "Thank you to Zimmerman, Jefferson, Reynolds, and Associates for a stellar design. The public consultation will last through April and May with last tweaks to the plans taking place this summer. We intend to put shovels in the ground mid-September."

There was applause from city staff and those who'd gathered for the announcement — likely Mortimer's employees, Rouleau thought. He searched past the first row to find Marci who already had her hand up to ask a question. Clement pointed at a reporter with his hand raised in the front row.

"Aren't there zoning issues with putting a casino on the waterfront?"

Clement motioned to the tall curly-haired man standing silently off to the side to take the mic. "City planner Mark Richardson will answer, and he'll be on hand afterward to show the plans."

Richardson had to bend to speak into the mic.

"Council approved the zoning change after a full environmental assessment. The building meets all restrictions concerning height and green space."

Marci's voice rose above the others. "There's been negative reaction from the public to building a casino downtown. Why are you going ahead with the location in the face of this strong vocal opposition?"

Richardson turned to look behind him and stepped aside as the mayor moved forward. Clement stared directly at Marci. "Of course, we've taken all the public's views into account, but we kept coming back to the need to revitalize the downtown core and to what makes the most economic sense. This project hits all the right buttons. Businesses are on board and tourism is going to boom. We were elected to show leadership, which is what we're doing." His gaze swung around the crowd. "Now, I know you have more questions. I'll be on hand to answer them after Acting Chief Ellington brings you up to date on the recent investigation into the tragic death of a young mother."

Ellington waited for the chorus of questions from reporters to subside. Beside the dais, Clement raised both hands and slowly lowered them to still the voices to a murmur. "Well, you're a hard act to follow this morning, Mr. Mayor, especially since I don't have a great deal to report except that my officers are making progress. As I speak, a person of interest is being interviewed at the station for the third time. I hope to have a positive lead or an arrest later today. In the meantime, we again ask members of the public to report any information they have about the movements of Nadia Armstrong last week and during the six months she lived in Kingston with her young child."

A reporter raised his hand and Ellington pointed at him.

"Is this person of interest a suspect for her murder?"

"I can't comment on that at this time. However, I can say that the team has been working diligently to make certain that Nadia Armstrong's death is solved. We have several leads and have been following up on each and every one. However, gaps remain in our knowledge about Nadia's wherabouts the day she died so I encourage anyone with information to step forward."

Marci stood up. "Mr. Mortimer, did Nadia Armstrong have any connection to Mortimer Construction? After all, her body was found on your new hotel site."

Mortimer took his time getting to the mic and when he spoke, Rouleau detected controlled anger in his voice. "Nadia Armstrong was not acquainted with me or my firm. I regret that she died on my construction site but there is absolutely no link to us or to our project. I send her family my condolences for their tragic loss." He stepped back and said something to Clement before the mayor again took the mic.

"We'll adjourn while the staff sets up the casino site plans. Thank you again for your patience."

Everyone stood at once and began milling about, voices raised in an indecipherable din. Rouleau found

Marci on her phone at the back of the room. She ended her call when she saw him.

"Well, that was a bombshell," she said.

"I'm guessing you mean the casino announcement, not the update on our investigation."

"Did you know that there's a Facebook page with over four thousand followers dedicated to stopping construction of a casino at the downtown waterfront?" Marci tucked her head closer to his. "The fallout from this announcement could be nasty for Mayor Clement and his council. The election is this November."

"The project will be well underway by then."

"I'd like to see how the contracting was handled. The casino was tendered without the media knowing. Mortimer has won several large projects of late. Makes one wonder."

"Your question to Mortimer about Nadia Armstrong came out of nowhere."

Marci shrugged. "I was trying to shake him up. By the pissed-off look on his face, I'd say I struck a nerve."

"No businessman likes to be tied to a possible murder."

"From what I hear, Harold Mortimer wields his power like an autocrat. His third wife is an ex-model who lounges around pools with a big martini problem. Sucks to be her."

"You seem to know a lot about his personal life for someone who handles the crime beat."

"My fashion and lifestyle colleague Rick keeps me informed of the gossip, whether I want to hear it or not." Her fingers touched the back of his hand. "This casino announcement came out of the blue, though. I called my editor and he's asked me to follow up. I was hoping to see you tonight but it looks like I'll be working late."

"Makes two of us."

"Oh yes, the person of interest. Anyone I know?"

"No comment. I promise we'll catch up when this investigation is over."

"That's a promise I look forward to cashing in. See you later, Rouleau."

He watched her stride confidently over to the crowd of people surrounding Mayor Clement and manoeuvre herself close to him. She was tenacious. He didn't envy Clement. He'd need to dig deep into his political savvy and media lines to keep her at bay. A tap on his shoulder made Rouleau turn.

"So nice to see you again, Staff Sergeant." Sally Clement extended her hand and shook his firmly. She wore a silk dress in a pale shade of blue, and her subtly applied eyeshadow matched it exactly. The blond streaks in her shoulder-length hair accented rather than masked the grey. Rouleau had chatted with her at other events and liked her open gaze and easy laugh.

"Nice to see you too, Sally. Quite a big announcement from Tom."

"Wasn't it? He wanted me here to show support from the business community. I believe a casino will be good for tourism and lucrative for all our shops and restaurants. Tom will have to convince the majority of citizens before the election, though." She looked across the room and dropped her voice to a teasing, intimate tone. "Don't look now, but he's coming toward us."

Mayor Clement shook Rouleau's hand and put an arm around his wife's waist. "Were you in time to hear Harold's announcement?" he asked her.

"I rushed in as you were introducing him."

"I think it went well."

"It went very well. And it's so nice to see Willy back in town. We must have him over for dinner."

Rouleau looked around the room until he found Ellington deep in discussion with one of the city councillors. He looked back at the Clements. "It was good to see you both, but I have to head back to the office."

"Don't be a stranger," Sally said. "I have a fundraiser for the Heart and Stroke Foundation coming up next month. Perhaps you can come by. I'll send the information."

"I'll do my best."

By the time Rouleau reached Ellington, he was alone. He spoke quietly to Rouleau so that nobody could overhear. "The Armstrong case will now take a back page to the casino — especially when the media gets wind of the fact that the girl was a sex worker. At least I've made one final attempt to get public input."

"Hopefully, someone will come forward."

"I wouldn't hold my breath but one can hope." Ellington waved at someone across the room and raised a finger to let them know he'd be right over. "Take the car back to the station. I'm having lunch with Tom after we wrap up here."

"I didn't realize you and the mayor were friends."

"Tom and I grew up playing in the same sandbox. In fact, I'm godfather to their second-born. Keep me in the loop if anything develops on the case."

So, no opportunity to raise the subject of Vera on the ride back to HQ. Rouleau had heard that she'd already accepted a job at the university and knew that she wouldn't appreciate his interference now that her mind was made up. Regardless, he'd raise the matter with Ellington at the first opportunity. He should be made aware of what an unprofessional asshole he'd been. He should know that Rouleau was going to report him to the police board.

Tanya Morrison was getting ready to leave early for the day when Fred Taylor approached her desk. "Where is everybody?" he asked.

She paused with one arm partly inside the sleeve of her jacket. "Rouleau's at City Hall, Stonechild is off talking to somebody about the case, and I have no idea where the others are."

"Then could you speak with a woman at the front desk? She called at four this morning to report that her daughter didn't come home last night and she wants us to track down the boy-friend. I guess she figures coming here in person will speed things up."

Tanya sighed. "I was off to pick up my kids for a wild night of pizza and Netflix but I suppose they can wait a while longer. Let me call my husband and I'll be right out."

"You're the best, Morrison. I don't care what anybody else says."

"Should I be taking offence?"

He smiled and disappeared out the door.

Tanya called Allen and left a message. What if he didn't check his phone? She hesitated before calling Sara's cellphone. After two tries, she got through. "What's that noise?"

"Daddy's vacuuming."

"Can you put him on the phone for a minute, please?"

"Are you getting us soon? Shandra's coming over and I don't like her."

"In a while. Put your father on." She waited, drumming her fingers on the desk. "Who's Shandra?" she asked when he picked up.

"My house cleaner."

"You're vacuuming for the house cleaner? Oh, never mind. I'm going to be later than I said. Can you keep the kids another half hour?"

"Sure. I'll put them to work."

"Good luck with that."

She hung up and stood still, looking at the phone. How in the hell had she let her life fall into this sad state? If it weren't for her job, she'd be completely depressed. She finished putting on her jacket and headed to the front desk. Taylor handed her a folder with the case details before she turned and scanned the lobby. Daria Jefferson was sitting in the waiting area and Tanya had a chance to look her over as she approached. Late forties, bleached-blond hair down to her shoulders, face aging prematurely from sun exposure. No wedding ring. She looked brittle and angry, as if she were barely keeping her rage in check. Tanya could have been looking in the mirror.

"I understand your daughter Vanessa didn't come home yesterday evening, Mrs. Jefferson," Tanya said after introducing herself. She sat down next to the woman. Good thing they were alone in the waiting area or she would have had to find a meeting room. She wasn't willing to waste any more time relocating them. "Can you tell me about her boyfriend?"

"Please call me Daria. No, I can't tell you anything about him." Daria gave a laugh that came out half-strangled. "I only just learned that she was dating him the day before she went missing. I grounded her and I suppose she defied me by running off with him when I thought she was in her room doing homework. My daughter is only fifteen, Officer. She turns sixteen in December. This boy, or should I say *man*, is in his twenties."

Tanya made notes in the file as Mrs. Jefferson talked. She looked up. "He could be charged under the *Criminal Code* if the relationship is sexual. She's under sixteen and he's more than two years older than her."

"She wouldn't tell me whether they were having sex. She wouldn't even tell me his full name. All I got was his first name: Leo. I finally convinced her father to come over yesterday afternoon for the 'big talk'" — she made quotation marks in the air — "with his daughter. He was supposed to drop by after supper. I was hoping she'd spill her guts to him.

She's rebelling against me because Mick and I are in the midst of a divorce and she blames me, even though he's the one who was getting it on with his colleague and doesn't want Vanessa living with him. Go figure."

And I thought I had it bad. "So you don't know the boyfriend's full name or what he looks like, is this correct?"

"It sounds ridiculous when you say it. Mick told me I was an idiot for coming here. I just don't know what else to do."

Tanya felt a pull of sympathy at the raw distress on the woman's face. What would she do if this were her daughter? "Teenage girls often tell their secrets to girlfriends. Have you spoken with them?"

"I called them both, but they said they didn't know anything about the boyfriend or where she is."

"Would you like me to speak with them? They might feel comfortable telling a third party, especially if they're made to understand that Vanessa could be harming herself in the long run."

"At this point, I'm willing to try anything. Emily and Chelsea have been friends with Vanessa since kindergarten. If anyone knows something, it'll be them."

"Well, give me their contact information and I'll drive over to talk to them face to face."

Right after I call my husband and break the news that he and Shandra are going to be entertaining Jack and Sara for the entire evening.

She set out at four-thirty after the call to Allen, who reluctantly agreed to keep the kids another couple of hours even though he stressed that he had important plans, and two more calls to make certain Emily and Chelsea were home and available. They'd agreed to meet at Emily's house west of downtown.

The house was a limestone three-storey set back from the street and surrounded by a high wrought-iron fence. A willow tree draped across one corner of the front lawn. Tangled brown flower stalks lined the walkway but someone had begun clearing the old, dead foliage in the flower beds near the fence to make way for spring planting. Closer to the front door, she spotted a few red tulips that had outlived their sisters. She'd like to return midsummer to see the place in full bloom. She imagined the grounds would be spectacular, not like her own overgrown yard, which she had no time to tend between work and shepherding the kids to their hockey, curling, soccer, and baseball games. As one sports season wrapped up, another began. She didn't begrudge the time, though. Keeping kids involved in teams was the best way to get them safely through the teen years.

A striking blond girl the same age as the missing Vanessa opened the door. Tanya could see her mother standing behind her: an older, stylish version of the girl. Tanya focused her attention back on the daughter. "I'm Officer Morrison."

"Hi, I'm Emily. Chelsea hasn't arrived yet but we can wait in the family room. Mom's made tea."

Emily's mother said hello and brought the tea into the family room, but she didn't linger. Tanya silently thanked her for realizing that her daughter might reveal more without her mother present.

Tanya was stirring cream and sugar into her tea when the doorbell rang. Emily jumped up to answer it. *She's as edgy as a cat*, thought Tanya. *I wonder what she knows.*

Chelsea was shorter than Emily but with the same shade of blond hair, although hers looked like it was enhanced from a box while Emily's looked natural. Tanya could see immediately that Emily was the dominant one in the relationship. Chelsea even waited to see where Emily sat before choosing her own spot on the couch.

"So, I'm here to get your help tracking down Vanessa. Her mother's worried and believes she's somewhere with her boyfriend. What can you tell me about him?"

Chelsea and Emily exchanged glances but as Tanya expected, Emily did the talking. "She called him Leo but we never met him."

"You never met him?" Tanya couldn't keep the surprise from her voice.

"No. We joked that he was her secret boyfriend."

"Surely you girls found that peculiar?"

Emily shrugged. "We thought she'd bring him around when she was ready. They'd only been going out a few months. I wasn't sure how serious Van was about him."

"You knew he was older than Vanessa?"

"Yeah, she said he was finished school and working. He drove a black car and picked her up in it after class almost every day to drive her home. She said he took her for coffee on the way but they never went to the same place we did." Emily chewed her bottom lip and looked at Chelsea before saying, "I thought she might be seeing him to get back at her parents. They've been fighting a lot and she hated it."

"Do you know the make of the car?"

"No. You, Chels?"

"Nope."

Tanya asked, "Have you anything to add, Chelsea?"

"No, except that Vanessa had never had a boyfriend before. Like, I didn't think this would last very long. She called him her boyfriend but I, like, thought he was just a friend."

"When's the last time you saw Vanessa?"

Again the exchange of glances with Emily doing the talking. "At school yesterday. She said that she was grounded because her mom had found out she'd been seeing Leo and that her mom would be driving her home all week. But she didn't seem to mind. She said she was okay breaking up with Leo."

"You're sure about that?"

"Yes."

"Did she contact either one of you by text or email or phone since school yesterday?"

Both girls shook their heads.

"Do you know anybody else she might have confided in?"

"No." Emily seemed about to say something more but closed her mouth again. Chelsea sat mutely next to her.

"I'm going to give each of you my cell number and I want you to call me immediately if Vanessa gets in touch. Can you do that for me?"

"Yes." Emily took both business cards and passed one to Chelsea. "You do think she's okay, don't you?"

The first sign of concern. Tanya decided to up the pressure. "I have no way of knowing but her mother is extremely worried. The fact that this boy is in his twenties and your friend is only fifteen could signal a problem."

"We'll ask around," said Emily quickly, her face flushing red. "If anyone else knows anything, I'll call you right away."

"I'd appreciate that, girls." Tanya was glad that Emily had picked up on the urgency of the situation. She wondered if Emily knew something that she wasn't willing to share until she spoke with someone else. The best she could do was leave the door open and hope that Emily got back to her right away — or, even better, that Vanessa showed up back home before nightfall on her own steam.

"What do you think?" asked Chelsea when they were alone. They'd gone downstairs to the TV room but hadn't decided whether or not to turn it on.

"Vanessa's acting stupid. When her parents get hold of her, she won't be allowed out for a long time."

"Like, she really changed this semester. Ever since her dad left, she hasn't wanted to hang out. She even ignores my texts half the time."

"Maybe we should have made her bring Leo around." Emily didn't know why she was so uneasy. "I have to talk to Dawn."

"Why?"

"She might have seen Leo. Vanessa told Dawn that Leo liked her and had a friend who wanted to date her. It sounded like they might even have met."

"You didn't tell the cop."

"I want to make sure Dawn wants to speak with her first. She might not know anything."

"You heard the rumour going around about Dawn's mother?"

Emily wasn't sure she wanted to hear, especially when she saw the look on Chelsea's face, like the cat that swallowed the canary. "No, I didn't. Who cares about a silly rumour?"

Chelsea kept talking as if she hadn't heard. "She's in a women's prison in Quebec for armed robbery. She won't be getting out for a long time."

"How would anybody even know that?"

"Amy Shuster's aunt works in Corrections and she told Amy, who told just about everyone in the school. How come *you* didn't know?"

"Because I don't listen to gossip. And it doesn't matter, anyway."

"Well, I'd be careful. Maybe Dawn knows Leo better than she let on. She could have set Vanessa up."

"Are you serious? Dawn wouldn't lie about something like that."

"Sure she would. She comes from trailer trash."

"Her aunt is a cop."

"Her aunt was a homeless drunk before she became a cop. There's a story in the newspaper. You can find it online if you do a search."

Emily stared at Chelsea, trying to make sense of the information. It was true that Dawn never talked about herself or her family. Never invited her over or even accepted a ride home. Why didn't she share this stuff about her mother if they truly were friends? Dawn should have known by now that she wouldn't have judged her. She'd confided her own personal problems to Dawn. Even about cutting herself when she'd been at her worst. Maybe she'd been stupid to trust her. Could Dawn really have known Leo all along? Vanessa had talked like they'd spent time together, and she'd waited for Dawn to say something but she hadn't. Maybe Dawn had even introduced Vanessa to Leo to get her away from her and Chelsea. Break up their friendship. But that seemed crazy — why would Dawn bother? Emily scratched the top of her head and ran her hand through her hair as she replayed old conversations between Dawn and Vanessa.

Out of the corner of her eye, she saw Chelsea glance at her and pick up the remote. Chelsea began scrolling through movies on Netflix before clicking on an icon and settling back into the couch. "Oh, goody. I've been waiting for this one to get added."

Emily looked at the screen without really seeing it. The sick feeling she'd had in the pit of her stomach since the cop showed up had turned into confusion and now anger at her friends. Vanessa was off with some loser guy and Dawn was keeping secrets. And Chelsea — well, Chelsea was being a smug bitch. She had always felt like a mother hen to the other girls, and this hurt like the worst kind of betrayal.

She knew that the logical thing to do was to call Dawn and find out what she knew, but evasions were easy on the phone. No, she'd wait to speak with her at school when they were face to face. It was harder to lie when you were looking someone in the eye.

Emily reached over to turn off the lamp as the opening music started. "I've been waiting for this movie too," she said, putting her feet on the coffee table and leaning back next to Chelsea. She'd let go of all the nasty thoughts running around in her head for a couple of hours and try to remember the things she liked about Chelsea. She'd step back from reconsidering her friends for tonight and face what she had to in the morning.

CHAPTER TWENTY-EIGHT

Kala was restless after her lunch with Gundersund. The knowledge that Nadia had been having sex with her landlord in exchange for discounted rent was unsettling on many levels. And yet, Kala understood about being cornered into bad decisions just to get by; she wouldn't condemn Nadia for it. A more pressing question remained, however: was Nadia a good mother, intent on turning her life around or a devious addict turning tricks and trying to seduce her brother-in-law? The answer could be key in understanding what happened to her.

Kala pulled up Bennett's report on his interview with the neighbour across the hall. Mrs. Greenboro hadn't seen any men enter Nadia's apartment except for Murray Simmons. She could have missed them, of course. She had to sleep sometime and at other times she'd be in the washroom or making lunch in the kitchen. She'd said someone from her church came to take her to bingo on Wednesday nights and grocery shopping Friday mornings. She attended church when she felt up to it. Kala read the name of the babysitter that Mrs. Greenboro had mentioned to Bennett. He'd made a note to follow up with Holly Tremaine but hadn't yet. He was helping Woodhouse with Murray's interview and wouldn't be free for the rest of the afternoon. Kala looked up Holly's address online and grabbed her jacket. She let Morrison know she'd be out for a bit. She'd inform Bennett later.

Holly lived in a small white bungalow wedged between a high-rise and a parking garage. The front lawn was little more than a short concrete-block walkway lined by a few feet of brown grass tufts on either side. She opened the inside door before Kala raised her arm to ring the doorbell.

"I was waiting for a mom to pick up her boy and saw you walking up the sidewalk," she said. "Are you looking for somebody?" Her middle-aged face was pleasant, her eyes curious but friendly behind blue-framed glasses. Her grey hair was cut in an asymmetrical bob, the bangs a swoop over her eye.

"I'm Kala Stonechild, one of the officers investigating Nadia Armstrong's death." Kala took out her badge and held it at eye level. "Do you have a few minutes to talk?"

Holly looked back down the hallway before pushing the door open wider and telling her to come in. "We'll have to sit in the living room, where I can keep an eye on Tai. He's a busy one."

Kala followed her into a room with coral-coloured walls and mismatched furniture of the cumbersome dark-wood vintage. An Asian boy aged about three was sitting on the middle of the hardwood floor surrounded by toy trucks. He made *vroom* noises as he crawled across the floor, pushing one of the trucks between the legs of the coffee table.

"I've just steeped a pot of Earl Grey. Would you like to join me in a cup?" Holly asked.

"I would, thank you."

Kala sat in a swivel armchair and waited for Holly to bring the two cups of tea from the kitchen. The little boy watched her shyly for a few minutes before coming over, setting a truck on her knee and silently staring at her.

"Is this your favourite truck?"

He nodded, solemn-faced. She thought he might say something before the doorbell rang and he darted away. Holly bustled in and set the teacups down. "That'll be Tai's mother. I'll be right back once I see him out."

Kala sipped the tea while she looked around the room. Holly was well set up for child care with a playpen in one corner, a high chair, and a bookcase stuffed with children's books and toys. Holly returned after shutting the front door and dropped onto the couch, spreading out her arms and legs in a parody of exhaustion. "My next charges arrive in half an hour for the whole evening. A brother and sister whose parents do shift work." She straightened and picked up her mug. "I'll need my energy. Now, what would you like to know about Nadia? I can't tell you how shocked I was to hear that she was the one murdered."

"I understand you looked after her baby while she was at work waitressing."

"Yes, but I looked after him a few evenings a week, as well, when she wasn't at work. She liked her free time." Holly drank from her cup but not before Kala saw her lips tighten.

"What were your impressions of Nadia?"

"I wouldn't want to say anything, you know, on the record. It doesn't seem right to talk poorly of her when she's dead."

"I understand. Let's agree that I won't make an official record of what you tell me unless it's absolutely required to move the case forward."

Holly appeared to weigh the idea. "I wouldn't want other parents to think I'm judging them too."

"I'll be as discreet as possible."

"Okay, then." Holly set her cup down on the coffee table. "I put some flyers up in the local shops with tearaways of my phone number at the bottom. That's how Nadia came to find me. She said that she was new to the city and would need my services at odd hours since she was waitressing different shifts and got called in last minute sometimes. I don't normally stray far from my house so I agreed."

"Did you form any kind of relationship with her?"

"We were friendly initially but our relationship cooled at the end because she was behind in paying me. The week before she died, I told her I wouldn't take Hugo unless she paid me what she owed. I think what sparked it was seeing her new coat and expensive handbag. I guess I won't be seeing that money now."

"How much did she owe you?"

"Three hundred dollars, give or take. I suppose it's partly my fault. I told her in the beginning that I didn't mind a bit of a delay in payment … but then, I'm working to keep afloat too."

"So you came to believe that she was taking advantage."

"I'd say that's a fair assessment. The strange thing is that I still liked her."

"Did she talk to you about her life at all?"

"She said that she was planning to go back to school and waitressing part-time for now. I believed she was struggling financially so I fed Hugo for nothing and didn't tell her. I respected her attempts to make a better life for the baby — at least, she told me that was her goal. I know all about starting over. My husband left me ten years ago without taking his debts with him and it took me a while to get back on my feet."

"I'm sorry to hear that."

"He didn't deserve me." She smiled.

"I'd like to ask what you meant when you said that Nadia liked her free time. Do you know how she spent it when she wasn't at work?"

"Not exactly. I did wonder though."

"About what?"

"Well, she'd bring Hugo over late some evenings, sometimes when I was getting ready for bed. She'd pick him up in the morning — I didn't like the idea of her showing up in the middle of the night to waken him so I said I'd keep him overnight for no extra charge. Those times, she'd look as if she'd been up all night. I wondered how she cared for Hugo in that state. The odd time, she'd ask me to keep him all day because she got called into the restaurant, or that's what she'd tell me on the phone. I always accommodated her because I was fond of him and worried about his welfare."

"Were there ever any signs of abuse?"

"Oh, no. Nothing like that and I don't want to give the impression that she wasn't good to him. I only worried about how she was looking after him when she obviously needed to sleep off the partying."

Kala thanked Holly for her time and left before her next children arrived. She ran through the rain to her truck, thinking about Nadia Armstrong and what made the girl tick. Was being a mother enough for somebody like Nadia, who'd preferred to live on the street rather than live by her parents' rules? She'd had regular sex with Murray Simmons rather than ask her parents or her sister for financial help. Was Hugo a noose around her neck or had she genuinely cared about him enough to completely change her life? So far, all Kala had were contradictions.

Kala's phone signalled a message and she jammed the keys into the ignition while she pulled the cell out of her jacket. The text was from Gundersund. The team was meeting at the Merchant for a beer and update in half an hour. She checked the time on her phone. It was late enough in the afternoon that she was happy not to have to drive all the way out to HQ. The Merchant was downtown, near the waterfront, and she could easily head home from there. Maybe a recap of the day and a brainstorming session with the others would jumpstart an idea for where to begin in the morning.

Fisher woke the second time that morning to rain dripping on his face through the branches of the pine tree that sheltered him from the worst of it. Still inside the sleeping bag, he rolled himself to a dry spot with a denser layer of branches overhead. He'd woken after sunrise and had a bite to eat and a drink of water before falling back to sleep. He stretched gingerly, pleasantly relieved when the pain didn't jolt through him like a sharp punch to the gut. The long sleep seemed to have been the ticket to recovery. His phone was long dead and he had no idea what time it was with the sun shrouded in dense cloud. By the hunger in his belly, he guessed mid to late afternoon. He eased himself out of the sleeping bag and pulled on his rain jacket, which had been tightly folded at the bottom of his pack. The ground smelled rich and dark and alive in the woods. Fisher breathed in deeply and held the fresh, moist air in his lungs. The feeling was good enough that he didn't even crave a smoke, which was great since he was out despite having carefully rationed them.

He'd hung the bag of food high up in a tree away from his bed and he hauled it down now, taking out the last of the sandwiches and chocolate bars that Dawn had brought on her last visit. He'd saved an apple and ate it last. If Dawn didn't come down to the beach after school, this meal would have to hold him until morning. He thought it might be time to pack up and move on. The itch to be back on the road was growing stronger as his body healed. It also wouldn't hurt to put more distance between him and Loot. He could catch a bus into town before Dawn got home and get on the Greyhound heading east. He liked travelling at night when most people were in bed asleep, the lights and miles zipping past while he sat up front talking to the driver; it made him feel as if he were going toward someplace good. Kept the black hole from eating him up. He had enough money to make it to the coast ... but he owed the kid a goodbye.

He moved close to the edge of the woods and looked up the beach toward the path leading to the house. The two men in the black car the day before had unsettled him. They didn't feel like the kind of friends either Kala or Dawn would tangle up with and he couldn't come up with a good reason why they'd be trying to get into the house with the occupants away. He pictured the money hidden in Kala's bedroom. The stash would buy him time to get set up in a new town. It would pay for a room and give him an address to use while he worked on landing a job. Employers liked a fixed address. Yet he disregarded the idea as quickly as it came. Stealing from family would be a bad start to cleaning up his life. He couldn't do that to Dawn.

He stared out at the flat grey lake and the dark underbelly of cloud hovering not too far above. The rain made circular divots on the water and played a continuous scale of notes on the surface. The fish would be biting in the bays. He'd have given anything to be out in a boat with his rod in the water. He wondered what kind of fish he'd catch trawling the shore of the Atlantic. The last he'd hooked had been a couple of rainbows near the Sault. He'd fried them over a campfire with onions in a slab of butter; he imagined the taste on his tongue.

The rain started to let up. He'd give it a bit more time before making a trek up to the house to see who was around. Dawn might be home from school and alone. He wanted to talk to her and let her know that he'd likely be gone the next day. She was better off here than with him, but he'd leave the door open if she ever changed her mind.

CHAPTER TWENTY-NINE

Kala was the last to arrive at the Merchant and found the others gathered around a long table in an alcove where they had complete privacy. Rain streaked down the plate-glass window in rivulets and the bar room was snug and warm after the wet dash from her truck. She took the empty seat next to Gundersund and felt his thigh momentarily press against hers before he shifted away. Woodhouse and Bennett were at opposite ends of the table with Bedouin and Morrison directly across. Jugs of beer and plates of nachos and chicken wings filled the table. The server set a cranberry juice and soda in front of her shortly after she sat down.

"I ordered for you," said Gundersund. "I hope that was okay."

She smiled and tilted the glass in his direction. "Thanks." She looked around. "No Rouleau?"

"He's stuck in a meeting with Ellington," said Bennett.

"And I'll be going back to HQ to update him," added Gundersund. "Apologies for mixing work with pleasure but I'll need to know what everyone's uncovered today so I have something to tell him."

"I've come from a visit with Nadia's babysitter, Holly Tremaine," said Kala. "Nadia would drop Hugo off on the spur of the moment, often overnight. She could have been meeting men for sex."

"I don't know," said Morrison. "Her friend Faz said she only did that when she was pressed for money. She didn't like the lifestyle."

"She owed Holly about three hundred bucks."

Bennett interrupted. "We got a readout on her bank account. She'd saved close to six thousand dollars."

Kala considered the implications. "She couldn't be making that much from part-time waitressing alone. Not with the bills she had to pay, reduced rent aside."

"I believe she was back hooking," said Gundersund. "Does everyone agree?"

"I'd like to say no but you're likely right." Morrison frowned. "I was rooting for her, you know? To try making something good of herself now that she was a mother."

"People aren't always what we want them to be," said Gundersund. He gave a slight nod toward Woodhouse who had his head down over his phone, typing busily with his thumbs and oblivious to the conversation. Everyone smiled, united in a moment of shared understanding.

"What?" asked Woodhouse as he set his phone on the table and saw them watching him. "Why're you all gawking at me?"

"Just wondering who's the lucky lady you're texting," said Bedouin.

Woodhouse reached for his beer. "It's nobody." He stopped talking and drank.

Kala studied him, assessing his discomfort. She pulled herself back to the conversation. "I don't think we can assume she was soliciting — not without proof. Someone she knew, like a family member, might have loaned the money to her."

"You're right," agreed Gundersund. "First rule of policing is to never assume. Do you have time to check with her family?"

"Of course. I'll call them tomorrow morning. She could have had a friend who loaned her money, though. The bank might have record of a money transfer. I'll check that too."

"Great." His gaze shifted. "How did your interview go today, Woodhouse?"

Woodhouse leaned back in the chair and rested the beer glass on his belly. "Murray Simmons lawyered up and refused to say anything incriminating. Bennett is going to dig around in the lives of the Simmons brothers tomorrow. We need more ammunition."

Bedouin looked at Morrison. "We received a few calls from people who think they saw Nadia in various bars around town. Should keep us busy tomorrow."

Morrison nodded. "I met with a family about their runaway teen before I came here. Unrelated to this case but it might take up part of my day tomorrow. I can help otherwise."

"Need any assistance with that?"

"I'll let you know, but I'm hoping the girl comes to her senses, ditches the loser boyfriend, and shows up at home tonight."

"You make it sound personal," Bedouin said.

"Let's say I'm getting tired of men and the power they hold over those of us stupid enough to fall for their charms." The noise coming from her throat sounded like a growl.

Everyone lifted their glass to drink, eyes carefully averted. Kala didn't blame the men for wisely staying silent on the issue. Even Woodhouse thought better of giving his opinion.

The meeting broke up soon afterward when Gundersund received a text that Rouleau was in the office waiting for the update. Kala walked with him to the door ahead of the others.

"I could come by with Minnie after I'm done at HQ," he said as he pulled the hood of his jacket over his head.

"I'll save you some supper."

He smiled and rubbed his hand up her arm before dashing out the door into the dusky night, the sidewalks and roads slick and shiny with rain. She turned to see if anyone had noticed the contact but the others were only just entering the hallway. She waved goodbye to Morrison and Bedouin and followed Gundersund through the cold rain to her truck. She climbed in, grateful that she'd found a parking spot within view of the Merchant's front entrance. Bedouin and Morrison left together with Bennett less than a minute behind them. Kala peered through the gloom and the rain-streaked windshield and waited. She texted Dawn to say she'd be home within the hour, feeling a twinge of guilt at leaving her alone again.

It was another five minutes before Woodhouse stepped outside the bar, pulling the collar of his jacket up around his ears. He stopped and looked up and down the street before turning toward the waterfront. Kala jumped out of her truck, locked it, and hurried down the street after him as he disappeared around the corner.

He was a block ahead by the time she reached Ontario Street. She saw him jaywalking across the road. She checked for traffic and ran to the opposite sidewalk, keeping a block back. The rain and the noise of passing cars covered the slap of her footsteps on the wet pavement. Woodhouse checked behind him once but his eyes didn't linger in her direction. He picked up speed and widened the distance between them. She cleared the rain from her face and panicked for a moment when he passed a group of university-aged kids clustered at a light and she lost sight of him. She jogged a block farther before realizing that he'd detoured into the Delta Hotel. There was nowhere else he could have gone. She backtracked and entered by the front door, shaking water out of her hair and hoping that he hadn't taken the elevator to some room where she'd never find him.

The reservation desk was directly ahead and the hotel lounge was to the left of the lobby. A long bar underlit by blue lights extended the length of the entrance to the lounge, dividing the tables with a view of the harbour from the hallway. She paused at the end of the bar and surveyed the room. Woodhouse had his back to her. Kala felt a stab of disappointment when he shifted sideways and she saw Marci Stokes sitting across from him. She'd half hoped that she'd misjudged him. He wasn't her favourite person by any stretch but feeding information to the press would bring trouble on his head. He was breaking the code of ethics that they'd signed before joining the force. She had no idea how Rouleau would take Marci's involvement, although Kala couldn't blame Marci for finding sources wherever she could. No, Woodhouse was the one who'd put his job on the line.

She took out her cellphone and snapped several photos of the two of them together, moving into the room but keeping out of their sightline. The lighting in the main room was dim and she wasn't convinced the photos were clear enough, but they'd have to do. The two were deep in discussion and Marci had her laptop open. She pointed at something on the screen and Woodhouse twisted his body to see. He nodded and she typed on the keyboard while continuing to talk. Kala would have given anything to hear what the two of them were discussing but she couldn't move close enough without exposing herself. She stepped back behind a large wooden pillar at the end of the bar and waved off the approaching bartender. "I'm just checking out the view of the lights on the water," she said. "Sending photos to impress my boyfriend back home."

"It's beautiful, isn't it? Take your time." He smiled and moved away.

She glanced across the lounge. Woodhouse was getting up. He said something to Marci before looking around the room. Kala slipped behind the pillar again. He strode out of the bar and past her without glancing toward her hiding place. She watched him cross the lobby and exit through the main door. His entire meeting with Marci had taken less than ten minutes. Marci was still talking into her cellphone and looking out at the boats moored at the dock when Kala followed Woodhouse out into the darkness five minutes later.

CHAPTER THIRTY

By the time Fisher reached the house, the rain had started up again. The back deck wasn't roofed but he didn't want to sit up there anyway. It felt too exposed if someone came around the corner unexpectedly. Dawn must have gone somewhere after school; he was going to have to wait. He'd packed up his few belongings and left them in the woods, but he'd retrieve them once she got home and he had a chance to say goodbye. His stuff would stay dry in the shelter of the trees and bushes where it wouldn't encumber him if he had to make a dash to stay hidden. He was antsy to get moving and decided to catch the night bus east. Loot and Ronnie would be searching for him by now and they'd had an eerie ability to find him in Toronto. He prayed their tentacles didn't reach as far as Kingston. He wouldn't feel safe until he was living somewhere remote on Nova Scotia's South Shore. He pictured a cottage in the woods near the sea. Nothing fancy, but a place with a woodstove and a view of the water. He'd find work on the boats or as a labourer and would hunt and fish to keep himself going. He didn't need much as long as he could see the stars at night.

He started down the driveway toward the road, keeping close to the line of trees. The rain pelted his face and ran off the hood of his jacket. It was probably earlier in the day than the light would have him believe, the clouds low and heavy, blocking out the sun. He heard the rumble of a car approaching on the road and ducked into the brush while it passed. From what Dawn had told him, Kala Stonechild was a loner and didn't interact much with her neighbours, but they might question a stranger walking up her laneway.

Dawn would be getting off the bus at the end of the road and walking the rest of the way home. He wasn't sure which direction she'd be coming from so he selected a spot directly across from the driveway under the shelter of a fir tree. He had a clear view up to the bends in the road in both directions. He crouched down, surrounded by the smell of wet moss and rich, damp earth. He inhaled as much as he could into his lungs and held it there, letting it out slowly, then taking in another big breath. All those years inside, he'd felt like he was suffocating. The institutional air wasn't fit for the living even though it had kept them alive.

When he'd first moved away from the bush and tried to make a go of it in the city, the pavement and concrete had felt like they were suffocating him too. He'd thought he'd get past the feeling during that first year with Rosie but he'd failed. Gotten into drugs and gambling when the panic set in. Started breaking into houses. He didn't blame her anymore for kicking him out. He was a bad influence on the kid. The funny thing was that he'd figured out what he needed in prison. It wasn't money or chemical oblivion. These had only masked what he was missing. He had to get back to the water and the land. Talk Rosie into coming with him once she got out of Joliette. She didn't belong in the city either. They'd be there for Dawn but he wouldn't force her to join them. She was on her own path.

He looked up and down the road, looking for his daughter through the thickening dusk and rain. He shifted positions and leaned forward when he made out the slight figure of a girl rounding the bend on his right. His breath caught at the sight of her. Dawn moved like Rose, and it cut him to his heart. He straightened from his crouched position, prepared to meet her halfway. Even if someone saw them together, he'd be gone within hours. Still, he was relieved that the road was empty. The spreading darkness would also make them difficult to see.

He was about to step out from his hiding spot when he heard a car engine revving loudly. He paused and cocked his head to listen. The rain and murky light made it hard to tell which direction it was coming from, but Dawn must have heard the car too because she stopped, moved closer to the shoulder, and turned to look behind her. The car's lights cut through the gloom and Dawn raised a hand to shield her eyes. Fisher squinted through the light and started walking toward her, keeping along the side of the road so he could jump for cover if it turned out to be Kala. The car stopped a few feet in front of Dawn and he watched the back door on the passenger side swing open. A young man got out and appeared to be talking to her. She started to back away and he grabbed her arm. It was the same car and the same men who had been casing the house.

Fisher started running.

Dawn was in the back seat when Fisher reached the Audi, her eyes enormous and scared. The man was pushing her back with one arm across her chest while slamming the door shut with his other hand. The car lurched forward. Fisher pounded on the front hood as it shot past, yelling at them to let her go. He thumped his fist on the window and kicked at the side panel before the car careered out of reach. He started to run after it but the ache in his side made him double over. He gulped air, trying to suck in enough oxygen to replenish his muscles and carry him forward.

The Audi was revving away, the noise getting fainter. Fisher stumbled but righted himself and half ran, half limped down the middle of the road. He couldn't hear the car's engine any longer but he kept going. He was nearly at the bend, staring into the darkness when he was blinded by car headlights snapping on and realized his mistake too late. The car sped forward. He felt the crunch of his bones as it struck him full, tossing his broken body into the air like a rag doll. He felt his hip and shoulder smack onto the pavement, water and dirt flying, stars filling his vision — and then nothing.

CHAPTER THIRTY-ONE

Kala hiked back to her truck through a break in the rain. She was chilled from the wet chase to the Delta and eager to get home for a hot shower and supper with Dawn. Even if Dawn had already eaten, they could share a pot of tea before taking Taiku for one last walk down by the water, or up Old Front Road if the yard was too muddy. She felt her phone vibrate in her pocket as she dug for her truck keys and pulled both out. She opened the text from Gundersund as she slid behind the wheel.

At HQ. Will bring dessert. Hope you and Dawn like chocolate.

Kala smiled. She checked to see if Dawn had been in touch. She hadn't. Kala almost pressed speed dial but thought better of it. She'd be home within the half hour and Dawn wouldn't appreciate being checked up on like a child. Kala knew that she herself hadn't welcomed parental oversight at that age, not that anyone had cared where she was. When she'd dropped out of high school and skipped out of her last placement, nobody had come searching. She never would have believed back then that she'd end up owning a house and property and looking after a teenager. Even considering a future with someone like Gundersund would have seemed fantastical during those years she was living on the street in Sudbury.

She opened the window halfway to let in the night air even though she'd turned the heater all the way up. She drove west out of downtown Kingston, enjoying the sight of stretches of lakefront on her left and stately limestone buildings on her right. When had she fallen in love with this university town? When had happiness wormed its way into her soul?

She kept the radio off, preferring the night sounds: the buffeting wind, the clanging of the harbour bell and the waves striking the breakwall. The houses gradually dwindled away once she passed the vacant Kingston Pen, now a tourist draw for the city. Night had settled in completely and woods and shadows replaced the city lights as she turned toward the lakeside on Old Front Road. The first stretch of road gave her an open view of the water, and she drove slowly to savour the fresh air and the wide expanse of sky before trees filled her sightline. She passed several properties and had driven most of the sweeping curve of road when she spotted activity ahead. A red light pulsed in the darkness, and she realized that the street was crowded with police cars, an ambulance, and a fire truck.

People stood in small groups at the ends of the closest driveways. In the sweep of red light, she spotted Frank from the house across the road. He was talking to a police officer. She backed up until she reached a driveway and eased the truck into the lane, not wanting to block the emergency vehicles' exit. Whatever was happening was on this side of her property so it wasn't a house fire. Perhaps someone had fallen ill or slipped on the wet roads.

She jogged back up the road and was in time to see the paramedics lifting a man onto a stretcher, though her view was blocked by their backs and by the others milling about. They hefted him into the ambulance and two paramedics got in with him before the door shut. The ambulance pulled away. The neighbours were off to the side and she was ushered that way by an officer whose job, it appeared, was to keep everyone away from the accident scene. She saw Frank standing alone and hurried over to him.

"Hey, Frank. What's going on?"

"Oh, hi, Kala. Looks like a hit and run. I found the fella when I drove home from visiting a friend. He was lying on the side of the road and it's a wonder I didn't run him over."

"Do you know who he is?"

Frank shook his head. "Never saw him before."

She squinted through the darkness at where the man had been lying. "Was he conscious?"

"He groaned a few times but seemed out of it. He was bleeding from his face and legs." Frank rubbed a hand across his forehead. "Seemed in bad shape. Good thing the paramedics showed up right away to give the poor guy a fighting chance. I thought at first you might have known him."

"Why's that?"

"He looked like he might be visiting." Frank started walking away from her without explaining what he meant. "Gotta get home and let the dog out. Take it easy, Kala."

She wanted to call after him to find out why he'd said that but he'd been swallowed up by the darkness. Instead, she moved closer to the activity and called over one of the uniformed cops.

"I'm sorry," he said, "but we're asking everyone to go home unless you have information."

"I'm Officer Kala Stonechild. I live up that driveway. Can I help in any way?"

"You're off duty?"

"I am."

He told her to wait and left to speak with another officer. A minute later he returned with his notepad out. "I can't tell you anything but let me take your contact information. My supervisor will speak with you later, if he needs to."

After giving him her cell number, she got into her truck and drove back the way she'd come. She could access Old Front Road by its other entrance off Front Road. The route was longer but she'd reach her driveway on the other side of the accident.

The rain started up again as she ran for the back door. The front light was on a timer but none of the lights in the house were on. Had Dawn already gone to sleep? Kala rounded the back of the house in the dark and stepped gingerly up the stairs, fumbling with the key to the back door. Taiku was waiting for her and he zipped past her to pee on the lawn before bounding back up the stairs. An uneasy feeling started in Kala's stomach. He hadn't been let out since morning by the look of it.

"Dawn!" she called, even though she knew there'd be no answer. She went from room to room anyway, finally returning downstairs to the kitchen with Taiku following at her heels. "Where is she, boy?" Kala sat and ran her fingers through his fur while she called Dawn on speed dial. A message told her that the phone was not in service.

Kala stood and began pacing. Why did she have the feeling that Dawn was in trouble? Was the hit and run related to her disappearance? She couldn't sit here doing nothing. She crossed to the back door and grabbed her coat, calling for Taiku to follow her. She'd drive Dawn's bus route home and check in at the art gallery where she sometimes went after school. She hit Gundersund's number on her phone as she locked the door and raced across the deck. Maybe he knew something that would lead her to Dawn.

CHAPTER THIRTY-TWO

Gundersund set the package of chocolate cup-cakes and sugar cookies down on the front passenger seat of his Mustang outside Sydenham Sweet Bakery, a delicious find located in a strip mall on the way home. His phone rang as he pulled into traffic but he ignored it for the time being. He'd be at Kala's within fifteen minutes; nothing could be so important that it couldn't wait that long. Likely, it was Fiona anyway. She had finely tuned radar when it came to him and Kala.

The rain had let up some but his headlights cut through a wall of mist that limited visibility. He checked the clock and turned on the radio. The news would be on in a few minutes and he'd get a weather report. Bryan Adams filled the cab, singing about his life peaking at sixteen. Gundersund sincerely hoped that he himself hadn't already passed the pinnacle of his life. He wanted to believe the best was yet to come. Otherwise, what was the point?

He pulled into his driveway, happy to see the Camero was gone. Fiona had talked about visiting some friends for supper, which made his life a whole lot easier. He opened the front door and whistled for Minnie. She did her greeting dance and then scooted ahead of him through the darkness toward Kala's, turning at regular intervals to make certain he was following, her tail wagging double time. "I'm excited too, dog," he said.

At Kala's driveway, he stopped and squinted up the road. A cop car straddled its width, and an officer was attaching police tape to a tree. Flares were positioned nearby. Gundersund called to Minnie again and lifted her under one arm before making his way toward the officer. It was a woman he didn't know.

"Something going on? I'm Officer Gundersund. I live up the road."

"Hit and run."

"Do you know who it is?" His voice wavered and he glanced back toward Kala's laneway.

"A man, early forties, not from around here, apparently."

Thank God. "No ID?"

"Nope. We believe he might have been a homeless man, based on the state of his clothes and hair. Indigenous."

"Are you sure?"

"As much as one can be from looking at him."

What were the odds of an Indigenous man being hit right outside Kala's driveway? "Did you speak with the woman who lives right there?" He pointed toward her property.

"Another officer took her contact info. She arrived after the paramedics took the victim to emergency but the neighbour who found him said the man wasn't from around here. I'm going to speak with her when I'm done securing the site."

"I'll let her know."

Gundersund set Minnie on the ground once he'd started up Stonechild's driveway and the dog raced ahead. It was only then that he noticed Kala's truck was gone. He followed Minnie around the back of the house and banged on the door. When nobody answered, he sat down on the wet step leading up to the back deck and tried to make sense of what was going on. Kala should have been at home. Had she driven off to buy something for dinner or to pick up Dawn? Taiku must be with her because he hadn't come to the door. Gundersund would have seen him through the window. He stared at the black line of trees at the end of the property and at the rim of sky. A wind had come up and the clouds were breaking up, scudding eastward. Clearing overnight and warmer tomorrow, according to the radio report. They could do with some better weather.

Minnie tired of racing around the yard and came to lie at his feet. He tugged gently on her ear while pulling out his cellphone. The missed call was from Stonechild. He kicked himself for not checking earlier. She hadn't left a message but had followed up her call with a text.

Dawn didn't come home from school. Gone into town to look for her. Let me know if with you.

Before he had a chance to call her back, he heard tires crunching up the gravel driveway. A door slammed and Taiku came bounding around the corner with Stonechild close behind. Taiku and Minnie chased each other into the darkness as Gundersund met her halfway.

"Any word from Dawn?" he asked, although he knew from looking at her face that there wasn't. He waved his phone. "Sorry, I just read your text a few seconds ago."

"I can't imagine where she is. She's not answering my calls — in fact, her cell is out of service. I went to the art gallery but nobody has seen her. I'm frantic, Gundersund. She should be home by now." The wind whipped Kala's long hair into her face and she held up a trembling hand to push it away.

"Has she ever gone anywhere without telling you before?"

"Not lately because she knows I fret. Her phone has never been disconnected before."

"What about her friends? Could she have met up with someone?"

"Emily!" Stonechild's face brightened. "Her number's on the list inside the house. I had Dawn write down her friends' phone numbers in case I ever had to track her down."

"Smart thinking."

They entered the house and Stonechild searched the desk in the front hall until she found an address book. "I've got it!" she called. Gundersund waited in the kitchen and listened to her place the call. She talked to Emily for almost five minutes. When she joined him in the kitchen, her brow was furrowed and eyes deeply worried.

"Emily said that another one of their friends went missing yesterday. Vanessa Jefferson. They think she ran off with her boyfriend, Leo, but Vanessa's parents were worried enough to call in the police. Morrison took the call. Vanessa must have been the missing teenager Morrison told us about at the Merchant."

"Leo who?" Gundersund had his phone out.

"Emily said they don't know his last name. She's never even met him. Vanessa has been dating him a few months behind her parents' backs and was keeping him something of a secret, even from her friends. He's older. Out of school."

"Did Emily know how Vanessa met him?"

"On the internet. She thought maybe he friended her on Facebook."

They stared at each other. Gundersund knew that Stonechild had noted the same red flags he had: a high school girl, lured into the lifestyle by a more experienced man, who kept her away from friends and family. Girls got tricked into the sex trade without knowing what hit them until it was too late. Being trafficked was a very real danger. "Dawn wasn't dating anybody, was she?"

"No!" Stonechild put a hand on her forehead. She moaned. "At least, I don't think so. Surely I would have known."

"Okay, let's think this through. I'm going to call Morrison to hear what she's found out. You check Dawn's room to see if you can find any clues as to who she might be with." He didn't say *in case she was seeing someone behind your back* but Kala was no fool. She nodded and ran up the stairs as he looked up Morrison's number in his phone contacts.

"Morrison," he said after she answered hello. "It's Gundersund. Kala's niece, Dawn, didn't come home from school today, and she's friends with Vanessa Jefferson, the girl you told us went missing yesterday. Have you made any progress locating her?"

Morrison's voice was worried. "No. There's been no word from her. We think she's with her boyfriend but nobody seems to know Leo's last name or anything about him."

"Well, now we have two girls missing."

"I don't like the sound of this."

"Me neither. I'm going to call Rouleau and get things escalated."

"I'll return to HQ. Have you got a photo of Dawn that I can distribute? Should we request an AMBER Alert? Both girls are under sixteen."

"Let me get back to you on that after I speak with Rouleau. I'll be in touch soon and I'll send over Dawn's photo."

Stonechild was still upstairs. Gundersund placed the call to Rouleau who listened without interrupting. He was silent for a moment after Gundersund finished.

"Have you checked the road and talked to the neighbours?"

"Not yet."

"I'll ask a patrol car to swing by and I'll also call Morrison. It looks like the two disappearances are connected. How's Stonechild holding up?"

"I think she's in shock, but she's upstairs searching for clues in Dawn's room."

"Okay. Tell her we'll move quickly on this." He paused. "Tell her not to jump to any conclusions. We're going to find Dawn."

"I'll tell her."

His phone rang as he was about to tuck it away. He checked the caller before answering. "Fiona, I'm a bit busy." He could hear the clink of dishes in the background and the murmur of people talking.

"Has something happened?"

"Dawn didn't make it home from school. Another girl in her class has been missing since yesterday so we're trying to find them."

The background noises faded and her voice sharpened. "My God. I saw Dawn walking home just a few hours ago, about four-thirty."

"Where?"

"She was turning the corner onto Old Front Road and I waved at her. I was driving toward downtown."

"Did she look upset or scared?"

"No. She smiled and waved back. Could this have anything to do with the hit and run on Old Front Road that I just heard about on the news? They said the victim wasn't from the neighbourhood."

"I don't think so." Even as he said the words, he hesitated. The fact that the guy was Indigenous made him wonder. He reminded himself to run the coincidence past Stonechild when she came downstairs. He asked, "Did you notice if anybody was following Dawn in a car or on foot?"

"Not that I saw. I'm sorry. It was raining and I thought about asking her if she wanted a ride but

I'd reached the main road and it was difficult to turn around. I wish now that I had."

"We might need to get a statement from you."

"I've got my phone handy."

"Well, I have to go. I won't be home tonight."

"Keep me updated. I —"

He ended the connection before she finished talking. Fiona always closed with a guilt trip and he didn't need it today. This latest piece of information was disturbing and he wasn't sure how to tell Stonechild. Dawn was nearly home before she disappeared. The possibilities were becoming more and more ominous with every passing minute. A knock at the front door stopped him from going upstairs. The dogs barked on the landing but he beat them to the door and opened it to find the female officer he'd spoken with earlier. A male officer stood next to her.

"I'm glad to see you," Gundersund said. "There's been a development that may or may not be connected to the hit and run." He called upstairs to Kala and they all gathered in the living room. Stonechild was calm on the surface but he knew she was churning inside. He filled in the officers about what they knew, including Fiona's sighting of Dawn. Stonechild looked stricken, and he remembered too late that he hadn't shared this information with her yet. Events were unfolding too fast.

"I didn't find anything in Dawn's room," she said. She turned toward Gundersund. "I sent a photo of her to Morrison. She texted me."

The female officer, who identified herself as Pagett, radioed her supervisor. Her partner, Officer

Chow, asked, "Have you looked on the waterfront and in the woods at the back of your property?"

Stonechild blinked twice. "No."

"We've got a few officers going to the beach now. I've asked others to search along the road."

Stonechild closed her eyes and swayed backward as if she was about to pass out. Gundersund grabbed her wrist and put an arm around her shoulders. He leaned close. Her voice was so low he could barely hear her.

"I should have been home. I should have been here for her."

Gundersund looked over at Chow. "Stonechild's dog, Taiku, could help with the search. He knows every inch of the woods and the beach. He'll take us to anything Dawn-related."

"Worth a try."

Kala straightened. The idea appeared to renew her resolve as Gundersund had intended. She took a step away from him. "I'll get my jacket. Come, Taiku."

The lawn was slick with rain and their flashlights crisscrossed on the ground as the four of them made their way to the lake, led by an eager Taiku. Gundersund had left Minnie inside so as not to distract Taiku. The wind was stronger than it had been when he'd walked up the road to Kala's house and he heard the waves battering against the beach as he climbed onto the rocky strip of shoreline. Taiku charged ahead and they chased after him, their way hampered by uneven rocks and long shadows piercing through the gloom and mist. Gundersund's flashlight cut left in time to catch the dog disappearing into the woods. They changed course after him and reached the edge of the brush. Chow took the lead. "Wait here," he said to Gundersund and Kala. "Come with me, Officer Pagett."

He took a few steps into the trees and squatted down while Pagett kept her flashlight pointed on the ground in front of him. "What's this?" He put on gloves and moved aside a sleeping bag to find a knapsack which he carefully opened. He looked back at their waiting faces. "Someone's been sleeping rough here. Without jumping to conclusions, it's a good bet it was the man who got hit by the car." Chow opened the side pocket of the knapsack and pulled out a wallet. He flipped through it. "Do either of you know a Fisher Dumont?"

Stonechild let out a cry. "He's Dawn's father." She stumbled back against Gundersund. "He's been hiding out in our woods and must have made contact. What the hell has he gotten her into?"

CHAPTER THIRTY-THREE

Shawn B. crowded uncomfortably close to Dawn and she made herself as small and still as she could, one hip pressed against the passenger door. She knew who he was because Leo had yelled Shawn's name to make sure he was in the car before hitting the gas. The guy who Vanessa said wanted to date her.

Leo clicked the locks down as soon as Shawn slammed the door closed and they sped up Old Front Road. She rocked against Shawn when Leo pulled a sudden U-turn. The car rocketed forward and she thought they'd struck something big from the sound of the thunk, but Leo let out a loud whoop and kept going, only slowing when they reached the turn onto the main road. He swivelled his head around and said to Shawn, "What in the hell was that all about?"

Shawn punched the back of the passenger seat. He looked daggers at the back of Leo's head. Dawn heard sarcasm with an undertone of anger when he spoke. "No idea, but I think you took care of the problem." He shook his head and dropped his voice. "You stupid motherfucker."

Leo let out another excited yell. "Woohoo! Are we having fun yet?" The tires squealed on the wet pavement as he braked. He swivelled his head to look at Shawn. "Shit, we were supposed to get her to write a note."

"Too late now. Cool it and stick to the plan," Shawn said. He turned to Dawn. "Hand over your phone."

"I don't …"

He grabbed her arm and squeezed. "Now."

She found it in her pocket and gave it to him without saying anything. He released her arm and fiddled with the phone, opening the back and removing the battery. He lowered the window and tossed it out.

These last five minutes since Shawn had forced her into the car had a surreal quality, as if she were watching herself from outside her own body. She felt the same fear she had when Gil had robbed a store with her in the back seat and then taken her and her mom on the road to escape the police. But the cops had found them anyway and chased them across half of Saskatchewan before arresting Gil and her mom. She hadn't spoken then either. It was as if her voice shut down and her brain went into slow motion.

Shawn slapped the back of Leo's seat. "Go the speed limit, idiot. You don't want to get pulled over now."

"Yeah, yeah." Leo raised a dismissive hand without turning around.

Shawn levelled his gaze on her. "You're a freakin' quiet one," he said, as if her silence irritated him. His tone was aggressive, meant to make her crumble.

She could feel him looking at her but she kept staring out the side window. He pinched her arm through her jacket and she jumped but swallowed the cry of pain before it reached her lips. "Why are you doing this?" she asked to stop him hurting her further. She knew from watching Gil with her mother that men wanted to feel like they'd scared you into submission. The worst beatings Rose had ever endured came after she'd stood her ground — but that was only at the beginning. After a few months of standing her ground, Rose had shut down and let Gil do whatever he wanted.

"Because lover boy up front had you in his car."

"Why does that matter?" She was honestly puzzled. Then she remembered that Vanessa was supposed to have run off with Leo to pay back her mother for grounding her. "Is Vanessa worried I'll say something? Where is she, anyway?"

Shawn was quiet for a moment. "She wanted us to come get you so she could tell you something."

Dawn knew that he was lying but she nodded as if what he'd said made sense. Like she'd forgotten already what he did to her phone. Leo was driving toward downtown Kingston, taking the street along the waterfront. If the door wasn't locked, she could have opened it at a stoplight and made a run for it. Shawn was checking the road through the back window. They passed Rouleau's condo building and kept going past the Holiday Inn. She tried to see if Kala's truck was parked near the Merchant, but the intersection came and went and then they were passing the Leon Centre and the ferry to Wolfe Island. They crossed the causeway onto Highway 2 and followed a line of cars out of town.

"Where's Vanessa?" she asked.

Shawn pulled his eyes away from the back window. "Not far. She'll be glad to see you."

Dawn was quiet for the rest of the ride and made note of the street sign as they turned onto Rudd Avenue. She'd never been in this section of town before. The houses on the right backed onto the lake but didn't have thickets of trees and bush like the ones on Old Front Road. These houses were a mix of cottages and fancier homes. The ones on the left were newer and set back from the road by long sloping lawns. Leo pulled into the last lane-way on the right. The one-storey house in front of them looked like a small cottage with yellow siding, a peaked, brown-shingled roof, and two small windows facing the road. Lights were on in the house next door but nobody was outside to see them leave the car. Shawn took her arm and walked her quickly through the backyard.

Dawn nearly gagged at the mess inside. The kitchen stank like mildew and rot. Dirty dishes filled the sink and lined the counter along with empty beer bottles. Takeout containers and pizza boxes were tossed on the floor near an overflowing garbage can. She saw a phone on the wall near the fridge and wondered if it worked before quickly lowering her head. She didn't know if Shawn had seen her looking at it.

"This way," he said, giving her a shove from behind. Attached to the kitchen was a living room with an old couch and a couple of tattered-looking chairs. A cheap coffee table held an overflowing ashtray and more empty beer bottles. He pointed to one of the chairs. "Have a seat."

She could hear Leo talking to somebody on the phone in the kitchen as she sat down. His voice rose in anger and then dropped to a mumble. Less than a minute later, he appeared in the doorway, tucking a cellphone into his pocket. He looked upset. "He says something's come up. We can't move them until tomorrow."

"What the hell?"

"I know. We have to keep them here tonight."

"I don't like this. We're deviating from the plan."

"Can't be helped."

"Then you'll be spending the night here. I have somewhere to be."

"Since when?"

Shawn glared at him. "Since I don't have to answer to you. And since I haven't seen any of the money you promised."

"You'll get your money." Leo looked over at Dawn. "Let's go see Vanessa. Sorry, you'll be in cramped quarters for tonight but we'll get you in a bigger bedroom soon." He grinned.

Dawn stood up. He told her to return to the kitchen and he opened the door to the basement. As she passed him, he ran a hand down her back and let it rest on her rear end. "Too bad we're not allowed to party," he said close to her ear. "But I have my orders." He motioned her to get down the stairs.

She knew the chances of making a run for it were slim and thought she might have a better opportunity once Shawn left. The steps were steep and narrow and the stone walls damp with mould. She shivered at the cold air that rose up to meet her from the concrete floor. A bare lightbulb cast minimal light and she felt her way carefully, testing each stair before putting her weight on it. The door slammed behind her and she heard the lock click.

"Vanessa?" she whispered, then repeated her name more loudly. She heard whimpering and tried to locate the sound. She waited for her eyes to adjust to the shadows. A cot was in the far corner of the room and someone was sitting up on it, their eyes glinting in the feeble light. Dawn moved slowly forward until she reached the figure. *Vanessa*. Dawn bent down and touched one of Vanessa's arms which were wrapped around her stomach. "Vanessa, are you okay?"

"I'm sorry. I'm sorry. I'm sorry." Vanessa was rocking back and forth, her voice breaking into a wail. Her hair was tangled and she clutched a filthy grey blanket. A sour smell came off her, like rancid milk and fear.

Dawn ignored the bad taste in her mouth and sat on a corner of the cot, wrapping an arm around Vanessa's shoulders. "You weren't the one who dragged us here. What's going on?"

"They're evil."

"What do they want?" Dawn felt Vanessa's body go rigid. She rubbed Vanessa's back, not knowing what else to do. Vanessa gradually relaxed against her.

"They're getting rid of us."

"I don't understand. Leo's your boyfriend."

"They made me do awful things. I'd rather die than let my parents know. I hate them. I hate them!" Her voice rose and echoed against the bare walls.

Dawn swallowed down the sick feeling in her stomach that made her want to vomit and waited for Vanessa to stop shaking again. "You don't have to talk about it. You're not to blame for anything."

"How do you know? Leo picked me. He must have known that I'd ..." Her voice trailed away. She shuddered and cried, "I didn't stop them from going after you."

Why *hadn't* Vanessa warned her? Dawn remembered her casually suggesting a "double date." She wanted to lash out at Vanessa but knew it wouldn't help anything. She said with more conviction than she felt, "I don't think you could have stopped them."

"Leo acted so crazy about me at first. I sent him photos like he asked because I thought he loved me. Then he made me do things with him and with Shawn and with other men at the Blue Nights."

Dawn stared at her, horror making her own body begin to tremble. "Is that where you went after school?"

"If my mother finds out ..." Vanessa was crying now. Big gulping sobs. Letting the tears roll down her cheeks without trying to wipe them away.

"I'm not going to say anything." *We might not have a chance to tell anybody.* Dawn looked around the basement and leaned her head back to look at the window. *Think about how to get out,* she told herself. *Don't think about what happened to her.* She waited until Vanessa's noisy crying had subsided before asking, "Have you tried to escape?"

"The door's locked."

"Did you try the window up there?"

"No. I can't reach it and it's too small to fit through."

Her voice had turned sulky but Dawn couldn't care about that now. She had to think of a way out of this. She needed to stay calm, to think through options like her aunt Kala would. "Maybe we can find something to hit them with when they come to get us. Have you checked the entire basement?"

"No, it's too creepy. I'll bet there are rats in the corners."

Dawn got up from the cot. "I'm going to see what I can find." She took a few steps and then turned around.

"Why did they take us?"

"I dunno."

"Leo was talking to somebody on the phone about what to do with us. Do you know who he was talking to?"

"No."

Dawn wasn't sure if she believed Vanessa; she'd hesitated before answering both times and Dawn bet she knew more than she was letting on. Rose had lied too when she felt cornered. She'd made stuff up to make Gil look less like the abuser he was. Rose had even blamed herself for provoking him. But Dawn kept her voice reassuring so she wouldn't alienate Vanessa. She would need her co-operation once she came up with a plan. "Try to remember what he told you before he brought you here while I check the room."

It took Dawn a while to make it through the entire basement. Concrete poles held up the ceiling at regular intervals and she clunked her head against one, making her slow down her steps even more. The musty, dank smell made her nauseous and she tried breathing through her mouth. The one bare lightbulb at the bottom of the stairs didn't cast any light into the corners, so she had to feel her way. An oil furnace took up one end of the room like a hulking dark monster. It wasn't turned on and she remembered seeing a woodstove in the living room. They probably lit it on cooler nights to warm the cottage. She was chilled through by the time she made it back to Vanessa. She knew that the temperature dropped to just above freezing on these spring nights. Vanessa's eyes were wide.

"Did you find anything?"

"No. Move over." Dawn climbed onto the cot and pulled a corner of the blanket across her legs. "It's freezing."

"At least we'll warm each other up."

"What about going to the bathroom ... and food and water? Have they given you anything to eat?"

"They've left cold pizza on the top step. When I pound on the door, they let me go to the bathroom and I get a drink then."

"In all the shows I've ever seen about kidnapping they tie people up."

"I guess they aren't worried about us escaping or about anybody hearing us. They seem to be improvising," she added as if the idea was only now occurring to her. She tugged the blanket from where she'd tucked it under herself and pulled it across Dawn's stomach. "I'm sorry," she said. "I should have stood up to them. I was just ... so scared ... and I didn't know what they'd do."

Dawn felt her shivering with fear or cold — she couldn't tell which. "We'll get out of this," she said, looking up at the window. It was narrow and out of reach, with bars across it. If they were going to escape, it would have to be through the door at the top of the stairs. She turned to say quietly into Vanessa's ear, "It's two against two. We need to bide our time and surprise-attack when they least expect it."

She thought about Kala and how panicked her aunt would be when she didn't come home. Would Kala think she'd run off like she had in foster care or would she know that something bad had happened? Dawn closed her eyes and pictured Kala and Taiku in the kitchen and wondered what they were doing at this moment. She'd give anything to be there with them, making supper and listening to music on the radio. No matter where Leo and Shawn took them tomorrow — or for how long — she could close her eyes and see home. She could feel Kala telling her not to give up.

CHAPTER THIRTY-FOUR

Rouleau looked around the meeting space at the team's grim faces. They'd put in a long night and only resolve, adrenaline, and strong coffee were keeping them all going. Bedouin had missed the overnight shift but he was ready to fill in for those needing sleep. Rouleau had sent Kala home a half hour earlier. She'd been at her breaking point and he'd told her that she would be of no use if she didn't get some rest. She'd finally agreed when he brooked no argument but he could tell she wasn't happy about it.

Woodhouse and Bennett had arrived minutes before the meeting, having combed the downtown streets through the morning hours for any sign of the two girls. Rouleau had unilaterally given the go-ahead for the AMBER Alert at 6:00 a.m. The missing girls' photos and descriptions were now being broadcast across media channels and a team of officers was manning the phone lines.

"We don't know if the girls are still in the city or if they've been moved," said Rouleau. "Two reported sightings from the alert haven't panned out. We need to consider the possibility that their disappearance is linked to Nadia Armstrong's murder, although there's no evidence yet."

"What about the hit-and-run victim? How's he implicated?" asked Bedouin.

"Fisher Dumont is Dawn's biological father. Kala shared that Dawn's mother, Rose, who is serving time for armed robbery, had asked her to keep Dumont away from Dawn. We're not sure if Dawn was in contact with him but he'd been camping out in the woods at the end of Kala's property."

From where he stood leaning against the wall, Gundersund added, "Dumont hasn't regained consciousness and his condition is critical. The doctor reports that he'd recently been beaten up and those injuries hadn't completely healed. He was living in Toronto, so we've put in calls to the Toronto police and to his parole officer."

"Was Stonechild aware —" began Bedouin.

"That he was hanging around her property?" finished Gundersund. "Of course not."

"No, I meant did she know that he was out on parole?"

"Yes."

Rouleau waited for Bedouin to look back at him before speaking. "Even if the abductions are top priority, we need to keep going with the murder investigation. Bedouin and Morrison, I want you to check up on the Simmons brothers and look through the apartment buildings again. Revisit the basement where Jeff Simmons keeps a cot. Show up at their homes and get inside if you can. The search warrants don't cover another entry so you'll have to be creative. You can take a couple of officers with you."

"Nadia's death is the pretext but we're actually searching for signs of the girls?" asked Morrison, looking up from her notepad.

"Yes. When you're done your search, Morrison, go home and get some rest. Bedouin, you can return to HQ."

Rouleau looked at Woodhouse and Bennett. "Both of you, go home and catch a few hours of sleep. You'll be on the late-afternoon shift."

Bennett frowned. "I planned to spend the rest of the day driving the streets."

"Every uniformed officer in Kingston, not to mention the province and across the county, is on the lookout. The public is also watching. The girls could be gone from Kingston by now. You'll be of better use to the team if you're rested."

Rouleau motioned for Gundersund to stay behind. "I've been called in to update Ellington. Can you manage the team coordination for another hour? Then you can get some rest too."

"Sure. I'll grab a few winks on the premises when you come back. You can call me if I'm needed."

"Take the couch in my office. I'll work at your desk."

"Good enough."

Vera was typing at her computer when Rouleau stopped at her desk. She looked up at him, her eyes troubled. "This is too awful to contemplate," she said. "How's Kala holding up?"

"No show of emotion whatsoever."

"She's probably in shock." Vera tilted her head toward Ellington's office. "He's been on the warpath."

"Why's that?"

"He believes you usurped his authority. He's been talking on his cell so I have no idea who's on the other end. Mayor Clement called first thing."

"I couldn't afford to waste time crossing all the t's for the AMBER Alert. Time is too important."

"The reason won't matter to him." She gave him a rueful grin. "Well, good luck in there. I'm happy to have only a few more days left putting up with his majesty."

"Oh, right." He knew that a surprise party was in the works. It would have to be delayed, what with the chaos going on. "Can I take you for a drink after your last shift?"

"I'd like that."

Ellington was holding a cup of coffee and staring out the window when Rouleau entered. He was an imposing figure, even if not in the best shape. His size and bulk would intimidate on the street and in a meeting room. He reminded Rouleau of that seventies TV cop character who sucked on lollipops — *Kojak*. Rouleau was surprised the name had come to him so easily. He waited for Ellington to sit before taking the chair across from him.

"Any progress with the missing girls?" Ellington asked.

"Nothing that has panned out. I understand Mayor Clement phoned this morning?"

"Yeah, he wanted to know why the AMBER Alert. I would have appreciated a chance to approve the request before you issued it."

"Sorry about that, but in my judgment timing was critical."

"Well, I've spent the morning explaining and calming people down."

Rouleau didn't bother responding again. One apology was enough. Ellington lost interest in staring him down. "You'll be called in front of the police board to explain your flaunting of the chain of command, so you'd better have your reasoning ready. Saying time was critical isn't going to cut it. You of all people should know the importance of following protocol."

"Understood."

"Have you made any progress with the Armstrong case?"

"Nothing to report."

"I want to hear as soon as you have anything … on Armstrong or the missing girls. I'm to be your first call, is that clear? I want my number on your speed dial."

"Clear."

"Okay, then."

Ellington stood and moved back to the window, turning his back on Rouleau and effectively dismissing him without saying another word.

Marci Stokes glared at her computer screen before deleting a line of text. She picked up a pencil and

threw it at the bulletin board. Rouleau and Woodhouse were ignoring her calls and she'd gotten little
from the police communications liaison unit about
the missing teenage girls. Her article had gaps you
could drive a truck through. It was shit, really. Her
phone buzzed and she looked at a text from Scotty.

Where is it? Deadline half an hour ago.

"It's right here," she muttered. "Looking back
at me like a piece of Swiss cheese." She skimmed
through the article again and typed a new final sentence before saving the story and emailing it to him.
The wretched attempt would have to do.

She sat back and sighed. She was being pulled in
too many directions at once. Whatever had possessed
Scotty to let most of the team go to a conference in
Vegas was beyond her. She'd agreed to cover the city
council beat for the week and then — sod's law — the
casino announcement had blown up and she'd needed
to dig around to find out how council had voted
that in, and how they'd managed to award the contract without the public's knowing. The Armstrong
murder and the missing girls were time-consuming
enough on their own.

She checked her notepad. Woodhouse had
told her to dig into the Simmons brothers. She'd
intended to visit Murray Simmons' workplace this
morning since Woodhouse had named Murray as
the prime suspect in Nadia's murder. If she hurried,
she'd make it to Mortimer Construction before
closing. They'd have insight into his character and
maybe give her something on the record that she
could use in an article. It would be good to have

an exposé ready once he was charged, although Woodhouse said not to rule out the brother Jeff, who'd committed a lewd act with a minor and seemed to be playing without a full deck. Big leap from that to murder in her opinion, but she'd keep an open mind. She might also get someone to talk about the contract for the casino, if she was lucky. So far nobody was saying much, at neither City Hall nor Mortimer Construction.

The drive to Mortimer Construction took twenty minutes. She was relieved to see cars still in the lot and the lights on inside the reception area. She parked and entered. Nobody was behind the desk, but a moment later an overweight older woman with impossible hair, red as brick and teased into a helmet, and acne-scarred cheeks entered from the back room, putting her coat on as she walked. Her voice was gravelly.

"We're closing up now."

"This'll only take a few seconds. Can you tell me how long Murray Simmons has worked here?"

"Why're you asking?"

"I'm a reporter with the *Whig* doing some background on the girl who was found dead recently. She was living in one of his apartment buildings."

"I wouldn't know anything about that."

"Is Murray a good guy?"

"Seems okay. He's worked here going on fifteen years, to answer your question."

"Look, could I buy you a drink? I don't know about you but I could sure use one. It's been a long day."

The woman hesitated and Marci pressed her advantage. "There's a pub just around the corner."

"Well, I guess one won't hurt."

The bar was dark and depressing, with people scattered at tables, hunched over their drinks. Was a time they'd all be smoking cigarettes too, but thankfully, those days were long gone. Marci collected a gin and tonic and a Scotch on the rocks from the bartender and carried them to the table with a view of the widescreen television that Gloria had staked out. She'd settled back in a chair, one foot resting on the edge of the seat next to her. The woman was at home in a drinking establishment, no doubt about that.

"Cheers," said Gloria, pointing her glass in Marci's direction before raising it to her lips. She swallowed and looked around the room. "Odd. Nobody I recognize."

"You come here often?" *Now I'm talking like a pickup artist.*

"Often enough." Gloria put her foot down on the floor, straightened in her chair, and faced Marci. "So, what do you want to know?"

"Has Murray ever had any issues with women around the workplace?"

"You mean like hitting on us?"

Marci nodded. She didn't trust herself to speak, stifling the urge to giggle at the idea of Gloria including herself in the pool of women Murray might hit on. Fatigue was making her giddy.

"Nah, nothing like that. Mind you, we don't have any young women working for us at the moment.

I'm as sexy as it gets and I'm not into men." Her laugh was deep and phlegm-filled.

Marci smiled, warming to Gloria's lack of filter. Gloria had quaffed the rest of her drink, and Marci signalled to the bartender to bring a second. After he'd delivered it and Gloria had taken another mouthful, she asked, "So what's up with the casino contract? I never saw *that* coming."

Gloria looked around as if to check whether anybody was listening before she leaned forward. The first drink had made her cheeks ruddy and her eyes sparkled. "Neither did I. But there's a lot goes on in the backroom under the table, if you get my drift."

"A bribe to get the contract?"

"You didn't hear it from me." Gloria winked and took another sip while Marci waited. "They're all tight with each other," she continued. "Have been since they were teenagers."

"Who would that be?"

"Harold Mortimer, Tom Clement, and that other guy. The cop whose name I can never remember. The bald one."

Marci stared at her. Could she possibly mean Rouleau? He'd spent some years in Kingston before moving to Ottawa and marrying Frances ... and he was bald.

"Staff Sergeant Jacques Rouleau?" she asked, but Gloria had pushed back her chair and stood up.

Gloria raised her voice above the Guns N' Roses song that the bartender had just jacked up on the house sound system. *Welcome to the jungle* ... "Can

I get you another?" she asked, signalling at Marci's glass in case she couldn't hear over the music.

"No, thanks."

"I'm going to the loo."

Marci sat back in her chair and watched Gloria strutting across the floor toward the back of the bar. She stopped to talk to two guys in work clothes sitting at a table pushed against the wall. By the time she returned from the washroom, a drink was waiting for her at their table. Gloria pulled out a chair and plunked herself down with her back to the room. Marci could see where this was heading. She drank the last gulp of her gin and tonic and stopped on her way out to give the bartender some money for Gloria's second drink.

The cool night air made her shiver, and she wished she'd worn a warmer coat. She'd never gotten used to this crazy Canadian weather that changed at the drop of a hat, and not usually for the better. The short walk to her car had her looking in the shadows to see if anyone was lurking there. This wasn't a neighbourhood that invited leisurely strolls after dark. The only romance going on in these back alleys would be the anonymous drunken kind with money exchanging hands.

Once inside the car, she locked the doors, turned on the heater, and considered her next move. She could go home and eat leftover Chinese food or follow up on Woodhouse's lead. She checked the time. What the hell. She didn't have anybody waiting for her and the cat she'd adopted couldn't care less when she showed up. One more stop at the end of a frustrating day wouldn't kill her.

She drove across the city to Bellevue Towers and was lucky to snag the last spot in the visitor parking. The lot was at the side of the building, with one street lamp providing inadequate lighting. She hurried to the front door, feeling spooked but not sure why. She waited inside the outer door for someone to let her into the building but nobody came or went. After another five minutes peering through the glass door, she pulled out her cell and searched for Murray Simmons's home address. He was in an upscale suburb north of downtown. *In for a penny*, she thought before opening the outer door and running through the murky darkness to her car.

This time, she parked across the street from Simmons's house and sat for a moment, getting the lay of the land. Simmons had one of the larger homes on the street. A modern boxy two-storey with lots of smoky glass and copper, the house was set back on a wide lot. The treed yard provided distance and privacy from the neighbours — more than usual, in this age of infill. If Simmons was home he'd parked his car out of sight in the garage. She was happy to see lights on as she climbed the wide stone steps to ring the doorbell. A woman in red leggings and a white hoodie opened the door. Her blond hair was pulled back in a ponytail but her face was older than the youthfulness of her attire. She looked Marci up and down with zero friendliness in her eyes before asking, "Yes, can I help you?"

"I'm looking for Murray Simmons. Would he be home?" Marci spotted a child at the end of the hallway watching them with a finger poked into his mouth. She estimated he was three years old, but she was no expert when it came to kids.

"Who should I say is calling?"

"Marci Stokes from the *Whig-Standard*."

"I'll see if he wants to talk to you." The door shut and Marci shuffled from foot to foot on the top step while she waited in the cold. She'd just about given up and had turned to return to her car when the door reopened.

"He'll see you." The same woman held the door open wide to let her in. She led Marci to the family room at the end of the corridor. Murray was sitting on the couch with a full bottle of beer in front of him on the coffee table. He didn't stand but invited her to sit at the other end of the couch. Their ghostly reflections were captured in the floor-to-ceiling window.

"Surprised I agreed to speak with you?" he asked.

"Somewhat, but I'm glad you did. This is a lovely home. Was that your wife?"

"Yeah, that was her."

"Does she know about your cheap rent arrangements with select girls?"

He didn't question how she knew. "Broad strokes only. Believe it or not, she doesn't care what I get up to as long as I keep bringing home the cash. We have an open relationship."

"So, what is the arrangement, exactly?"

"I'm what you'd call a good Samaritan. I give a couple of women a discount on their rent and they agree to give me sex. That's it. A business transaction. I'm not the only landlord doing it and the girls know full well what they're getting into. Nothing for the Me Too movement to get their panties in a knot over."

"One might say you're taking advantage of vulnerable women who have no real choice." She thought she'd managed to keep the revulsion out of her voice, but he recoiled at whatever he saw in her eyes and turned his head to look out the window.

"Yeah, well, they could find somewhere else to live. I didn't force them. There's a selection of slum-lords in town. Shelters. Any number of places."

"I'm curious. Why did you let me in?"

"To convince you that I had nothing whatsoever to do with Nadia Armstrong's death. Sure, I gave her the business discount on her rent but I never killed her. In fact, we were both preparing to end the arrangement. She wasn't enthusiastic and said she could pay regular rent, and frankly, I was bored with her lack of energy. The cops want to believe the worst of me."

"Were you planning to raise her rent?"

"Crossed my mind, but not until the end of the lease, which comes up in September. She'd kept up her end even if the sex was lacklustre." He looked Marci full in the eyes. "I'm not as big a creep as you might think."

"You're too modest," she said, deadpan. "What about your brother? Is he in on this arrangement too?"

"Keep Jeff out of this. He's got a social gene missing and never meant to scare that girl."

"What did he do exactly?"

"He followed her around like a puppy dog. Her mother told the police that he was stalking her and had touched her inappropriately. I know for a fact she made that up."

"Aren't you worried that he might have become obsessed with Nadia?"

"He wouldn't have. I warned him about what would happen if I caught him following around any girl ever again. Believe me, he does not want to go back to live with our brother Lenny again."

"Why not?"

"Lenny owns a hog farm in Nebraska and Jeff thinks of going there as being banished. He'd do anything I say not to have to go back."

"So it's do as I say and not as I do?"

"Look, how many times do I have to tell you, the women agreed to the terms. I never did anything against their will."

"Technically speaking. Aren't you worried about your reputation after I write about this?"

"Not if you tell the truth."

She looked pointedly around the room. "You've done well for yourself. Accumulated lots of expensive stuff for a guy working at a construction company."

"I make a good salary and invest wisely. The apartment buildings bring in decent rent."

"How did you afford them in the first place?"

"My father also knew how to make money. He bankrolled the first one."

"Lucky you. Were you by any chance involved in landing the casino contract?"

"Not me. That's above my pay grade."

Marci stood to leave. She looked down at him. "You know anything about the two missing high school girls? If you have any leads on who took them, I won't say where I got the information."

The surprise that showed on his face didn't seem to be feigned. Was he surprised because he really hadn't known about the missing girls or because this turn in the conversation was unexpected? She believed he was being straight up about Nadia but she'd been fooled by liars before. Not often, but enough times to make her cautious.

"What missing high school girls?"

"You don't know about the AMBER alerts?"

"Sure, I heard something, but those girls got nothing to do with me."

"If any of your associates hear anything, let me know. Your co-operation could help your case."

"Like I said, I'm not up on the girls who disappeared, but I'll put out feelers."

She reached into her pocket and pulled out a business card. "Don't hesitate to call me when you have something."

"And in the meantime, you can convince that Woodbrain cop that he's barking up the wrong family tree."

She stared at him, looking for a trace of guile, but could see none. He was an abhorrent individual, but was he a killer? Her reporter's gut said no and yet Woodhouse was convinced that one of the brothers had murdered Nadia. She had a lot to mull over before deciding which way to go with this story.

There was no sign of his wife when she let herself out. The wind had come up and mouldy autumn leaves left unraked from the winter swirled in front of her as she hurried across the lawn to her car. She wanted more than anything to call Rouleau for an update on the search for Dawn and the other girl, Vanessa, but his recent coolness held her back. Their relationship had soured for a reason she couldn't identify. She'd have to contact her other sources when she got home. Scotty might have accepted her meagre offering on the missing girls today because of the time constraints but he'd be less accommodating two days in a row.

Pulling into her parking spot at her downtown half double, she remembered Gloria's comment about the bald man on the force who'd been a childhood friend of Mayor Tom Clement and Harold Mortimer. Was he in fact Rouleau? If so, why hadn't Rouleau mentioned their friendship whenever she'd talked about City Hall or the Mortimer projects going on around town? She'd made another connection since hearing the name Vanessa Jefferson. Mick Jefferson's architectural firm had designed the new casino for Mortimer Construction. Was this bit of business tangential to his daughter's disappearance? She thought about pointing out the connection to Rouleau but he might see that as interfering. She also knew more than she should about the case because of Woodhouse, so she had to be careful.

She replayed her many wide-ranging conversations with Rouleau when she finally sat down with a cup of tea in hand and a purring cat in her lap, but when she climbed the stairs to her empty bed an hour later, she was no closer to understanding the man whom she'd come to love and despair of in equal measure.

CHAPTER THIRTY-FIVE

Janet Dodd looked down at the Indigenous man lying on a gurney in intensive care. He was hooked up to an oxygen mask and a heart monitor that kept track of every beat. Five hours of surgery had stopped the internal bleeding but he'd lost a large quantity of blood. She adjusted the tubing running to his hand before turning to look at the police officer named Stonechild, sitting in the chair at the foot of the bed. She'd been asleep, her chin resting on a fist with her elbow propped up on the thigh of a crossed leg, but now her black eyes were open. Watchful.

"Is there any change?"

"No. His heart is holding steady, though. He's very weak." Janet was moved by the pain she saw in the officer's eyes. "Do you know him?"

"He's the father of someone I know. She's disappeared and he might have information that will help us find her."

"Those two teenage girls who've gone missing?"

Officer Stonechild didn't respond, and Janet straightened the bedcover before making one last check of the man's vital signs. She took another look at the officer. "It's late. You should go home and get some sleep. He could be out of it for a long time yet."

"I'll wait."

Janet could tell from the officer's face that arguing would be pointless. So instead, she went to the supply shelf and returned with a blanket, which she handed to Stonechild. "I'll be keeping a close eye on him, if you want to sleep. I can wake you if there's any change."

Officer Stonechild nodded and spread the blanket across her lap. She was soon dozing again in the chair, chin tucked into her jacket. Janet alternated between her two critical patients throughout the early morning. The officer was awake more often than she was asleep but she finally fell into a deeper slumber around 3:00 a.m. when Janet was spelled off for her break. Janet left instructions to waken Officer Stonechild if Fisher Dumont regained consciousness but she knew that the chances of that happening were slim.

In the small staff kitchen, she sat with a cup of coffee and the egg salad sandwich she'd brought from home. Someone had left a newspaper on the table and she reached for it. The teenage girls' disappearance was the front-page story but the article was short on details. Vanessa Jefferson and Dawn Cook. One white with blond hair, the other Indigenous with long black hair and bangs. They looked so young and earnest. There was no mention of the man lying in the intensive ward. The link between him and the missing Indigenous girl had not been made by the reporter. She wondered how the beat-up, emaciated man in the bed could possibly be this beautiful young girl's father. And where did Officer Stonechild fit in the chain of relationships? Janet finished her coffee and washed her hands before returning to relieve the nurse covering her break.

At 5:00 a.m., Stonechild stirred and Janet sensed her gaze before turning to her.

"Any change?"

Janet took a quick glance at the heart monitor. "His blood pressure is low but he's maintaining. He hasn't regained consciousness."

"I can't believe I actually slept." Stonechild stretched and asked, "Can I get you a coffee?" She pushed aside the blanket and got to her feet.

Janet smiled. "This is almost my bedtime but thanks for the offer." She glanced at the door. A tall, broad-shouldered man with curly blond hair and a beard stood framed in the small window. "I believe someone is here for you."

Janet saw Stonechild's troubled expression relax at the sight of the man. For some reason, knowing that the officer had someone to help her through this horrible time comforted Janet. Stonechild had seemed so solitary, so alone. She hadn't wanted to tell her that Fisher Dumont might never recover from his injuries. The surgeon had not been optimistic before releasing him to her care. Janet didn't want to be the one to extinguish the last vestige of hope in the officer's eyes.

Gundersund tried to keep the concern off his face as he pulled Stonechild into the visitors' lounge at the end of the corridor. Those who didn't know her well would wonder at the lack of emotion on her face but he wasn't fooled. She was coping the only way she knew how. Compartmentalizing and dealing with her fear by throwing herself into finding Dawn. He knew that she wouldn't allow herself a moment of weakness until this was all over.

"Sit with me for a bit," he said, and was relieved when she lowered herself next to him on the couch even though she kept a little distance from him. He wanted to wrap his arms around her but knew he shouldn't. He understood that she needed to stay within herself to keep going. "We will find her."

"I know."

"The entire country is watching for them; someone will see them. Somebody knows where they are. The team is personally reaching out to police across the province and into Quebec. We won't stop until we connect with every force."

"He knows something."

"Who?"

"Him." She swivelled her head toward the door. "Fisher Dumont. I feel it in my gut."

"Do you think he was part of it?"

"I don't know. Maybe he wanted to take her away and something went wrong."

"Rouleau is sending an officer to spell you off. They'll be here soon." He saw the stubborn look on her face and added gently, "You can't sit in there all day and night."

"I don't know what else to do."

"You can go home and get some real sleep. I'll let you know as soon as we find out anything."

She leaned closer and touched the scar on his cheek, running her fingertips along its length as lightly as a whisper. "You haven't slept either."

"I had a rest at work."

"Okay," she said pulling back. "I need to let Taiku out anyway."

He wasn't certain that he should trust her to sleep but he was glad that he'd convinced her to step away from the hospital and from work. "I promise to call you as soon as we have any news."

Her black eyes were exhausted but determined. "I'm going to get her back," she said. "If I have to track whoever took her to the ends of the earth, I'll do it. And then I'll make them pay."

"You won't be alone. I'll be right beside you." He kissed her on the mouth and promised again to call her the moment he got a lead. No matter how small.

CHAPTER THIRTY-SIX

Kala went home as she'd promised but not to rest. She fed Taiku and let him roam around outside while she had a quick shower and changed her clothes. After pouring a cup of coffee, she put on her jacket and sat outside on the back step as she worked through what to do next. She tried to set aside Rose's anger when she'd called to tell her Dawn was missing. She was barely able to deal with her own. If Fisher Dumont was behind Dawn's disappearance, she'd put him away for the rest of his life … if he recovered.

The blazing sun seemed like a rebuke. How could this be such a promising spring morning when all she felt was misery? The warming temperature and new growth in the garden that she and Dawn had planted together only added to her pain. The crocuses and daffodils were poking through the rich loam. She imagined Dawn's delight and blinked away the tears that threatened to fall. Taiku came bounding from the woods and ambled over to her, resting his head against her leg. He was out of sorts, waiting for Dawn to come home. She reached down to scratch his head. "We'll find her, boy. She's counting on us."

In the hospital, Kala had thought about Dawn's behaviour over the past week — stalling in the mornings before school and trying to out-wait her. Reluctant to take a ride when she was running late. Evasive and jumpy. She'd thought Dawn was hiding something but hadn't thought it was a person. Kala was convinced now that Dawn and Fisher had met up. Dawn hadn't told her that Fisher was camping out in the woods. The question was why not? Had he been threatening her or had he secured her silence for another reason? More importantly, why had he been struck and left for dead on the road if he was behind Dawn's disappearance? The facts didn't add up. She tried to take herself out of the equation and be objective. She kept returning to the idea that Fisher had actually been trying to prevent the abduction, that whoever took Dawn had run him down — but she needed confirmation.

Her phone buzzed and she looked at the call display. *At last.* "Yes, Dennis Wilburn? Thank you for getting back to me. As I said in my voicemail message, I need to know more about your client, Fisher Dumont."

"I've spoken with his doctor," Wilburn said. "His chances of ever waking up aren't good. Did you know that, Officer Stonechild?"

She squeezed her eyes shut. "They didn't tell me in so many words but I guessed."

She heard his sigh across the miles. "Fisher had so much potential but trouble had a way of finding him. I truly thought he might make it this time. He was off drugs and had this bit of hope about him that I hadn't seen before."

"Did you know that he has a daughter, Dawn?"

"He talked about her once. Said he'd screwed it up with the mother and wished he could go back and redo that period in his life. Be a better husband and father."

"I'm sure you've heard others say the same thing."

"Like variations on a theme? Yeah, the cynic in me understands talk is cheap and a tool of manipulation."

"I need to know if Fisher would ever hurt his daughter."

"My honest gut reaction? No. Fisher was a passive kind of guy. Fell into stuff but didn't initiate. He was genuinely regretful about missing out on Dawn's childhood."

"So somebody else might be calling the shots?"

"If he's involved, but I honestly don't think he'd jeopardize his daughter's well-being. Not knowingly. I'm sorry I can't help you further. Fisher worked as a dishwasher at the Venice Café but didn't associate with anybody after work. He kept a low profile since his release. I wouldn't even know who else you could talk to about him."

"If I have more questions, can I call you?"

"Any time. I hope Dawn is safely returned to you soon."

Feeling sick at heart, Kala ended the call and called for Taiku to come. *Now is not the time to give up*, she told herself. She'd walk the route that Dawn had taken and inspect the location where Fisher had been struck.

Hopefully she'd find something to shed light on the sequence of events.

She heard a car pulling into the driveway as she was locking the back door. She ran down the steps and across the lawn to greet her visitor. Taiku was ahead of her, already nuzzling his head against Marci Stokes's hand. Marci straightened and walked quickly toward Kala, embracing her for a long moment. "I'm so sorry this is happening," she said. "I want you to know that I'm poking around too, trying to find out where Dawn and Vanessa might be. I'm also after more information for today's article if you have anything to share that could help find them."

"I was going to walk up the road to see if I can piece any of it together."

"I'll come with you."

Kala felt comfortable striding alongside Marci, whose trademark trench coat flapped around her legs. Her auburn hair was a messy tousle that she ran her hand through periodically. She was wearing what looked like army boots over black stretch pants and her long red sweater had a snag below the neckline. She must have swiped a pen across her cheek because a streak of blue ink stained the skin below her left eye.

"Do you want to brainstorm?" Marci asked when they reached the end of the driveway. She linked her arm through Kala's.

"Are you writing about Nadia Armstrong too?"

"I am. Also, the casino contract that went to Mortimer Construction." She was silent a moment. "The Armstrong girl's body was found on the Mortimer building site."

"That's always bothered me," said Kala. "Why there?"

"Nadia was sleeping with her landlord, who works at Mortimer Construction, and it's a safe bet she didn't stop there. I looked at the map and there are a few motels out that way."

"She might have met a man for sex. They did drugs and her heart gave out so he panicked and shoved her off the seventh floor — that is, if the half-built hotel had been the rendezvous site."

"Could have happened that way."

"But why meet there and not in a motel?" asked Kala. "A bed is way more comfortable than a concrete slab."

"I don't know … for the thrill of it? Or maybe one of the workers wanted to give his boss the proverbial finger by screwing a hooker on the site."

"Or she was murdered somewhere else and the killer tried to make it look like a suicide."

"Another possibility."

They'd reached the location of the accident and stopped talking while Kala inspected the ground where Fisher's body had been found. She also checked the brush lining the road. "Nothing," she said. "I'm going to backtrack in the direction Fiona saw Dawn walking from the main road."

"I'll take the other side," said Marci.

They silently studied the pavement and scanned the bushes. When they reached the main road, they switched sides and retraced their steps back to Kala's laneway.

"Nothing," said Kala.

"What were you hoping for?"

"Signs of a struggle, maybe an item dropped by her or her abductor."

"You're sure she was taken against her will?"

"I'm certain of it. She must have seen something or known something about Vanessa's disappearance so they came for her too."

They'd stopped walking and were facing one another. Kala kept talking. "I think all the evidence points to human trafficking. An older man named Leo met Vanessa online. She was struggling with her parents' divorce, angry and ripe for the picking. This Leo kept his real identity a secret from everyone who knew her. Isolated her."

"And now she's missing."

They stared at one another. "Could the girls' disappearance be connected to Nadia Armstrong?" asked Marci, "All three are young, vulnerable women."

"You're making connections that have no basis," said Kala, "but you're not going anywhere I haven't been myself, trying to figure this out."

"What now?"

"You've given me an idea worth pursuing. I'm going to the hotel construction site to speak with the foreman, Bill Lapointe. He might know of any workers who'd want to stick it to Mortimer Construction. What about you?"

"I have a couple of articles to write and deadlines to meet." Marci pulled her car keys out of her pocket. "You be careful. The person angry with Mortimer might even be Lapointe. These people aren't fooling around." She took a step toward her car and stopped. "The receptionist at Mortimer Construction told me something odd. She said that Harold Mortimer, Mayor Clement, and a bald cop on the Kingston force have been tight since they were kids. My first thought was Rouleau but he's never acted as if he knew them that well. I was thinking that Woodhouse is bald and could have been in with the others, even though he's younger."

"Why would that be important?"

"She said that they fixed the contract for the casino. I need more proof before going public but I thought the announcement smelled fishy from the start. I'm going to keep digging. One more oddity: Vanessa Jefferson's father is the architect who drew up the plans for the casino. That's a lot of connections, don't you think?"

Kala had a sudden premonition that sent a chill up her back despite the warmth of the day. "You need to be careful too. These are powerful men and a lot of their money hangs on keeping their reputations unsullied. They won't like feeling threatened."

"I know, but somebody has to hold them to account." Marci gave her a grim smile before getting into her car. She waved after she backed out of the driveway and then drove slowly up the road they'd just walked searching for signs of Dawn.

Kala heard construction noise through her lowered window before the dark towering skeleton of the hotel came into view above the pine trees. More of the openings had been bricked in and the roof was one-third complete. She parked along the side of the road and walked past the line of trucks that fed onto the construction site. She stopped for a moment to study the workers on the roof and the inside of the structure. Electricians were running wires and she heard intermittent hammering and drilling coming from different floors. She spotted Bill Lapointe's white hard hat on the ground level, through what would be the main entrance to the hotel, and crossed the uneven dirt walkway toward him. A man standing next to Lapointe pulled on his sleeve and pointed toward her before she entered. She watched Lapointe roll the document he'd been reading into a tube. He said something to the man who'd alerted him to her presence before walking over to her.

"I'd like to ask you a few more questions," she yelled above the construction racket. He motioned for her to follow him back down the road. The cacophony dropped several decibels, enough so they could hear each other. Lapointe pulled out a pack of cigarettes and lit one while he waited for her to talk. Kala opened her notebook and felt for a pen inside her jacket pocket.

"How do you like working here?" she asked.

"Well enough. Construction's no picnic, but it pays the rent."

"Have you been with Mortimer long?"

"Eight years, give or take. I was working on a project in Ottawa and they moved me here last year to handle this build."

"Mortimer has an office in Ottawa?"

"Yup. We'll take on projects around the valley too. Got a condo job on the go in Brockville and a fire station in Pembroke."

Kala filed away the information and watched him as she said, "Nadia Armstrong's body was dropped off of this hotel, which has always struck me as an odd choice of location. They'd have to have known it was here and how to get to the seventh floor in the dark. Do you know of any workers who might be angry with the company or who might want to stick it to Mortimer for some reason?"

Lapointe laughed. "You're not always dealing with the most upstanding segment of society when it comes to some of the trades. Several of the guys have done time, but I have to say, they aren't likely to bite the hand feeding them. They also wouldn't be stupid enough to kill a woman where they work. That'd be like shitting in your own nest."

"You're right." She watched an eagle soaring high above their heads, its wings spread wide, riding a current. "Anyone quit recently?"

Lapointe scratched his temple. "We hire from a union pool now and then, so they come and go. Fired a guy a few months ago. He wasn't too pleased."

"Do you have a name?"

"Uh, Lenny somebody. I don't remember."

His gaze shifted away from hers. Kala detected a lie. "Do you recall what he looked like?"

"Not really. I don't spend much time getting to know the occasional workers. He was a labourer brought in on someone's recommendation. He was lazy and had zero skills so we let him go."

"Would any of the other guys know more about him?"

"Maybe, but I doubt it."

"You must have his contact info."

"The office would have it. You sure this is important?"

"We're looking at all angles."

"Makes sense, I guess." He sucked on the cigarette like a baby with a pacifier. Smoke poured out of his nose. "Anything else? I have to get back to work." He tossed the cigarette butt onto the gravel.

"Do prostitutes come to the site?"

Surprisingly, he wasn't taken aback by her question. "Not here."

"Then where?"

"Some of the guys talk about going to the Blue Nights Motel, not far from the site. To be clear, I have no personal knowledge."

"Are we talking young girls?"

"I wouldn't know."

"Well, thanks for your time."

She got into her truck and called Morrison to contact the Mortimer office about the elusive Lenny. She deliberately chose Morrison, knowing Gundersund or Rouleau would tell her to stay home and rest. "I'm going to the Blue Nights Motel," she added before hanging up, "to check out a tip."

"Stay in touch," said Morrison. "And call me if you need backup."

CHAPTER THIRTY-SEVEN

Fisher was breathing on his own but an oxygen mask covered his mouth. Woodhouse sat in the chair vacated by the last officer on watch and stretched out his legs while crossing his arms across his chest. He'd agreed to a two-hour shift over the supper hour after which he planned to cruise the streets on his way home to look for the missing girls. More than twenty-four hours without sleep ... the warm hospital room was making his eyes close. He felt himself dozing and jerked himself awake, staring at the man in the bed who was not expected to survive. Woodhouse forced himself to stand up and moved to the head of the bed.

"You're one poor miserable bugger," he said. "What were you doing that got you into this condition?"

Woodhouse had heard that talking to comatose patients sometimes brought them around. He wasn't convinced but talking would help him to stay awake. The word from HQ was that this sad specimen of a man was Dawn's father and that he could have witnessed something that would lead to her whereabouts. Woodhouse had met Dawn a couple of times and knew she'd had it rough. He'd never admit it to anybody but she reminded him of his own little sister, Cassie, who would have been thirty-five now if she'd lived past her sixteenth birthday. She'd had that same quiet exterior you could read as strength but that he'd known was an illusion. He was twenty-four when Cassie took her own life. He'd moved into his own apartment six months before she died, leaving her alone with an alcoholic father and a bitter mother who hated every person in her life by that point, her children in line behind her husband. He'd thought his dependable sister would be able to handle them with him gone. His mistake was his burden.

The nurse made a drive-by, checking Fisher's vitals and reading the heart machine before she moved on to check her other patients. They hadn't wheeled Fisher out of the critical care ward yet. Gurneys with fresh patients were being rolled in and out. The luckier ones stabilized and got moved to another floor before too long. When Woodhouse have first arrived to take up watch, he'd witnessed a frantic flurry of white coats working around one man before the sheet was pulled up over his face and he was taken away.

"I'm going to check Fisher's temperature," said the nurse close to his right ear. She'd come up behind him on silent feet.

"Is there any change?" asked Woodhouse, taking a step back but remaining standing.

"He's still critical."

She made notes on his chart and straightened the sheet after she was done. "I have a new patient being brought in from surgery so we'll be busy for the next while."

"I don't know how you do it. This steady stream of patients and no time in between."

Her serious face relaxed into a smile. "You get used to it."

He wanted to ask her if it was true that speaking to a comatose patient could help bring them around but she'd already gone. He moved back into position near the head of the bed. Sitting down would mean instant sleep so he'd keep upright even though his legs ached and the chair was looking damn attractive. He thought he heard a groan coming through the raspy breathing rising up from the bed and he leaned closer.

"You okay there, buddy?" Of course he wasn't. Woodhouse checked to make certain nobody was close enough to overhear him. He felt stupid enough talking to a guy who was unconscious without getting razzed about it later. "Thing is, we need you to wake up so we can find out who's taken your daughter. Dawn's in trouble and you're the only one who can help."

This time he knew he wasn't imagining the eye movement and the sounds coming out of Fisher's mouth. He kept going. "Dawn's missing, man, and we've got no leads. You were the only one to see her get taken and we need you to wake up and tell us who's got her. She's counting on you, Fisher. Talk to me, man." He was guessing about Fisher being the last one to see her but Stonechild seemed to think he knew something.

Fisher was trying to get some words out and the line on the heart machine was going crazy. Woodhouse knew this might be his only chance. He lifted the oxygen mask and put his mouth next to Fisher's ear. "Dawn needs you. Who took her? You've got to give me a name. Dawn's counting on you."

"Bruuu."

"I need a name. Try harder."

"Braaa ... ggg."

He could hear the nurse's footsteps thumping toward him. "What are you doing?" she asked, her voice low and angry. Woodhouse chanced her ire and blocked her view of Fisher for a few more seconds. "Come on, Fisher. Give me something to save Dawn." The nurse was looking at the heart machine and buzzing for assistance. Woodhouse leaned closer and Fisher's eyes flickered open. He made a couple of new sounds that sounded like numbers. His eyes rolled back. The nurse elbowed her way between them and all but shoved Woodhouse out of the way as he let the oxygen mask drop back into place on Fisher's face. "You'll have to wait outside," she ordered. "Go now and stay in the waiting room until we allow you back in."

He took one last look at Fisher but left without argument. Once in the hall he pulled out his note-pad and wrote down what he'd heard before he felt the nurse's elbow in his ribs. He tried to make sense of it. Thought of what Fisher might have witnessed as Dawn was being taken and where he'd seen this pattern before. "Why, you wily old bastard," he said, recognition dawning on him. "If this bears out, you'll be my new hero."

He took out his phone and scrolled through to his buddy's number. It was late but he'd still be able to track this down and it wouldn't take long. The guy owed him a few favours. He sure hoped he was right about what Fisher had been trying to tell him and that he wasn't off on a wild goose chase. He'd wait for the info to come in to make sure he'd cracked this before phoning it in to HQ.

Dawn and Vanessa huddled together on the couch and watched Leo pacing in front of them, talking on his cellphone. He was upset and distracted and Dawn considered how she could use this to their advantage. "I'm not evil," he'd said when he let them out of the basement after a full day of shivering in the cold. "This is just business."

Vanessa had roused herself enough to say, "I thought I meant something to you."

"You do, baby, but I can't let my feelings get in the way. It might have gone differently if you hadn't seen that dead girl at the motel."

Dawn kept her eyes straight ahead. Kala was working on a case about a woman who'd been found dead on a construction site. Was Vanessa holding something back about why they'd been brought here? She wanted Vanessa to respond but she stayed silent. She'd have to wait until Leo left them alone.

"I want them gone," he said into the phone. "Shawn is bailing. Yeah, he says this is all bullshit and I'm starting to freak." He listened and paced and then said, "You make sure and it better happen soon." He shoved the phone back into his pocket and glared at them. "What're you two looking at?"

His phone buzzed a message and he pulled it out again, standing in place as he read. "Shawn'll be here in an hour. What am I going to do with you until then?" Leo's gaze settled on Vanessa. "This could be our last chance to say goodbye." His smile was more of a leer and Vanessa flattened herself against the cushions. Her eyes looked wildly around the room for escape.

Dawn grabbed onto Vanessa's arm as Leo pulled her up from the couch, but he wrestled Vanessa away from her. "Stand there," he told Vanessa, pointing to a spot on the floor. He backed into the kitchen and returned with a knife and some twine. He cut off a few lengths and told Dawn to sit in the straight-backed chair near the doorway. He tied her wrists together and then tied her arms to the chair. "You sit here nice and quiet, and this won't take long."

Vanessa was waiting silently behind him, not even trying to get away. Dawn wanted to scream at her to do something but she had that same faraway, dead look in her eyes, just like before. Leo turned when he was done with his knots and shoved Vanessa forward in front of him to the bedroom off the side of the living room. Dawn waited until the door was shut before she began working at the knots. Lucky for her, Leo clearly hadn't been a boy scout and she'd managed to hold her wrists apart slightly as he tied them together. It didn't take her long to worm one wrist out of the twine. A minute later and she was free.

She stood and looked at the closed door. Should she try to rescue Vanessa or get out while she could and find help? She had no idea how long she had before Shawn showed up and she couldn't fight off two of them, especially with Vanessa acting like a walking zombie. A quick scan of the room didn't reveal any handy makeshift weapons and the thought of using a kitchen knife on Leo didn't appeal to her. She made her decision and moved silently toward the back door.

The kitchen was still a mess and smelled of stale pizza and beer. She tiptoed across the floor, holding her breath. The phone on the wall made her pause but the urge to flee kept her moving. She unlocked the deadbolt as quietly as she could and collided with the screen door before she realized it was also locked. Her frantic fingers found the hook and then she was outside, pulling the doors shut quietly. She turned and scanned the darkness, letting her eyes adjust for a moment. The back-door light of the neighbour's house was on and she started running in that direction. Halfway across the yard, she could see that the inside of the house was in darkness and her spirits dropped. She'd have to keep going and hope someone was home farther on.

Before she made it past the leading edge of the house, a car slowed on the main road, the arc of its headlights barely missing her as they swung up the driveway between the two houses. Dawn flattened herself against a wall and stayed motionless while she watched Shawn jump out of the black car that had brought her here. As soon as he entered the back door, she ran across the neighbour's yard in the direction of the water and the temporary safety of the trees.

CHAPTER THIRTY-EIGHT

The man behind the counter at the Blue Nights Motel was an innocent babe in the woods, if Kala was to believe his version of the truth. He'd never seen any prostitutes on the premises, let alone under-age girls. Mind you, he only worked nights and most patrons were already tucked safely in their rooms by the time he took over. "Sure, have a look around," he said to her at the end of his stream of bullshit.

Kala tried unsuccessfully to get a view of the TV screen behind the desk. "What about security cameras? Do you have tapes of people coming and going?"

"Nah, we live stream to the office but don't keep any of the feed. It's not like we're a high-security building." He laughed, showing teeth browned from nicotine. "I can let you into a room if you want but they're basic places to sleep. No frills."

"If it's not too much trouble."

He jangled a ring of keys as he led her to room eleven. He hadn't padded his description of the decor. Her eyes took in the off-orange bedspread, scarred brown headboard, and green-and-gold patterned carpet. The desk under the window had a vinyl-covered chair and a small fridge tucked underneath. She remembered seeing the black-and-white flower pictures hanging above the bed at Ikea. She checked the bathroom. Cramped shower, toilet, and sink with a yellowish stain surrounding the drain.

"Do people pay by the hour?" she asked as he locked up.

"Not that I'm aware."

"Do you know a guy named Lenny?"

"Lenny?" he turned, a puzzled expression on his face. "No, can't place anyone by that name."

She pulled out her phone and showed him photos of Nadia Armstrong, Vanessa Jefferson, and Dawn Cook. He shook his head each time. "Like I said, I'm not here during the day."

Kala knew that he couldn't be that unaware of what was going on but she had nothing to use to leverage the truth out of him. The innocent look on his face was at odds with the cunning in his blue eyes, magnified to an owlish intensity by his black-rimmed glasses.

"I'll be back tomorrow," she said.

He nodded. "I'll leave a note that you're coming."

She had no doubt that he was on the phone to his boss before she even reached her truck. She slammed the steering wheel with the heel of her palms. The answers felt close and yet out of reach. Taiku got up from where he'd been lying on the passenger seat and began licking the side of her face until she flung an arm around him. "It's okay, boy. I'm not upset with you."

Now what?

She turned on the engine and let the truck idle while she considered her next move. Her phone vibrated in her pocket and she pulled it out. "Yeah, Stonechild here."

"And Woodhouse here. I have something. Can you meet me in front of the Merchant in ten? Park your truck and we can take my car. It's less obvious."

"What are you talking about?"

"I have a lead we need to check out."

Kala started to ask him again what was going on but the line went dead in her ear. "What the hell, Woodhouse?" she muttered. She had nowhere else to be so she put the truck in gear and started downtown. At least this errand would keep her from thinking too much about all she was in danger of losing.

Woodhouse was waiting for her at the main entrance, his car idling in the no-parking zone. Kala settled Taiku in his back seat before climbing into the front. Her phone rang as she was buckling up her seatbelt and she answered after glancing over at Woodhouse. He was doing a shoulder check and pulling onto the street.

"Hey, Gundersund," she said. She kept her eyes on Woodhouse. "Yes, I'm with Woodhouse and we're going to check out a lead." She listened for a moment. "I'll put the phone on speaker. Where are we going?" she asked Woodhouse.

"Fisher gave me the licence plate number of the car that hit him. At least, I'm hoping that's what he told me. I got a name and address for the owner of a black Audi and I thought Stonechild and I could go have a look. I could be totally wrong, however, so I didn't want to raise the cavalry yet, especially considering the name of the owner."

"Who?"

"Leonard Clement."

Gundersund was quiet as Kala connected the name to her leads. "Leonard, Lenny, Leo. Is he the guy Vanessa was dating?"

Woodhouse glanced at her. "That was my thought. He's the mayor's youngest son, if you haven't pieced it together yet. Living in a family rental property at 533 Rudd Avenue, east of the city off Highway 2."

Gundersund's voice filled the space between them. "Bennett and I will meet you there. Wait for us before you approach."

Kala pulled the phone back. "Don't tell anybody else." She wasn't sure why the thought came to her but mention of the mayor made her wary. He had connections everywhere, and she didn't want this Leonard to get advance warning. "Let's make sure we've got the right guy before we bring any others into it."

She ended the call. Woodhouse drove slowly across the causeway but picked up speed as they passed the military college.

"Did Fisher wake up?" she asked.

"He surfaced for a moment, but I wouldn't say he was completely conscious. He might have woken up after I left."

She sensed a curious tone in his voice and wondered what he wasn't telling her. "Did he say anything else?"

"No. Dawn must have been on his mind."

She looked out the side window and let his statement hang unquestioned, like the opening to a hornet's nest that she couldn't allow herself to explore. They drove farther into the country, Woodhouse following his GPS but staying on Highway 2. The lights inside houses and businesses zipped past, breaking up the stretches of pitch black. "Never been on Rudd Avenue before," he said, slowing down and scanning the road in front of them. "Looks like it has two exits off the highway. GPS says to turn off at the far one."

He veered right at the last second onto Park Place, a narrow, paved side road blocked on both sides by spindly black elm trees and brush. It jogged to the right and short driveways led to small houses on either side, separated from each other by long hedges or pockets of woods. Kala knew that the properties on the left trailed down to the water even though the darkness hid the lake from view. She strained to see the house numbers under the porch lights. They rounded a bend lined with trees and kept going. The houses were eclectic, some small ancient cottages, others new constructions set farther back from the road. Another swoop right and the trees were thicker, the buildings more spread out, with longer stretches of lawn.

"It's that small place on the left," said Woodhouse. "The Audi is in the driveway. Licence plate BRAG 213," he said under his breath. He slowly reversed and pulled onto the shoulder, where a wide stretch of pavement sat empty in front of a two-car garage. They could observe from a distance without being obvious.

"It's got no neighbour on this side and looks to share a driveway with the house on its left," said Kala. "Lights are on inside."

Woodhouse lowered his window and they listened to the wind. Kala felt a damp breeze moisten her face. Taiku was restless in the back seat and moved into position behind Woodhouse with his nose close to the window.

"I'd like to get out and have a look around," said Kala.

"Gundersund said to sit tight so we probably should."

She thought about ignoring him and taking a walk down the road on the shadowy side of the street. Sitting here doing nothing was not her style. She had her hand on the door handle when she heard a vehicle approaching from the other direction. Its headlights rounded the corner and Kala and Woodhouse slumped low in their seats. "Down, Taiku," Kala ordered and heard him drop onto the back seat. The car pulled into the driveway of the house they were watching.

"Can you see who it is?" Kala asked.

Woodhouse had his phone out and was taking pictures even though the lack of light would likely make the images useless, in Kala's estimation. That and the bushes blocked most of their view. The front door of the house opened and a young man in his midtwenties with longish hair, wearing a black jacket and jeans, emerged and ran down the walkway to lean in the front passenger window of the car. The driver kept the engine running while they talked. The young man pointed toward the neighbour's backyard. A second man who also looked to be in his midtwenties came out of the front door of the house and approached the car. He was wearing a ball cap and a thick beard covered most of his face. Both men looked toward the woods.

"Do you think one of the girls got away?" asked Kala.

"Something out there definitely has their attention."

As they watched, the car backed out of the driveway and started slowly up the road in the same direction as it had come. They were too far away to read the licence plate or to see inside the car. Leo and his friend were running toward the neighbour's property.

Woodhouse and Kala opened their doors at the same time, but before Woodhouse got his closed, Taiku pushed past him from the back seat and leapt out of the car, disappearing into the darkness.

Kala whistled for him to come back but he was gone.

"Don't yell for him," said Woodhouse. "They can't know we're here."

"I'm going after them," said Kala.

"Then I'm coming with you. We can split up when we get closer and be backup for each other." Woodhouse pulled his service revolver out of the holster inside his jacket and Kala did likewise. She'd been carrying her weapon ever since Dawn went missing.

She checked to see whether Gundersund and Bennett were approaching as they ran toward the house but there was no sign of their car. "Should we look inside the house first?" she asked. The wind was whipping her hair around her face and the cool air made her shiver inside her jacket.

"We don't have a warrant."

"Probable cause. Don't you think you hear a girl screaming?"

"I think I do."

They approached the front door cautiously, one on either side of the entrance, guns pointing at the ground. Kala turned the handle. The door opened into an empty front room. "Do you want to wait here and I'll do a check?" she asked.

"I'll go straight ahead. You get the door on the left." He strode past her without waiting for a response. She opened the door to a bedroom: a depressing, claustrophobic room with a small window high up, a bare lightbulb on the ceiling, and a smell of mould and sweat that made her eyes water. Sheets and blankets were bunched up at the bottom of the bed but nobody was in it. She looked inside the small closet. It was filled with men's clothing. A second door opened on a bedroom much the same as the first although the bed was made and there were fewer clothes in the closet. She shut the door and hurried into the kitchen. The stink of stale food and beer was strong and she wasn't surprised to see stained pizza boxes and empties stacked on the floor and on the grey linoleum countertop. The door to the basement stood ajar.

She approached and looked down into the murk. Another bare bulb hung from the ceiling at the bottom of the stairs. "Woodhouse?"

He appeared under the light. His face was ashen in the harsh glare. "Dawn made a run for it. I have the other girl here and she needs an ambulance."

"I'm going to find Dawn."

"I can't leave this one down here alone."

"I know. You stay. I'll be okay on my own."

Even if I'm not.

Kala unlocked the back door and stumbled across the uneven yard toward the woods, fear pulsing in her throat. She flashed back to the cottage in Smiths Falls when Bennett had been shot, and even further back in time to her and Rose running from the man in the van. Anyone could be hiding in the woods, waiting for a chance to kill in the dark. But Dawn needed her to be strong ... and Taiku. She couldn't lose either one of them. She saw the arc of a flashlight bobbing far off in the direction of the water. Resolve made the panic disappear and her feet begin running toward the light.

CHAPTER THIRTY-NINE

Dawn quickly realized that she couldn't outrun them or hide for long. The woods were not thick or extensive and the lake cut off her exit path. She could keep going and hope somebody took her into their house, but she didn't feel safe exposing herself on the open stretch of lawn that she'd have to cross to get to a back door. Would she be putting somebody else in danger? How many people would Leo be willing to hurt to get her back?

I won't let them take me to the cottage or do to me what they were doing to Vanessa. They'll have to kill me first.

Once she knew in her being that she was prepared to die, the terror went away and she was at peace with whatever was to come. She stopped at the edge of the wood and bent over to catch her breath with her hands on her knees.

But I won't go easily. What should I do, Aunt Kala?

She straightened and looked up at the sky for an answer. That was when she spotted the pine tree at the edge of the clearing. If she could get high up in the tree, they might not think to look for her there. She'd fight them every inch of the way down if they did find her. It took a few tries to find a toehold, but luckily, the lowest branch was in reach once she hoisted herself up a few feet. She pulled herself over and continued climbing, testing each branch before putting her full weight on it. She settled on a bough and wrapped her arms around the tree, taking comfort from its solid strength. They would probably be able to see her from the ground if they shone a light upwards but she'd sit perfectly still and hope they didn't.

Not long afterward, she counted two flashlight beams metres apart, criss-crossing the ground in the darkness and coming from the direction of Leo's house. They were slowly moving her way, searching for her like bloodhounds on the trail of her scent. She heard a rustling in the bushes before a sharp bark rose up from the darkness below the tree. She looked down and thought she was hallucinating. The dark shape standing under the tree looked a lot like Taiku. The animal had its front paws on the tree trunk and was staring up at her through the branches. She blinked twice and rubbed a hand across her eyes. The dog was still there. Dawn's heart lightened even though her whole body began to tremble.

"Taiku," she said. "Go find Kala. Go, go." Fear made her voice high and shrill but she couldn't have them find Taiku or her hiding place. "Go! Away and find Kala!" She said it with more authority and Taiku dropped his paws to the ground. He whined and looked up at her before running off into the trees.

Kala is nearby. Vanessa and I are going to get out of this.

The wind was strong enough to make the smaller branches sway but the larger boughs remained relatively still. The clouds that had covered the moon were scudding eastward and the night was brighter. One flashlight beam stopped at the spot where she'd first spotted the pine. The second flashlight made its way to the same place and she could hear the low murmur of their voices. She knew they were deciding what to do next, which direction to track her. One of the flashlight beams swung in an arc beneath her tree and across the backyards of the closest houses. She sat as still as she could, willing them to leave. Instead, the lights moved closer until they were almost directly below her. She prayed that Taiku wasn't in the bushes nearby.

"I'm doubling back to my car." A voice that she didn't recognize. "Don't return without her."

"What if she's in somebody's house?"

"Christ, you've really balled this up." A long pause. "Call me if it turns out she's talked to somebody. I'll have to handle it."

"Shit, what's that?" Leo's voice, startled and full of fear. "Where did this crazy dog come from?"

Taiku was under the tree barking, defending her, sensing the danger. She squinted as the flashlight beam swung upward and impaled her in its glare.

"She's up there." The flashlight beam arced down and back up again. "In the tree."

The light was blinding her; she covered her eyes with her hand. The panic that surged through her was as much for Taiku as for herself.

"Get out of the tree or we kill the dog."

She wasn't sure which one of them had spoken but she could tell he wasn't making an idle threat. "I'm coming down," she said. "Don't hurt him." She felt for toeholds and lowered herself from the tree, landing with a thump on her feet next to Taiku. The ground jolted up her backbone but she remained upright.

"You stupid bitch," said Leo. He was shining the flashlight in front of her and she could see him and Shawn with another man a few steps back. Leo made a move to grab her arm but Taiku got in front of her and bared his teeth, a low rolling growl coming from his throat. Dawn looked past Shawn to the third man who'd receded into the shadows.

"You've set us behind schedule," said Leo. "You must have known you wouldn't get away. What, were you going to leave your friend back there all alone? Not very nice." He turned his head to look at Shawn. "Do something about the dog."

"*You* do something about the dog."

"Either one of you touches the dog and you'll regret it." Kala stepped out of the darkness and stood with her gun levelled at the ground between Leo and Shawn. "Taiku, down. Come over here, Dawn."

"There's another one," Dawn said. "He was with them a second ago."

Kala was surveying the woods but seemed satisfied there was no immediate danger. "He's making a run for it, no doubt. Left the two of you to clean up this mess, right, Leonard Clement?"

Shawn shoved Leo against the tree with both hands. "Just great. I'm not taking the fall for any of this."

"Shut up."

"I'm not doing time for you or your seriously fucked-up family."

Leo shoved him back. "I said shut up!"

"Both of you put your hands on your heads and face away from each other."

Shawn put his hands up but stayed in place. "I knew I shouldn't have come back. I *knew* this shit show was going to hell."

"I *said*, turn around." Kala tucked her gun into her belt and pulled out handcuffs. She grabbed their arms and yanked them close to each other, snapping the cuffs on their wrists so that they were attached together. She patted them down roughly.

Gundersund emerged from the woods with his gun drawn just as she finished with Leo. The tension in his face relaxed when he took in the scene. "Looks like you have it all under control, partner," he said. "Dawn, are you okay?"

"I'm okay."

Kala nodded at Gundersund to take over and stepped back to wrap her arms around Dawn. She didn't say anything but Dawn felt her aunt's heart beating hard against her own.

"I knew you'd come," she said. "I knew …" Dawn stopped. "Vanessa. She's in the house."

"We've got her," said Gundersund. "You're both safe now."

Kala gave her one more long squeeze before letting go. Dawn dropped down to rest her head on Taiku's. "Such a good boy," she said into his ear. "You're such a good boy." He licked her cheek and stayed by her side as Kala led them out of the trees to the road.

CHAPTER FORTY

Rouleau decided to question Shawn Baxter alone in the interview room with a video camera rolling and a mic recording every word. Shawn had the look of a tough street thug but the possibility of life inside had him rattled. Like he'd do anything to shift the blame away from himself. Rouleau offered Shawn a soda and something to eat. Made sure he was warm enough. Comfortable. Then he began to work Shawn in earnest, maintaining a low-key, friendly tone, like a father talking with his son. His patience began to bear fruit around the two-hour mark.

"Yeah, Leo was dating Vanessa and he brought up the idea of making money for sex."

"She was willing?"

"She was hot for Leo. Yeah, she went along."

"Did you pay her for sex?"

"No, man, nothing like that." Shawn was sitting back in the chair with his legs spread wide apart. He held on to his Coke can with one hand while his other hand rested on his thigh. "I only partied with her the one time and she was, like, more than willing."

"Do you know how old she is?"

A too-earnest furrowing of the brow. "Seventeen? Eighteen?"

Rouleau pulled back. Pointing out that Shawn knew Vanessa was fifteen would only put him on the defensive, break the rhythm they'd established. Instead, Rouleau changed the line of questioning. "Why did you agree to take Dawn on her way home from school?"

"Leo said he wanted to talk to her, and she got in the car."

"You didn't help her get inside?"

"No. I opened the door and she got in by herself."

Another lie that Rouleau let go for now. "So Leo was driving."

"Yeah."

"He was driving when the car struck a man named Fisher Dumont."

"Yeah. I told him to stop and check it out but he said he'd hit a deer and it got away into the woods. I didn't question it, man."

"Fisher Dumont is still in a coma."

Shawn dropped his head and shook it back and forth. "That blows. That really blows."

Rouleau looked at the top of Shawn's head for fifteen seconds before checking a message on his phone. "Why don't we take a short break. Would you like a sandwich?"

Eyes up. "Another Coke would be good too."

Gundersund was waiting for him in the hall with an update on Woodhouse's interview with Leo.

"He's lawyered up and his father the mayor is in the building putting pressure on Ellington, who's putting pressure on us to get this settled."

"That's all we need. Has Leo said what he was doing with Vanessa in his basement and Dawn running to get away?"

"Only that the girls were there of their own volition. He says he told them they could leave whenever they wanted. He'd be happy to drive them home."

"Did Woodhouse point out the evidence to the contrary?"

"He did."

"And?"

"Leo claims the girls know they'll get into trouble, so they're lying." Gundersund's voice was worried. "There's one more thing. Shawn's lawyer is on her way and you're not to continue interviewing him until she's here."

"He was just starting to talk. I'm going to have a chat with Ellington — I need more time. Can you have another Coke and a sandwich brought in to Shawn?"

"Sure thing."

Rouleau was heading to his office when Bennett called him over. "Morrison is getting Dawn's statement and she thinks you should step in for a minute."

"Did Dawn get medical attention?"

"She refused to go to the hospital with Vanessa but a paramedic at the scene took her vitals and said she's fine. She wasn't raped."

"Thank God for that."

Rouleau found Morrison and Dawn in his office, sitting on the couch. Dawn smiled when she saw him and he wondered at her strength. She reminded him of Stonechild, who was sitting in a chair close by. Taiku was lying at Dawn's feet. Rouleau crossed the room and took Dawn's hand. "How are you?"

"They didn't hurt me. I wish I could say the same for Vanessa."

"We'll make sure Vanessa is well looked after. You've both been extremely brave."

"Leo was making her have sex with other men, but I don't think that's why they took us. Vanessa saw the dead girl with a man at the Blue Nights Motel. She told Leo that she didn't get a look at the man, but she told me that she lied about that. They didn't believe her, anyway. They thought she'd recognized the man, and she had. She said there was no way he'd let anybody find out."

"Did she tell you this man's name?"

Dawn shook her head. "But Leo was on the phone a lot with somebody who was telling him what to do. They were getting ready to move me and Vanessa somewhere away from Kingston."

"Do you know why they took you?"

Dawn looked at her hands. "I got in the car with Leo and Vanessa after school one day. They drove me to the library. I think they were worried I'd talk about Leo and the car once Vanessa went missing for good. Shawn was mad at Leo for giving me a ride. He said this was all his fault for being so stupid."

Rouleau met Kala's eyes. He could see a cold anger in her that worried him. She was capable of setting out on her own to make these people pay. He asked her to walk with him.

Stonechild waited until they were alone in the hallway before speaking. "The third person was in the woods where we found Dawn but he slipped away before we caught him. Woodhouse and I saw him pull up in a car and talk to Leo and Shawn before they went looking for Dawn. He stayed in the car and drove up the road, away from us, so we didn't see him."

"You're sure it was a man?"

"Quite sure. He might be working for somebody else but I can't believe a woman would be behind this." The uncertainty in her voice belied her words.

"I need to get Shawn to talk."

"He's the weak link, as far as I can see."

Rouleau paused. "Dawn is a remarkable kid. You're doing a great job raising her, Kala."

"I can't take credit but thank you. If they'd laid a hand on her …"

"Justice will be done. We have to play this by the book."

She nodded, but Rouleau wasn't convinced she agreed. "I'm taking Dawn to see Fisher when she's finished giving her statement," she said. "No matter what mistakes he made in his life, he saved hers."

"Call me later. And Stonechild …"

"Yes?"

Rouleau swallowed his warning. "Nothing. Check in from the hospital."

He watched her walk away. He couldn't shake the feeling that more bad stuff was coming but he didn't know how to head it off.

Vera was at her desk and told him that Ellington had gone to a meeting off-site. Rouleau had no choice but to follow orders and stop his interview with Shawn until his lawyer arrived.

"We could go home if you don't feel up to seeing your father now," said Kala, glancing at Dawn. "It's almost midnight."

Dawn looked out the truck's passenger window. "I want to see him." She knew that he was still in a coma and that the doctor wasn't optimistic. He'd suffered severe internal injuries. Kala had told her straight up without sugar-coating the truth. This might be her last chance.

They parked in the hospital parking lot and took the elevator to the third floor. Dawn waited by the desk until Kala had cleared their visit with the intensive care nurse. The adrenaline and fear that had carried her over the last few hours had been replaced with sadness for her dad. She'd only begun to get to know him, and now, like everyone else in her life, he was being taken from her.

"I'll come in for a minute and then wait for you in the hall. You can take as long as you need," said Kala.

"You can stay with me if you want."

"I think you should have some time alone."

Kala didn't add, *to say goodbye*, but knew she didn't need to. Dawn walked slowly up to the bed. Fisher looked so sick and smaller than she remembered. An oxygen mask covered his mouth and nose, and he was hooked up to some machines by a tube taped to his hand. Kala's fingers rested lightly on her back. "He's not in any pain."

"I'll sit with him for a while."

"I'll check on Vanessa and get a coffee. Then I'll be back. Take as long as you need," Kala said again.

The room was bright and warm but Dawn didn't take off the jacket Kala had lent her. It felt like protection against the night and all this suffering. She'd never touched her father before but she didn't feel weird taking his hand now. His skin was rough and dry against hers. She gently squeezed to let him know she was there. She watched him for a minute. When it felt right, she said, "I'm here, Dad. Kala got me."

She thought she saw the trace of a smile. Thought she saw his eyes flutter and try to open — but knew they couldn't have. It must have been a trick of the light because a nurse was suddenly next to her, and then another, and then a doctor. They all checked machines and Fisher's pulse and felt his neck.

"I'm sorry, honey," said the nurse who'd let them into the room. "Your father's heart has stopped beating. He's passed away. Is your aunt still in the building?"

Dawn nodded.

"Would you like to sit with him a while longer?"

Dawn nodded a second time and the activity around Fisher ebbed away. She was left alone with him again, like when the two of them were on the beach. A kind of peace came over her even as she tasted the salt from her tears. She touched his forehead and bent low to kiss his cheek above the rough line of stubble. "I love you, Dad," she whispered into his ear before straightening and looking at him one last time.

Kala wasn't back yet so Dawn walked to the washroom at the end of the hall and took a moment to cry and to wash her face. She hadn't seen herself in a mirror since she'd been taken by Leo and Shawn and she hardly recognized her tired, haunted face. She raked her fingers through her messy hair, pulling her bangs straight down her forehead into her eyes. Her hair hid the redness if she kept her neck slightly tilted downward.

She left the washroom and looked down the length of the hallway, still not seeing Kala. She didn't have a phone to text her and thought maybe she was with Vanessa on the floor below. She didn't want to stop moving and she needed to be with Kala. The door to the stairwell was behind her. She opened it and stepped through; the door slammed shut behind her. She stood still and listened to the sounds of the building for a moment before hearing another door slam a few flights below her. She stepped back so she couldn't be seen, not feeling ready to meet other people.

"You've broken up. Damn it." A man was clomping up the stairs. He stopped at the second floor. Dawn sank to the floor, wrapping her arms around her knees. She should run but then he'd know she was there. She squeezed her eyes shut. Fear kept her frozen in place. She heard a door creak open and he began speaking into his phone again. "I'm in the stairwell now. Are you still there? I gave an order for the cop to go home. Just checking he's vacated ..."

The door shut.

It's the same voice I heard in the woods. It's the man who was giving orders to Leo and Shawn before he slipped away in the darkness. And now he's on the same floor as Vanessa.

Dawn got to her feet and started quietly down the stairs.

I need to find Kala and warn her.

CHAPTER FORTY-ONE

Kala checked in with the officer sitting outside Vanessa's room after speaking to the nurse on duty. They'd examined Vanessa thoroughly. She was bruised and scratched up but she'd recover — physically, at least. The hospital psychiatrist had visited earlier and prescribed a strong sedative to help her sleep. She'd been adamant that there'd be no questioning for now, not while Vanessa was so exhausted. There'd be time tomorrow to get her story and to start therapy. Her parents had agreed, united in their resolve to protect her.

"Where are her parents now?" Kala asked.

"The doctor sent them home to sleep. They're going to need their strength as well to hear the details of the trauma she's suffered and all that lies ahead. You can imagine how devastating this type of information can be to absorb."

"Only too well."

Kala stepped into the room but didn't approach the bed. Vanessa looked so young sleeping on her back with her freshly washed hair fanned out on the pillow. Kala wished she could take away all the pain of what she'd lived through and of what was to come. Vanessa was fortunate to have her family's support, and a key piece of her recovery would be her friendship with Emily and Chelsea — and Dawn.

After listening to the steady in and out of Vanessa's breathing, Kala went in search of coffee. The cafeteria was closed but she found a coffee machine in the basement that dispensed a thick black brew. She added three creamers and rode the elevator back up to reception on the main floor to call Gundersund. Her strength was crumbling but she had another hour or so to last before she could get Dawn safely home. More than anything, she wanted to hear Gundersund's voice.

The elevator door slid open and she scanned the lobby. Her gaze landed on a curly blond head. He was leaning back in a seat, eyes closed. She smiled and walked over to sit in the chair next to him. "Hey, Gundersund."

He opened his eyes and his arms, and she rested her head on his chest. "I could go to sleep right here," she said.

"Soon."

She looked up into his vivid blue eyes. "Yeah … soon." She patted his chest and moved away. "I left Dawn with Fisher but I need to get back upstairs."

"Should I come with you?"

"I think Dawn would like that. This isn't easy for her. She and Fisher had made a connection."

In the elevator, Gundersund drew her close. He kissed her until the door opened onto the third floor and she broke away. "You make me forget where I am," she said.

"That's the idea."

The nurse on duty met them in front of Fisher's room. "Isn't Dawn with you?" she asked. "I thought you'd come back for her already."

"I wanted to give her some time alone."

The nurse's expression was apologetic. "Fisher died soon after you left. She wanted to stay with him and I had another patient who needed attention. She said you'd be back and she'd tell you."

"She can't be far. What a sad end to this awful week." Kala pushed open the door to the room, stepped inside, and approached the bed. She bowed her head to say a silent prayer for this man whom she'd never gotten to know. "Thank you for Dawn," she said.

Gundersund was waiting in the hall. "Could Dawn be in the washroom?"

"I'll look. She might have gone in search of me. I told her that I'd be visiting Vanessa's room and then grabbing a coffee before I came back to wait for her here." The expression in his eyes made her pause. "What is it?"

"I don't like her being on her own tonight."

Kala caught his worry. "I don't either." She ran to the other end of the empty corridor to look inside the washroom. She checked for Dawn's feet under the stalls but didn't find her. Gundersund was waiting at the door to the stairs.

"She's not in there. Let's go down to the second. An officer is on duty — he's likely seen her."

"Why don't I check the basement while you look in on Vanessa," said Gundersund. "She could have gone to search for you in the cafeteria."

"It's closed, but you're right. She wouldn't know that."

Kala entered the stairwell and stopped for a second to listen before descending. She was the only one on the stairs as far as she could hear. *Why oh why did I leave Dawn alone?* She tried to stifle the panic that started with Gundersund's concern. They'd both been cops long enough to know when something felt off. She could only hope their gut instinct was wrong this time and Dawn wasn't in danger.

She stepped into the second-floor corridor and felt the eeriness of the late-night hospital. The lights in the hall had been dimmed and most patients were asleep in their rooms with the doors shut. The nurses who should have been at the desk were either making tea in the kitchen or attending to patients in their rooms. The chair outside Vanessa's room where the uniformed cop had been sitting was empty. Kala's heart lurched.

He should be at his post. Why did he leave her alone?

She walked softly down the hall and stopped in front of Vanessa's door. Slowly, slowly, she pushed it open and stepped inside. The sight that greeted her was surreal, shocking, and it took a moment to understand what was happening. A bear-sized man in a long black coat was bending over the bed, his back to Kala. His large hands were holding both sides of a pillow and pressing it down over Vanessa's face.

Adrenaline kicked in. Kala lunged across the room, tackling the man at waist level with all her strength. The impact knocked him sideways into the bedside table and she was falling with him, her chin banging against his leg, her right arm taking the brunt of the impact. She barely registered the sharp edge of the table cutting into her forearm. He managed to hang on to the pillow and it buffered his fall as the metal table and the carafe of water that had sat on it clattered to the floor.

Kala tried to roll upright without success. She screamed as the man pulled himself forward and head-butted her into the wall. Momentarily stunned, she stared at him with dawning horror. None of this made sense — but murder never did. Her fingers blindly searched the floor beside her until her hand found the water jug. She rolled onto her side and lifted it as high as she could, heaving it with all her might at his head. The half-full metal container bounced off his temple but barely slowed him down. He'd scrambled to his feet and he viciously kicked her in the side. His second kick landed on her thigh. She somehow got her hands free and grabbed his foot, wrenching until he fell backward onto the floor. The sound of his head cracking against the bed frame was as loud as a gunshot. He made as if to rise and Kala crab-crawled backward until her back slammed against the wall. She watched Ellington's bald head loll back as the impact of striking the metal bar made him lose consciousness.

She grimaced when she raised her arm in front of her. Dark-red blood drenched the sleeve of her jacket and dripped to the floor. A wave of nausea rose up from her stomach and she pressed her arm across her chest to stop the flow. Panting hard, she slid herself up the wall. She ached in every part of her body, but she couldn't give in now. She steeled herself to step over Ellington and get to Vanessa when the door to the room slammed open. Gundersund's bulk filled the doorway, his face fierce, his eyes afraid for her. Kala glimpsed Dawn in the hall behind him and the tightness in her chest eased. Ellington hadn't gotten to Dawn. She could breathe again. She kept herself upright, propped against the wall, gritting back the pain. "He was smothering Vanessa with that pillow. Gundersund, make sure she's still breathing. Dawn, run for the nurse."

They did as she ordered, not stopping to question who lay unconscious on the floor. Gundersund glanced at Ellington and back at Kala with incredulity in his eyes before stepping over him to check on Vanessa. "She's alive. You stopped him in time."

He took out his handcuffs and squatted to secure Ellington's wrist to the bed frame. He looked up at her, then spun around and stood up in one quick motion. "I've got you," he said as she felt herself free-falling into a blessed, pain-free darkness. Later she was uncertain whether she'd heard him add, "And I'm never going to let you go."

CHAPTER FORTY-TWO

Rouleau spent most of the early morning at the hospital, not leaving until Stonechild ordered everybody out so she could get some sleep. Gundersund had already gone home with Dawn and Taiku and planned to spend the day looking after them. Rouleau's father, Henri, arrived at the hospital at 3:00 a.m. with Marci, who'd picked him up on her way. Rouleau didn't realize until he saw her how much he'd missed her. The trauma of the past few days was a wake-up call. People could be lost to you without warning. They hugged warmly and made plans for later in the day. Then she and Henri left for breakfast, which she promised to treat him to after she filed a brief story for the morning paper. Rouleau knew he had to go in to HQ to deal with Ellington and all the fallout. He'd fielded phone calls from the police board members all morning.

Shards of pink and orange filtered through the dark morning sky. Rouleau rolled his window partway down so that cool air filled the car. He inhaled deeply, forcing himself to work through his fatigue. After picking up a large coffee at the Tim Hortons drive-through, he arrived at the station shortly before 6:00 a.m. Vera met him in the hallway on his way to his office.

"Did you get my text?" she asked.

"Yes, thanks. I'll interview Shawn Baxter as soon as his lawyer arrives."

"She's already here. Shawn wants to get this over with so he can go home."

"A long shot for him, surely?"

"His lawyer thinks a judge will grant bail after Shawn signs a statement."

"Well, let's hope he's stopped playing games. Is this your last day?" Rouleau called after her as she started back down the hallway.

She turned and smiled. "Yes, but don't worry about the drink today, with everything going on. I can always meet you another time." She disappeared around the corner before he could respond.

Shawn was subdued and much paler than he had been the day before. "This is all sick, man," he said when Rouleau sat down. They were alone in the room except for Shawn's lawyer, who sat off to the side, effectively giving Rouleau free rein for the interview. Shawn started right in.

"That girl, Nadia, she was dead when Leo and I picked her up. Natural causes. She took some drugs and convulsed and that was it. Pfft! Gone."

"Were you with her when she died?"

"No. See, she was … with a client, and we got the call from Ellington to dispose of her somewhere so's nobody would be implicated."

"Who was this client?"

Shawn hesitated for the first time and glanced over at his lawyer. She had her head down and didn't offer any advice one way or the other. "You aren't gonna believe me."

"Try me."

"It was Leo's old man, the mayor. His wife was out of town overnight and Nadia went up to his house for some partying. She died in his bedroom, on his big ol' king-sized bed. Clement freaked."

"So he called Ellington?"

"Willy Ellington lined him up with Nadia in the first place, so yeah, that's who he called. Scandal and all that. Ellington couldn't get caught with her body, either, so he sent me and Leo. We were supposed to get paid for disposing of her or I wouldn't have had anything to do with it. Leo was the one who came up with the idea to leave her at the construction site since they fired him after a week on the job. He was royally pissed about that."

"Throwing her off the building ..."

"Overkill, yeah. Ellington and Clement wanted to kill Leo too when they found out he didn't just leave her in an alley somewhere." Shawn dropped his head but not before Rouleau saw him grin, either at his own wordplay or at the men's anger.

"How did Ellington come to use Nadia's services?"

"They met in Ottawa through Harold Mortimer. He had this fling with her one summer while he was back and forth working on a government building, and you'd think he was in love with her, the way he talked. He introduced her to Ellington and *he* started pimping her around after Mortimer dumped her. Mortimer wasn't happy when she showed up in Kingston 'cause of his wife. It was as if Nadia thought they'd live happily ever after like they were in some Walt Disney movie. She even said the baby was his. Mortimer met her at a bar to try to get her to see reason but they had a big fight and she tossed her drink at him. She took up again with Ellington after that."

"How does Vanessa fit into this scenario?"

"Leo strung her along until he could get her to do anything he wanted. He did it to impress Ellington. Leo would do anything to get Willy's approval. They had this odd connection, you know? Ellington is his godfather, even. Let's face it, pimping was the perfect line of work for a loser like Leo."

"And how did you become part of all this?"

Shawn shrugged. "I met Leo in high school and we hung out. Now I wish we hadn't. Anyhow, Vanessa happened to see Nadia in the parking lot of the Blue Nights with Mayor Clement and made the mistake of telling Leo. His dad and Vanessa's dad the architect had done work together and Leo was pretty sure she'd recognized his dad, even though she clammed up when he asked her. When Ellington found out, he said they couldn't take the chance of Vanessa talking and she needed to disappear. He had contacts in the sex trade in Vancouver so he was going to ship her out there. That other Indian girl …"

"Dawn Cook."

"Yeah, idiot Leo picked her up and drove her somewhere once. She could have identified him and his car so Ellington decided she had to go too. He said you might figure everything out if Dawn talked. He called her a loose end."

Rouleau tried to control his voice. "Did Leo assault Dawn?"

"No. Ellington told him not to cause he could get a better price for her if she was a virgin."

Rouleau checked over his notes from the previous interview, buying himself a moment to regain his temper. "You said earlier that Leo thought he'd hit a deer. Is this still the case?"

Shawn hesitated and his lawyer looked up and stared at him. "No, I was mistaken when I said that. He turned his car around and hit that guy on purpose."

Shawn's lawyer followed Rouleau out into the hall. "He's given you Willy Ellington and Leonard Clement on a platter. The mayor's career is all but over too. I hear his wife kicked him out. For what it's worth, I think Shawn's salvageable if given some counselling and direction."

Rouleau thought about how close they'd come to disaster. "The judge will decide. At this moment, the way I feel, he's lucky it's not up to me."

The acting chief job was once again vacant. He'd jump in for a few weeks to keep the work moving but he'd already told the board to keep looking for a replacement. Now, more than ever, he knew that his place was with his team.

Kala woke from a long nap and lay listening to Dawn and Gundersund talking in the kitchen. The sun shone pale yellow into the room and the clock confirmed that the day was waning into evening; she'd been asleep on the couch for almost three hours. It had been a week since Ellington was arrested. Seven days with two broken ribs, a stitched-up arm, and a thankful heart that Dawn had come home to her.

She worked her way to a sitting position and swallowed a painkiller tablet that would allow her to breathe deeply without excessive pain. She rested ten more minutes to let the medicine kick in and then pushed herself to the edge of the couch. Taiku padded into the living room and licked her hand before lying down at her feet. He'd been vigilant all week, not letting her or Dawn stray far from his view. Minnie was in the kitchen with Gundersund.

Dawn appeared in the doorway and called over her shoulder, "Gundersund, she's awake. We made tea, and Gundersund picked up pizza," she told Kala.

"Aren't you going to a sleepover with Emily, Chelsea and Vanessa?"

"Gundersund's driving me after we eat."

Gundersund appeared with a tray, his eyes assessing her as they did every time he entered the room. He'd been so attentive to them both that she'd slept worry-free, knowing he was looking after Dawn. He was working from her kitchen when she slept; the team was uncovering Ellington's secret life making money off prostitutes. "We're gathering enough evidence to put him away for a long, long time," said Gundersund when she asked.

They ate in the living room with supper on their laps before Dawn ran upstairs to pack an overnight bag.

"We've only had a week to recover … I'm not sure this is a good idea," Kala said to Gundersund. It would be Dawn's first night away from her since she'd gone missing. Her worry was still strong.

"I hear you, but the girls need a chance to work out what happened in their own way. Dawn has to get her life back to normal. She needs to get over Fisher's death."

"You're right. I'm being overly anxious."

"You're allowed." He smiled and leaned in to kiss her. "Do you think you could stand a bedmate tonight?"

"I'd like that."

Her phone rang soon after he'd left with Dawn and the dogs. She checked the caller ID before answering. "Hey, Woodhouse. What's up?" She hadn't seen him since they'd tracked down Leo on Rudd Avenue.

"I'm outside. Do you mind if I come in?"

"The back door's unlocked."

A moment later, Woodhouse stood uncomfortably in the hallway, holding two bottles of beer. "I thought you might want a brew."

"I don't actually drink."

"I'll leave it in the fridge for Gundersund, then."

"Have a seat."

He set the two bottles on the coffee table and folded himself into a chair that was too small for him. He crossed his legs and feigned being relaxed. "So, how're you doing?" he asked.

"One week into six weeks of lying around. I'm going to be stir-crazy by the weekend."

"That's good," he said distractedly, not listening. She waited.

"I was wrong about those Simmons brothers," he said.

"Murray gave you reason. He's a slimy piece of work. Marci's writing an article that doesn't cast him in a flattering light." She shifted positions, trying to ease the pain in her side. "I want to thank you for finding out where Dawn was and for going with me to find the girls."

"Yeah. Glad it all worked out. The bit with Ellington was a shock. I looked up to him when I started on the force. These charges shook me."

"Are you questioning the order of things, Woodhouse?"

"Maybe. Maybe I am."

She'd been mulling over what to do about him leaking information to Marci. She felt as if she owed him but she had to make sure he wouldn't do it again. "I know you've been giving case information to Marci Stokes."

He met her eyes. "What are you going to do about it?"

"Nothing, if you promise me you've stopped."

He bowed his head and sat silently while she watched him. Finally, he nodded. "This makes us even then." He smiled at her and got to his feet. "You're all right, you know that, Stonechild? I'll see myself out."

I hope this isn't the drugs making me hallucinate, she thought as he walked out of the living room. *Because I could have sworn Woodhouse just gave me a compliment.*

The back door shut behind him and she poured the last of the tea into her cup. She took her time getting to her feet and shuffled over to look out the half-open window. The moon was bright tonight and this felt like a hopeful omen. It wasn't only her body that needed to heal. Her spirit did as well. The line between happiness and hell was razor-thin and she'd been waking to panic attacks, knowing how close she'd come to total despair. She returned to the couch, lowered herself by increments and lay her head against a pillow. She gasped from the exertion and let her breath out in a long, thankful sigh.

She looked around the room and let the calm of the evening fill her being. In this moment of stillness, she could see a future in this house, in this town, and she knew that this was where she was meant to be. Looking after Dawn and Taiku. Planting a garden and putting down roots. Waiting for the sound of Gundersund's car in the driveway.

Knowing in her soul that this was enough.

That, for now, this was more than enough.

ACKNOWLEDGEMENTS

Thank you to all the readers who have engaged with this series and who continue to support my work. I appreciate every email, tweet, and in-person encounter. As in past acknowledgements, I would like to thank a few constant friends and supporters: Kelly MacNaull, Barbara Woodward, Ann MacDonald, Madona Skaff, Brenda Muir, Wendy Sinclair, Catherine Ginn, Suesan Saville, Catherine Brown, Paulette Nicol, Jim Napier, Gail Bowen, Ann Cleeves, Grace Johnston, Estella Arlott, Rick and Shelley Adamson, Brian Neale, and Sean Wilson and the Ottawa International Book Festival. I owe a huge debt of thanks to countless bookstores for promoting my series, in particular, my friends at Perfect Books, Books on Beechwood, Coles Carlingwood, Chapters Gloucester, Sleuth of Baker Street, Novel Idea, and Let's Talk Books. My thanks also to the many book clubs that I've visited these past few years — I've been wined and dined while meeting some mighty fine readers!

I am indebted to the team at Dundurn for all of their work on my behalf: freelance editor Shannon

Whibbs, assistant project editor Jenny McWha, free-lance copy editor Catharine Chen, designer Laura Boyle, and publicist Michelle Melski. Thank you also to Dundurn president and publisher Kirk Howard for your belief in the power and magic of Canadian stories.

A special thank you to my brother, Ian Black, who is, fortuitously, a retired RCMP officer and was always available to answer my questions about polic-ing and investigations.

The characters and storylines in this series are completely fictitious, although the beautiful city of Kingston, Ontario, is a very real and lovely place to while away a summer's day or two.

Love to my husband, Ted, our daughters, Lisa and Julia, and our son-in-law, Robin Guy, for mak-ing this journey so much fun.

Book Credits
Project Editor: Jenny McWha
Developmental Editor: Shannon Whibbs
Copy Editor: Catharine Chen
Proofreader: Megan Beadle

Cover Designer: Laura Boyle
Interior Designer: Lorena Gonzalez Guillen